PRAISE FOR BOOK OF DAYS

Wow. A brilliant book. Perfectly paced, incredibly engaging, and entirely satisfying. It's one of those rare stories that settles comfortably in the deepest corners of your imagination and simply will not leave until long after the final page has been turned. With Jim's first book, *Rooms,* we were introduced to a budding talent; *Book of Days* establishes Jim as the real deal. If you love suspense, intrigue, adventure, romance, and a solid dose of spiritual wonder, then this book is a must read.

—The Miller Brothers, award-winning authors of the Hunter Brown book series

I devoured *Book of Days* by Jim Rubart in one sitting. It is an exciting but poignant novel about how truly important our memories and choices are to who we become. It's still resonating in my heart. Highly recommended!

—Colleen Coble, author of *The Lightkeeper's Bride* and the Lonestar series

No sophomore slump for James L. Rubart! *Book of Days* is actually better than his best-selling debut, *Rooms.* Rubart crafts a terrific story that is equal parts fast-faced thriller, thought-provoking allegory, and moving drama. Don't miss this one!

—Rick Acker, author of *When the Devil Whistles*

It's very rare that a novel makes me cry—really have tears running from my eyes, but *Book of Days* did. I laughed and cried right along with Cameron on his quest to find the Book of Days. And just when I thought the plot couldn't possibly be wrapped up in a way that would satisfy, Rubart pulled out all the stops to create the perfect ending to a heartfelt story. This is a journey not to be missed!

—Robin Caroll, author of *Deliver Us From Evil* and *Fear No Evil*

Great cover, great concept, and great fun to read! *Book of Days* blends Peretti's *The Visitation* and Jordan's *The Miracle of Mercy Land* and explores biblical ideas in a modern context. Rubart is for real and his writing is fast-paced and readable.

—Eric Wilson, *New York Times* best-selling author of
Fireproof, Expiration Date, and *Valley of Bones*

A story intricately woven with God's truth and human frailties, *Book of Days* is what I call a "living book"—a story able to reach across time to significantly effect the hearts of its readers. James L. Rubart is a master storyteller with an unparalleled style and oomph that drags you back to his stories time and again.

—Ronie Kendig, author of *Dead Reckoning* and *Nightshade*

James Rubart is officially now one of my favorite writers. He takes grand concepts, weaves them together with mystery, suspense, some mischievous fun, and a serious thread of hope. *Book of Days* is a great read . . . why people buy novels.

—Dan Walsh, award-winning author of
The Unfinished Gift and *The Homecoming*

James L. Rubart's stories are clever and creative. He's a storyteller who pricks the heart of our generation and causes us to think about where we've been and where we're going. He weaves it all in the cotton of a great book. *Book of Days* is a must read.

—Rachel Hauck, best-selling and Carol award-winning author

Book of Days is an imaginative, adventurous, and compelling read. Rubart's attention to plot and character, while weaving in spiritual truth, gives an already terrific premise dimension and depth. Rubart's talent is undeniable, and his ideas are pure wonderment.

—Rene Gutteridge, award-winning author of *Listen*

Book of Days

JAMES L. RUBART

Book of Days

A NOVEL

Nashville, Tennessee

Printed in the United States of America

978-1-4336-7151-7

Published by B&H Publishing Group
Nashville, Tennessee

Dewey Decimal Classification: F
Subject Heading: ADVENTURE FICTION \
MEMORY—FICTION

1 2 3 4 5 6 7 8 • 15 14 13 12 11

For Dad

ACKNOWLEDGMENTS

I thought *Book of Days* would be the novel I saw in bookstores first. All the major publishers had passed on *Rooms* (in the fall of '08) so I put it on the shelf and started working on *Book of Days*. But B&H reconsidered, *Rooms* came out first, and I'm grateful.

Book of Days was inspired by my dad's illness, and it feels right that it should come out after he's gone to be with Jesus and the chapter of his life on Earth is over.

Again I'm thankful to all those who helped take *Book of Days* from a scattered idea to a completed novel:

To Jaime Wright-Sundsmo for lending her time and extensive expertise to make my climbing scenes accurate (and for telling me it was okay to stretch the authenticity in places where I needed to).

To John Olson for telling me I had to flip my original vision of *Book of Days* and make Cameron my protagonist. (He was right.)

To my readers of my first draft: Debbi Anderson, Jamie Carie, Ron DeMiglio, Jennifer Fry, Ronie Kendig, Bob Lord, Pat Rubart, Jim Rubstello, Tina Sander, Ruth Voetmann, and Katie Vorreiter. Your stellar critique and comments smoothed out many rough edges.

To my incredible team at B&H Fiction, you're awesome! Special thanks to Kim Stanford for being so great at doing the final polish, Diana Lawrence for my outstanding covers, Karen Ball for her vision, and Julie Gwinn for her wisdom and bucket loads of talent.

To Royce Cameron who was there "where it all began," brainstormed on the original idea, and walked every step of this novel with me.

To Andy Meisenheimer, for being instrumental in shaping the plot and pushing me to go deeper with the story, then deeper still.

To my editor Julee Schwarzburg for being brilliant and a joy to work with.

To my prayer team for warring for me in the heavens: Allen Arnold, Twila Belk, Nancy Biffle, Jamie Carie, Jeff Conwell, Ron and Tina DeMiglio, Mary DeMuth, Eric and Jennifer Fry, Randy Ingermanson, Susan Hill, Keith Horner, Ronie Kendig, Tosca Lee, Bob Lord, Dineen Miller, Cec Murphey, Don and Heidi Myers, Glen Peterson, Peter Prinos, Steve Price, Cynthia Ruchti, Jim Rubstello, Darci Rubart, Taylor Rubart, Micah Rubart, Pat Rubart, Jim Rubstello, Jeff Scorziell, Mick Silva, Jeff Stucky, Carla Williams, and Jim Vaux.

To my wife Darci and sons Taylor and Micah, for their constant support, encouragement, and unwavering love.

To my mom for loving me like only a mother can.

To my dad. I love you. What a day it will be when I see you again.

To the Father, Son, and Holy Spirit for your grace, mercy, and letting me live my dream.

All my days were written in Your book and planned before a single one of them began.

Psalm 139:16

PROLOGUE

Summer 1853

A stone slammed into the side of Hassun's head, sending him to his knees. Pain exploded like lightning and streaked down his back as he slumped forward onto his hands. Careless. His moccasins must have left a trail. Foolish. How could he have let that happen?

Have to move! His assailant's next attack would most likely be to his ribs.

Hassun spun to his left, sending up a thin curtain of dust from the ledge overlooking the cliff, and caught the man's dark leather moccasin as it flashed toward his face.

Hassun twisted his attacker's leg and the man sprawled on the ground, his head inches from striking a rock.

Not close enough.

The man leaped to his feet, stepped back five paces, and snatched a bow and a pine shaft with a brilliant black arrowhead off the ground. By the time Hassun staggered to his feet and shook his head, the man had nocked the arrow.

"Nukpana? Why?"

"You are surprised?"

"You were my friend."

"I am still your friend and ever will be." Nukpana drew back slightly on the bowstring, the arrow pointed at Hassun's chest, and laughed. "Do not worry, I am not going to kill you. I could have done that easily with a larger rock a moment ago." He released the pressure on the bowstring and stroked the arrow's white feathers. "You never could hide your tracks. I only need to know where the Stories are and I will leave you."

Hassun should have seen it. The rage two summers past when he was chosen guardian instead of Nukpana, then the false praise for having been given the honor. Being badgered almost daily ever since in a half-joking, half-serious manner about the location.

"And if I do not tell you where they are?"

"I will see how much pain you can endure before you die. But know before you join our ancestors, you will tell me."

"The Stories are not for your eyes."

"But they are for yours?"

"I am not the one who made that choice."

"And who is?" Nukpana pierced the tip of his forefinger with the point of the arrowhead and a drop of blood seeped out.

"You know."

"But those who chose you are gone, and the understanding now only remains with you."

Hassun nodded, his long black braids hanging over his muscled shoulders.

"What if something happens to you? Another must retain the knowledge."

"That is not for any man alone to decide. You know this also."

"Think, Hassun. We could use its power for so much good. Together. You and I. Blood brothers since our youth. We could wield the insights and foretelling it offers to—"

"No. That is not its purpose."

"If you will not tell, then give me the stone." Nukpana spread his feet wider, one in front of the other, renocked the arrow and drew it back.

"I cannot. Even if you do not yet know how to decipher the markings, it would be the same as telling you." Hassun massaged the small stone that hung from his neck on a thin leather cord under his buckskin shirt. "You know this."

"Enough. Give me the stone." Nukpana drew the bowstring back further, his first two fingers turning a deep red where the string bit into them.

Hassun stared into Nukpana's eyes as he lifted the stone from around his neck and let it hang from his upturned palm.

"Yes, throw it to me and there will be peace between us."

"No." Hassun wrapped the cord around the stone and closed his fist around it.

"One more chance. Tell me where the Stories are or give me the stone. Either one and you will live. Now."

Hassun closed his eyes. "For You, I choose." He opened his eyes and gauged the distance between Nukpana and the edge of the cliff. Three paces, maybe four. The distance might be short enough. Nukpana would not shoot to kill, only to maim. "As I have told you already, it is not possible."

"Is it worth your life?"

Hassun drew in a deep breath and whispered, "Yes."

"So be it."

Nukpana drew back fully on the bow at the moment Hassun lunged forward and sprinted toward his friend, little puffs of dust rising from where his feet dug into the ledge above the cliff.

Nukpana's fingers loosed the arrow and time slowed.

As Hassun hurtled toward the arrowhead streaking toward him, he hurled the stone over the edge of the cliff.

Nukpana's head snapped to the left to follow the arc of the stone against the blue sky, shock splashed across his sun-browned skin. "No!"

The arrow entered Hassun's chest just above his heart, making him stagger, the darkness of unconsciousness rushing into his mind. No, he wouldn't give in.

Two paces to go. Yes. He would make it.

Nukpana turned back the moment Hassun slammed into the bigger man, driving him back, then over the edge of the cliff.

Sound vanished as Hassun wrapped his arms around his friend and the forest floor spread out below him.

"I have protected that which was entrusted to me. Now I come."

CHAPTER 1

Cameron Vaux stepped into his dad's room and tried to push the regrets into a dark corner of his mind. They'd never go on the backpacking trip he'd planned for his dad's fiftieth birthday. Never take the sailing trip from Seattle to Alaska. The cruise around Italy would be a grand intention never fulfilled.

The what-should-have-beens had vanished.

Just like his dad's mind.

It had been a year since his dad knew who Cameron was. The doctors said the grains of sand still in the top of the hourglass were few, which made the call he'd received that morning from one of the nurses surprising.

"Your dad is more coherent than we've seen him in a long time. He keeps saying, 'I need to see him now. Right away. I must tell him.' But when we ask who 'him' is, he says he doesn't know. We're guessing it's you."

Cameron stood just inside the door, stared at the back of his dad's graying head, and watched him study the business section of the paper as he'd done his whole life. Pouring over the stock charts to see who was up and who was crashing. Ready to steer Cameron's economic choices down the straight and financially rewarding. His house and his healthy IRA were due to his father's fiscal acuity and passion to share what he'd learned with Cameron.

He sighed. There would be no more lessons on navigating the investment waters.

"Hey, Dad, how are you?" Cameron eased over to the windows and pulled open the beige curtains. Early May sunshine filtered through the emerald leaves on the maple tree outside and filled the room.

His dad sat next to the window in his dark blue leather chair, feet propped up and covered with the Washington Huskies slippers Cameron bought him last Christmas.

"Well, I'm still alive. It's so good to have you here." His dad adjusted his glasses and squinted. "Now tell me again who you are . . . ?"

"It's me, Cameron. Your son. You asked for me?" He couldn't help hoping the tumblers inside his dad's mind had magically clicked back into place, and he could have one last conversation where his dad knew him. *Please?*

His dad set aside the business section he'd probably read twenty times already that day and stuck out his hand. "Put 'er in the vise, pal."

Cameron took his dad's hand and cried out in mock pain. "Ahh, wow, you haven't lost your strength, Dad."

His dad smiled, a hint of water in his eyes.

"You know, sometimes I look in the mirror and say, 'Hey, you old buzzard, what are you still doing here?'" His dad's eyes lit up and he laughed like stones skipping on a pond.

"You're not old." Forty-nine was not old. Certainly not old enough to have a disease that made Swiss cheese of his dad's memories.

"We'll be home before dinner at this pace." His dad nodded. "Yep, we're making good time."

The familiar sadness tried to rise from Cameron's heart and smother his mind, but he blocked it. He didn't need the emotion. He didn't need tears right now. There had been enough of those over the past six years to fill Puget Sound.

"The nurses said you needed to see me."

"Well, it is so very good to see you."

"They said you needed to tell me something, Dad."

His father lifted his glass of orange juice and toasted Cameron. "Have I told you how proud I am of you?"

Cameron smiled, closed his eyes, and let the words sink in. His dad used to say those words ten times an hour two years back, but the frequency had dwindled to almost nothing. It was a gift to hear the phrase again.

Cameron glanced at the pictures on the walls. Of family. Of friends. Of his mom and dad playing tennis when they were first married. Cameron picked up a photo sitting on the coffee table of his mom and dad swimming across the Smith River in the redwoods and drew his finger across the surface of the glass.

"I miss her so much."

"Who?"

"Mom." He held out the frame for his dad to see.

His dad took the picture and stared at it. "That's me! Isn't it? And who is that with me?"

Cameron closed his eyes and sighed. Not mom, he couldn't let his dad forget her.

"It's mom. You have to remember her. You loved her very much."

"I did? And what did you say her name was?"

How could he forget the woman he'd been married to for twenty-seven years? Yes, the disease, but their passion for each other was the type that nothing should ever be allowed to steal. There had to be something he could say to trigger his dad's memories of their love.

"Camping in the redwoods. The Big Rock. We went there every year till I was ten. You can lose all the other memories, but not of her. You have to remember Mom. You always said living without each other would be a Siberian existence."

"Okay, and I'm living here with you right now, pal."

Cameron slumped into a chair next to his dad and dragged his teeth over his lower lip. "Where have your memories gone, Dad?"

"Well, I don't know, but you're here and I'm so glad you stopped by."

Cameron stared into his dad's eyes until his father looked away.

"Are they lost forever? Maybe when this life is through you'll get them back. Maybe you'll find them in whatever comes next."

His dad smiled, the hint of laughter playing at the corners of his mouth. "Heaven is coming, you know."

"You looking forward to heaven, Dad?"

"Oh yes, indeed. He's coming for me." His dad glanced around the room until his gaze settled on Cameron. "Well, I'm glad you've come by, but remind me again, how are we acquainted?"

Cameron's chest tightened and he tried to smile. "I'm just a kid who loves his dad with all his heart."

"That's good. Very good."

Cameron scooted his chair closer to his dad and leaned forward. "I'm sorry, Dad. Sorry you have to go through this. I don't think I could handle getting this disease of yours. I'd be tempted to end things early, you know? Did you ever consider it?"

Not a chance. His dad would have obliterated the thought the instant it appeared. "At least you have your God-thing going on, so you feel like you know where you're headed."

"God is so good."

"Yeah." If only God was real. Maybe He was, maybe He wasn't. It took a leap of faith to believe, his dad always said. But how could you know for sure before leaping? And Cameron wanted to know. A never-ending circle.

Cameron picked up the myrtlewood cribbage board that sat on the coffee table next to his dad's chair. "We played a few hundred on this board, didn't we? Or was it a few thousand? I'd love to play one more game. Wouldn't you?"

"We could play now if you like."

"Should I set up the board?"

His dad grabbed Cameron's hand and smiled wide. "Tell me exactly what are we doing here today."

"Talking. Just two guys hanging out together talking."

"And you are?"

Cameron set down the board, rubbed its smooth surface with his finger, and circled the word *Finish* carved into the end of the wood. "The product of an awesome father."

Outside his dad's room an orderly's tennis shoe squeaked on the linoleum as she passed the door. At the sound his dad jerked his head up and his eyes cleared.

"When it starts happening to you, you must find the book with all your days in it, Cameron. It might cure you. Do you understand?"

Cameron raised his head. "What did you say?"

"When you start losing your memories, you must find the book. Everything will make sense to you then. Find it for me, will you? Promise me you'll find it."

"Are you with me here, Dad?" Cameron's mind reeled. He couldn't tell if his father was lucid, but his eyes were clearer than he'd seen them in ages, and the countenance of his face said he knew exactly what he was saying.

"Did you know you can see the future? I saw it once. It's not a real book, of course. I even touched it, when I was a kid. Did you know that?" His dad rubbed his hands together and chuckled. "Of course you didn't. I never told you that. I never told anyone except one person right after it happened. People would have thought I was crazy. But that doesn't matter now."

"What are you talking about?"

"Do you understand? Find the book, Cameron." His dad took Cameron's face in his hands. "Did you hear me? The book of all days. Find it for me. Find it for you." He released Cameron's face and rubbed his eyes with the palms of his hand.

Cameron shook his head, as if it would cause his dad's words to make sense. Was this real? Did Dad have any idea what he was saying? "Why do you think it will happen to me?"

"Not a question. It will happen; it will. I've seen it." His father patted Cameron's hand. "I'm so sorry."

Cameron blinked and a trickle of fear wound through his mind. He wasn't ready for a conversation out of *Alice in Wonderland*.

"What is this book? Where would I find it?"

His dad grasped Cameron by both hands and nodded once. "You know what I love about us? We both have beautiful blue eyes."

Cameron leaned in. "Why do I need to find this book?"

"You know what I love about us?" A smile lit up his dad's face as he squeezed Cameron's hands. "Both of us have beautiful blue eyes."

"Stay with me, Dad. You just told me I'm going to start losing my memories like you and about a book I have to find. Where is the book?"

"Well, I'm very proud of you, you know."

Cameron let his head fall back and he closed his eyes. It was over. No matter how hard he tried to massage the conversation back to whatever this book was, and why his dad thought Cameron would get the disease, it wouldn't happen.

He wanted to have one last conversation with his dad about the important things in life, so why did he end up with his dad rambling about nonsensical things instead?

A few minutes later Cameron let it go and told the story about the two of them skiing from nine in the morning till ten at night up at Stevens Pass without a break.

"Do you remember the next day? We couldn't move!"

For the next half hour Cameron didn't stop the tears when they pushed out and didn't stop the laughter when his dad talked about some random comical event from decades back.

After the light outside his dad's room had grown black, Cameron slid his arms around his father and whispered in his ear, "I love you, Dad. Always have. Always."

His dad held him for a moment, then patted Cameron on the back and took him by the shoulders, a wide grin on Dad's face, moisture in his eyes.

A week later his dad was gone.

CHAPTER 2

Eight Years Later

"Come on, remember!"

Cameron stared at the phone number on the yellow sticky note, willing himself to recall who it belonged to. He pressed the Post-it note onto the middle of his MacBook's screen.

What was wrong with him? It was his handwriting. No one else had scrawled those numbers half an hour ago. He remembered jotting it down. It was someone he needed to call back. But the memory of whose number it was had disappeared.

His face grew hot.

"Remember what?"

Cameron looked over at Brandon slumped in front of his computer, a pen whirling around his fingers like a minibaton on steroids.

"Where'd you learn to do that?"

"YouTube." Brandon glanced up at the clock on the wall of their production studio. "If we're going to get this vid finished, we gotta jam. You're almost done with edits, right? Tell me yes."

"Another hour at the most."

"Cool." Brandon sat up and whacked away on his keyboard. "So have you decided, Cam? Are you headed to the fifteen-year this weekend?"

"We just had a ten-year reunion. Besides, July is too early to have a reunion. It should be in August."

"Did I ask you if you'll do a couple of tunes again? Just you and a piano up there onstage, nothing fancy."

"No chance. I haven't played for eons." Cameron rubbed his eyes. "I can't believe high school is already fifteen years in the rearview mirror."

"Thirty years is coming in a flash." Brandon grinned. "Old man time will be here before you know it. Hey, remember, I need you to get that voice-over on the Crystal Mountain video laid down by the end of the day."

"Right."

Cameron turned back to his screen and stared at the number. What if old man time had already shown up? He tried to laugh at the idea. So he'd been forgetting a few things lately. Big deal. It was probably the stress of working sixty-plus hours every week and still finding time to coach Little League baseball.

Plus the added bonus of the anniversary date looming like a storm over his heart. Less than a month away. Couldn't the pain stay buried till a few days before the seventeenth arrived?

But it hadn't been a few things he'd forgotten and it hadn't been lately. It had been going on for at least a year. And it was getting worse.

Go to the reunion? Yeah, it would be a blast answering questions about Jessie's death.

"Cameron! What is going on?"

He turned toward the sound of the voice.

A bald guy ducked under a sagging streamer that said, "Class of '95, About to Come Alive," threw open his arms, and grinned as he stutter-stepped up to Cameron in black dress shoes that were out of place with his jeans.

"These reunions can't come fast enough for me. I love seeing everyone. I can't believe you and I haven't seen each other since the last one. That's just a wrong song."

"Hey," Cameron said. Not even a glimmer of recognition. "Great to see you. You are . . . ?"

"You crack me up, Cam." The guy grabbed him in a bear hug, and when he pulled away the grin left his face. "Hey, I heard about Jessie. Sorry, man. Really."

"Thanks." Why couldn't people read his mind and realize he didn't want to talk about Jessie? Maybe he should have worn a sign that said, *I'm doing as well as I can, but my heart was shredded when she died, and I'd rather not talk about it with you because the pain is still extremely ripe even after two years.*

"Are you still climbing?"

"Yeah." Had he gone rock climbing sometime in the past with this guy?

"It seems like yesterday you and I and Jessie and Gina Stewart learned to climb together. When was that? Two summers out of high school? You'd just met Jessie and her sister—what was her name? Ann? And if I remember right, you couldn't decide which one to ask out." The guy gestured up and down with his palms like a scale. "Then Jessie asked you to take the class, and you didn't want to go 'cause you're scared of heights. But you liked Jessie so you decided to gut through it. That cracked me up, you pretending the whole time that you weren't terrified so Jessie wouldn't know, but I knew you were freaking out . . ."

Ann, Jessie's foster sister.

Cameron hadn't thought about her for at least six months. She probably hadn't thought of him since the funeral. He'd tried to get along with her the whole time Jessie and he dated, but Ann had never warmed up to him. She'd stood there, maid of honor at Jessie's and his wedding, glaring at him through the entire ceremony.

". . . and Jessie blows all three of us out of the water the way she took to climbing. And I loved her laugh; it was so totally uninhibited, you know? She's hanging out over a two-hundred-foot cliff cracking up like she's at a party, telling us to climb faster."

A rock-climbing course after high school? Is that when he started? Images flitted through his brain, then the memory of the summer rushed in. Yes. Jessie calling him with an invitation to take the class together. Him deciding that was a sign to pursue her instead of Ann even with his aversion to heights.

How could he forget that? It was his first date with Jessie, if you could call it a date. He didn't want to learn to climb, but he wanted to get to know her. So he went and fell in love with both the sport and Jessie.

"I remember." Cameron pursed his lips, nodded, and rubbed his face.

"Hey, I'm an idiot, I shouldn't stir up . . . talking about Jessie . . . I mean, I don't want to—"

"It's okay, really."

They said good-bye and Cameron watched his old friend dance up to a group on his left.

"There he is," said a voice to his right.

Cameron turned to face a man with slicked-back blond hair and a goatee already flecked with hints of gray.

"Hey . . . hi." Who was he? *Here we go again.*

"Cameron, how are things going for you? It's my fault for not calling you. It's been too, too long since we talked."

"Yeah, it's been a while."

"When Jessie, uh . . . I should have called, and really I should have come to the service, but I'm just weird when it comes to—"

"Death." *Think, Cameron.* He knew him. "It's all right."

As they talked Cameron tried to picture the guy fifteen years younger. They were in some kind of group together . . . weren't they?

"Are you doing your films yet? I bet you are."

He jerked his head back. "What?"

"Aren't you making films and doing the Steven Spielberg directing thing? You always said you'd have your first one finished by the time you reached the age of thirty-two. You were so convincing. Some of the stuff you did back in high school was pretty impressive, so I figured thirty-three means you're a year overdue, if you haven't done one yet."

A chill washed over Cameron. That was indeed the plan. Two years ago he was on track to jump into the Hollywood circus, but the plan didn't include losing Jessie. The dream crashed and burned after that.

"No, I'm behind schedule."

"I understand." The man nodded. "You ever want to talk about it, call me. I mean it."

As the man sauntered off, the pieces inside Cameron's brain snapped into place.

A moment later Brandon came up to him with two drinks in his hand.

"That was Donnie Taggart," Cameron said.

"Uh, yeah it is."

"It took me a second to remember—"

"Well, he's pretty forgettable. We only played in a band with him for two years."

Donnie Taggart was in their band? What? No. Wait. That's right. How could he forget that? "He played bass. Sang a killer version of 'Better Man' for us and sounded just like Vedder. He lived a few miles away from you in a house painted a muted yellow. Didn't he have a boxer that snagged Frisbees out of the air no matter how far you threw it?"

"Look out Jeopardy, here comes Cameron. Nice to know your steroid-strength memory is still functioning. You know I hated you in high school 'cause of that. I don't think you ever studied."

If only it were as simple as taking steroids to get his memories to return and fix whatever was malfunctioning in his mind.

Brandon clapped him on the back. "Have fun, bro. I'm going to go catch up with all my old girlfriends."

"That'll take, what, five, ten seconds?"

"Ha." Brandon punched him in the arm. "Be good."

Cameron breathed deep and it seemed to clear his head. As he scanned the room, he recognized almost every face. He remembered names and even the classes he'd taken with them. The memory loss had to be due to stress and lack of sleep more than any kind of encroaching disease.

His gaze settled on a dark-haired woman who stood next to the small stage they would probably use for giving out awards for having the most kids, the farthest distance traveled to get here, and married the longest.

As he studied her profile, a wave of heat washed over him. He should know her. *Concentrate.* Something about their junior year. She was part of it.

She turned and spotted him.

Oh no. He needed to figure it out before she reached him. But his mind was blank.

She shimmed up to him and gave him a sideways hug. "Hey, handsome. I was hoping you would be here."

"I was hoping the same." Cameron bit his upper lip, as if the shot of pain would tell him who this woman was.

"It is so great to see you. You know, I meant to come to the ten, but life was pretty crazy in those days." She pulled on her earlobe. "I'm so sorry about your wife. I read about it. It was a small plane accident, right?"

Cameron nodded.

She stepped back a few paces. "Let's see, your black hair is just as black and thick, no discernible extra girth around the middle yet, and only a few laugh lines around your gray-blues." She laughed and leaned closer to him. "I thought all the guys were supposed to come to the fifteen-year reunion bald and overweight."

A moment later he knew her. "Tonya!"

"Cameron!" She pointed at him, smiled, and studied his face. "You okay?"

"I'm just tired; my job has been nuts lately. For the past year actually."

By the time they'd finished talking, he remembered every one of their dates. But it didn't help the big slug of lead in his stomach get any lighter.

Two weeks later on a sun-soaked Saturday afternoon, Cameron packed the last of his climbing gear into the back of his MINI Cooper and fired up the engine. He felt good. Strong. His mind hadn't shifted into hibernate mode even once since the reunion, and he tried to believe the incidents were over.

But part of his brain still felt like he was watching a 3-D movie without the glasses.

He hit Highway 2 out of Monroe at two o'clock and glanced at his watch. Should be to Leavenworth by four or four thirty. He might even be able to get a climb in before dark and make camp on top.

As the little town of Gold Bar slid by, his dad's words from eight years earlier echoed in his mind: "*When you get it . . . when you get it . . . You will . . . you will . . .*"

"No, Dad, I can't believe that." Cameron popped his steering wheel with his fist. "It's just the anniversary of Jessie's death and the pressure of work. That's all."

The stress-O-meter had been pegging red for far too long. Brandon and he had become master jugglers with twenty video projects in the air at all times. That extracted a high price at life's tollbooth.

"Nice try," said the other side of his brain. Stress alone wouldn't make his mind take as many vacations as it had during the past twelve months. Neither side of his mind could claim victory. But in his heart there was already a clear winner.

The fingers of his right hand started shaking, and he clamped his left hand on top it. That didn't accomplish anything except make both hands quiver. *Relax!* His mind was fine. He probably just needed food.

A burger at the Alpen Drive-In took care of his hunger pains, but it didn't quell the gnawing feeling running through his mind.

As he waited to pull back onto Highway 2, Cameron stared at the license plate in front of him and played the game he amused himself with on long car rides when he was a kid.

LIO A33.

Liking intelligent orangutans after thirty-three.

Launching igloos over a thirty-three.

Life is over at thirty-three.

CHAPTER 3

Cameron sat on a cliff overlooking Icicle Creek watching the glacier-fed stream wind its way toward the Wenatchee River.

He stared at the outline of a boulder buried under the surging river as he pulled off the stone hanging around his neck and massaged its smooth surface. When had Jessie given it to him? Not long before she died, he was sure of it.

Why hadn't two years taken away more of the pain from Jessie's death?

Two years?

The accident felt like two days ago.

Like two seconds ago.

Fragments of the scene tried to rush into his mind, but he forced them into the deep recesses of his heart like he'd been doing for the past twenty-four months. He wouldn't let himself relive it again. Ever. Jessie's accident was the one memory he wished he could forget completely.

Hadn't someone told him after the accident that it would be okay?

Okay?

It would never be okay.

Fairy-book marriages snuffed out after only five years were not okay.

Wild Turkey whiskey should have given him an award for the amount of their booze he bought and drowned in after Jessie's death.

Then on a Friday night, a little over half a year after he lost her, he quit drinking. When he came within inches of hitting an SUV head-on, he was convinced. Part of him wished his MINI Cooper had wound up the size of a microwave—with him inside.

That same weekend he started rock climbing again. It didn't cause his forehead to split open the next morning like drinking did, and although the sport wasn't quite as adept at helping him blunt the pain, it was a way to be with Jessie.

He looked up from the edge of the craggy rock face as the last sliver of a mid-July sun vanished behind the Enchantments, leaving strains of orange, cotton-candy clouds. The temperature dropped and Cameron rubbed his bare upper arms. Tank tops were ideal for climbing but not for watching the sun set.

Six months after he stopped drinking, well-meaning friends started the blind-date merry-go-round. He went on three dates. The first yakked about her divorce two hours nonstop; the second spent the evening asking herself questions, then laughed at the answers like a bored late-night talk-show host. The third woman was perfect. Smart, funny, pretty, and she loved the outdoors.

But she wasn't Jessie.

Nobody could be, and after he turned down the next five set-ups, his friends stopped playing matchmaker.

In the movies when the hero loses the love of his life, another perfect girl comes along full of liquid light and fills all the dark places. It didn't work that way in the real world.

Three or four times a week a dream of Jessie wrenched him from sleep. In those moments he wondered if his memories were true, or if the passage of time had made their marriage more wonderful than it really had been.

And now he'd started losing those memories of her. And some days—he clenched his teeth—he couldn't quite capture her face.

These days when he pulled up photos of Jessie and him together, he sometimes couldn't even remember where they'd been taken. Most times when he concentrated, the memory rushed back into his mind like the ocean filling a tide pool. But other times . . .

Cameron lingered on the edge of the cliff a few more minutes and gazed at the valley three-hundred feet below. He sucked in a breath and held it as long as he could before releasing the air.

Wasn't heaven in the clouds? He massaged his arms and stared at the darkening sky. Was that where Jessie was?

To his right a squirrel screeched. Cameron squatted and peered at the animal who sat ten yards away at the base of a western larch. The life of a squirrel. Simple. No pain. No maddening mysteries. Few questions and an answer with every acorn. He dug into his day pack, pulled out a large handful of trail mix, and tossed it toward the creature.

"You'll be able to feed all your kids for a week on that."

The animal squealed and skittered around the trail mix and stuffed its cheeks full before scampering off.

Cameron reached down and grabbed a baseball-sized stone, stood, and hurled it with all his strength at a quaking aspen. It smacked into the tree and tore off a section of bark. Strike. He picked up another rock. Then another.

Smack! Strike two.

Strike seven, eight, nine. *You're out.*

He ignored the pain knifing through his arm and shoulder and didn't stop throwing stones till the water in his eyes blurred his vision too much to see.

First Dad, then Jessie. People died. Why couldn't he get over it and move on?

Cameron slumped to the ground and massaged his eyes with his palms and tried to recall the first time Jessie and he had met.

The memory wasn't there.

Here we go again.

Cold sweat broke out on his forehead. What was going on with him? Impossible. How had his dad known? How could this be happening to him at thirty-three?

Cameron pounded his forehead with the flat of his palm. "You can't lose your mind, Cameron! You can't."

A few seconds later their first date surfaced like the sun cresting a mountain ridge at dawn. It didn't help the panic pinging through his mind.

One year for Christmas he'd framed a collage of all their most memorable days leading up to their wedding. First real date . . . their trip up to Vancouver, B.C., where they'd visited Flintstone Land and he danced with Wilma and stepped on her toes three times. First kiss . . . Larrabee State Park in Bellingham, wasn't it? First time they'd said I love you. First . . . The canvas of his mind went blank after that.

He used to know all the dates better than Jessie ever had.

Now all he had were fragments.

Cameron trudged back to his amber one-man climbing tent, pulled his iPhone out of his climbing pack, sat, and scrolled through his favorite pictures of Jessie and him.

"Where are you now? If you're in some blissful afterlife, can you see what's going on down here?"

A picture of Jessie holding her pilot's license, a big grin on her face, slid into view. Immediately he was back at the scene of the crash, and the memory surged up from his heart like a flash flood.

This time he couldn't stop it.

"Let me talk to her!" Cameron shouted into his cell phone. Through the phone he heard a siren wail through the night.

"I'm sorry, sir. Her condition isn't . . . she can't—"

"Please put her on the phone. Please."

Cameron heard muted voices and then rustling.

"Hey." Her voice sounded soft and muffled, as if she were speaking through a thick blanket.

"Jessie!"

"Hi, Sweet-dream." A labored breath. "I love you." Silence. Then barely a whisper. "Hurry, baby, please?"

He hung up and tossed his cell phone onto the passenger seat.

Sweat dripped off his forehead into his eyes as he alternated between crushing the accelerator and mashing the brakes. Swerving around and through light traffic on I-5, he felt like he was in a movie chase scene on double speed. Rain hammered against the windshield and "Don't Fear the Reaper" played on the radio, the perfect soundtrack to the nightmare he was living.

Breathe, Cameron.

This couldn't be happening.

But it was.

He wanted to call her back, tell her something, anything, to keep her alive.

Jessie was dying.

No. Impossible. They were meant to be together always—till they were old and gray and it was time to lose their minds.

This wasn't the end. It couldn't be. There was so much life left to live.

By the time he reached the off-ramp that would take him to Paine Field, the rain had shifted from a downpour to a fine mist, as if a giant spray bottle pumped out little bursts overhead.

As he skidded around the final corner leading to the air strip and straightened his MINI Cooper, the lights of the police cars and ambulance lit up the horizon like the Las Vegas strip. But the lights pulsed with death.

He rolled down his window as he approached the scene, and the silence struck him like a wall. No sirens sliced into the night. No one spoke, no one shouted, no one ran back and forth between the ambulance and the mutilated metal that had been Jessie's midnight blue and white Cessna Skylane.

As Cameron got out of his car, he tried to take slow breaths. He'd imagined running for Jessie the moment he arrived, but his feet felt bolted to the asphalt.

A medic squatting next to the wreck glanced at him, then nodded toward the inside of the ambulance and spoke to someone inside.

A medic appeared from the ambulance, jogged up to Cameron, and stuck out his hand. Cameron didn't take it.

"Mr. Vaux?"

"Yes."

"She only has minutes left. You need to come."

"Now?" As Cameron uttered the word he realized how stupid it must sound. But everything was out of rhythm, out of body, far past surreal.

"Yes, you need to come now. Right this way." The paramedic took his arm and guided him toward the mangled Cessna.

Part of him wondered why he didn't sprint to the plane, cradle Jessie in his arms, and somehow pull her back into this life.

"How did it happen?" Cameron mumbled as the medic guided him toward Jessie, his hand still on Cameron's arm.

"You need to talk to her now."

Cameron scuffed up to the plane and stopped just before reaching it.

"Is she . . . ?"

"Her body has been . . . her upper body is okay. She can talk to you."

Jessie lay inside the plane, her head resting on the passenger's seat, eyes closed. No cuts, no bruises, dark hair framing her face like a work of art. A tiny speck of blood on her chin was the only imperfection.

But what must have been the cockpit lay buried in her torso, her blouse dark red from blood already starting to dry.

As Cameron reached out with his pinky finger and stroked her chin, Jessie's eyes opened.

"Hey, baby. You're here." She coughed lightly.

"I'm here, you're going to be—"

"Shh, only moments now." She coughed. "I was never completely sure it was real, but it was. What I saw. Death brings clarity. It sweeps away all the doubts, you know?"

"What—?"

She laughed but the blood mixing in her lungs made it sound like she was gargling. "Mortality makes many things clear, my love." She swallowed. "One is I love you more than life. The other is, the book is real. I know it is. I saw it."

Cameron braced himself against the plane's frame. The book? Too weird. The memory of his last conversation with his dad flashed into his mind. Dad had talked about a book he'd seen that he wanted Cameron to find. It was a nightmare version of déjà vu. It couldn't be the same book, could it?

"Jessie, are you talking about a book with all days in it?"

"No time." She coughed again. "You have the stone, yes?"

"What stone?" He stared into her eyes, as if he could do it with enough intensity to climb inside her mind.

"I gave you . . . before I left . . . this afternoon." She sucked in a stilted breath. "You must not lose it. It's the key."

"Yes, I have the stone, but a key to what?"

She closed her eyes and her head slipped back.

"Jessie!"

Her eyes fluttered open and she gasped for air.

"Use it to find the book, okay?" She blinked and drew another breath.

"What book? My dad's book?"

"He saw it too? You never told me." She coughed out a barely audible laugh. "That's God. He loves you so much, Cameron."

"I thought Dad was crazy."

"Promise you'll find it." Her eyes closed. "It's okay."

Tears fought their way onto his cheeks.

"No. No tears, Aragorn." The most precious name she had for him.

"You can't leave me, Jessie."

"I have to. It's going to be all right, I promise." Her grip on his hand faded. "Someday you'll know that it's okay."

Jessie drew one more breath and locked her eyes on his. "I love you, Cameron. Always and forever."

He blinked back tears as he shook his head.

Unbelievable.

Jessie and his dad both saw this book, whatever it was, or at least they believed they saw something.

Cameron stood and wiped his moist palms on his shorts as he paced back and forth on the top of the cliff near his tent. Was the book real?

He had to find out.

Now.

And he needed help.

But from whom?

Someone who wouldn't think he was nuts when he told his dad's and Jessie's story. Someone he could trust. Someone who knew Jessie almost as well as he did.

He sighed and slumped forward.

No, he wouldn't call her.

But he had no choice. He picked up his iPhone and scrolled through his contacts. If she was still in Portland, her number would be in there.

"Hello?"

"Hi, Ann, it's Cameron Vaux."

"Yeah, I saw that on caller ID."

"It's been a long time. How are you?"

"Fine."

Cold as ever. What was he doing? He could hang up right now and Ann wouldn't call back. He needed another option. If only there was one.

"Cameron?"

"Yeah, I'm here. Are you still doing investigative reporting?"

"No, I'm hosting *Adventure Northwest*. For almost two years now."

"That's right, I'd heard that." He rubbed his forehead. "Today's the anniversary of Jessie's—."

"What do you need, Cameron?"

"I thought maybe you would want to talk about—"

"I'm sorry, I don't mean to be rude, but we haven't had a conversation in two years, and it seems a little strange that you want to talk about Jessie all of a sudden."

Cameron massaged the back of his neck and walked to the edge of the cliff. No choice. He had to tell her. "I have to talk to you about something important."

"Okay."

"When my dad was forty-two, forty-three, his mind started slipping."

"I remember Jessie mentioning something about that, but I never knew the details."

Did he really want to get into this with Ann? Cameron glanced at the river below surging with the spring runoff. No choice.

"Are you there, Cameron?"

"I'm not sure I want to talk about this."

"So why'd you call?"

"I don't know." A red-tailed hawk soared above him screaming *kee-eeee-ar* as he tried to make a decision.

"Do you want to call me back?"

"I . . ."

"Look, Cameron, I know we've clashed in the past, but if you want to talk I'm willing."

He pressed his lips together and drew a deep breath. "I need to tell you the last thing my dad said to me."

"Okay."

"It was bizarre at the time, but now I'm not so sure." Cameron paused. This he needed to remember with as much accuracy as possible. "He said I would get the same disease he had. Not *if*, but *when*."

"I'm sorry."

"I went to my fifteen-year reunion a few weeks ago and didn't remember people."

"I'm going to mine next year. I'm sure I'll forget people too. You hadn't seen some of them in fifteen years."

"I didn't remember a girlfriend I had for a year, a guy I played in a band with for two years."

"You had no memory of them the whole time?"

"No, I mean, yeah I did . . . but it took a while each time for the memories to kick in. It's like it was locked up somewhere in my mind. I stared at this person, knowing I should remember them and just couldn't."

"And now you're thinking you're going to go down your dad's path?"

"Yeah, but there's more. At the same time he told me my mind would start going, he said I had to find a book with all the days in it. That he saw this book when he was a kid. That when I found it, everything would make sense; everything would be all right."

Ann didn't respond.

Great. He needed video conferencing on his phone. Was she surprised? Amused? "Are you there?"

"You're saying he was coherent when he laid all this *Twilight Zone* stuff on you?"

"He was clear, Ann. It was only for a few moments, but he was all there."

"It's been eight years since you had that conversation with him. Is there any chance time has tainted your memory of it? Given what you've, uh, been going through lately?"

Maybe. It was a fair question. But Cameron knew what his dad had said.

"No, I remember." He kicked at a rock, then said, "Here's where it gets a little bizarre. Jessie said the same thing on the day she died. She said I had to find a book, and if I did, it would be okay." Cameron swallowed hard. "What if they were talking about the same book?"

"Jessie was on the verge of dying; the mind can come up with fantastical things in those moments."

"But they both came up with the same story." Cameron shuffled back to his tent and sat next to it. "Jessie also said her stone was one of the keys to finding the book."

Again, Ann didn't answer.

"Did Jessie ever talk to you about a book or her stone?"

"What does all this have to do with me, Cameron?"

"I have to find the book. For my dad, for Jessie, for myself."

"But why are you calling me about it?"

"I need someone who knew Jessie to help me. Who might know something more about her story."

"I don't think I'm the person you're looking for."

"You know you are. Who else can I trust?" He scratched at the dirt with his forefinger. "Who else do I know who has a background in investigative reporting?"

The silence lasted more than thirty seconds.

Ann sighed. "What do you want me to do?"

The next morning his cell phone shattered the silence. Who was calling this early? He fumbled through his pack to find his phone. Ann. Cameron unzipped his tent and glanced outside. Not a hint of dawn. He might be able to get back to sleep.

He slid his Bluetooth over his ear. "Why are you calling me at this hour?"

"I thought you wanted answers."

"It's four forty-five, Ann."

"My foster dad always said, 'Never any point in burning daylight.'"

"It's not light," Cameron muttered.

"Do you want to know what I've discovered or not?"

He blinked and shook his head to wake up. "I want to know."

"Your dad said he found this thing when he was a kid?"

"Yes."

"Did he ever talk with you about his childhood? His early childhood when he lived in Central Oregon, in a town called Three Peaks?"

"No, I knew he grew up in Oregon . . . and I remembered him saying it was a strange time for him, but I didn't remember where. Where is Three Peaks?"

"I just told you, Central Oregon."

"Hey, I'm still waking up." Cameron crawled out of his tent and sat cross-legged.

"How long did he live there?"

"Till he was nine. What does this have to do with—?"

"Remember what he said to you?"

"About?" He scratched the back of his head.

"Wake up, Cameron. You need to be on point for this. Your dad said he saw this book thing as a kid."

"Yeah."

"I got up early and dug through the Internet, grabbing everything I could find on Three Peaks, which wasn't a lot. But I did find one item worth mentioning."

"What?" Cameron massaged his feet and slipped on his shoes.

"Have you ever heard of Future Current?"

"No, should I?"

"Probably not. It's not that well known outside of New Age circles. But in that subculture it's pretty well known. Their whole focus is unlocking memories from the past as well as trying to look into the future. Know it, tap into it, control it, use it to shape future events. And their headquarters are in—"

"Three Peaks, Oregon."

"Yep. For them to choose to locate in a town of only seventeen-hundred people . . . seems like a pretty interesting coincidence. Why there, you know what I mean?"

Cameron started breaking down his tent.

"So what's next?" Ann asked.

"When can you meet me in Three Peaks?"

She sighed through the phone. "Sorry, Cameron. Why don't you check it out and call me if you need help once you get there."

"Ann? Please?"

"I'll think about it."

"Ann, I really—"

"I said I'll think about it."

The line went dead.

He didn't need her to think about it; he needed her to come. Cameron dug his fingers into his knotted shoulder and stared at the horizon, now a lighter gray streaked with hints of gold.

I have to find the book, huh, Dad? That will bring my Jessie memories back and keep them intact for the rest of my days? Will it keep me from losing any more of my mind? He rubbed his brow as the cords in his neck tightened. *I can't afford to lose my brain, Dad.*

Cameron finished breaking down his camp and glanced at his watch. He could be back to Seattle and packed for a trip to Three Peaks by early afternoon.

As he stuffed his tent into his pack, Jessie's stone around his neck fell out of his shirt. He dropped his pack and held the stone, staring at the markings on its surface.

This was the key?

All right, Jessie, if the wild goose is running, I'm ready to go on a chase.

All he needed to do on Monday morning was convince Brandon he could handle an extra fifty hours for the next couple of weeks.

Piece of cake.

Yeah, right.

CHAPTER 4

Cameron sat in his office on Monday morning, chewing espresso beans and getting more irritated by the second. Brandon and he played tug-of-war over his going to Three Peaks, and Cameron was getting tired of the rope burns.

"You can't go now, bud, we've got five jobs on the front burner. They're jumping off the stove, they're so hot. I'm supposed to shoot, edit, write, and do the voice work all by myself? Oh, that's right, I forgot, I don't do voice work. And I can't animate like you can. But other than that, sure, count me in for a 120-hour week. Sign me up, lock and load, make it happin' captain." Brandon did a bad version of The Twist.

"Stop."

"Huh, what? Say again. One more time?"

"Stop talking. Now. You're not funny and your dancing makes you look like you've got the dry heaves."

"That's your big comeback for why you have to go?"

"I have to do this, Brandon."

"Listen, sarcasm aside, I get it. Great. Go. That's why we started this biz. Have the freedom to get out of here and go without checking with some corporate suit. But hello, uh, not when we're in the heart of the game. Two months, then you're outta here for three weeks. Four. Six. Whatever."

"I need to go now."

"Okay, okay, I'm with you. Just give me a good reason why, and I'm on the team."

"I think I'm . . ." Cameron stopped himself. Right. As if he could tell Brandon he was losing his mind. And his dad's whacko last words and a recent recollection of Jessie's accident were about to send him on an insane goose chase to find some book that would restore his memories, cure his mind, and maybe answer ninety-nine of the other one-hundred questions of life.

"I can't tell you."

Brandon slouched back in his chair and locked his fingers behind his head. "Oh, great. Let me guess. It's some weird trek, like the time you were convinced Bigfoot had visited your campsite up near Tumwater Canyon and you needed to hang out up in the pine trees for three days trying to get his picture."

"I was seventeen when I did that. I was a little more impressionable in those days."

"So you don't believe in Bigfoot anymore?"

"No, I've shifted my focus to something fully based in reality—the Loch Ness Monster."

Brandon laughed and slumped back in his chair. "It's hard to stay ticked off at you, even when you're being an idiot."

Cameron smiled. "Thanks, I think."

"So why can't you tell me what's going on?"

"Three Peaks is where my dad grew up till he was nine. Something he said to me might be a clue as to why he died so young. I need to check it out."

"You're killing me, Cam."

"I have to go now."

"You already said that." Brandon sighed and pulled up a calendar on his computer. "How long?"

"A week, maybe two."

"This be July 19." Brandon pointed to the date on his computer monitor and then moved his finger down two weeks. "This be August 2. You gotta be back at de veddy, veddy latest by that date, cool?"

"It'll probably be sooner than that. I just want to see if there's anything of my dad's history there that will explain how Jessie and he ended up talking about the same . . ."

"How Jessie and he ended up talking about the same what?"

Cameron dug the nail of his forefinger into his thumb. He needed to be careful. He wasn't ready to tell Brandon what was going on. He had hardly come to terms with it himself. "I need some space on this one. Okay?"

"You got it. No worries."

No worries? Right. They were the only thing filling his mind.

~

An hour later Cameron checked to make sure his mountain bike was securely mounted on top of his MINI Cooper, then slipped behind the wheel. He tossed his briefcase into the passenger seat on top of a couple of books on Central Oregon history and buckled up.

The backseat was stuffed with his laptop, video camera, clothes, and climbing gear: ropes, carabineers, tapered wedges, SLCDs, harnesses, shoes, and chalk. Always lots of chalk, so he wouldn't slip. Climbing safe meant climbing in control. No emotion, only execution.

Even the adrenaline rush that coursed through him when he climbed wasn't emotion. It was a drug, an endorphin high that buried his pain. A way to keep the loss of Jessie at bay for at least a few hours. And a way to be close to her at the same time.

His mind shifted to Ann. She had finally relented and agreed to meet him, saying she'd been meaning to come to Three Peaks anyway on a personal matter. She would arrive in Three Peaks in a couple days but could only stay for a week at the most. Fine with him. All he needed was a little help.

He fired up his car and headed south on I-5 toward Oregon. Wispy clouds moved across the sky, covering and uncovering a brilliant sun framed by a sapphire sky. That old sixties song nailed it: the bluest skies were in Seattle. He glanced at his dashboard temperature gauge. Seventy-seven degrees. A perfect summer day.

He'd read that depressed people killed themselves more often on sunny days. They were supposed to feel better when the sun was out. When they didn't, any remaining hope died, and so did they.

He'd traveled that road hundreds of times in his imagination. When Jessie died, the idea shoved its way into his mind at least a few times a day.

The blackness had tried to draw him in. It invited him to a place with no pain, no emotions, no longings—nothing but sweet relief from despair, so thick every day felt like he was slogging through waist-high tar.

The past year had been better. His mind said ending his life wasn't the answer, even if his heart continued to argue back.

These days whenever the dark thoughts surfaced, he shoved them underwater till they drowned.

He shouldn't worry about it. If he ever got serious about the idea again, Jessie would probably swoop down from heaven or wherever she was, stop him and say, "How can you think about destroying your life? You have a destiny. One that no other life can fill. Live free, Aragorn."

A king that loses his mind. Yeah, what a great tale that would be.

"Where are you, Jessie? Are you and Dad together? My heart is so barren without the two of you."

Cameron pulled into Three Peaks late that afternoon looking for Dream It, Do It Hardware, the place he'd get his first shot at finding answers.

A hair salon anchored the corner of the first building. Midway down the street was Bronco & Buster's Grill & Saloon and a sporting goods store with rubber canoes out front and a basket of clearance items spread out on the sidewalk.

On the other side was Palino's Pizza, the town hall, and Java Jump Start. At least he'd be able to get a decent caffeine jolt each morning.

At the end of the next block was the Ponderosa Lodge Best Western. He glanced at the name of the hotel on his itinerary. Yep. The Ponderosa would be home for the next two weeks.

Across the street stood the hardware store. He pulled into the parking lot on the side of the building and sat in his car, fingers tapping lightly on the steering wheel. One minute. Two. Probably the place where his journey would end before it started.

Jessie loved her dreams and visions. About God, about life, about all things spiritual.

Maybe the book was just another one of her fantasies.

Maybe his dad's words were the final ramblings of a mind shutting down forever.

Only one way to discover the truth. Start asking questions.

Lots of questions.

As he stepped through the door of Dream It, Do It Hardware, chimes announced his arrival. He scanned the store. No customers. To his right a small fan pushed a faint smell of sawdust and grease into his nostrils.

"How can I be of help to you today?" said a man with thinning, dirty-blond hair. He sat behind a low counter on a tall maple stool and pecked at a computer keyboard with his forefingers. He wore a rumpled blue polo shirt with a *Benjamin Moore* logo and khaki shorts. Cameron guessed the man was in his late fifties, early sixties.

He eased toward the man. "I'm looking for Mayor Kirk Gillum."

"Mind if I tell him who it 'tiz that's searching for him?" The man stepped out from behind the counter, his eyes narrow.

"My name's Cameron Vaux, I'm—"

"Right, we met on the phone. I'm Kirk." He folded his arms across his chest. "You don't look like you sound on the phone, Mr. Vaux. You've got one of those deep radio voices, so I thought you'd be six foot ten or something. Of course, I probably don't look like I sound either. People rarely do." He unfolded his arms and gave Cameron a weak handshake. "I suppose I should offer you a drink."

Kirk moved back around the counter and opened a small refrigerator. "I've got Diet Mountain Dew; that's about it."

"Mountain Dew is fine."

He tossed a can to Cameron who snagged it with one hand.

Kirk stepped back to the counter and leaned forward on his elbows. "You mentioned you're a videographer, right? Will you be doing any filming while you're down here?"

"Probably not."

"Too bad. It would be a real treat to have someone make a documentary about our town," Kirk said.

"Treat?"

"The wonderful things about a small town outweigh the downsides, without question, but one of those downsides is wheelbarrows full of monotony. Three Peaks is great for tourists, but sometimes we locals like a little shot of excitement. Having a film crew here would be kinda fun."

Cameron took a swig of Mountain Dew. "Sorry to disappoint you, but maybe someday."

"No problem. So you want some history on Three Peaks, huh?"

Kirk didn't wait for Cameron to answer. "Like I said when you called from Seattle, I'm not much of a historian, but a few folks around here can tell you everything, from the highest and lowest temperatures for the past fifty years to who won the Doggie Dash ten summers back. I've already told them you'd be coming."

Kirk yanked a folded piece of paper from his back pocket and handed it to Cameron. On it were three names with addresses and phone numbers.

"They're looking forward to meeting you. First is Arnold Peasley. He's a little off center—most folks around here would say he's certifiably peculiar—but he knows his history like I know nuts and bolts.

"Next is Laura Moon. She was the mayor here before me and owns the crystals store in town. She runs the local theater and writes her own plays sometimes. Her plays are about as exciting as bird-watching, but we like her too much to complain."

"I know some people who really enjoy birding."

"Sorry to hear that." Kirk almost smiled. "Just kidding."

He tapped the next name on the list. "Then we've got Susan Hillman, the best of the bunch. She works at the library, so she can point you to the history books. She's a rock, solid as they come, and is one of the keenest observers of people you'll ever meet. A little whacked out when it comes to her spiritual beliefs, but we overlook that as best we can."

"Thanks, I appreciate all the help."

"No problem, young Cameron." Kirk attempted another smile. "Anything else you want to know before we say good-bye?"

Should he tell this guy the real reason he was here? Kirk Gillum wasn't exactly heating up the hardware store with his warmth. But what could it hurt?

"I want to talk about my dad."

"Your dad?"

"He lived here till he was nine."

Kirk rubbed his chin. "Interesting. It is indeed a small world. Is this the first time you've visited Three Peaks?"

Cameron nodded. "First time."

"And you wanted to see where he spent his early years? Is that what this history thing is about?"

"That and hopefully a little bit more."

"More?" Kirk leaned back and folded his arms again.

"My dad died eight years ago, but before he did, he said something strange. His mind was gone at the time so I didn't pay much attention then. But some recent . . . circumstances have made me think again about what he said and take it a little more seriously."

"And what did he say?" Kirk titled his head.

"That I needed to find the day's book. I have to find out if it exists."

"The day's book? Hmm . . . ?" Kirk squeezed the tip of his tongue between his lips and looked like he'd taken a bite of lemon pie without any sugar.

"Does that mean anything to you?"

The mayor stared at him with a condescending smile. "Don't take this the wrong way, Cameron, but why in the world would you want to go searching for something like that? Trust me, leave it alone."

"So it does mean something to you."

"Of course it means something to me, or I wouldn't have suggested you drop it." Kirk stood and strolled toward the front door of the store. "But since I'm one of the friendliest people you'll meet in this town, young Cameron, I'll say it again. You might consider just leaving it alone."

Cameron planted his hands on his hips. "Mind telling me why?"

"You are a free citizen and can do whatever you want within the confines of the law." Kirk pushed open the front door. "But I do hate to see anyone in my town, especially a fine new friend, waste his time chasing down some fairy tale that is none of his business when he could be out doing so many other interesting things." He motioned through the door toward Cameron's car. "Thanks for coming by."

Cameron took the not-so-subtle hint and walked out. He climbed into his car and fell back in his seat.

Until that moment, he hadn't given his dad's and Jessie's words more than a fifty-fifty chance of having any validity. No longer.

A fairy tale? Not to Kirk it wasn't. So what was this book?

Cameron pulled Gillum's list out of his pocket. Time to meet quirky Arnold Peasley.

CHAPTER 5

"What are you still doing here?"

Ann Banister looked up from her desk to find Drew Silster standing in the doorway of her office, arms spread to both sides of the door frame, his eyes twinkling behind his squared-off glasses. Good boss. Good friend.

"I was plowing through a few e-mails and wrapping up a few last-minute details," Ann said.

"You mean you were stalling?"

"You're funny." Ann smiled. "I mean I was wrapping up a few details."

"Anything I can do for you while you're gone?"

She shut down her e-mail. "Yes. You could pray for my trip. I'll need it."

"Excellent suggestion. I'll get started on that as soon as I figure out how that whole prayer thing works." Drew stroked his chin.

"When you get back, I've got a stupendously stellar story for you to work on."

"That's the twentieth time you've used that line this year." Ann leaned back in her chair and folded her hands across her dark blue Nike jacket. "And it's only July. You're addicted to alliteration."

"I can't believe I'm giving you three weeks off in a row."

"Sure you can, I've earned it." Ann grinned. "And you love me."

"True. And so do they." Drew stepped inside and pointed at a map of the United States on the far wall of Ann's office. "Did you see the overnights? The TV audience in Miami loves you. As they do in Philadelphia, and San Francisco, and Nashville.

"But they're not so sure about you in Dallas or right here in Portland, Oregon." He walked to the map and circled the cities with his forefinger. "The show has plummeted all the way to number two in its time slot in both markets."

"I still wonder why I got in front of your cameras that first time." Ann shook her head, even though now she couldn't picture herself doing anything else.

"You're finally going to tell me why you agreed? Ever since I've known you, you've never wanted anything to do with the outdoors or thrill seeking, then all of a sudden two years ago, boom, you transform from Ms. Investigative Journalist into Adventure Girl."

"I think you know why." Ann touched the tip of her forefinger to a framed picture on her desk.

"I suppose I do."

"It's the same reason I started rock climbing. It's a way to feel close to the true adventure girl. I think about Jessie with every story I do. She would love to be cohosting the adventures with me. And she'd be better at it."

Ann picked up the photo of her foster sister and clutched it against her chest. "I pretend Jessie's doing the stories with me, laughing, teasing me, pushing me to do even crazier things."

She set the picture back on her desk and swallowed. No more tears. Enough had come a few days back on the anniversary of the crash. "So what's the stellar story you'll have me dying to develop when I get back?"

"Rock climbing. Since you're a pro now, it's time." Drew waved the production schedule in his hand. "I've been producing *Adventure Northwest* for three years, and we've never done a show on rock climbing."

"I didn't realize that. What a riveting revelation." Ann clicked off her desk lamp.

"That one was better than your last two."

"Thanks. Listen, I'm still pretty new to the whole climbing thing. Maybe we could wait another six months or a year even."

"Nah, you'll be great. Knowing you, I'm sure you're better than you're letting on."

She scooted her leather chair up next to her desk as she watched Drew gaze at *The Princess Bride* poster on her office wall.

"Still waiting for Wesley, aren't you?"

"Absolutely." Ann flipped her shoulder-length auburn hair behind her shoulders. "Nothing can stop true love."

"Don't you have to find him first?"

"I'm working on that." But she wasn't working on it. Was she supposed to meet someone online? Not a chance. Ask friends to set her up? No. Finding true love wasn't as easy as scripting a movie where the handsome hero suddenly appears.

Drew rapped a rolled-up tube of papers against his palm. "Speaking of romance, I'm going to surreptitiously stick my snout in where it doesn't belong."

"You already did with your stalling comment." Ann folded her arms across her chest.

"Are you seriously going down to Three Peaks to meet Cameron?"

"No. I'm not going there to meet him. He'll just happen to be there at the same time I'm finding out where I came from." Ann raised her eyebrows and tilted her head.

"You sure you want to dig into your family history?"

"Positive."

But she wasn't positive. Why try to find relatives who might not want to be found? Why uncover a past that might be better off buried? Because she had to know if she was completely alone in the world. And the timing of Cameron's call might be God's way of saying it's time.

"You just happen to be going down there at the same time as Cameron? I thought he called and asked you to come." Drew slumped into the chair in front of Ann's desk.

"He did."

"I'm confused."

"So am I." Ann pinched the bridge of her nose. "But I've been meaning to go there anyway, so the timing worked out. What was I supposed to say?"

"No."

"I tried, Drew."

"Not hard enough apparently."

"He's almost like a brother-in-law. And it has to do with Jessie too. Something I need to find out about her."

Drew nodded. "You're not worried about any emotions that might surface again being around Cameron?"

Ann rolled her eyes and sighed. Yes, she was fully worried. "That was seven years ago." She slammed her laptop shut and stuffed it into her briefcase.

"So you don't have those feelings anymore?"

"No." *Ann, you are such a liar.*

"I'm only going to say this because you're one of my closest friends. I can tell when you're lying."

"Well, this time you're wrong." She slung her briefcase strap over her shoulder and glared at him. "I'll be fine."

"What kind of friend would I be if I didn't at least tell you to be careful?"

"I'm always careful."

"I know." Drew stood, walked through the doorway, and said over his shoulder, "Be extra careful this time, okay? I don't want you getting hurt."

Neither did she. But it wouldn't be easy.

Hearing Cameron's voice and having the old feelings surge to the surface was bad enough. Now she'd have to be around him for a week or more.

Why had God stuck him back in her life? Even if Cameron caught a clue and realized how she felt, she could never let herself get involved with him.

Add in the possibility that Jessie's book was real, and she had a recipe for severe psychosis. How many times had she teased Jessie about that fantastical story? Probably every day after they ended up together in the Busby's foster home.

Ann strode out of her office, tears threatening to spill onto her cheeks.

She had the feeling this adventure would wrack more nerves than any on-air story she'd ever done.

CHAPTER 6

Cameron rang Arnold Peasley's doorbell as he examined the chipped pea-green paint on the siding determined to get answers. He wouldn't let Arnold shut him down as fast as Kirk Gillum.

Ten seconds later the door swung open and a spry man wearing a plaid long-sleeved shirt and an ancient-looking pair of Adidas sweatpants stood in front of him. He held a worn basketball under his arm.

"Arnold Peasley?"

"Yep."

"My name is Cameron—"

"I know precisely who you are." Arnold tapped his foot double-time on the faded hardwood floor in his entryway. "Gillum said you'd be coming by to converse with me about Three Peak's history."

Arnold led Cameron through a six-foot-tall corridor of stacked newspapers bound with twine. Piles of papers lined every wall.

"Quite a collection of newspapers you have there."

"I keep telling myself I should toss 'em, but I consider myself the town's unofficial historian, and a newspaper is the best history you can have. Books have a tendency to filter out all the interesting details." Arnold ran his fingers through his hair three times in rapid succession.

"Don't they have microfiche of all these papers?"

"Oh, probably, but there's nothing like having the real McCoy, you know what I'm saying? I think you do." Arnold stopped in front of two rocking chairs, only a few patches of varnish still on them, sat, and motioned for Cameron to do the same.

A few moments later Arnold smacked the arms of his chair three times and popped back to his feet. He strode toward the kitchen dribbling his basketball. "Come along, Cameron; don't just sit there."

He smiled to himself and followed his host.

"I do know the history around here," Arnold said over his shoulder, "so fire away. What would you like to know?"

Everything. No point in being subtle; he needed answers now. "Before my dad died, he told me about a book with all the days in it. Does that mean anything to you?"

Peasley stood in front of the refrigerator dribbling the basketball. "Why should I tell you?"

"Because I—"

"Can you take the time to explain what the book has to do with finding out about the history of Three Peaks?"

"I'm not—"

"You're not really here to find out the broader history of our town, are you?" Peasley glared at him as he shifted his weight from one leg to the other.

Cameron sighed. "No, I'm not."

Peasley squinted at him as if he were studying a map, deciding on the best route to his destination. "Since you've come clean with me, I'll be fairly transparent with you. Yes, I know exactly what you're talking about."

"And?" Cameron raised an eyebrow.

"I said fairly transparent. Not fully. There's a couple of people to talk to, but you might want to start with him."

"Him?" Couldn't he get a straight answer from this guy?

"Yes, there's always been rumors that he knows more about the book than the rest of us, but he won't talk about it. Maybe you can get him to open up." Peasley drummed his fingers on the counter.

"All I want to know is what the book is."

"Ah, so disappointing. We were doing well, and there you go lying to me again." Arnold shook his head. "No, no, no, you want to know far more. And if you knew what the book really was, you'd want to know far more than you're imagining right now. You'd want to know it all."

Cameron gritted his teeth. Yes, he wanted to know everything about the book. If he confessed that, would Peasley stop talking like Mr. Cryptic?

Arnold opened his refrigerator and grabbed a pitcher filled with something light brown. "Can I interest your taste buds in something cool and refreshing?"

"Sure." Cameron nodded and swallowed. He'd better choke down at least a little of what looked like well-aged iced tea, or Arnold might stop talking altogether.

Peasley poured two tall glasses and handed one to Cameron. The other he left on the counter. "I grew up around here. I never left."

Cameron took a sip of the tea. Not bad.

"I played guard on the high school basketball team in '68 and

'69 you know. You're staring at the Three Peaker who took the assist record to new heights those years."

"Who scored the points?"

"Taylor Stone did, of course, but if I hadn't seen the lanes with my eagle eyes, he wouldn't have gotten the ball. Taylor always mentioned that about me when he was talking to the paper about his record-breaking performances. Always. Good man, Taylor was. We had the most consecutive wins in the history of the town. The '82 team came close to breaking it but didn't quite make it. They missed the record by two games."

Arnold Peasley undoubtedly knew his history. Basketball at least.

"I have pictures of the team from both seasons I played, both seasons—did you know that? And the photographer those years? Whew. Good photos. Action photos."

"Will you tell me anything about the book my dad told me about?"

For the first time since their conversation began, Arnold stopped fidgeting. He turned and stared straight into Cameron's eyes, basketball clasped between his palms. "Maybe later. But I'd start with him, and if you get anything interesting from him, we'd love to hear about it."

"Who is 'him,' Arnold?"

"Taylor Stone, of course." Peasley shook his head. "I was giving you clues the whole time and you didn't pick up on them. Are you going to go see Taylor?"

"I'll think about it. Thanks."

"I probably wouldn't waste my time trying. He most likely won't talk to you. Certainly not about the book."

"You just said I should talk to him."

"I said you *should*, I didn't say you *could*. In fact, it's pointless to try and if I were you, I'd head back to Seattle as soon as you can."

Arnold bounced his ball once. "Did you play basketball growing up? You're going to love these pictures. C'mon, I'll show them to you. Come along."

Arnold Peasley grabbed his iced tea and clipped back into his living room.

Cameron grabbed his notepad and started writing. Why was Arnold driving him to talk to this Taylor Stone? He didn't think it was Peasley's altruism. And why hadn't Kirk Gillum mentioned the guy?

Ann Banister poked her trip counter on her dashboard on Tuesday evening at five thirty, cranked the volume up on her Maroon 5 CD, and pulled onto I-5 heading south. She should be in Three Peaks in three hours.

Cameron flashed into her mind and she sighed.

Three days wouldn't be enough time to figure out what she would say to him when she saw him. Why did he have to ask her to come? Wasn't it enough to talk on the phone?

"Why am I doing this, God?" She smacked her steering wheel. "I could have said no. I should have said no."

But it was about more than Cameron. Why should she be burdened with only one unpleasant task when she could be weighed down by her mysterious past as well?

Ann glanced at the photo on her passenger seat. "Did you love me, Mom, in the short time we had together? Do I have any aunts or uncles out there thinking about me? Wondering about me? Do I finally get to find out?"

She sighed and stomped on the gas. *Fine. Let's go.* It was time to uncover the past, face Cameron, see if any of Jessie's story of the Book of Days held any truth, and determine what all three things would tell her about the future. But she didn't have to like any of it.

Ann passed through Marion Forks at seven thirty and flicked on her headlights against the growing dusk. Another forty-five minutes and she'd be there.

The highway was nearly empty. She rubbed the back of her neck. It would be okay. What was the worst that could happen? She'd see Cameron, get over it, confirm that Jessie's tale was another instance of her imagination spinning out of control, find out she had no living relatives, and be done with it. Then head back to Portland to move on with life.

Simple.

Ann closed her eyes for a second. She was tired. Emotionally, physically . . .

What was that—?

No!

A deer stood in the middle of the highway, fifteen yards ahead, eyes wide.

Ann swerved into the oncoming lane of traffic, a horn wailed at her, and she yanked the wheel back to the right. The car on her left passed her by inches at the same time her right bumper clipped the deer's back leg.

She screeched to the side of the road and grabbed her legs in an attempt to keep them from shaking. It didn't work. Ann rubbed her face. "Oh, no, no . . . deep breath now. Get out, see if it's okay. Come on."

It was one of her worst nightmares. Her passion for animals overrode most other things in life.

She fumbled with the release on her seat belt, flipped it back, and stumbled out of her car.

"Please don't be dead."

When she reached the spot where she'd hit the deer, there was no sign of it. No blood, no fur, nothing.

Was the deer all right? She glanced off the road on both sides. "Please let it be okay."

Ann returned to her car and eased back onto the highway. Was this a sign of how much pain she'd have to go through before she was done with Three Peaks, or Three Peaks was done with her?

CHAPTER 7

Cameron looked at the address on Gillum's piece of paper and then gazed at the numbers on the two-story house in front of him. This should be the home of Susan Hillman.

Thirty seconds after the chime of the doorbell faded, Susan opened her door. Her short, tossed brown hair made her look like she'd just come in from a windstorm.

She offered iced tea—must be the official Three Peaks' drink—which Cameron declined explaining he'd had a glass during his last visit. But he did accept two cookies and a glass of milk, making him feel six years old again. They sat outside on her covered redwood front porch and made small talk for a few minutes about the heat of a Three Peaks summer and how long she'd lived in town.

"Fifty-seven winters." A smile played at the corners of her eyes. "But my age and how warm it gets here isn't what you want to know, is it?"

The small-town gossip grapevine must be on overdrive. "No. I'd like to talk about my dad. About his childhood."

Susan nodded.

"His name was Boscoe Vaux and he lived here till he was nine."

Susan laughed. "Well, fancy that." She leaned back in her chair till it bumped into the planter behind her filled with blue Larkspur. "I remember him."

"You what?" Cameron jerked his head and squinted. "You remember my dad?"

"Isn't that funny? I haven't mulled over the memory of Little Boss for ages. And you're his son. He was one of my closest friends in those days. Fascinating." Susan ran her hands through her hair. "God has a sense of humor, yes? Little Boss and I shared the same paint set in first and second grade."

"Little Boss?"

"That's what we called him, due to his being named after your grandfather, who of course was Big Boss." She smiled again. "Boscoe wasn't the best name for a little boy to have. I think he appreciated being called something different." She shook her head. "That takes me back a few years. If Little Boss went two minutes without laughing that was a long time. And what a great smile. Everyone loved him. So tell me, how is your father?"

"He passed away eight years ago." The familiar ache settled in his stomach as an image of his dad and him standing on West Seattle's Alki Beach filled his mind. Cameron missed that grin and the hearty laughter that always accompanied it.

"Oh, Cameron, my heart hurts for you." Susan blinked and covered her mouth. "So young."

"Thanks." They sat in silence for a minute, and it seemed to fill a dark corner of his heart with light, if only slightly. "My dad said when he was a kid, he saw a book that showed him the past and the future. Do you know anything about that?"

Susan stared into Cameron's eyes, then looked down and smoothed her forest green shorts. "I haven't thought about that for years, but I do remember a few things. Wow. Funny how it's stayed with me." She tilted her head back and scanned the ceiling, as if she would find what to say etched on its surface.

"Boscoe and Big Boss were involved in this group called Indian Guides, and they'd go on all these hikes and adventures together. Every Monday morning at lunchtime in the school's orange cafeteria, Little Boss would report what they'd done and where they'd gone.

"Well, after one of their weekend hikes, he started acting all closed up and wouldn't talk to me or anyone else. After a few weeks of that I finally asked him, 'Why are you being so quiet all of a sudden?' or something like that. He poked his straw up and down in his chocolate milk and said, 'I know when I'm going to die.'

"It was a strange thing to say coming from a nine-year-old kid, and I didn't know how to respond. Then he said, 'When I grow up I'm going to have a son and I know things about him too.' I laughed but Little Boss just kept staring at his milk carton.

"I asked him where he saw these things, but all he would say is, 'I don't know if I could find it again. Maybe I dreamed it all up.'"

"We never talked about it after that. Back then I thought he was making up stories, but over the years I've often wondered what he saw. Looking back with an adult's perspective, he certainly believed he saw this book you're looking for."

Cameron shuddered. His dad had seen something. Maybe he was just a kid, but what he saw had changed him. "I have to find that book."

"Why is this book so important to you, Cameron?"

"My dad said I needed to find it to understand."

"Understand what?"

"What would happen to me. Or what is happening to me. What he thinks he saw."

"And what is that?"

Cameron stared at Susan Hillman. Wisps of her brown hair hung over her eyes. This was a woman it would be easy to slide into friendship with, a woman he'd be tempted to spill his guts to. "I'm not sure."

"I see." And by the way she looked at him, it seemed Susan truly did see.

"Are you hoping that if you find this book Little Boss spoke of, it will give your life meaning?"

"No." Cameron held his breath and looked away, as if turning could deflect the question. How could he tell her he had to find the book because he was scared he was losing his mind and he was hoping his dad was right and the book would cure him?

How could he describe losing his memories of Jessie and tell how he would try anything to get them back? How he was terrified of ending up like his dad, talking about nothing and everything mixed up into a mess the best linguists in the world couldn't decipher? How he'd promised his father he'd search for a book that probably only existed in his dad's mind and Jessie's imagination?

Susan looked at him with compassion. "I had a son about your age. Are you thirty-four? Thirty-five?"

"Thirty-three." Cameron shifted in his seat. "Had?"

Susan nodded as she brushed back her hair. "I'd like to offer you a stone."

Interesting. Susan understood loss but didn't want to talk about it. Part of him didn't want to talk about Dad and Jessie, but she had a choice. He didn't. "Offer a what?"

She reached over and opened an old dark mahogany cabinet sitting next to the front door and brought out a bowl made of stained glass. It was full of rocks, all polished to a brilliant shine.

"This one is pretty." Susan picked a piece of jade. "I found it myself. I let it scuttle around in the polisher with all that fine sand working on it, rubbing off the rough spots, for three straight weeks." She handed him the bowl and he set it on his knees.

"You know more about the book, don't you? Will you tell me what it is?"

"Pick a stone, Cameron. To keep." Susan grabbed the edge of the dish and rattled the stones inside it.

He settled on a flat stone the color of crème brûlée streaked with black lines. Peppered along the lines were tiny red specks, connecting them, making it look like constellations of another world.

It made him think of Jessie's stone. His hand pressed against his chest and felt it under his shirt. For a moment he thought about telling Susan about the stone. Not yet. It wasn't time.

"That stone is a good choice." A pleased, almost joyful look passed over Susan's face. "A very, very good choice. Do you know where I found it?" She spoke as if talking directly to the stone. "Right here. In Three Peaks. I've never seen another like it."

She nodded twice and stood. Cameron took his cue and walked toward her porch steps. "So will you tell more about the book?"

Susan smiled and patted his arm. "You're a good man, Cameron. Keep hope, always hold on to hope."

Cameron jammed his notepad into his back pocket, clomped down Susan's stairs and toward his car. He did have hope mixed in with a full helping of discouragement. Cryptic answers was all he was getting. He didn't have time for Three Peaks' version of *Where's Waldo*. He needed answers before his mind went on permanent hiatus.

Movement in the corner of his eye caught his attention.

A man clipped along the sidewalk directly across from Susan's house.

Who? . . . Gillum, it was Kirk Gillum.

"Hey, Kirk." Cameron gave a quick flick of his hand in greeting. "As you've probably guessed, I just met with Susan. Thanks again for the introduction."

Gillum nodded in return and kept walking.

A little more of that mayoral warmth to brighten Cameron's day.

It didn't matter. Tomorrow he'd employ an old-fashioned method of discovering what he needed to know. And he would find answers.

CHAPTER 8

On Wednesday morning Cameron headed for the Three Peaks Public Library determined to find answers. Looking in books and old newspaper articles might tell him something the Internet and the people of Three Peaks hadn't relinquished.

Five and a half hours later, after pouring over every history book housed on the sagging shelves and every article available, all he'd achieved was exhaustion. And a neck that felt like guitar strings tuned three octaves too high.

Cameron slammed a book on the history of early Oregon shut and squeezed his temples. Why couldn't he find anything? Why was this town such a vault when it came to this mysterious book?

He looked at his notes spread out on one of the library's tables in front of a huge picture window and watched a shadow creep across them as the sun started to set.

It was pointless.

"You're not getting anywhere, are you?"

Cameron turned at the sound of the voice behind him.

A young man with sky-gray eyes, a Caterpillar baseball hat and a thick black goatee sat in a corner of the library, worn cowboy boots propped up on a chair in front of him. A decades old copy of *Life* magazine rested on his chest. Jimi Hendrix was on the cover.

"No one is tossing out straight answers, are they?"

"About?" Cameron raised his eyebrows.

"Don't insult me." The man laughed. "News travels in a small town even faster than Twitter."

Cameron rubbed his chin and studied the man. His eyes were mischievous. "You really want to find out about this Book of Days nonsense?"

Cameron frowned. "Book of Days?"

"Yeah, that's the official title. What have you been calling it?"

How much should he tell Cowboy Bob? At least enough to keep him talking. "My dad said 'book of all the days.'"

The man set his boots on the ground and sat up. "Your dad?"

"That's what he called it."

"Close enough. Some people call it the 'Book of Memories.'"

He leaned in. Finally someone who didn't talk in circles. "Book of Memories?"

"Sure, supposedly it's the book where everyone's life is recorded. All their memories."

His dad's memories. Jessie's. His own.

"I need to find that book." Cameron looked directly at the man. "I have to find that book."

"Take a number."

"What do you mean?"

The man took off his hat and leaned forward. "I've wondered about the legend myself for years."

"Can you tell me the legend?"

"I just did." The man flicked his hat. "It's Native American. At least that's where they say it started. But some people in town get pretty private about it. The New Agers mostly. I don't know why. It's not that big a deal. The few outsiders who dig around and figure out what it is, come to the conclusion it's a joke and they wander off."

"So where do I go from here?"

"Talk to Jason. He's the expert on the Book of Days." The man closed his *Life* magazine and tossed it onto the end table next to his chair.

"Where do I find . . . ?"

"Jason Judah. Three Peaks' most prominent self-appointed spiritual leader."

"Self-appointed?"

"You answer every question with a question? You some kind of Socrates fan-boy?" The man broke a toothpick in two and started cleaning his teeth. "Just a little small-town humor for you."

Or small-town strangeness. "I see."

"My name is Johnny. People around here call me Johnny."

"You should have stopped with the first joke."

"I like you, Cameron." Johnny chuckled.

"Thanks." Cameron rose to his feet. "Where can I find Jason?"

Johnny pointed out the window in front of Cameron to a building on the corner across the street.

"See that tiny door between the two windows? The white one with the dark blue trim? That's where the faithful gather."

Cameron stared at the dark blue door hoping that stepping through it would change his life forever.

~~~

The door said Future Current.

Future Current? That sounded familiar. Cameron looked at his notes. Right. It was the New Age group Ann told him about. Yes. Finally he would get answers. Cameron stepped into the room, slid a few feet along the flaxen-colored back wall, and leaned against it. Jazz-rock—Joe Satriani maybe—played just loud enough for the melodic bass line and an occasional guitar riff to be heard.

Jason Judah stood in front of a polished steel podium, looking like an aged and heavier version of the Norse god Thor with curly hair, his thick dirty blond locks hanging down just below his ears.

His sixty-plus disciples leaned forward in their chairs, taking copious notes as their leader's voice rose and fell in a gentle cadence.

Two of Jason's followers he recognized: Arnold Peasley and his buddy Kirk Gillum.

"We are looking for answers. The answers are out there. We are looking for direction. The path is right in front of us. We are looking for meaning. The meaning of our lives is calling to us in every moment. We are looking for our bliss. Our bliss is waiting for us to take action.

"What do you want? You don't have because you don't ask. You can make what you want reality. We must understand that the power of the mind is limited." Jason smiled and waited, probably for the questioning looks that appeared a few seconds later.

"You expected me to say *un*limited, yes? But the mind is indeed limited; by fear, by worry, by doubt. It is time to put fear aside. To push through the doubts to the other side. To give anxiety no place in your heart ever again." Jason motioned with his hands as if beckoning his followers.

"Come now, come. Believe. Believe you can create the reality
~~~

you've always dreamed of. Believe you can use the Book of Days to make everything you've ever wanted come true. Believe you can tap into its vast knowledge of yesterday, today, and tomorrow. The book is here. And if we believe, we can move mountains with its power."

Jason closed his eyes and tilted his head back.

"The book is our guide." Jason paused, then opened his eyes and grinned. "And with it we will become unstoppable."

A rush of adrenaline coursed through Cameron. Either the man was a nut case or this was the breakthrough he'd hoped for.

Jason's gaze swept slowly back and forth over the faction in front of him. On his second pass he locked on to Cameron. One by one, Jason's group followed his gaze till all eyes were riveted on Cameron.

"Are you a seeker or a believer?" Jason asked.

"Neither."

"An honest man." Jason held out his hand, palm up. "That is refreshing." He strode over to Cameron. "If you are neither a seeker nor a believer, tell us what brings you here and what we might do to help make your life more full."

Cameron couldn't tell if Jason was kidding or not. Did he make up a line like that or read it in some self-help guru's book? Neither the man nor the smile on his face moved. Jason must be serious.

"My name is Cameron Vaux."

"Welcome, Cameron."

"I'd like to talk to you about the Book of Days."

"Excellent. You've come to the right place. Let's step outside for a moment." Jason led Cameron back through the door he'd come in. After they'd walked five yards Jason said, "The book, why do you seek it?"

"My—" He glanced at Jason. A hunger in the man's eyes made him stop. "Some friends of mine mentioned it before they died.

They said it was important that I find it. I promised them I would. So I'm honoring their request."

"Wise friends. And I respect your honoring their desire." Jason smiled. "I think having a discussion about the book can be arranged. Breakfast tomorrow morning, perhaps? Say seven thirty at the Outland Café?"

"I'd like to talk to you about it right now."

"Not now. Tomorrow morning."

Cameron nodded. Jason didn't seem the type to be coerced into anything he didn't want to do.

"Our journey together begins, Cameron. I believe you will find it an extremely fascinating one."

CHAPTER 9

Ann sat in her room on Wednesday morning holding a cup of bad hotel coffee as she tried to ignore the cloud of doubt that hung over her head, sending drops of anxiety into her heart.

You're supposed to be here . . . you're supposed to be here.

Repeating the phrases like a mantra didn't help.

She'd slept late, went for a run, and showered, thinking it would help her figure out if she should call Cameron. He wasn't expecting her till Saturday. Part of her wanted to announce her early arrival, and part said wait.

She decided to check in with Drew, then grab an early lunch. Getting out among people would help clear her head.

"How was the drive down?" Drew asked.

"Fine." Ann took a sip of coffee and grimaced.

"You're still feeling this is the perfect path for you to be on?"

"No, but I'm successfully ignoring all those negative thoughts." She paused. "At least I wish I were."

"Are you thinking of heading back?"

"No, I need to do this, Drew."

"Hey, do me a favor. If you have it in your laptop, could you look up the e-mail address of that photographer who came by the office last month? I want to have him take some new head shots of you and the rest of the crew."

"RonnieD@JadeShot.com." Ann grabbed her keys and slipped out her door into the hotel hallway.

He chuckled. "It amazes me every time you do something like that."

"There are some advantages of having a photographic memory."

"What, there are disadvantages?"

"Remind me to tell you about them sometime."

"So have you figured out what you're going to say to Cameron when you see him?"

"I'm thinking about hello for starters." Ann reached her car, opened it, and slid behind the wheel.

"Hah."

"Hey, I worked on it the whole trip down."

"Seriously, what are you going to say?"

"I'm not thinking about it." Not at the moment. But she'd been debating what to say since that first disconcerting phone call four days ago. Ann jammed her keys into the ignition, started her Prius, and yanked the gearshift into Reverse.

"In other words, you have no clue how you'll greet him."

"I have nothing."

"I think you should take the blunt approach and tell him the reason you haven't had a relationship last more than nine months ever since you met him."

"I already told you, those feelings vanished years and years ago." A grocery store slid by on her left. Lunch. She needed some.

"I think the lady doth protest too much."

"Leave it alone, Drew." She didn't need him needling her about it. Especially when his needles were hitting such tender spots.

"Does anyone in Three Peaks know you're coming?"

"Who would even care if I'm coming?"

"Small towns make big stars like you even bigger."

"I'm not a star. I hate that."

"It's true."

"Fine. I'll get my pen prepared."

"I caught that alliteration. Nicely done."

"Thanks, I'll be in touch." Ann hung up and her stomach took advantage of the pause in the action to shout, *Food! Now!*

The Darn Good Deli caught her eye and she slammed on the brakes and turned hard to the right. Behind her a horn screamed at her.

"Yeah, sorry, my fault." She squeezed into a parking spot on the far side of the lot and grabbed her purse. As she stood in line trying to decide between the barbecue chicken sandwich and the turkey melt, the mumbling behind her grew in volume.

"It is!"

"Here? Nah. It is not."

"Is!"

Ann turned. Two women, one blonde, one brunette, both in short-sleeve blouses squirmed behind her. They looked to be in their midforties, carrying a few extra pounds, but their features were striking. Take twenty years and twenty pounds off and they could have been models. Who did they remind her of? Some old comic book with a blonde and brunette in it. Bingo. *Archie.* Betty and Veronica hit middle age.

The brunette spoke first. "Hi, sorry to bother you. We're not exactly the outdoorsy types, but we love reading and watching shows about it. And, well, there's this national TV show we're hooked on called *Adventure Northwest*. They do shows on white-water rafting, and paintball, and hot-air ballooning, and kayaking, and skiing, you know, that kind of stuff. Well, we think you look just like the host, Ann Brewster."

"Banister!" Betty whacked Veronica on the arm.

"A lot of people tell me I look like her." Ann nodded toward the sandwich menu on the wall. "What do you recommend?"

"I always get the turkey melt; it's never let me down," the brunette said.

"I'll take that one," Ann said to the man behind the counter. She winked at Veronica. "Thanks."

After giving him details on how she wanted it—mayo, mustard, no pickles, olives, lettuce, and tomatoes—she felt a tap on her shoulder.

"Are you sure you're not Ann Banister?"

"I'm pretty sure. But it's difficult to be absolutely one-hundred percent positive."

"I think you're her. She's my favorite person on TV."

Ann smiled. "Okay," she whispered. "I'm me. I mean, I'm her. I'm Ann. But it's not a big deal. Really."

She paused to watch the absurdity of fame engulf the women.

"Ahh! I knew it was you!" The brunette drilled her finger into the blonde's shoulder like a woodpecker trying to get at a beetle. "See! See! I was right."

"Ouch! Stop it!"

"Can I let you in on a little secret?" Ann said.

Both women leaned in, their mouths twittering with nervous grins.

"I'm no more special than you two, just a bit better known. Really." Ann might as well have mentioned aliens just landed in town square for all the effect her words had. The ladies nodded and kept grinning.

By the time Ann paid for her sandwich, the women had calmed down. Thankfully the two workers behind the counter had obviously never seen her show.

After creating a mix of Diet Mountain Dew, Cherry Coke, and raspberry iced tea, Ann waited for her two new friends to pick up their sandwiches.

"Can I ask you a favor?"

"Hi," the blonde said. "I mean, yes, of course."

"I'm visiting in town for a few days and haven't connected yet with the person I'm meeting here. Do you mind if we eat together? I would love to find out a little bit more about your town."

After almost dropping their drinks the two women agreed, and the three found a table in the back.

"We'll introduce you to Jason Judah, absolutely for sure we will," Betty said. "He's the most spiritual man you'll ever meet and knows just about everyone in town. In fact, he's having a get-together tonight at the town hall. It's an open invitation and you'd get to meet everyone. You know what I mean? You should come."

Veronica gave her the address and time.

"Okay, I will." Ann noted them on her cell phone. "But for the moment, all I want to know is if there are any good swimming holes around here where the kids hang out during the summer."

"You came all the way from Portland to find out where the local kids go for a swim?" Betty tilted her head and frowned.

"It's pretty important to me to find out the answer." Ann reached into her purse and pulled out the picture of her mom.

"Oh my." Veronica stared at the picture, then slid it over to Betty. A few seconds later they both scooped up their sandwiches and grabbed their drinks. "We're so sorry, Ms. Banister. We just remembered something. There's somewhere we have to be right now. Gotta go."

Ann stared at them as they scampered out the door without looking back. Interesting. There were obviously some dark rabbit holes in Three Peaks. She looked forward to seeing how deep they went.

CHAPTER 10

As Cameron trudged down Main Street on his way to breakfast with Jason on Thursday morning, he stared at a sign in the window of Step on the Field Sports that reminded him of Jessie. It said, "You gotta believe! The Outlaws will take State this fall!"

Three months after they'd started dating, Jessie had stood on the top of Mount Si thirty miles east of Seattle, gazing at the miles of trees laid out in front of them like a patchwork green carpet.

"Looking at this splendor, you just gotta believe." She turned to him, eyes lit up like diamonds reflecting morning sun.

"In what?"

"Something and Someone greater than yourself."

"What do you believe in, Jess?"

"I haven't told you enough already?" She laughed. "God loves you, you know." Jessie took his hands. "What about you? What do you believe in?"

"Us."

"Me too." She snuggled into his chest as he watched an eagle canter on the winds that swirled up the side of the mountain.

"That's it? No more questions? Aren't you supposed to try to save me?"

"That isn't in my job description." Jessie poked him. "God handles that part."

"So He's slackin'? I haven't felt anything yet."

"Someday He'll reach you, Cameron. I know it." Jessie pulled back, her hazel eyes gazing into his, her countenance suddenly serious. "He's not hung up on time like we are."

"Good to know." Cameron stroked her hair. "So there's a God and a heaven, huh?"

"Oh yes." She said it without a trace of doubt.

Maybe Jessie was there now, looking down at him as he tried to believe the book wasn't on the level of the Loch Ness Monster. And hoping Jason wasn't a quack.

Cameron stepped into the Outland Café and scanned the restaurant. Dishes clattered and an intense tang of bacon crept into his nose. Growing up, he'd been given two pieces of bacon every day before school. These days the smell made him nauseous.

He shook his head and waited to be seated. Two families sat at tables along the wall to the right, underneath a large picture of the three snow-capped peaks the town was named for. To Cameron's left, two men, who looked like they stepped off the pages of *Field & Stream*, each downed a three-inch-high stack of pancakes doused in maple syrup.

The hostess led Cameron to a table at the back of the café. After settling in, he glanced at his watch. Another two minutes and Jason would be late.

He wasn't.

As Jason stepped through the doors of the Outland Café, the majority of eyes turned toward him. At least six foot five and probably 260 pounds, the man was Mount Everest, or K2 at least. People acknowledged him with either admiration or thinly veiled disgust in their eyes. There didn't seem to be any middle ground. Jason's eyes seemed to say "love me or hate me, just don't ignore me."

Spying Cameron, he burst into a wide grin and sauntered toward the back of the café, stopping along the way to greet his admirers with an encouraging word. He ignored the ones who glared at him or had a sudden interest in the food on their plates.

"Good morning." Jason stuck out his frying-pan-sized paw and Cameron shook it.

"Thanks for talking to me."

"The pleasure is mine." Jason sat across from Cameron and beamed. "Cameron Vaux. How are you?" It was a statement, not a question.

"You're popular around here."

"With some." Jason smoothed back his thick hair and nodded at two women three booths down who gazed at him with dopey looks on their faces. "Others not so much."

"Why not?"

"I make people uncomfortable." He paused and a thin smile appeared on his face. "Do I make you uncomfortable?"

Cameron considered Jason Judah. He formed an impression of most people quickly. Jason was not most people. He exuded confidence, yet below the surface floated insecurity, maybe even anger. Cameron saw it in the way Jason continued to glance around the room, attempting to catch the eye of a fan, frustration rising when it didn't happen quickly.

"What's your technique for making people uncomfortable?"

Jason looked him straight in the eye. "I tell them the truth."

A waitress filled both their oversized brown mugs with coffee. Cameron ordered the Three Peaks Scramble. Jason waved her off, saying coffee was enough.

"There are people here in town and across the country who don't like what we're doing at Future Current."

An emotion flashed across Jason's face. Sorrow? Self-pity? It was gone instantly, but in that moment Cameron got an impression of what Jason had looked like as a little boy—frightened and longing for the red wagon or train set that never showed up on Christmas morning.

"Maybe they don't like it because of the hospitality of your followers. I tried to talk to your friend Kirk Gillum, and he didn't exactly set up tea and biscuits for me."

Jason laughed. "I'm sorry about that. Kirk is a little protective. He's had a number of organizations come in and call us a cult and try to rough him up a little because he's the mayor of the town."

Cameron raised his eyebrows.

"No, not physically, but they've hassled him. Little grousing fundamentalist groups around here calling for his resignation, saying he's part of a religious order trying to take over the town and all that. But now that you've checked out, I'm hoping he'll warm up."

Jason had done a background investigation on him? This guy might be over the top and down the other side. "Checked out?"

"Of course. I had one of my people do a quick background check on you to make sure you're who you say you are and aren't part of some right-wing religious group trying to denounce us and make our work out to be a blight on Three Peaks. It's why I couldn't meet with you last night."

"Thanks for delving into my life without my permission."

"You're welcome." Jason took a drink of his coffee and smiled. "Don't you research clients before you start working with them?"

"Sure."

"Then don't begrudge me for doing the same."

"I'm not going to become a client."

"But you might become a follower."

"I doubt it."

"You never know, Cameron. This book is not for one man; it's for all of us. You, me, my followers."

"Why is it for everyone?"

"Because with this book we can change the world." Jason ripped open five sugar packets simultaneously and dumped them into his black coffee. "It tells the past, and more important, what is to come."

"You're saying your Book of Days tells the future?"

Jason leaned back. "That's exactly what it does. Once we learn to access its secrets more fully, we will change lives all over the planet. Imagine if you knew ahead of time that Hurricane Katrina would hit New Orleans. Or an earthquake was about to level Haiti. Or that a cruise ship would sink with your loved ones on it. With this book, you could shape your own destiny far beyond imagination."

Cameron poured a splash of creamer into his coffee. It sounded wonderful. Like a fairy tale. But the book didn't keep Jessie's plane from smashing into the ground and stealing her life, and didn't keep his dad's mind and days from disappearing far too early.

"We're getting better at reading it every day. And we will once again learn to read the book like those who did hundreds of years before us. We will know the past in complete detail. We will know the future with blinding clarity."

The guy was serious. It sounded ludicrous. But at the moment ludicrous had appeal. *Lead me to it.* "What exactly *is* the Book of Days?"

"Oh, you've got to be kidding." Jason laughed and slapped his palms on the table. "No one has told you yet?" He stared at Cameron, a smile growing on his face.

"What is it?"

Jason shook his finger. "Not so fast. First, I want to know why you want to find it so badly when you don't even know what it is."

"I told you already, some friends asked me to locate it."

"And if you don't mind me asking, when did these friends ask this of you?"

"Eight years ag—" Cameron stopped himself. He saw exactly where this was leading.

"Uh-huh. Thank you for your honesty, even if it was a slip of the tongue." Jason leaned in and replied in a mock whisper, "You found out about the Book of Days eight years ago. Yet you've done nothing about it till now.

"Don't you find that fascinating?" Jason addressed the table next to them, but the two teenage girls sitting at it ignored him. He turned back to Cameron. "I find that fascinating. I wonder what the answer is. Hmm?"

Cameron stared at the man across the table. He was a manipulator, someone who got what he wanted, when he wanted it. Not his kind of person.

"See what I mean, my new friend? About people not liking me because I tell the truth? And now you're wondering about my motives."

"All I want to know is what the Book of Days is. If you're not going to tell me, fine. I'm outta here."

"Cameron, please. Do you really want me to call your bluff? You're not 'outta here.' You need to know what the book is, because something stirring inside you is so great it will burst out unless you get your answers. That much is obvious. But I'm not one to pry into another's affairs without an invitation. I apologize. Your forgiveness, please?"

"Sure." Jason was a certifiable piece of work.

The waitress arrived with Cameron's meal and Jason said, "Thank you, sweetheart." She ignored him.

He smiled at Cameron. "The Book of Days is power. Ultimate power. Ultimate knowledge. A book from God's own pen."

"God? I haven't ever had much use for religion."

"Neither have I. That doesn't change the fact that a book exists that was written by the hand of God."

"I think people call that the Bible."

"This book is different. That book was written by men under the inspiration of the Holy Spirit—that's what the Christians say. God penned *this* book Himself in which He has recorded the past, present, and future of every life that has ever lived or ever will live. Look it up. It's right there in Psalm 139:16."

"Sounds like an urban legend."

"No, not this. This book is real. I promise you."

Real? Cameron hands tingled as if all ten fingers were tiny cell phones on vibrate. "Can you take me to it? Can I see it?"

Jason raised his eyebrows and laughed. "I think you've misunderstood me. The Book of Days isn't a physical book, just as love is not physical. Yet love's power is greater than a nuclear bomb. The Book of Days exists on a spiritual plane. If we only believe in the things we can see on a corporeal level, we are indeed blind."

"What?" Cameron closed his eyes and sighed. The wild goose died. "The book is all in your head? Are you joking?"

"Not in my mind, just as coincidence and intuition aren't in my mind, but are waiting to be acquired if we have the eyes to see and ears to hear."

"Fine. Then how do you use it?" Cameron sat back and folded his arms. "Look at the silverware, plates, glasses, salt-and-pepper shaker, and the fake rose in front of you.

"Now watch." Jason placed his massive arm on the right side of the table and slid everything he'd just mentioned to the left. "Now, don't think about what you see, but ask yourself what you feel.

"Suddenly there is an openness between us that was not there previously. We spoke, we saw, yet with those items removed we feel closer to the other, with a greater ability to communicate, wouldn't you agree? The simple act of removing those things between us made our connection stronger.

"It is the same with the book. To access it fully, we must rid ourselves of the things in the world that block us. E-mail, Facebook, TV, movies, our fears. We must get rid of the noise and free our minds."

Jason placed his hands on the table, leaned back, and took in a long breath through his nose and let it out even slower. "When we slow down, we start to receive the spiritual impressions all around us in every moment. We see pictures in our mind's eye; visions that are sent to us from the book fill our hearts. Visions of our past and future. We record them and test them against what the rest of us have seen and heard."

Jason waved his hand through the air. "The curtain is thinner here in Three Peaks than almost anywhere else, making it easier to access God's book."

Cameron felt like he'd been dropped in a glacial lake. So the Book of Days was just another made-up religious fantasy? No wonder his dad had talked about it. God was his whole life. Same with Jessie.

Cameron swallowed hard and rubbed the back of his neck with both hands. He'd wanted so badly to believe it was real.

"What's wrong?" Jason said.

The book was a figment of Jason's imagination, another eccentric chapter from the pantheon of New Age mysticism. So what had his dad seen? Jessie? What had they *thought* they'd seen?

"I thought the book was real. Physical. Something you could see."

"It is real. It's—"

"No, not your kind of real. My kind." Cameron picked up his cup and his napkin. "Something you could get a coffee stain on."

"And what made you think it was that kind of book?"

"My dad said he'd seen it, touched it."

"Touched it?" Jason leaned forward and an eager look flashed through his eyes. "And you believe your father?"

"I believe he believed it when he told me."

"When did he say he saw it?"

"When he was nine, before his family moved away from Three Peaks."

"Fascinating." Jason steepled his hands and rubbed the bottom of his chin with the tips of his fingers. "There are some who believe as you do. I've never been able to decide one way or another.

"I've prayed for evidence that the book exists on more than just the spiritual plane. I even dug into old Native American stories from these parts, thinking I might find something there. The Paiute tribe who filled this land is full of them."

Jason leaned forward.

"But the only thing I've found on the book is a scant legend that tells of a place where stories are told of the past and the future." Jason slumped back in his seat. "I tracked down a few of the older members of the Paiute tribe still living in these parts, but they apparently don't know their own history, at least not this legend.

"The only semiverification I found was from one old-timer living in the mountains near here who said, 'Yes, I have heard of the legend, but that is all I can tell you.' Hardly substantive confirmation of a physical Book of Days."

"What was his name?"

"George or Graham or something like that. Does it matter?" Jason drummed his fingers on the table hard enough to make the silverware rattle.

"But in my wildest dreams I've always hoped the book was existent, and you have now fanned the flames of that emotion. I believe we've been brought together to explore that possibility, yes?"

Cameron stared at Jason. Brought together? No. The man had a vibe about him that said sprint in the opposite direction, as if a swarm of wasps were closing in. But if Jason could help find out if his dad's last words were real . . .

"So will you join me, Cameron?"

"I'll consider it."

"I served in Vietnam." Jason twirled his knife around on the table with his forefinger. "I dispatched men there. I would be a formidable collaborator."

"You're saying you'd kill to find this book?" Cameron cocked an eyebrow.

Jason smiled and shook his head. "I simply want you to realize the passion I bring to this quest. This book is far more than simply a tome of answers about the past, about the future. All the tormenting questions that pound your mind in the deepest shadows of the night. Every one of them answered. This book holds all the memories you've ever created."

Jason drew his knife slowly across his palm and then placed the tip of it on his forefinger and pressed until it appeared deep enough to be touching bone. "If it exists on a physical plane, it's worth doing almost anything to find it."

A surge of hope filled Cameron and caught him off guard. He closed his eyes and tilted his head back.

"Are you quite well, my friend?"

Cameron nodded. But he wasn't okay. His rational, logical side said the book couldn't exist—that his dad was delusional, that

Jessie had been speaking out of the emotions surrounding imminent death—but his emotional side screamed of what the book could do for him if Jason's claims were true.

Until that moment he hadn't admitted, even in his darkest moments, how much the idea of this book meant to him. He would get his memories of Jessie back, know if he would suffer the same fate as his father, and even see what he could salvage of the rest of his life.

His dad said it might heal his mind. Finding the book meant everything.

"I'm fine."

"Passion is the fuel that drives great discovery." Jason waggled his forefinger back and forth between them. "I think our passions can complement each other."

"I don't know."

"You will join me, Cameron, if not now, then someday. You want the book too much. You need me. It's only a matter of time."

"If we were to work together, what would the next steps be?"

"Good, good." Jason patted the tips of his fingers together three times, then pointed at Cameron. "There's a man in town I've always wondered about. Things have happened around him that have always made me ponder if he knows more about the Book of Days than he's told."

"Like?"

"He grew up with Midas touching his every choice. As if he knew what would happen before it did. It's always caused my curiosity to be stirred."

"So why don't you talk to him?"

"I've tried, many times, but the best of friends would not be the language used to describe our relationship. He likes to control people, and I'm not one who can be controlled."

"What's his name?"

"I think you can guess. Arnold Peasley should have given you a clue."

What was the name he'd written down after he'd talked to Arnold? "Taylor Stone."

"Have you talked to him?"

"I'm intending to."

"Good. We should chat again after you do." Jason stood and dropped fifteen dollars on the table. "That should take care of breakfast and provide a healthy tip for our waitress. Pay it forward can work wonders, don't you think?"

A short time later Cameron stood on the sidewalk outside the Outland Café and stared at the mountains looming over the town like a guardian. Apparently all roads led to Taylor Stone.

It was time to find the man and get him to talk.

CHAPTER 11

"Have you read the online version of the *Post* today?" Tricia Stone asked on Thursday afternoon as she leaned back from her computer screen and looked at her husband.

It was a rhetorical question. Taylor had run the *Three Peaks Post* for eighteen years, and when it arrived each week, he scoured every story, brainstorming out loud how it might have been improved if he were still there. And wishing they'd never developed an online version.

Tricia tapped her monitor. "Jason Judah just posted an op-ed piece about this video producer from Seattle, Cameron Vaux, coming here to search for the Book of Days. He ends it by inviting people to a town hall meeting tomorrow night. Jason says he has an astounding announcement to make."

Taylor didn't respond except to shift in his dark brown leather chair and turn a page of his fly-fishing magazine.

Tricia took off her slipper and tossed it at Taylor. It smacked him in the belly. She crossed her arms and waited till he looked up. "Are you talking to me today?"

"I'm sorry, hon. I'm more than a little wrapped up in this article. It talks about a way to create makeshift flies from things in the woods."

It was a lame attempt at covering up. Even though they'd married later in life—three years after her first husband had died—she'd known Taylor since third grade. And after five years of marriage, she knew when he was hiding something.

"You've never liked talking about Jason's Book of Days religion. Why?"

Taylor raised an eyebrow. "Anything written about the Book of Days should be on the *Weekly World News'* Web site, not the *Post's*. I can't believe what's happened to that paper since I retired." Taylor took off his wire-rimmed glasses and cleaned them on his 501 Levis. "I should have stayed on till I hit sixty-five."

"Maybe they truly are tapping into some mystical knowledge, some spiritual plane we don't know about that shows the past and the future. A lot of Jason's followers believe in the idea, and they're not bad people."

"A lot of nice people believe in Bigfoot too, and they can show you a great deal more evidence than anyone can show for a book with the past, present, and future recorded between its covers." Taylor put his glasses back on. "It doesn't make Bigfoot real or a book that exists only in the spiritual realm real either."

Tricia got up from her chair, padded across their hardwood floor to Taylor, and wrapped her arms around his shoulders. He patted her forearm and picked up his magazine, blocking his face from view.

Later that night, toward eleven o'clock, just before sleep took her, Tricia felt Taylor slide out from under their goose-down comforter. A floorboard squealed and he stopped. A few moments later their bedroom door opened and closed.

She eased out of bed, put on her lavender robe, and opened the door a crack. Taylor sat in front of their kitchen computer, his face bathed in the stark light from the monitor.

She eased across the floor till she saw what he was reading. The online version of the *Post*. She squinted. No surprise. Taylor was reading Jason's post about the Book of Days.

Taylor rubbed his face three times, then pressed his knuckles into his lips.

He'd carried whatever it was for so long. If only he'd tell her.

The man stared at himself in the mirror, at the lines under his eyes, at the softness of his flesh. Where had the years gone? The late fifties weren't middle age. If they were, he'd live to 120. Life was running out.

He strode out of the bathroom and onto his deck overlooking Three Peaks. A breeze kissed his hair and he allowed himself a grim smile.

So close, he was so close to finding the book. He felt it. With it he would set things right. Expose the lies. And then protect it for the rest of his days. And he wouldn't let some punk kid from Seattle sweep in and find the tome while he stood screaming on the sidelines.

He would watch Cameron. Where he went. Who he talked to. What people would or wouldn't tell him. He would use whatever Cameron discovered to find the Book of Days.

And then do whatever was necessary.

CHAPTER 12

Cameron sat in his hotel room Thursday night chewing on espresso beans, studying his notes of Jessie's words from when she lay dying in the plane.

"The book is real. I know it is. I saw it."

But did she mean physically or with what she always called her spiritual eye?

That was the hard place between the rock. He had no way now of knowing what she meant.

Peasley, Susan Hillman, the mayor—what was his name?—none of them had said anything that would indicate the book was real, had they?

But his dad said the book was physical: *"I saw it once . . . I even touched it, when I was a kid. Did you know that?"*

Think. Come on. Of course his dad wasn't lucid. His brain was gone. Spinning make-believe. Cameron had no way of knowing if his dad's words were fact or fiction. So his story happened to match up with Jessie's dying visions. So what?

Cameron walked back to the oak veneer desk and slammed his laptop shut. Then he went down the hall to get a Mountain Dew. "Will this Stone guy give me the answer, Jessie?"

Cold drink in hand, Cameron trudged back into his room and slumped into the chair next to his window.

Was his dad thinking straight when he talked about some book he'd seen as a kid? That was the hard place between the rock. He had no way of knowing if his dad's words were fact or fiction. So his story happened to match up with Jessie's dying visions. So what?

But maybe the book was real. It was possible, wasn't it? Peasley, Susan Hillman . . .

Cameron bolted upright. Didn't he just have this conversation with himself? A surge of heat pulsed through his body. *Stop it.* He couldn't let himself go there. "You are not losing it, Cameron. Your mind is fine."

Cameron stood at the window and recited long passages of Henry David Thoreau he had memorized in college. After reeling off the top-ten grossing concerts of the last year, he launched into naming the places Jessie and he had gone on their first five hiking trips together. He made it to number two.

Cameron raked his fingernails across his head, as if he could dig the memories out of some hidden chamber in his mind. A groan escaped his lips as he pressed his head against the glass and gritted his teeth. *Think!*

Just after midnight he gave up and wiped the cold sweat off his forehead. He'd tossed on a rocklike mattress every night since getting to Three Peaks. He'd read that lack of REM sleep could have a devastating effect on memory. That had to be it. Had to.

He flopped down on his bed, yanked the covers over his body, and let exhaustion carry him away.

The dream started almost immediately.

Three Years, Two Month Earlier

A hint of barbecued salmon lingered in the air long after Jessie and Cameron had cooked and eaten their dinner in Wilmot Park on the north shore of Lake Chelan. The lake turned from gray to black as the last light of day faded from the sky, light ripples the only movement on the water. The first star broke out of the dusky twilight and neither of them spoke till three more had appeared.

Cameron pulled Jessie against his chest. "It seems ridiculous to believe we're the only beings in this universe, don't you think?"

"Does it matter?"

Cameron frowned. "What do you mean?"

"Does it matter if we are or we aren't? Isn't the deeper question if we'll go on once this existence is over?"

"You're thinking it's time for a little God-talk?" Cameron stroked her hair. "Lay it on me."

Jessie's breathing settled into a steady rhythm, and Cameron consciously caused his pace to join hers. It was a way to feel as one. Neither spoke.

She finally turned her head slightly and broke the silence. "You know how you always said you couldn't live without me?"

Cameron kissed her forehead. "True."

"You can." She took two long breaths. "You will."

"Uh-oh. This is where you tell me you've fallen in love with your old high school tennis coach and you're about to leave."

Jessie didn't laugh. "You'll make it without me." She gazed up at him, eyes sad.

"I'm not going anywhere, sweetie, and neither are you."

"Okay." Jessie buried her head in his chest. "I want to believe that."

"Why wouldn't you?" He leaned over and looked into her eyes.

She closed them and pressed her lips together. "It's just that sometimes I get scared."

"Of what?"

"Being separated."

"No fear, we're going to be together for a long, long time." He squeezed her tight. "That tennis coach isn't nearly as handsome as me."

Again, Jessie didn't laugh. "It's still years away. I'm not going to think about it."

What was she talking about? "What's years away?"

"Death."

A heaviness fell on Cameron as if a backpack full of stones had been thrown on his shoulders. She was serious. Death? "What's going on with you?"

"I'm fine."

"Then why are you talking like this?"

"I just want to be with you for a long, long time," Jessie said.

"It'll be decades at least."

"Okay." She nuzzled in tighter.

He stroked her hair again. "I love you, Jess."

"Always, Cam-Ram. Always and forever."

The melancholy tone in her voice echoed in his mind for the rest of their vacation.

Cameron woke early on Friday with images of Jessie in his mind.

Had he dreamed about her? Yes. They'd been somewhere together. Near a lake? On vacation? The last images slipped from his mind like sand through his fingers. He gritted his teeth.

He had to find the book. See if it could—

No.

Cameron threw on his biking shorts and ignored the thoughts galloping through his mind regarding the Book of Days. Not today. At least for a few hours.

Twenty minutes later he panted out a rhythm in concert with the spinning pedals of his Novara road bike up the McKenzie Highway. He glanced at his odometer, then his watch. Another hour and he'd reach the summit of McKenzie Pass. A perfect distance for pushing his lungs and muscles to the breaking point.

Which is exactly the point his head was at.

When he reached the Dee Wright Observatory, he stopped and sucked in big gulps of air. The site offered a panoramic view of the Cascade Mountain Range as far north as Mount Hood.

Beautiful, but it didn't ease the squeezing feeling in his stomach.

Cameron got back on his bike and headed back, quads burning, lungs burning, mind burning, as he glanced at the cars rushing past him in the right lane.

No one would guess.

It would be so easy to swerve in front of one of them. In seconds it would be over and he would be free. His heart rate kicked into another gear.

No way. Knock it off.

But what choices did he have?

Slowly lose his mind like his dad had? *No thank you.* Keep digging for fantasies here in Three Peaks and continue to get nowhere? *Sorry.* Follow Jason? A questionable plan at best. *Option number four, please.*

Find out more about Taylor Stone? *Definitely.*

As soon as he got back to his car, he pulled up Safari on his iPhone and went to www.whitepages.com.

She would know Taylor Stone.

Cameron dialed Susan Hillman's number as he sat at a red light at the north end of Three Peaks and stared out the window at a banner hanging over the street. "Meet You in the Park!"

The banner promoted the sixty-ninth annual Three Peaks Jazz Festival. It boasted itself as the Biggest Little Jazz Festival in the World. Might be worth going to.

Three rings. Four.

"Hi, Cameron. Nice to hear from you."

Cameron pulled his cell phone away from his ear and stared at it for a second. "How'd you know it was me?"

"Even out here in the sticks, we have this nifty little invention called caller ID."

Cameron smiled and thumped his head with two fingers. "You probably have microwaves and cable TV too."

"What can I do for you?"

The light turned green and he stomped on the gas a little too hard. *Slow down*. He needed to relax. "I've had some intriguing conversations with someone named Jason Judah."

"Ah yes. Interesting man."

"You know him?"

"In a town our size you know everyone. I've known Jason since grade school, but my guess is you didn't call up to get a deeper understanding of the man."

"True." Cameron braced his yellow notepad against his steering wheel and scratched *Susan Hillman* and the date at the top. No point in forgetting anything.

"Jason says I should talk to a man named Taylor Stone who knows a lot about the Book of Days that he's not telling."

"That's Jason's opinion." Susan laughed.

"So you know him?"

"Taylor? Very well. He ran the *Three Peaks Post* for almost twenty years. I think it's an excellent idea that you meet him."

"Okay."

"I'm curious, have you figured out why this Book of Days is so important to you?"

Cameron hesitated. As much as trusting Jason seemed like foolishness, trusting Susan seemed like great wisdom. "Yeah. Because of . . . I need to find it for my dad, and for my late wife, and also for me." He pulled into the parking lot of the Best Western and killed the engine.

The crackle of the connection was the only sound.

"And why is that? Why do you need to find it for yourself?"

Cameron paused a long time before saying, "Because I'm afraid I'm losing . . ." He didn't finish and didn't know what words to use to fill the silence.

"Did your dad say who wrote his book?"

"No, Jason says God did."

"What do you think?"

"I'm not sure if I believe in God."

"That doesn't prevent Him from believing in you."

Cameron smiled. "Thanks, Susan. I'll be by for another peanut butter cookie soon."

"I'll hold you to that. Now, here's Taylor's phone number and address. Ready?"

Cameron said good-bye, hung up, and stared at the information scrawled on his yellow notepad. Another dead end? Or a highway to answers?

After a quick shower he studied his notes and his eyes stopped on the verse Jason had told him to look up.

Why not?

He strode to his laptop and Googled *Bible* and *Psalm 139:16.*

Strange. His heart rate accelerated as the verse popped up on screen.

"Your eyes saw me when I was formless;
all my days were written in Your book and planned before
a single one of them began." (Psalm 139:16)

Impossible. That couldn't be the book they'd asked him to find. Bible tale, urban legend, a Noah's ark-type story dressed up in New Age clothes.

Cameron went to the bathroom, doused his hands with water, and slicked back his hair. He walked back to his laptop, hunched over the monitor, and stared at the verse again as he massaged a double knot in his right shoulder.

. . . were written in your book . . .

Could it be real? Little chance. It felt like *Indiana Jones and the Last Crusade*, searching for cinematic artifacts. But this wasn't a movie. So what did Little Boss and Jessie see all those years ago?

Cameron went to his window and stared at the tourists sauntering up and down Main Street, the sun flashing against their cameras as they snapped pictures every few seconds trying to capture a memory.

Susan's words about meeting Taylor Stone played in his mind: *"I think it's an excellent idea."* She knew more than she'd told him. He'd heard it in her voice.

Time to find Taylor Stone. Now.

CHAPTER 13

There was no answer on Taylor's phone, and no one there when Cameron stopped by the man's house. He caught a break when he dropped in at the *Three Peaks Post* and chatted with the receptionist.

"You're looking to find Taylor?" The young redhead set down her nail polish and pointed to a county map on the wall behind her. "I know where he is most days from May through September, and since it's July I should know where he is. And I do." She tapped her pen on the counter making little black dots someone would have to wipe off. "You wanna know too?"

"Yes." Cameron forced himself to be patient. The ache in his gut said every moment counted, and while he could force himself to be light on the outside, it wasn't an easy weight to carry.

"On the river." The receptionist made a motion of casting a line, then reeling in a fish. "They tell me he's very good at it."

"Any idea which one?"

"Sure." She stepped over a stack of papers and tapped a tiny blue squiggle on the map on the wall. "Either the Metolius or Squaw Cre—I mean, Whychus Creek. It used to be Squaw Creek, but a lot of people still think of it as Squaw Creek 'cause we called it that for a long time, know what I mean?"

"Sure. Any idea which one he favors?"

"Well, there's great fly-fishing on both of them, but the fish are smaller on Whychus Creek and this time of the year the water level there is dropping, but of course it's more private there and Taylor likes his privacy, so all things considered, I'd—"

"So you think he'd be on Whychus Creek, then?"

"If I were in your shoes, that's the one I'd try first. But you never can know for sure till you start searching, know what I mean?"

"Thanks for all your help. I appreciate it."

Later as Cameron hiked from the trailhead past thundering Chush Falls to the stretch of the creek where the fish would be running, he mulled over what he would do if Stone turned out to be a dead end. No idea.

And even if Stone led him to the book, what guarantee was there that it would fix whatever was eating away at his brain like a piranha?

As the first shards of the creek materialized through breaks in the trees and underbrush, he stopped and listened to the silence. An occasional call from a red-tailed hawk broke the still canopy overhead but that was all.

Intellectually he knew this was a place of peace, but the emotion eluded him.

As he pressed through the bushes, breaking into the rocky sun-soaked beach that bordered the creek, Cameron looked right, then left. Nothing. Wait. Two hundred yards downriver Cameron saw a flash. Yes. The sun glinting off a fishing pole.

The figure whipping the pole back and forth glanced his direction from time to time, but it wasn't till Cameron trudged down the creek bank and stood directly across from him that the casting stopped.

The man was tall and wore an Oregon Ducks baseball hat. He had a black goatee with more gray than black, and his eyes made Cameron think of Sean Connery.

Cameron eased forward till he was inches from the crystal water that gurgled in front of his boots. He glanced at the photo Susan had e-mailed him earlier. The man who stood twenty yards away on the other side of the creek was definitely Taylor Stone.

"Greetings!" the man called across the glassy creek. "You lost?"

"Not if you know where we are."

"Well said." The man smiled.

"You're Taylor Stone."

"Is that a statement or a question?"

"I'm Cameron Vaux."

"Ah, I see." Taylor whipped off his hat to reveal a shock of salt-and-pepper hair to match his goatee. He bowed, his hat across his chest. "You're correct. I am Taylor Stone. It is interesting to meet you."

He put his hat back on, turned, and whipped his arm back and forth three times in smooth succession, the fly at the end of his line settling on the water for only a few seconds before a flick of his wrist snatched it off the surface. "Are you a fly fisherman, Cameron?"

"I've always wanted to learn."

"Do you mean that?" Taylor stopped casting and stared at him, a twinkle in his brown eyes.

Cameron had wanted to learn since his dad and he had backpacked a section of the Pacific Crest Trail and stumbled on a fly fisherman who had given them part of his catch for dinner. "Yes."

"Well, well. Then perchance I'll teach you someday, Mr. Cameron Vaux."

He studied Taylor. "For someone so well known in Three Peaks, you're a difficult man to track down."

"Do you believe in God, Cameron?"

He almost laughed. Three Peaks: spiritual central. Did everyone here ask about a person's spiritual life so freely?

"My dad did. So did my wife."

Taylor pointed at him. "You know what I'm going to say next, right?"

"You're going to say, 'I wasn't asking about them, I was asking about you.'"

"Correct."

"I don't know." Cameron looked down the creek and gave a tiny shake of his head. "I really don't know."

"It's born into us. We're not humans with a spirit. We're spirits with a body. We're made to follow something bigger than ourselves. So we latch on to things to fulfill the way we were made."

"Your point?"

Taylor chuckled. "For some people around here, that 'something' is a magical, mystical book that exists only in their minds."

"Can we talk about that?"

"Why do you want to talk to me?"

"All roads seem to point to you."

"All?"

"Many."

"And do those roads say I'm a hermit?"

Cameron laughed. "I was going to say reclusive."

"How long after meeting someone is it before you form your own opinion of him?"

Cameron sat on a boulder and rested his elbows on his knees. "Jason says you're Machiavellian and control the people in this town; that you try to keep people from talking about the book."

"Machiavellian? I'm impressed. I didn't think Jason capable of coming up with such a precedent metaphor." Taylor winked.

"Most men's vocabulary and elocution don't allow the use of words with such eloquence."

Taylor nodded. "I like you, Cameron."

"Would you be willing and able to answer a few questions about the history of the Book of Days?"

"Able? Sure." Taylor pulled a ten- or eleven-inch redband trout out of the creek, removed the hook from the fish in one swift motion, set it back into the shallow water at his feet, and watched it swim away. "Willing? Nope."

Cameron assumed he was kidding. "I imagine you know why I'm here asking—"

"Yes. You've talked to Jason, maybe Arnold Peasley or Kirk Gillum, and they've told the young video producer, whose dad claimed to have seen the book, to ferret out the hidden knowledge buried deep in the cranium of Taylor Stone."

Cameron stared at the man. Had he been tracking Cameron as much as Cameron had been tracking him?

"Would you like to hear some hard, cold reality?" Taylor continued without waiting for Cameron to comment. "Although it's a truth you know well, allow me the liberty of stating it. Life for the majority of Americans is exceedingly boring. Work, eat, sleep, then hit the repeat button. It's why legends like the Book of Days bloom and multiply like dandelions. It makes life more interesting. And when you add in the New Age element that is rampant in Three Peaks, a cottage industry is created. People see things they want to see. They start hearing voices that don't exist and see pictures and visions in their minds that aren't real. They believe things that only reside in their imaginations, and they create evidence for past and future events where there isn't any."

Taylor caught and released another trout.

"So the Book of Days is a hoax?"

"You can find Web sites that prove Paul McCartney died in 1966 and was replaced by a look-alike, but I'm one of those who says he's still alive and well."

"So the Book of Days is a hoax."

"Not a hoax, a fable. A made-up story Jason and his followers have tried to turn into a religion.

"Do you believe in those books that say we can tap into a hidden power floating beyond our vision? That we can create our own reality just by thinking of it?

"Millions of people bought those books and believe the message. They are spiritually starving, so when a book like that arrives, promising to fill their empty souls, the unsuspecting lap it up like a starving cat in front of a bowl of microwaved milk."

Taylor turned from his casting and drilled Cameron with his eyes. "This Book of Days nonsense is no different."

"Then why keep the lid on it? Why not promote the idea that an amazing book that tells the future exists in your town and build the legend rather than keep it quiet? It would boost tourism."

"Because working, eating, and sleeping with contentment as your constant companion is not entirely bad." Taylor leaned his rod against his body.

"A great majority of the people who live in Three Peaks take for granted that they've known three-quarters of the town their whole life. They take for granted the gift of being able to call most of those neighbors in the middle of the night and see them come running to help."

Cameron nodded. "Community."

"Exactly. Yes, we could create T-shirts and posters and Internet ads telling people to come search for the legendary Book of Days and create a tourist trap that would rake in thousands daily. But it would become a trap for us as well. Do you think the Scots like the proliferation of tourists searching for Nessie? Some do, I'll grant you. The ones selling the T-shirts and DVDs wouldn't mind seeing even more seekers. But the majority of the towns around the lake would like to simply be left alone."

Taylor sat on a large boulder and set his fly rod across his leg as he worked on securing a new fly to his line. "I have some power in this town having been mayor a few times and having run the paper for more than a few years. And yes, I've tried to keep people from talking about the Book of Days or sticking their nose in where it doesn't belong so that we can keep our sleepy little town sleeping. If that makes me Machiavellian, so be it."

The confidence Taylor spoke with made his words ring true and washed away what little belief Cameron had held of the authenticity of the book.

The river between them seemed to grow wider. But he wasn't ready to give up without one last try.

"Before my father died, he claimed to have seen the book. He says he touched it."

"I'm sorry for your loss. I can't comment on what your dad saw or didn't see, and I don't know what has driven you to talk me today. But I do know people can be led down false paths when their souls are searching, and I would pray you do not take that path." Taylor finished tying on the new fly and began casting again.

His words settled on Cameron like a three-hundred-pound anchor. No one with a shred of rational thought would entertain the idea of a physical book that told the future and recorded the past existing on Earth. He himself had chalked his dad's words up to the disease until he'd become desperate. Even Jessie's words hadn't spurred him into action.

So was his own fear clouding his judgment? Undoubtedly. But he didn't care. Taylor Stone wasn't God. He didn't have all the knowledge of the universe at his fingertips. Maybe Jason was right and this guy was wrong.

"What if the book is real? You can't know with one-hundred-percent certainty it isn't, can you? I have to at least try to find it."

"That book will bring you nothing but death, Cameron."

"How can a book that doesn't exist bring death?"

Taylor's next cast fell far short of the deep hole he'd aimed for. He cast three more times before answering.

"I see your passion and can appreciate it. And I feel for you as you go on this quest. But I think we're done talking for the day." Taylor set his rod down and stared at Cameron. "Unless of course you're ready for that lesson."

"Maybe later."

Taylor nodded good-bye and Cameron turned away from the creek. He slogged through the underbrush arguing with himself. *Believe Taylor. Believe Jason.*

He replayed the conversation with Taylor in his mind. Something was off. Not off exactly, but slivers of Taylor's speech didn't ring true. Was it a hint of concern in Taylor's eyes? Maybe it was Cameron's feeling Taylor was protecting somebody. And what about his line, *"That book will bring you nothing but death"* Freudian slip?

He stopped, turned, and hiked back up the trail the way he'd just come. He slowed as he approached the creek and watched the ground in front of his hiking boots to avoid snapping any twigs. As he got closer to the river bank he scrunched down and eased forward, taking only one step every few seconds.

A rock shifted under his weight and cracked against another stone. Cameron froze and didn't move for thirty seconds. He sank to his knees and crawled up to spot where he could see the creek.

A few more yards, yes, he spotted Taylor. He wasn't fishing. He stood, hands on hips, looking toward the three peaks the town was named for.

Cameron was only slightly surprised when a few seconds later Taylor bent over a large boulder, arms extended to hold himself, and muttered something too quiet to hear. The next moment he straightened and kicked at the rocks in front of him. Then he picked up a stone the size of a cantaloupe and hurled it into the boulder in front of him. It shattered and Taylor turned and fell back against the boulder, arms folded, head looking up to the sky.

So Stone wasn't as self-assured as he liked to project. If Cameron's interpretation was right, he'd just ripped the door off a house that Stone wanted to keep hidden from everyone, maybe even himself.

The man deserved credit. Taylor Stone was quite an actor. The fisherman had almost convinced Cameron there was nothing to the legend.

Machiavellian? Probably not. But there was a very good chance he was the Book of Day's key master.

CHAPTER 14

Cameron arrived at the Three Peaks Community Hall on Friday night a few minutes before six o'clock, ready to see a skirmish. It seemed like a third of the town or more had responded to Jason's open invitation to hear the new revelation he'd discovered about the Book of Days.

He suspected Taylor Stone would show up to promote his opinion of keeping a proverbial lid on the whole Book of Days nonsense. At the very least he'd be there to see what Jason would say and refute anything he didn't like.

Rock 'Em Sock 'Em Robots, Three Peaks' style.

While waiting for the meeting to start, Cameron munched on the abundant hors d'oevres and surveyed the crowd.

As his gaze swept back and forth over the crowd, he spotted Kirk Gillum standing in a corner of the hall next to Arnold Peasley. Kirk's eyes locked on to Cameron's for a moment, he blinked, then looked away. The guy couldn't have been elected mayor on his charm.

Where was Stone? The man had to be here. Cameron spotted Taylor on his third scan. There. Over near the restrooms, leaning against the wall with a woman in her late fifties by his side—probably his wife. What was her name? The receptionist at the *Post* had told him, but he couldn't remember.

Cameron eased through the crowd till he stood ten or eleven feet from Taylor. He caught Taylor's eye just as Jason stepped to the microphone. Taylor winked at him.

"Friends and neighbors, seekers of the truth, and those who are merely curious. Welcome! Thank you for coming." Jason paused and looked over the throng, those with folded arms mixed in with those with adoration on their faces. "We have a packed house tonight. I think even my worst enemies must be here!"

The crowd chuckled politely as Jason's eyes swept the room. When his gaze reached the far right side of the room, he stopped and raised his eyebrows.

"Well, this is interesting. It seems we have a distinguished individual here this evening from Portland—Ms. Ann Banister."

Cameron closed his eyes and let his head flop to the side. Great. She wasn't supposed to arrive till tomorrow. Gear up. It would be fine. She might have grown a new personality since last time he saw her.

The crowd followed Jason's gesture toward Ann.

She waved and offered a half smile.

"Welcome!" Jason boomed as he led the crowd in light applause.

"Now, Ms. Banister, I don't mean to put you on the spot, but would you like to come up onstage and say a few words?"

What was Jason doing? Why would he want Ann up onstage? Did he expect her to uncover the location of the book on the spot?

Sure, she used to do investigative reporting, but she wasn't Scully from the *X-Files* or Olivia from *Fringe*.

The guy was rocking on a chair with no legs.

Ann waved Jason off. "That's okay, thanks."

"Come now, I think you have some fans here who would love to hear from you."

The crowd laughed and broke out into a louder round of applause.

"See?"

As Ann made her way to the stage, Jason gave an impromptu introduction. "If you don't know already, Ann hosts a very popular cable program that I believe is seen weekly across the country. Please welcome to our town, Ms. Ann Banister."

Ann sprang up the stairs in jeans and a maroon polo shirt with an *Adventure Northwest* logo. She walked over to Jason, shook his hand, and turned to wave at the crowd.

"Hello, Three Peaks!" A big smile creased her pretty face. "I didn't dress tonight with the idea of being onstage. I hope this works for you." She smiled again as the crowd applauded and nodded their approval.

A sudden movement to his left made Cameron pivot.

Taylor Stone stumbled forward and hunched over, as if he was choking on one of the mini crab cakes Jason had provided for the event. His wife steadied Taylor, and after a few seconds he stood erect again, apparently recovered. But his face wasn't red as it should be from choking; it was stark-white. His eyes narrowed and his lips parted, the look on his face was one of shock.

No question as to the source of his surprise. Stone stared directly at Ann Banister.

Taylor finally turned to his wife, who glanced rapidly back and forth between Ann and him. After sharing ten or fifteen seconds of intense whispers, Taylor and his wife eased out the back door.

The Taylor Stone saga had just added a fascinating new chapter.

Taylor Stone, you and I are going to get to know each other much, much better.

Cameron looked back at the stage and listened to Jason banter with Ann about life as a television-show host and his favorite episodes of *Adventure Northwest*.

"Now friends, I want to bring up a subject dear to my heart and many of yours. Ann, I'd love to have you stay onstage and answer a few questions if you don't mind." Jason turned, opened his palms, and tilted his head.

Ann gave a quick nod.

"Great." Jason turned back to the crowd. "I know some of you think Future Current is a joke and that the Book of Days is a figment of my overactive imagination. But I recently met a man whose father saw the book in physical form. And *touched* it. He carried this secret till just before he passed on."

Wonderful. Of course Jason couldn't keep his mouth shut about what Cameron had revealed. He glanced at the back door. If Jason threw out an invitation for Cameron to come up onstage, he didn't want to be in a position to accept.

"I believe this man told the truth. It brings to light something I've hoped for for years. That the book is not just real on a spiritual plane but in the physical realm as well. Are you ready to read about your future? Remember your past? With this book we can change mankind forever." Jason grinned. "Friends, please show your appreciation to this man's son for bringing us renewed hope. I give you Cameron Vaux."

Cameron gave a quick wave as a smattering of applause filled the room. He looked toward the door again. Kirk Gillum stood at the door glaring at Jason. A moment later he shoved his shoulder into the door and strode out.

"I'm sure Cameron will be interested in talking to any of you as soon as I'm finished."

Right. Maybe he should follow Kirk out onto Main Street.

Jason paced the stage, his head moving down then up then down again, then he turned to face the crowd. "I know many of you have heard the legends of the book since childhood, and the claim of someone who has seen the actual book in living color does nothing to bolster your faith.

"Regardless of where you stand, it is time to address the pink elephant that has taken up residence in the middle of our town. I haven't spoken of the book in a public gathering such as this for a long time. But now the time is right. It's time for you all to join us in our quest for the truth."

Cameron stared at Ann. Her face looked like she'd just stepped off a dingy that had been navigating twenty-foot swells.

"Friends, I don't think the timing of Ann coming to our town is coincidence. She's dug into stories around the Northwest as an investigative journalist for many years now and has found some intriguing and unusual things during that time. So now I ask you, Ann, from someone who has seen their fair share of strange stories, is it possible the book actually exists? That it is genuine?"

A wave of concern washed across Ann's face but she recovered a moment later. "Would you like me to give my professional or personal opinion?" Ann tilted her head to the side.

The crowd chuckled.

Jason tilted his head to the side. "We'd like to hear both."

"Okay, reporter first." Ann pretended to crack her knuckles and lowered her voice. "Since I am completely without bias and entirely objective," Ann smiled, "I don't know whether a Book of Days exists or doesn't exist. It would be fascinating if it did, but I will, of course, keep all emotion out of my mind as this story unfolds. And if you find it in the meantime, can you let me know if my show is going to be canceled next season? I'm a little worried."

Jason gestured toward Ann as they both joined the crowd's laughter.

"Sure it would be wonderful to find a book that told the unique story of every man, woman, and child on earth and explained the whys of their past and what will happen in their future. There are things I'd love to know about my past . . ." Ann cleared her throat. "And, of course, my future."

Jason's slight smile grew into a grin. It was obvious he considered Ann's words so far an endorsement of sorts.

"But to be serious for a moment"—Ann turned to Jason, whose smile froze on his face—"having talked to a great many people over the past ten years that have had, um, fascinating beliefs, I have to confess I think we all have a better chance of finding the lost city of Atlantis out back than finding a hidden Book of Days written by the hand of God."

Jason swallowed. "But you are here to scout out what could be the story of the century before bringing in the cameras, correct? This is the ultimate adventure."

"No, actually I'm not. I'm here entirely on a personal matter. Sorry." Ann held up both hands and grimaced playfully.

Jason's eyes clouded over. "But if the book is discovered, certainly many people would want to broadcast the story, yes?"

"Yes, of course, I'm sure a hoard of TV reporters would race directly here, right after finishing up their interviews with King Kong and the Abominable Snowman."

Laughter erupted through the crowd and Ann smiled kindly at Jason. "Sorry, Jason. I couldn't resist."

A wave of anger flashed across Jason's face. "I'm serious. If we showed you hard evidence, would you cover the story?"

Ann looked at him and it seemed for the first time she realized the level of intensity he carried regarding the book. She took a half step away from Jason. "My apologies. I didn't realize this search was quite so serious."

"Deadly."

"Okay." Ann took another step away from Jason. "If you find a genuine book of God, your town's population will make Woodstock look like an empty field."

Ann left the stage, the look of concern back on her face.

Jason answered questions for the next ten minutes before he wrapped up his talk and stepped down from the stage where his followers gathered around him and offered congratulations.

Ann was surrounded by people as well and Cameron moved near her to watch her work the crowd.

She was as charming to others as he remembered. Why couldn't she treat him half as kindly?

She smiled at the right times and always asked the people around her at least two follow-up questions, unlike most people who asked one return question to be polite but really didn't care what the answer was. She looked into people's eyes when they spoke, as if they were the only other person in the world, and her laugh was addictive.

No wonder she'd been Jessie's best friend.

"Have you met her yet?"

Cameron gave a start. Jason had sauntered up to his side without him noticing. "Yes."

"Do you know each other?"

Cameron nodded.

"Really. How?"

"Mutual friends from our past." Cameron rubbed his temple. He didn't want Jason to know his connection to Ann. Jason seemed much too interested in her. "That shouldn't surprise me. You're in the same type of business, and you're ambitious like she is."

"Not really."

"Oh yes. I Googled you myself last night. Three years ago you entered a short film in five different contests and you finaled twice. Your Facebook page is full of links and likes within the film industry." Jason clapped his back. "You've made no secret of the fact you want to move up in the world of video. Scrap it altogether and move into making feature-length films."

"What's your point?"

"If we find the book, you could make any film you wanted. You would never have to concern yourself with money again. You'd know the future. What if you knew which script Universal Studios would approve and which ones they wouldn't? What if you knew which films would be a massive success? You'd be planets ahead of every other director in the world.

"I'm going to use this book to help the world, but I'm only going to let a few people have direct access to it." Jason paused a moment. "You need me."

Cameron walked away. Jason was right. If the Book of Days was authentic and they controlled it, it could make his career. But his dream of making movies had faded. All he wanted now was to remember Jessie and find a cure for his disintegrating brain.

He filled his punch glass and went to study the core teachings of Future Current spelled out on two four-color posters sitting on large easels.

"Are you learning anything?"

For the second time in the past ten minutes Cameron was startled by someone sneaking up on him. He spun on his heel.

Ann. He tightened his grip on his plastic cup and it snapped, a trickle of punch wound its way down the cup's side. Great.

Where should he start? Seeing her in person was different than talking on the phone. Far different. Those eyes. Captivating. He'd forgotten how beautiful she was. And she looked leaner than when he'd last seen her. Maybe hosting *Adventure Northwest* required more than just standing in front of the camera.

"Hey, Ann, hi." Cameron leaned in to give her a quick hug at the same time she extended her hand, which caused her to poke him in the stomach.

She pulled her hand back. "Sorry."

"No, my fault, I wasn't sure if I should . . ."

Awkward. Just like the last time they'd seen each other.

"Thanks for coming down here," Cameron said.

"Sure." Ann nodded.

"I'm thinking we'll connect tomorrow late afternoon and talk about our game plan. I have some things I need to do the first half of the day."

"Good. Perfect. What time were you thinking? Three? Four?"

"Let's say four. I'll call you around three thirty and we'll pick a spot."

"Fine." Ann turned and waltzed back into the crowd, greeting fans along the way. She'd never been athletic like Jessie, but she moved with a fluid grace that was a bit mesmerizing.

He slogged back toward his hotel and stopped to look at the Three Peaks Bakery. Closed. A sign said the building was constructed in the mid-1920s. In the window were three apple fritters that looked like they needed a home.

He patted his stomach. Jessie and he used to have an apple fritter night two or three times a year where they'd gorge themselves on the treats and curse their decision the next day.

Had Jessie done the same thing with Ann when they roomed together in college? Probably. He turned and trudged on. Five days already in Three Peaks. And little to show for it.

"I'm not getting much of anywhere, Jess. You think a fritter could make me feel better?"

By the time he stepped into the lobby of the Best Western, his legs wobbled. His exhaustion was more emotional than physical, but his body still felt like he'd spent the day climbing Mount Kilimanjaro.

He fumbled in his front pants pocket for his hotel card and couldn't locate it. Where . . . ? Right. Back pocket. Cameron pulled it out and stared at the green stripe.

What was his room number? 304? 324? *Think!* He popped himself in the forehead twice with his fist. He looked over at the hotel's night host who stared at him with raised eyebrows.

Why couldn't he just ask the night guy behind the counter? No, he'd figure it out; he just needed to stop thinking about it for minute. He glanced around the lobby for a distraction.

A rack of brochures next to the check-in desk caught his eye. He wandered over to it and found leaflets that boasted of guided hikes that would fascinate him, a Bavarian Village fifty miles down the road that would fill him with unforgettable memories, white-water rafting that was the "trip of a lifetime" and world-class golf courses that promised to "Take you away from it all." He was ready to be taken away from it all and checked into a new life. One with a brain that wasn't missing a spark plug or three. *Where do I sign up?*

After five minutes of pretending he was reading the brochures, he broke down and approached the front desk. "Hey, can you remind me what room I'm in? Too many hotels in too many weeks and all the numbers start to blend together."

"No problem, Mr. Vaux."

Eschewing the elevators, he took the stairs to the second floor, the whole way fingering the rock Susan Hillman had given him. He rolled the cool, almost cold surface of the stone around his palm and stared at its intricate pattern of red lines, each one ending at a black spot on the stone. It was comforting.

On impulse he pulled Jessie's stone out from under his shirt and held the two stones side by side. They looked good together. Jessie had said her stone was a key, but he had no idea what that meant. He'd shown the stone to three northwest historians just before he left Seattle, but none of them had any idea what the markings were. If it was a key to finding the book, he needed some way to locate the door.

When he reached his floor and finally his door, he stuffed his card into the lock and pulled it out. The green light flared. He pushed the door handle and trudged into his room, not bothering to turn on the light. All he wanted was for sleep to consume him.

Let me escape. Sleep come quick, okay?

As soon as he plopped onto the russet bedspread, he jerked back up and rubbed his neck. A sharp corner of something had poked him. He fumbled for the light on the nightstand and snapped it on. A square dark maroon envelope held a thick red card inside. As he slid the card free, he couldn't help but think of Ann. She'd worn a maroon polo shirt at Jason's gathering. A great color on her.

> *My dearest Mr. Cameron,*
>
> *I hope you have enjoyed our hospitality during your short visit to our town. If you don't leave within the next day, and instead choose to prolong your unwarranted escapade here, the consequences will be, shall we say, disagreeable.*
>
> *Regards,*
> *A friend*

Cameron crumpled the note in his hand, his eyes darting around the room as his smile turned into laughter. Excellent. He was on the right track. And he had a pretty good idea who that trail would lead to.

CHAPTER 15

Midmorning on Saturday, Cameron unclipped another nut from his rack, jammed it into the crack and clipped in with a carabineer. He wedged his chalk covered fingers into the crack and adjusted his foot so he could stick the hold.

He was seventy-five feet above the forest floor and trying to keep his fear in check. Another hundred feet or so and he'd crest the ridge of the cliff and have a look at the amber and green valley below without a cascade of adrenaline pumping through his veins.

Right now the adrenaline was a torrent because the fear he'd confronted when he and Jessie learned to climb together had never left him. Could he manage it? Yes. Conquer it? Not even close. Even looking out a window from more than three stories up filled his stomach with stampeding butterflies. But the price was worth it. When he climbed, he felt Jessie and nothing else. Every other extraneous thought vanished as his concentration narrowed. And he didn't have to remember anything except how to stay alive.

His next move was a micro hold about two feet above his head. With a shove off the edge with his foot, he should be able to reach it with his fingertips. He stiffened his left hand in the crack, bending his fingers to create a human anchor, then released the wall with his right hand. Cameron plunged his hand into his chalk bag then returned to his hold; trying to ignore the burn in his arms and calves.

He took a breath and focused on the wall a quarter-inch in front of his nose.

The climb was listed as a 5.9 in *Spectacular Northwest Climbs,* but it seemed closer to a 5.10. The difficulty of finding decent holds increased the higher he got. Always have three points of contact; it was a fundamental of beginning rock climbing, but this route wasn't for beginners. And while Cameron wasn't a beginner, no one would describe him as advanced.

Squinting into the sun he saw his next hold and stretched out for it. Short by at least five inches. He reached the crux. The hardest part of the climb; the spot where the 5.9 rating came from. The only way to reach it was to shove off with his foot. His anchors would hold.

He was taking too long deliberating the next move. Momentum. Climb with momentum, few pauses. Just go!

Cold sweat broke out on his forehead.

Should he descend? No. He was almost halfway up and down-climbing would be harder than moving up. As his options pinged through his mind, Cameron looked down. A tactical error. Sweat seeped through the white chalk on his palms and fingers. Not good.

To think people free climbed this route without ropes. Insane. His right leg started bouncing, the panic inside pushing its way out.

Closing his eyes he sucked in a deep breath, then let it out slow. He laid his cheek against the cliff face and took another breath. Then another.

You want to live without me? You want to live with your memories vanishing? You want to try to live without a mind?

The thoughts flashed through him like they were spoken.

"Jessie?" Her name escaped his lips before he could stop it.

Join me. It would be simple.

Yes. It would be so easy. He could unknot himself from the rope—his toes the only thing keeping him on the cliff—then slowly lean back till the wind whistled past his ears, faster, faster, eyes closed, not knowing the moment of impact until . . .

Progress on finding the book was moving like a glacier, and he still had no gut feeling one way or another if it would turn out to be the answer to all his hopes or an illusion that would leave his soul even emptier than it felt right now.

He couldn't live with his mind slowly melting away like early winter snow.

He looked down again and his stomach knotted tighter, then reached toward his harness to undo the rope.

No one would ever know. It would be declared an accident, case opened and closed before sunset. Brandon could find another partner.

Cameron blinked rapidly and waited for his panic to settle, for the voice that couldn't be Jessie's to stop whispering at him—for the rational part of himself to grow strong again. But it didn't. He tried to swallow, but his mouth was too dry and a cough rasped out.

He should join her. Why not? Before all memory of her vanished.

Join her.

He reached toward his harness to undo his rope. He watched his fingers, as if detached from them, start to undo the knot. His toe slipped and he instinctively reached up to grip the wall. Wait, what was that?

Cameron started as he spied a figure on top of the cliff looking down at him. He or she was silhouetted by the blazing sun behind her, the outline of a rope around her shoulders. Female? Looked like it. The figure turned and he caught the outline of shoulder-length hair and a slender, athletic figure. Definitely a woman.

A witness.

Thank you.

Whoever it was had just restored a spot of sanity to his brain. What was he thinking?

Cameron sucked in a breath, shoved himself upward, and snagged the next hold with his fingertips.

"I hope I'll see you again someday Jessie, but not yet. Not yet."

An hour later he reached the top and slumped to the rocky ground breathing hard. After catching his breath, he glanced around for his lone spectator.

No one.

He slid out of his climbing gear, settled down on a boulder, and grabbed his water bottle. After five gulps he dumped the rest on his head and studied the drops of water as they fell from the ends of his dark hair.

They trickled onto the ground, sending up little puffs of dust. He couldn't keep his legs from shaking. Not from fatigue—from the fear of his near embrace with death.

"Cameron?"

He twisted to see who it was.

Unbelievable. Ann. Maybe there was a God. And Cameron was the ant under the magnifying glass. *Thanks for the torture, Book of Days Author.*

He shook his head. "You never wanted anything to do with climbing. I never imagined you would get into it."

"That makes two of us." She walked toward him, auburn hair bouncing on her shoulders.

"But you did."

"I hated it at first. I think I still do. But it's a way to be close to Jessie. You know what I mean?"

Cameron nodded. He knew.

"I didn't know you were climbing again."

The fear from the climb still hung on him like a concrete robe; she had to see it in his eyes and notice his leg bouncing like a jackhammer. But if she did, Ann didn't let on.

"I only stopped for about six months." He shifted, stretching his legs out in front of him. "What about you?"

Ann folded her arms and tapped her foot. "I started a year and a half ago. I still have a ton to learn."

"Hey, I'm assuming you just scaled this peak solo since no one else is up here, and if you did, you've got a pretty fast download going."

"That climb was a bit outside my comfort zone. Actually a lot outside." Ann paced, five yards away. "It's interesting to see you up here."

Interesting? What, she didn't think he could handle the climb? "You too." Cameron gazed out over the valley spread out below them like a golden-brown silk river, splotches of green spread randomly throughout. She was probably waiting for him to say something, but what? The only noise was a light wind straining to get through the pine trees dotting the ridge just behind them.

"I watched you catch your breath for a few minutes about a third of the way up. How long did it take you to get up here?"

Cameron's face flushed. If she only knew. He rubbed his forehead and coughed. "About an hour."

"I wish I could climb with that speed. I've focused on the sport intensely for the past eighteen months, but I feel like I've plateaued." She pulled her hair into a ponytail and secured it. "I've heard of climbers with natural talent. I am not one of those fortunate souls."

Ann offered him a bottle of Powerade from her climbing pack

and he accepted. After a few moments of silence, she got up, eased over to the edge of the cliff, and sat with her legs hanging over it.

After a few seconds' hesitation, he got up and joined her.

Ann peered at him out of the corner of her eye. "So, will we be able to get along for the next week or so?"

"You tell me, Banister. Our relationship has never been bathed in a great deal of warmth."

She shrugged. "I think we'll be fine."

"I hope so."

"I should let you know, I'm not here just to help you find out more about your dad's and Jessie's book."

"Really."

She folded her hands and looked at the sky.

"Are you going to tell me about it?"

"I want to try to find information on someone who lived here in the sixties and early seventies." She tapped the tips of her fingers together.

"Who?"

"My mom."

Interesting. "Okay."

"Jessie never told you my history?"

"Not much."

"I'm an only child and I have no idea who my dad was. He was gone before I was two. When I was seven, my mom hooked up with a loser from Shelton, Washington, and we lived there with him till I was eleven." Ann pulled at the thin band of silver in her right ear. "That's when my mom abandoned me for good."

"It was a drug overdose if I remember right."

Ann nodded. "I was so angry at her I refused to go to the funeral." She closed her eyes. "I'm still angry."

She shook her head. "Two months later I came home from school one day and found all my things on the front lawn. The guy was gone. Ten minutes later it started raining just like in some sappy movie.

"But for me it wasn't sappy. In that moment I realized I was alone in the world. I cried nonstop till Mrs. Carie next door came over and took me in for the night. The next day I was baptized into the foster-care system. As you probably remember, that's where I met Jessie. She's the only family I had."

Wow. She was an orphan.

Ann leaned forward, head down. "Once I was in college I never looked back. Until now. I don't know if I have any uncles or aunts or cousins, and at this stage of life—you know, turning thirty-two, thinking about having kids of my own—I'd really like to know something of my family history."

In that instant Ann became utterly human. It didn't matter that she'd never liked him. She knew pain, loneliness. The same pain he carried, the same loneliness. Cameron started to speak, then thought better of it. A disclosure of that nature needed a moment to settle.

Ann stood and brushed nonexistent dirt off her climbing shorts. She walked over to her pack and grabbed two PowerBars. She tossed one to Cameron and unwrapped the other in a swift motion.

"Both sets of my grandparents died before I was born. What are the odds of that? So I have no family. Period. Now you'd think someone in the media would be able to find the story of who my grandparents were and some history on my mom, but it didn't turn out that way. She wasn't exactly what you'd call a record keeper. But I've kept digging and finally a bit of luck led me here." She wiped her nose with a tissue. "I'm hoping to find someone who knew my mom before she left for Washington."

Cameron stole a quick look at her profile as she watched a white-throated swift flit about the ground, searching for anything the climbers might have dropped. Ann's lack of makeup allowed her freckles to stand out and it made her more beautiful than he'd ever seen her.

As Ann asked questions about the town, the sensation of knowing exactly what she looked like as a little girl immersed him. The innocence that growing up pushes out of most men and women still flitted behind her eyes and into her smile.

Cameron told her what he'd learned so far about the town and when he'd finished, she sat back and pulled one knee up to her chest and simply said, "Thank you."

"You're welcome. I hope you find what you're looking for."

Ann turned and leaned in toward him. "Now, it's your turn."

"Mine? For what?"

"To tell me about your plan for finding the book and what you've discovered already."

When he finished she said, "So you think Jason is the key?"

"No." Cameron rubbed his kneecaps and smiled. "Taylor is. With him it feels like I've made progress, and with you here I'm hoping we'll make even more."

"I used to read Taylor Stone's syndicated column in *The Oregonian*."

"He's a writer?"

"He ran the *Three Peaks Post* for years."

That's right. Cameron knew that.

"You don't really think there's anything to this Book of Days story, do you?"

"It depends on the moment you ask." Cameron sniffed a laugh. "Sometimes I can't believe I'm doing this; other times I think there actually might be something to the legend." Cameron whapped himself on the head with both hands. "Am I crazy? What do you think?"

Ann shrugged. "I believe what I said at the party last night. It's gotta be a legend."

"Even with Jessie saying she saw it?"

Ann stood and folded her arms across her chest. "You and I both know Jessie occasionally saw visions from God."

"But you believe all the God-things that Jessie and my dad believed."

"Jessie wasn't a full-out Christian mystic, but she liked reading them and that's the way her faith leaned. I've never gone down that path."

Cameron rubbed the ring finger on his left hand. "She was always asking me to go down that road with her."

"Why didn't you?"

"I've never had anything against God. It was great for Jessie, great for my dad, probably good for you too. I've just never seen how He could exist."

"What about now?"

It was an excellent question. "Maybe He's out there. But I wouldn't know where to start looking."

Ann cracked her knuckles and smiled. "I could offer some suggestions."

The fights they'd had over his marrying Jessie raced into his mind.

"You're a good guy, Cameron, but you don't follow Jesus so you shouldn't marry Jessie."

"All you're going to do is hurt her."

Cameron turned and raised his eyebrows. "Like the suggestions you used to give me all the time when Jessie and I were dating?"

Ann clasped her hands. "I see some of your memories from the past are still crystal clear."

Cameron rolled his eyes.

A few moments later Ann stuck out her hand. "Truce?"

Cameron looked into her riveting green eyes as he took her hand. "Sure."

He watched the late-morning sun play tag with the clouds as a breeze brought the perfume of ponderosa pine up from the valley. Cameron let his senses get swept away in it. It felt strange sitting next to Ann, alone, miles from anyone or anything. It also felt comforting.

And wonderful.

And wrong.

What if years ago Ann had invited him to a play before Jessie asked him to learn to rock climb? Would he be sitting here with a ring on his finger?

Stop it, Cameron.

He needed to keep his distance from her. Find out if the book was real as fast as possible, then get back to Seattle. He would never betray Jessie by having feelings for Ann. Never.

CHAPTER 16

On the drive back to Three Peaks, Cameron popped his steering wheel with his palm and blew out an exasperated breath. He'd told Ann he was making progress. What progress? If he could get Stone to talk, Cameron might get somewhere. But what if he couldn't?

"Jessie, what would you do?"

He laughed and contemplated having a conversation with God. That's exactly what Jessie would do. Could he do that while driving? How important was it to pray with eyes closed? Was that a requirement? Of course Jessie had prayed all the time with her eyes open, so it was probably all right.

He pulled up to a stoplight and rubbed his neck.

Two adults and three kids on matching bikes crossed in front of him, probably on their way to Indian Loop Road. The Fun To-Do guide in his room said it was a favorite of locals and tourists. The kind of trail he'd dreamed of going down with Jessie and their kids someday. "Thanks for killing that dream, God." There, he'd prayed.

The light turned green, and as he eased down on the gas, he decided to give prayer a real shot.

"I have no concept of how to talk to You. But if You really wrote a book, stuck it here in Three Peaks, and it's the one my dad and Jessie talked about and it really exists, I'd appreciate some help finding it. Thanks."

Ironic that he would end up here trying to find the answers to life. Jessie had loved Central Oregon as a kid. She came down at least twice with her church group, or was it Girl Scouts? She'd even asked him a few years ago about going back. Hadn't she? Didn't she say it was important they come here together? He gritted his teeth. He couldn't remember. Too much fuzz covered what little was left of the memory.

What should be his next move? On the cliff they'd decided Ann would stop by the library that afternoon and see if she could dig up anything he hadn't been able to find, but what should he do? He'd talked to all the possible leads in town—which had gotten him nowhere—except for his conversation with Taylor Stone. But getting Stone to help with his quest would be like swimming through concrete.

"I'm getting tired, Jessie."

He wasn't any closer to the book than when he'd arrived, and Brandon expected him to be back in Seattle in a little over a week. Cameron popped the steering wheel again. He needed answers now. Somehow. Some way.

He stopped for a long, late lunch and didn't arrive back at his hotel till four thirty. He tossed his keys and wallet on the desk and scanned his room. Something was out of place. Wait, not out of place—missing.

Where was his notebook? Didn't he leave it on the desk? It wasn't there. He glanced at the floor. The cleaning staff might have knocked it—no, not there. Not on the nightstand either.

He sucked in a breath and blew it out quickly as heat filled his body. *Think!* Where was it?

He wiped his forehead as he strode into the bathroom. Had he set the file on the sink?

Nothing. Not there.

Come on . . . Ah, there it was, resting at the base of the overstuffed chair next to the window. He snatched it up. "Don't go disappearing on me. I need y—"

Cameron stopped as he flipped it open and stared at a blank notepad. All his notes were gone, ripped cleanly out.

Another wave of heat coursed through him. A threatening letter was one thing; stealing his notes took things to another level.

He glanced around the room. Nothing else was out of place. At least that he remembered. And everything in the closet seemed to be there.

Cameron strode to the window and yanked back the curtains, as if the intruder would be standing under a streetlamp staring up at him.

The street was empty, but it didn't stop a shiver from running down his back.

He spun and smacked the chair.

He needed his notes!

He flopped into the chair and didn't know whether to scream or laugh. He was getting behind somebody's curtain, and that person wanted to kick him out of the theater. But Cameron had a ticket and wasn't about to leave.

After a long shower he glanced at his watch. Five thirty. Too early to catch a movie in the Five Pine campus at the east end of town.

He stared out his window and saw the banner promoting the jazz festival. It had just started. Hadn't he looked at the banner a few days ago? Yes. He remembered. A miracle.

Why not stroll down and listen for a while? It was better than sitting in his hotel room, wondering who had broken in for a second time and trying to ignore the nauseous gurgling that seemed to have taken up permanent residence in his stomach.

About halfway to the park, he caught the sound of a band. A guitarist was playing riffs in fine Robert-Cray style, and the faint smell of barbecued chicken tantalized his taste buds.

There had to be at least five-hundred people spread out on blue and green and red checkered blankets or sitting in lawn chairs, bottles of red wine at their sides or pitchers filled with what looked like iced tea.

People sat in large groups, talking and laughing, kids running from blanket to blanket acting like everyone was their mom or dad, sister or brother. One of the amazing aspects of a small town. Community was real. You knew your neighbors and everyone in town was a neighbor.

So different from his life in Seattle, where he had a lot of acquaintances but not many deep friendships. He'd always envied Jessie in that regard. She had a big group of God-buddies who would do anything for her.

Cameron was about to sit on a gray, faded picnic table on the edge of the crowd when he noticed two familiar profiles to his left: Taylor Stone and the lady who must be his wife.

As Cameron eased over to them, she smiled, whispered something to Taylor, and motioned for Cameron to join them on their checkered picnic blanket.

Taylor glanced at Cameron as he approached but stared straight ahead as Cameron sat next to him. "Still in town I see," Taylor said.

"For a while longer."

"Hello, Cameron. I'm Tricia, Taylor's wife." She leaned across Taylor and offered her hand. "I've heard positive things about you."

"Really?" Cameron grasped her hand. "Good to meet you."

"Are you a jazz aficionado perchance?" Taylor continued to stare straight ahead at the five-piece band.

"No, but I have a few CDs of the legends."

"Who do you consider legendary?"

"Coltrane, Miles Davis, Charlie Parker . . . and a few others."

Taylor raised his eyebrows.

"If Taylor were to admit it, he'd heartily approve of your choices. Good to have you join us." Tricia patted Taylor's knee as she looked at Cameron. "How is your search going?"

"For?"

"The Book of Days, of course."

"Everyone knows everyone else's business in a small town, don't they?"

"For the most part." Tricia smiled. "And your search?"

"Stymied. The people who talk about it only say the same things Jason says."

"Not surprising." Taylor eyes stayed locked on the band.

"Oh, really?"

"If you go to Roswell and asked about the alien landing, the only people who are talking about it are the ones trying to make a buck by plucking it from your wallet. The others are bored with the whole thing." Taylor sipped his tea. "Now that you've sliced open the hornets' nest with talk of your dad touching a real book, Jason and all the other whack jobs associated with Future Current will be searching for this genuine Book of Days till they bring Walt Disney's frozen body back from the dead. But they'll never find it."

Tricia offered Cameron a glass of iced tea, which he accepted.

"Once Jason drops out of sight, another New Ager will dig up the Book of Days story and continue the quest. We'll probably never be rid of it." Taylor drilled him with a frown and turned back to the band.

"Do you think Jason wants me to leave?"

"Are you kidding? You've handed him what he would call solid evidence that there's a physical book . . . No, he'd be the first member on your Book of Days Facebook fan page."

"I see. So it doesn't make sense that he or one of his followers would send me an unsigned note that somehow showed up on my hotel bed, threatening me harm if I don't get out of Three Peaks?"

An emotion flashed across Taylor's face, almost too fast for Cameron to see it. If he hadn't been staring right at Taylor, he would have missed it. Concern? Recognition? Anger? He couldn't tell. But it was enough to decide Taylor had sent the note.

"When did you get the letter?" Tricia asked.

"Yesterday."

"Did you report it?"

"No, I took it as a positive sign. That I'm on the right track. A hornet doesn't sting unless you're pounding on the nest."

"Why is it so important for you to search for this book?" Tricia asked.

Was it the town edict that everyone asked that question? Cameron let his head fall back and he stared at the thin layer of clouds above, growing pink. Why search? A moment later, Cameron found himself spilling his heart out to the two strangers beside him.

"Before my dad died, he said finding the book would answer my questions. My wife said the same thing before she died in a small plane crash. Maybe they were deluded, but I promised I'd search."

This time the emotion across Taylor's face lasted a full second, and Cameron didn't have to guess what the man felt: surprise and then conflict.

Tricia glanced at Taylor, then slid her hand on top of Cameron's and squeezed.

Taylor turned to him, a curious look on his face. "I'm sorry about your wife and the plane crash. Dying in an accident is . . . for the person who stays behind . . . It's not . . . I'm sorry for your pain."

Cameron nodded. Where had that bucket of compassion come from? Not exactly the Taylor Stone he'd met so far. It was Cameron's turn to study the band.

After the next set ended, Tricia and Taylor gathered their things and got up to leave.

"Best of success, Cameron, hang in there." Taylor bent down to shake Cameron's hand.

"Thanks, maybe we'll talk again."

"Maybe."

The park shadows grew till Cameron was the only one left in the park. The band had packed up and the last stragglers had ambled back toward their homes or hotels.

Wait. He wasn't the only one left. A figure in shadow leaned against a tree on the opposite side of the park. It was too small to be Jason. Was it a man? A woman? He couldn't tell, but he knew the person was staring at him.

Cameron stood and called out, "Hello."

No response. No movement.

"Can I help you?"

The figure shifted his weight and pulled his hood further down on his face.

As Cameron started walking toward the figure, the person walked backward a few paces, then turned and sprinted away.

Cameron raced toward the fleeing figure, but he had too much of a jump on Cameron. By the time he reached the spot where the person had stood, he had vanished.

The temperature had dropped at least twenty degrees since Cameron first arrived, or maybe the appearance of someone watching him made it seem that way.

Threatening notes. Someone stealing his research. Stalkers trailing him. Great. It added a nice flavor of fear to his quest.

But it also added validity. He was getting closer.

And Jason was right. Taylor Stone was far more tied into the Book of Days than he was willing to admit. Cameron would stay close to Taylor and somehow find a way to get the man to confess.

As he crawled under the sheets that night, hope fluttered up from his heart.

"I'm making progress, Jessie." He clicked off the lamp next to his bed. "I know you're with me. I'll see you in my dreams."

Three Years Earlier

Intermittent breezes had buffeted Cameron and Jessie as they hiked the two miles up Mount Erie in northern Washington. They could have driven, but they were considering entering their first triathlon, and the exercise would be a good addition to the mountain-bike ride they'd taken earlier in the day.

He grabbed her hand and gave a quick squeeze. She smiled, let go of his hand, and sprinted up the path. "Think you can catch me?"

Maybe not, but she'd caught him. All of him. Forever.

They crested the top of the trail and gazed down on the farmland a quarter-mile below.

It looked like a postcard, pencil-thin dirt roads separating bright green fields as far as they could see, with inlets of Puget Sound reaching out like fingers into the rich green-and-gold ground.

The sun would set in two hours, so they couldn't linger long before heading back down. They'd had one of their first dates here, and he'd taken her back once a year ever since. He would keep bringing her here till they had to drive to the top and get to the viewpoints using walkers.

They found their traditional seat, an outcropping of rocks with just enough room for both of them to sit, and dangled their legs with four hundred feet of open space below them.

"Perfect day?" Cameron asked.

"Only one thing would make it better."

"That is?"

"When we get home we find out a major studio wants to buy one of your short films, make it feature length, and have you direct."

The wind continued to swirl erratically, pushing Jessie's hair back in bursts, then dying so it fell on her shoulders like wayward feathers seconds later.

Perfection in human form.

She turned toward him. "What if I told you something you'd never believe?"

"I'd believe it."

"No. This is something I know you could never accept."

"I would accept it, because it's you."

"You wouldn't. It's the unanswerable argument. If I know you won't . . . it's like saying God, who nothing is impossible for, can make a stone too heavy for Himself to lift."

"Easy answer." Cameron laughed. "Since there probably is no God, he wouldn't be able to lift it."

Jessie ran her fingers over the top of his hands, then intertwined their fingers. "You promise to believe me?"

"Yes, tell me."

Jessie closed her eyes and smiled.

"What? You're pregnant? You were abducted by aliens? What?"

"Later."

He laughed and pulled her in tight, nuzzling her neck with his lips. "Now."

She tickled right under his arm where he was most sensitive, and he leaped back as if he'd stuck his finger in a light socket.

"I've seen proof. God is real."

"Really."

Jessie nodded.

"If you say so."

"He is."

"If you say—"

"No, Cameron, look at me. I know He's real."

"Uh-huh." Cameron drew her back into his chest and stroked her hair. "You're going to tell about this proof I suppose."

"Yes. I've seen something He made. Something amazing."

"What? The stars? The ocean?"

"Something even better."

"Tell me."

"I will, when it's time." She folded her arms across her chest, dropped her head, and leaned into him hard.

"I love you, Cameron. Always and forever."

CHAPTER 17

The oak door into Taylor's workshop creaked as Tricia opened it just past eight o'clock Sunday morning with one goal pounding through her heart—get her husband to talk. He didn't turn from the crinkled instructions laid out in front of him, but that didn't mean he hadn't heard her come in.

She watched him fiddle with an ancient-looking fly rod, probably from the midfifties, reading glasses perched on the end of his nose. He hated those glasses. They labeled him as middle-aged plus, which he refused to admit to.

The walls were covered with maps and pictures of hidden rivers and fishing holes that took three days of backpacking through the wilderness to reach. Most of the time Taylor took his trips solo, "to escape" he'd tell her, but what he was escaping from was never clear.

Even though they'd known each other since junior high, he'd never fully opened up to her. He held secrets that she'd learned to accept. But ever since Cameron Vaux had arrived in town, Taylor had been escaping from her emotionally as well. It wasn't like him.

The secrets weren't about another woman or some hidden addiction. Something about Cameron had pushed him into his workshop—or as she liked to call it, his cave—more frequently these past seven days.

"Hello, my wonderful Tricia," he said, his head still buried in the instructions, his hands holding two pieces of the rod together. "The glue should be dry here in another forty seconds or so."

Tricia eased up next to Taylor's workbench and leaned on her elbow. "Let's talk." She waited a few seconds for him to look at her, but he didn't budge. "I know you're doing your caveman want-to-be-alone thing right now, but I need to ask you something."

"I'm not caving; I have to get this done by the weekend."

"Uh-huh." Tricia straightened, turned, and leaned back against the workbench. "Are you going to help this Cameron kid?"

"Help him what?"

She would smack him on the head if it would stop him from playing dumb. "I know you better than you think I do."

"I'm sorry, hon. We've just registered ten pounds on the confusion fish scale. That's two pitches over my head, third strike, yer out."

"You're mixing metaphors."

"I know."

"Look at me, Taylor Stone." She placed her forefinger under his chin and lifted till he looked into her eyes. "I think both pitches hit you right in the heart, sweetie." She let his chin go.

Taylor harrumphed. "In other words you think I know something more about this book business than I'm telling him?" He sat up and pulled off his reading glasses.

"Thank you for stating the obvious."

"What gives you that idea? Yes, David says in the Psalms all his days were recorded in God's book before he was born. He didn't say everyone; he said for himself. And I highly doubt David was describing a physical book that just happened to be plopped down in the good ol' US of A and land in little ol' Three Peaks, Oregon. He was speaking metaphorically about God knowing the past, present, and future because God is omniscient. He wasn't talking about a book you can order on Amazon.com with the click of a button."

"Forgive me. I didn't know the depth of your knowledge when it came to that particular passage of Scripture. I'm sure you can tell me with complete certainty that God would only do that for David and no one else, and that there's no way He created a literal book and placed it somewhere on earth where man might find it."

Taylor shook his head and focused on his fly rod. "It would have to be a pretty big book."

"Since you were the voice of this town for eighteen years, you know more of its secrets than anyone." Tricia folded her arms across her chest and leaned in. "So if there is even a shred of a chance this book is genuine, any real evidence to back up Jason, then you would know it. And you like helping people. So if you try and tell me all you know about the Book of Days is that it's a strange legend and nothing more—"

Taylor spun toward her in his chair and locked his hands behind his head. "So I should just grab a three-cheese pizza with Cameron and hand over whatever knowledge I possess, whether it's garbage or not? Maybe spend a few days brainstorming with him, doing research, hiking in the woods with him looking for this thing since deep down he reminds me of myself and I'm always such a helpful guy?"

Tricia patted his shoulder. "Well said."

"Thank you."

Taylor returned to his fly rod and scraped off a tiny bit of excess glue. Tricia knew he considered the conversation finished, but she didn't. And she could always outlast him in the icy stare-down contest.

He slapped his modeling knife on top of the workbench. "If it's that critical to your happiness, I'll dig through my old notes and see if I can find anything. Okay?"

Tricia whirled, marched out, and didn't look back. Taylor wouldn't be grabbing the trowel anytime soon. Again, it wasn't like him. Finding out why leaped to the top of her mental to-do list.

On Sunday night Cameron drove into Bend to catch a movie and escape his crumbling world. He needed to wrap his mind around something more than the question of whether or not he'd be wrapping his mind around anything at all a few years into the future.

Tomorrow he'd meet Ann, see if she found anything at the library, and decide what to do next.

As he walked through the parking lot toward the theater, a familiar face moved toward him.

Ann.

"Cameron, what a nice surprise." She sashayed up to him and fell into step alongside him.

Was she kidding, or had the truce they'd established on the mountain kicked into effect? "I thought you were going to see that play in Bend."

"I changed my mind."

"I see." Cameron stuck his hands in his pockets and walked faster.

Ann took a few quick strides, then she was next to him, matching his pace. "You're going to a movie?"

Cameron nodded. "Yep."

"By yourself?"

"I think it's the best way to take it in. No distractions, no having to talk to anyone about it till you've had a chance to process it." He glanced at her. "And you're headed . . . ?"

"The same."

"To a movie?"

"Yes."

"By yourself?"

She nodded and smiled.

"And I thought all we had in common was rock climbing and—" Cameron stopped himself. No parents, brothers, or sisters for either of them. Both missing Jessie. Both looking for answers.

She raised her eyebrows.

"Rock climbing," he finished.

The line to buy tickets was long, and Cameron didn't try to break the awkward silence till it had stretched past a minute. "Have you found anything more about your family?"

"I'm getting almost nowhere."

He could relate.

Ann stepped out of line and folded her arms, probably to see why the line was moving so slow. She wore faded Levi's and a dark blue Nike sweatshirt, her hair cascading over it like water.

Beautiful. He locked his hands behind his head and put his chin down. *Stop it!* The feelings were wrong. This is the way to honor Jessie? To remember her? By letting possible emotions for Ann dance around in his head like a tango? He had to get a handle on it.

"Do you want to help me investigate?" She stepped back into line beside him. "The way I see it, we have similar skills. Find the interesting angle to a story whether it's with words or with the lens of a camera. We know how to draw the deeper parts out of a subject or a scene. It's always easier to find the answers with two minds focused on the story. I help you with the book; you help me with my family history. So?"

Great. More time with her. That wouldn't help. But it was fair. "Fine. I'll help."

"Thanks."

Cameron gave Ann a thin-lipped smile and half a nod.

She stepped in line in front of him and whispered over her shoulder, "When can you start helping me?"

"You're up." He motioned toward the cashier window with his eyes.

Ann bought her ticket and eased over to the right as Cameron stepped up to the window. He glanced at her face as he bought a ticket to a different movie. It was blank. If she felt something either way she didn't show it.

He shoved his wallet into his coat and walked with her toward the ten-foot high glass doors leading into the theaters. "What have you uncovered so far?"

"I think my mom was born in Three Peaks and lived here till she was at least a teenager."

He raised both eyebrows, an invitation for her to elaborate.

Ann glanced at her watch. "My movie's starting. Next time I'll give you the gory details." She winked at him, not a flirtatious wink, but certainly playful.

All it took was a truce on the mountain for her to get a personality transfusion?

He watched her till she disappeared into theater number seven, then tapped himself hard on the forehead when she turned back and gave a little wave, as if she knew he'd be watching. He spun on his heel and strode toward theater number two.

Cameron left the theater two hours later. He glanced around the lobby looking for Ann. Why did he do that? Would he ask her to go for ice cream if he found her? Hardly. She was wrong for him, not even close to what he would want because no one could ever take Jessie's place.

He needed to get his mind back on the book. Tomorrow he would take another run at getting Taylor Stone to talk. A hard run.

CHAPTER 18

Ann chose the wrong movie. A romantic comedy was the worst salve possible for a heart aching over a guy she couldn't have. She tried to keep from putting herself onscreen, but it was impossible when the male lead reminded her of the Cameron she knew before Jessie died.

When the lead started to throw away his collection of classic baseball cards to prove his love—with a smile on his face—Ann laughed and cried at the same time. That scene was Cameron personified.

And she would have stopped him just like the scene played out onscreen.

After the closing credits, Ann strode out the theater with her head down. "Get out of my heart, Cameron!"

A couple walking out of the theater with her tried to hide their laughter.

She turned her head toward them. "I'm thinking about the

classic girl-loves-boy-but-there's-no-way-they-can-ever-be-together-but she wants-to-be-more-than-anything storyline."

"And you're the girl?" the woman asked.

She was the girl.

He took one more glance at Cameron's notes, then let out a chuckle as he lifted them from under his reading lamp and filed them away inside his oak cabinet. It was such good news. Cameron's late wife had a stone she gave to him. And it was the key to finding the book?

Fascinating.

But where was the stone? Cameron must have it with him. It certainly wasn't in the hotel room.

Didn't matter. The stone was another confirmation the book truly did exist in physical form. He would keep watching. And waiting. And learning. Young Cameron was doing his work for him.

Thank you very much.

He picked up his Glock and looked at it from all angles, the oil he'd used earlier allowing the gun to spin easily around his fingers.

"We haven't played together in a long time, have we?" He laid it on his desk and spun it counterclockwise. "Have patience. We will dance together again soon. I can feel it. Can't you?"

He leaned back, smiled, and gazed at a map of Three Peaks and the surrounding land. He picked up his knife by the point, let it settle into his callused fingers, then flung it at the map.

Thunk!

It pierced the center of the map and sunk into the wood paneling behind it. "Wherever you're hiding, I will find you. And you will be mine."

CHAPTER 19

The Monday morning sun was bright as Cameron approached Taylor's house, the late model Ford truck out front throwing off little bursts of light like a disco ball from the seventies. The guy must polish it every day.

When no one answered the doorbell, he walked around the back of the house and found Taylor sitting on his back deck, wearing a tie-dye T-shirt, khaki shorts, and nothing on his feet.

He didn't acknowledge Cameron but had to know he was there. The boards on the deck squealed as Cameron walked across them, announcing his arrival as loudly as the mermaid wind chime would have if a wind had been blowing.

Cameron grabbed one of the Adirondack chairs against the house and pulled it within a few feet of Taylor and sat. A few minutes later, Taylor broke the silence.

"My feet roast in anything but sandals, still. Till age five I don't remember wearing shoes at all from April through September, except in church. Maybe sitting on those church pews—hard as granite, mind you—shoved the memory right out of my mind."

Taylor reached in and pulled something metal from his pocket. "I hated church. Not just 'cause of having to wear shoes. Every Sunday morning Pastor Davis Darton ranted about God's love and God's forgiveness but with a red face that looked like an overripe tomato ready to burst. I couldn't figure out how God could forgive anyone if He was perpetually angry.

"One Sunday after service, I snuck up to see if the spot where Pastor Darton pounded on his podium each week was dented. It wasn't, but the wood in the middle was a lighter color than the rest of it. To me, church wasn't a building; it was Annie singing one of the hymns we both loved or lying in the meadow with my eyes closed listening to her read from the Bible."

Interesting. Ann. Annie. "Who's Annie?"

Taylor sat without moving or speaking for at least two minutes. Finally he opened his hand and stared at the object resting on it. A window crank. He brought it up to his face and pressed it into his cheek until his skin turned bright red.

He sighed, dropped his hand, and began spinning the crank around his fingers. The sun flashed off it with each rotation, and with each rotation Taylor winced. After the seventh or eighth turn, Taylor squeezed his eyes shut and dropped his head.

Cameron shifted in his chair and tried to find something in the yard to focus on. It felt like he was sitting in on a Catholic confessional. Whatever crime Taylor was in the midst of paying penance for was serious.

Taylor raised his head and looked at Cameron. "Would you like to see it?"

"The . . . what?"

"This."

Cameron nodded and held out his hand.

Taylor held up the window crank for Cameron to look at but didn't hand it to him.

Cameron studied the crank and the blood rushed from his face. Why would Taylor have one of those?

"Do you know what this is, Cameron?"

He swallowed hard. "It's a window crank made sometime between 1965 and 1967. Standard on Ford Mustangs during those years."

"Not bad." Taylor squinted at him. "How'd you know that?"

He hesitated, then said, "I restored a '65 Mustang and gave it to my wife for a Christmas present one year." He didn't add that the only time Jessie drove it was to the airfield on the day she died.

A wave of what looked like surprise washed over Taylor's face, but he recovered a moment later. "That model was a great car." He sighed and laid the window crank on his knee.

They returned to silence and watched the wind blow through the pine trees bordering Taylor's property sixty yards away.

"Do you think God really forgives everything, Cameron? And if He forgives, does He forget? Or does He write everything down in that book of yours so it lasts forever?"

What was Taylor asking him about God for? Or was the question directed more toward Taylor himself?

"I don't know if He forgives, forgets, remembers, keeps track . . . God and I have never done a lot of communicating."

"Annie said He forgives it all. Past. Present. Future. For everything we've done that we're ashamed of. And remembers it no more. Our part is accepting it."

"Nice thought."

"If it's true, He must have to take a big spiritual eraser to those parts of your amazing Book of Days."

"Industrial-strength eraser." Cameron smiled.

"Annie would have forgiven me for what I did to her. In an instant. My head says that. But my heart . . ."

It was the third time Taylor had mentioned Annie. Cameron couldn't help asking again, "Who is Annie?"

"I've said way too much. Waaay." Taylor took in a deep breath and let it out slowly. Then he propped his elbow on his knee and spun the window crank again, faster this time. When he finished, they sat in silence for a long time.

Finally Taylor said "Here" and handed the crank to Cameron, as if it were a gem-encrusted dagger.

"Who did it be—?"

"Belonged to me. Off a car of mine." Tears threatened to spill onto Taylor's cheeks. Cameron couldn't be sure if Taylor's tears came from the pain of the sunlight flashing off the crank into his eyes or from remembering. Maybe both.

"When something you would die for is destroyed by the hand of another, you can almost learn to live with it. When you do the destroying yourself, it's impossible."

Exactly. *Almost* learn to live with it. And the part that remained was brutal. "What was destroyed?"

"Cameron . . ." Taylor stood and offered his hand. Cameron took it and found himself yanked to his feet with a surprising strength. "Tricia asked me to talk to you about some things I know about. But I can't. It's nothing against you. You're a good man, and we have some things in common. More than I thought. But some things are meant to be sealed forever. Do you understand?"

Taylor strode into his house without waiting for an answer, without looking back. The screen door smacked shut with a sound like the blast from a .22.

Cameron stared at the door and took two steps backward. He had the sensation of being watched and looked toward the upstairs windows. Tricia Stone gazed down at him, her face expressionless. Then she slowly mouthed the words *I'm sorry* before turning away.

As Cameron made his way back to his car, he ran his hands through his hair. The scene in Taylor's backyard was another confirmation that the man was in the thick of the Book of Days' mystery, but prying that door open would take a crowbar the size of Paul Bunyan's ax. So be it.

But Cameron hoped the crowbar wouldn't break before the door opened.

After leaving Taylor's house, Cameron headed for the mountains and did a climb rated a 4.5. It wasn't technically difficult, just a good workout. The air was absolute crystal, something Seattle's skies still aspired to, but they didn't reach this level of purity.

As he gazed out over the trees below, he pulled out the stone Susan Hillman had given him and watched the sun bounce off its surface.

He turned it over slowly in a continual motion, studying the intricate pattern the red sparkles made. It was like a map. A treasure map. Yeah, right. Wouldn't that be nice? When he was a kid—eleven, maybe twelve—he'd made a treasure map and hidden it in his fort, twenty feet up in the maple tree in his backyard. He looked at Susan's stone again. A map to the Book of Days? If only it were that easy.

Maybe it wasn't a map; maybe it was a road sign. On impulse he snatched his cell phone out of his climbing pack.

"Hello?" said a low, booming voice.

"Hey, Scotty, it's Cameron."

"Who?"

"Cameron Vaux. In college we—"

Laughter. "I'm just messing with you, man. I'd know your voice even after four and a half years of silence, which, by the way, it's almost been."

"Sorry."

"Why?"

"I, uh . . ."

"Shut up, Cameron. My fingers can dial too. Hang on a second." The sound of Bono singing "I Still Haven't Found What I'm Looking For" in the background snapped off.

Cameron snorted out a laugh. The timing of the song would be much funnier if he wasn't the butt of the joke.

"Okay, tell me what you want."

He smiled. When it came to geology, few were better than Scotty. When it came to tact, no one was worse. He wouldn't be able to look up *subtle* in a dictionary for a thousand bucks and Cameron loved him for it.

"I need a favor, Scotty."

"Anything."

"I'm going to overnight you a rock. I need you to examine it fast, see what kind of stone it is, that kind of thing . . ."

"No problem. I'll get you the composition, age, where it's from—"

"I know where it's from. Three Peaks."

"What state?"

"Oregon."

"What're you doing there, Cam?"

"Looking for a book God wrote, that records the past and tells the future."

Scotty snorted. "That's how you're wasting your time these days? If I thought you were serious, I'd tell you how stupid you are."

"Thanks."

"Your timing is decent. I can do it tomorrow afternoon and give you the stats tomorrow night. Will that work?"

"Perfect. I owe you."

"If I added up all your IOUs, Vaux, I'd be traveling in Europe forever and you'd never be able to reach me."

Cameron hung up, watched the wind rustle the tops of the trees, and smiled. The pieces were appearing. Maybe he was losing his mind, but he wouldn't stop trying till this puzzle was locked into place.

CHAPTER 20

Ann slowed her pace slightly on the dirt road on Monday afternoon and glanced at the woods around her. Why had she let herself get so far from civilization? She wasn't worried about being alone in these woods. It was just . . . Okay, she was worried. She'd seen too many stories of women who disappeared in her exact situation.

Her pedometer said she'd come 4.7 miles. Time to head back to Three Peaks.

But the solitude of the rutted logging road and the pines sending out waves of perfume muted her fear and pulled her around one more corner, then one more, and one more.

Out here she could think. About the multiple reasons she'd come to Three Peaks—but mostly about the game she was playing with herself when it came to Cameron.

In her mind there was no game. The answer was clear. Stay away. God was her life. Cameron wasn't even sure God existed. Never the two shall meet. But her heart said game on.

Why not? Jessie had done it.

Yeah and Ann had seen what it did to her. Jessie prayed for Cameron daily, waiting for him to fall in love with Jesus, but he never did. And though she'd kept it from him, it broke her heart.

Ann picked up her pace, timing her strides so her feet landed on the shadows the trees cast on the dirt road.

She'd relaxed too much at the movie theater and let her feelings seep out of her heart, into her mannerisms and reactions. Did Cameron notice?

And what about him?

Sideways glances at her when he didn't think she saw. The look in his eyes last night when she turned to wave good-bye. On top of the mountain he looked at her the way he used to look at Jessie.

She slapped her hip hard. What was she thinking? In a few days he'd be back in Seattle, she'd be in Portland, and they would go back to pretending they didn't know each other.

It wouldn't go anywhere. It *couldn't* go anywhere. Not with his agnosticism—

Behind her an engine surged. She grabbed her iPod and put Josh Groban's crooning on hold and looked for cover. *There!* An opening a few yards ahead. She sprinted for the horseshoe-shaped clearing, scampered off the road, and squatted behind a large juniper tree.

Ann laughed at herself. *Relax.* Yes, the road seemed abandoned, but that didn't mean cars couldn't drive on it. But something inside her pinged danger and she obeyed the sensation. She peered toward the path, hoping nothing more than her eyes would show through the underbrush.

Ten seconds later a Ford Expedition bounced into view,

pounding over the washboard road. Ann held her breath as the SUV passed her hiding spot. What was wrong with her? Cars were allowed to drive on dirt roads. The road seemed like it would be difficult to traverse by car and had been tough to find. But she was the one from out of town. The road might be frequently traveled by the people of Three Peaks. It probably was.

The sound of the Ford's engine faded.

Easing out from her hiding place, she breathed deep and looked up. *Thank You, God.* She didn't feel like having company out here.

Her mind returned to Cameron and what he—

The whine of the SUV accelerating pierced her thoughts. The Expedition was backing up. A second later it came into view; too fast for her to scurry back behind the juniper tree. A tinted window rolled down revealing the wide grin of Jason Judah.

He parked, eased out, and sauntered around the side of the Ford. Leaning against the passenger side door, he lit a cigar and took off his shades.

"You are a hard woman to track." He spread his arms. "But here I am. I can't deny that Nam gave me a few useful skills."

"What are you doing here?" Adrenaline pumped through her. This was not the scenario she wanted to be in with Jason. Menace oozed out of the man. She'd felt it the first time they'd met, and being miles from anywhere, from anyone, the feeling intensified.

During her years of working in television, she'd been in the center of hostile gangs in downtown Portland, been in white-water rafts where she'd come a razor's edge from death—but this man made those situations seem mild. The inner bell of intuition that screamed danger rang double-time.

"How are you, Ann?" Jason took two steps forward.

"You followed me. What do you want?"

"Tracked. Followed. I suppose it's the same thing." Two more steps.

Ann planted her hands on her hips. "What do you want?"

"Are you this abrupt with all your interviewees?" Jason tapped his cigar, too early for any ash to come off; it seemed to be a part of his act. "All I want is a little chat."

"Why not talk to me in town? Why here?"

"Fewer distractions."

Ann watched the last of the dust settle that had been kicked up by Jason's Expedition. She looked at his hands. No keys. There were twenty, maybe twenty-five feet between the SUV and him. She was fast, but she'd spent her energy on the five-mile run getting up here. She wouldn't be quick enough to make it around him and to the driver's side of the car before he got in the passenger door.

"I think you can help me."

"I doubt it."

"I knew it from the moment we met." Three steps forward. "We'd make a good team."

"I disagree."

"Why are you afraid of me?"

Afraid? No. Terrified. She'd seen a madness in his eyes when she'd teased him onstage during his town meeting. Out here it had ramped up to maximum intensity. "You're wasting your time."

"I don't think so." One more step. "I wonder how many people have taken the time to figure out you're the foster sister of Cameron's late wife."

She shuddered. He'd been researching her? She hugged herself as if she'd be shielded from his gaze. "So what."

"From what Google and Facebook tell me, the two of you were close. Not only foster sisters, but best friends. I believe it highly probable Jessie talked to you about the book. I think you know more than you're telling. Maybe even more than you've told Cameron."

Ann backed up and stumbled over a pine branch.

"Relax; I'm not your enemy. I'm not anyone's enemy."

"Fine. What do you want?" Ann repeated for the third time. *Keep sounding confident; keep your eyes locked on his.*

"I want you to tell me everything Jessie told you." Jason took a long drag on the cigar, blew out a perfect smoke ring, and watched it melt into the sky. "I've come to believe her and Cameron's father. The book is real."

"How do you know?"

The trees on both sides of the clearing hemmed her in. The cliff in back of her formed the third wall. And the fourth, a steadily advancing Jason lessoned her options with every one of his steps.

"I admit I'd never seriously considered there was a book in physical form till Cameron showed up with the story of his dad and wife. I mean, who are we kidding? A real book of God here on earth? Now mind you, I had hoped and prayed and dreamed of it, but did I truly believe it possible? No. But after Cameron and I talked, I did a little digging. And I've discovered something very interesting. Would you like to know what it is?"

Ann shrugged. "Sure."

"There are six other spots in the world with a similar legend to the Book of Days. The Middle East, South America, China, Scotland, Turkey, Egypt, and of course the seventh location is in the United States, right here in Oregon."

"How did you find this out?"

Jason took three more steps forward. "Every one of the legends talks about a book with recordings of days in it. They don't use that exact language, but that's the general description. And they're not describing an idea, but a physical book."

"A book that tells the future." *Keep him talking. Find a way to get out of here.*

"Yes. That has recorded every event of every man and woman's life. Those that have been, and those that are to come."

"So what? Multiple stories about a book that tells the future doesn't make it real. You can find stories of a massive flood in nearly every culture. It doesn't mean a man named Noah really floated above it all with a boat full of all the animals in the world for forty days."

"That's amusing. I know you're a Christian. Which means odds are you believe the Noah story."

"Fine. I believe the flood story." Ann glanced to her left then her right, as if she could find an escape route she missed earlier. "If it's in the Bible I believe it, but I'm not prone to fantastical meanderings and chasing way-out legends like this book nonsense."

"This is the story of the century, Ann. Pulitzer-prize material." Jason tapped his cigar again. This time a spot of ash floated down. "Consider what this would do for your career. You wouldn't be limited to doing little featurettes on thrill seekers around the Northwest. If we find an authentic book, you'll want to be the one who reveals it to the world."

Jason waited for Ann to respond. She didn't. Reveal it to the world? For what purpose? Fame? Notoriety? No thanks. If there was a genuine Book of Days, she'd let someone else announce it and she'd keep her sanity.

She'd watched too many people in television grab for the brass ring of stardom only to find out it was really a brass handcuff. One that dangled a person's self-worth over a fickle fan base that loved you one moment and despised you the next.

"Cameron has to be getting some useful information with all the people he's talked to, especially Taylor Stone. Has Cameron told you everything? Find out all he knows, we'll add to what I know, and let's dig this thing up. Even if it turns out to be nothing, what have you lost?"

Jason was right. If a Book of Days was found, even if it was written by the hand of man, it would be an intriguing story. Worst case, it would be comic relief to tell Drew and her other friends; best case it would be *Raiders of the Lost Ark* come to life.

"I'll think about it."

"Excellent. That's all I'm asking." Jason walked around the Expedition and opened the driver's side door. "Very, very good, Ann Banister." He paused before getting in. "Would you like a ride back to town?"

"No thanks."

"You're probably right." He tilted his head and eyed her slowly up and down. "You could use the workout."

Ann smashed her tongue against her teeth to stop from seething out something she'd instantly regret. Her heartbeat didn't slow till the dust from Jason's SUV settled on the road two minutes later. What was wrong with her? Relax. He hadn't threatened her.

She squatted and held her head between her legs. Yes, he most certainly had.

What had she gotten herself into?

CHAPTER 21

Cameron glanced at his watch late Tuesday morning as he sat in front of his laptop, studied climbing routes on www.smithrock.com, and waited for Scotty's call. A few more moments and he'd know if his hunch about the stone was right. Scotty prided himself on being on time—precisely on time, which meant the phone would ring in thirty more seconds.

It didn't.

After Scotty pressed in on being two minutes late, Cameron reached for his iPhone at the instant it lit up with Scotty's caller ID. "Hey."

"Sorry I'm late."

"Are you changing personalities?"

Scotty cleared his throat. "I'm not surprised easily." The line went silent.

"What has you in shock and awe?"

"Where did you say you got this rock?"

"Three Peaks, Oregon."

"Impossible."

"Why?"

"This rock only exists in six places in the world and central Oregon ain't one of the places."

"You're kidding." Then where did Susan Hillman get a hold of that stone? "Where are the places?"

"The Middle East, South America, China, Scotland, Turkey, and Egypt."

Cameron opened Word on his laptop and started taking notes. "Spread out all over the globe."

"Very spread." Cameron heard Scotty tapping a pen or pencil against his desk. "That's where it gets weird." Again the line went silent. Cameron watched five seconds tick by on his watch.

"This type of stone is somewhat the holy grail to geologists. When I say this type of rock exists in only a few places in the world, I don't mean there are big deposits of it. I mean in each of those places, there are two, maybe three pounds of this type of rock, and while it has no intrinsic value like gold or platinum, its rarity makes it highly desired among us professional rock hounds.

"Carbon dating says these rocks are only around five thousand years old, so where did they come from? What made them? Volcanoes? No one knows.

"And for the final chapter in Weird Rocks of the World, their basic properties are almost the same as diamonds. They look pretty ordinary, but guys like me would pay hundreds for a piece. Where did you say you got the stone?"

Cameron felt light-headed. The words Susan Hillman had said skittered through his mind. *"A good choice, Cameron. A very, very good choice."*

"I need to get that rock back, Scotty. As soon as you can."

"You wouldn't be able to get another one, would you?"

Cameron pulled out his brown leather notebook and started jotting down every detail of his conversation with Scotty. This was a revelation he couldn't afford to forget.

"Cameron?"

"Huh?"

"Get me another stone, okay?"

"Sure. Gotta go, Scotty."

He ended the call and punched up Susan's number. It was time to find out exactly what she knew.

Moments later Susan answered. "Hello?"

"Hi, it's Cameron. I have to talk to you about the rock you gave me."

"I wondered how long it would take you to figure it out."

From behind a cluster of western larch, Jason watched Taylor Stone apply his ax to a pile of pine stumps with considerable force and waited for the right moment to step into his line of vision. Stone hadn't lost much size since their football days; Jason had surrendered even less.

If it came to blows, both would have a shot at taking the title. Taylor a mite quicker, Jason certainly holding the size advantage. But it wouldn't come to blows between two middle aged men. Ridiculous.

This was his time. He and his followers held their destiny in their hands. The universe had spoken through Cameron—telling them the book was real—and Jason would not be stopped from responding with a shout that would reverberate through the ages.

All he needed were a few answers.

Cameron would provide none. He would have joined Jason by

now if he was going to. Banister? She might be wavering, but she considered the book a fairy tale. Plus she feared him. Which he enjoyed, but she would stay away because of it.

He needed to break Stone, chip his resolve into grains of sand he could sift through his fingers. Taylor knew hidden things about the book. Jason was sure of it.

"Stone!" He stepped into view, his hands on his hips.

Taylor squinted into the setting sun. "Well, Jason. What a pleasant surprise."

"It's been quite a while, hasn't it, Taylor? Just the two of us chatting about life, with no one else around to distract us from meaningful conversation."

Taylor stared at Jason, his face like granite, the ax held stiff in his dark-brown leather gloved hands.

He strolled across Taylor's lawn. "It's been interesting to have some new blood focused on the book, this time searching for a real one, wouldn't you agree?" Jason folded his arms, smiling. "There is so much out there for us. Such power that is drawing us. It is time we looked into those pages of power and let people control their own destiny."

Taylor slapped the ax handle against his palm. "I suppose at some point you'll tell me why you're here, but why don't you stop the pompous guru bit since none of your flock is around to hear you." He narrowed his eyes.

Jason grinned and sat on one of the stumps dotting the backyard, clasping his hands together. "To the point as always."

"Why the obsession with the idea of finding a physical book, Jason? You know it's a myth."

"Do I really need to give an answer to you of all people?"

"Humor me."

Jason rubbed his hands together as he stood and strode over to Taylor, stopping inches from Taylor's face. "You know that in the right hands this book could do great things for the world, old friend. Things never before conceived by the mind of man."

"*Your* hands."

"Yes, mine." Jason circled Taylor like a boxer. "I would bring healing to so many and prevent so much future pain."

"You would bring sorrow. Knowing the future isn't for us to obtain. With our finite view, we would use the knowledge the book contains to twist things into a tapestry of knots that could never be untangled."

"Freudian slip?" Jason pursed his lips. "'The book contains?'"

"It was a figure of speech to point out your—"

"I think not." Jason put his hands behind his back and tilted his head back, his eyes staying focused on Taylor. "Come now, old chum. Talk to me."

"Even if there was a book, you'd set yourself up as the gatekeeper, the only one who would know its location."

"It's a role someone has to fill. To keep away the crazies. But I would share what I learned with all."

"Leave it alone." Taylor raised his ax to his shoulder. "There's nothing to tell."

"Have you told Cameron Vaux what you know?"

Taylor's only response was a deep breath.

"I believe you've known exactly where the book is ever since we were kids and could lead me to it right now if you wanted to. I believe you found the book years ago and used it over and over again as we grew up. To be the football star, the basketball star. Class President, mayor of Three Peaks. The editor in chief of *The Post* where you could manipulate the lives around you and make yourself the most golden boy in the history of this town. You had the Midas glove on when you touched anything. Because you always knew what was coming next and you changed it to fit your dreams.

"And I believe the book—and you—were intimately involved in a certain mysterious death thirty-three years ago that no one talks about anymore. When I find this book, I will systematically bury you, golden-boy."

Stone said nothing, but the pallor of his face told Jason he'd hit a nerve.

Taylor smacked the ax handle into his palm. Then again. And again. And again. "Time for you to leave, Jason."

Jason glanced at the ax before riveting his eyes on Taylor. "Are you threatening me?"

"Without question."

As Jason strode away, the sound of splitting wood seemed to grow faster and louder. Yes, he'd definitely hit a mother-lode nerve. He would track Taylor twenty-five hours a day. Along with Cameron, and Ann just to be thorough.

Cameron flopped back on his bed at the Best Western early Tuesday afternoon. Two hours until he saw Susan. Enough time for a nap. He could use it with how poorly he'd been sleeping. He stared at the small water stain on the wall next to the bed that resembled the undulating curves of the Columbia River, closed his eyes, and imagined himself floating down a river with nothing on his mind. Peace like a river, Jessie used to sing a song about that.

Just a few minutes rest couldn't hurt.

The vibration of his cell phone in his pocket snapped him back from the edge of sleep. He blinked, sat up, and looked at caller ID. *Brandon.*

He should take it. This was his partner's third call. The first one he'd forgotten about till he looked at his phone's recent-calls list. The second one he hadn't listened to yet.

"Hey, Brandon."

"Why haven't you called me back?"

"Sorry, I've been busy down here."

"Don't sweat it. I've got great news, bud."

"Yeah?"

"More than great. We've been invited to submit to *Thrill Junkie's* Grand Canyon wild-water adventure. And they're doing a celebrity version. We get to bid on the job, so they're asking us to put together a killer demo reel on why we should get to film the Stars on the River Reality Trip. Celebs on the river with you and me. If we get on that river, it will lead all the way to Hollywood."

"Are you serious?" Cameron sat up.

"That's the good news."

"I don't need the bad."

"Yin and yang. Gotta take 'em both."

"The bad?"

"They need the bid a week from this Friday."

In ten days? "Wow. They want it that quick?" Cameron clenched his teeth. Wrapping up his search in five days wasn't going to happen. But this is the kind of job that could put their company on rocket sleds. "I might need more time down here."

"Sorry, dude, no more time to spare. This gig could be huge. Gigantor huge."

"I know, we gotta do it. But part of me is thinking this Book of Days thing could be genuine. I'm not kidding. Can you imagine knowing your future?"

"What are you talking about?"

Whoops. He'd forgotten he hadn't told Brandon anything about his dad, Jessie, and the book. "Sorry, I thought I'd told you." Cameron rapped his forehead with his fingers. "Look, when I get back, I'll do my Paul Harvey impersonation and tell you the rest of the story."

"Who?"

"Paul Harvey, he was a radio legend. Don't tell me you don't know who he is."

"No clue. You're the ex-broadcaster, not me."

"Just a little bit longer."

"Soon, Cam."

"Don't worry."

"I am worr—"

"I'll be back the first instant I can." Great. Gig of a lifetime and he was searching for some fantasy book.

Susan had better be willing to give him some rock-hard answers.

CHAPTER 22

Two hours later Cameron glanced at his watch, swore, and mashed his gas pedal. Three thirty-five. He should have been at Susan's five minutes ago. She probably wouldn't care, but he hated being late. Probably because it irritated him so much when people made him wait.

Cameron reached over to flick on the radio, but before he could, his cell phone buzzed. He picked it up and looked at the number. Ann. "Hey, how are you?"

"Great, how was your movie?"

"Fine. Yours?"

"Excellent." She paused. "Maybe next time we'll choose the same one."

There it was again. Friendly Ann was still onstage. Why? "Sounds good." What else could he say? *Why are you suddenly being Cinderella to me after seven years of playing the Ice Queen?*

"Guess who met a stalker this morning."

He clutched his steering wheel as an image of the figure from the park flashed through his head. "Are you okay?"

"Fine."

"Was it Jason?"

"You win."

"Where?"

"In the mountains on an old dirt road. I went for a run and he followed me there. He's a whacko, Cameron."

Traffic in front of him stopped and as his MINI Cooper slowed to a halt, Cameron looked to his right. Climb-It Sports. A poster in the window showed a climber dangling from an overhang by his fingertips. There was no rope. The caption on the poster said, *Leave It All Behind*.

He thought of his moment on the mountain before he'd seen Ann in silhouette and how close he'd come to leaving it all behind. The thought still niggled at him, tempted him. He was making progress on finding the book, but to what end? Even if he got to the finish line, he might not have enough of a mind left to know if he'd won the race. His dad didn't say the book would cure him, only that it would be okay. What did that mean? Who would really miss him? Brandon, of course. And . . .

"Cameron?"

"Yeah, I'm here."

"Did you hear what I said?"

"No, sorry."

"After making me feel like I wanted to take three showers in a row, Jason told me something interesting."

"Talk to me." Cameron glanced at the chipped street sign a half a block ahead as the light turned green and traffic lurched forward into a lazy curve in the road. River Street. That was his turn to get to Susan's house.

"Did you know according to Jason, there are six spots in the world with a legend about a book that tells the future?"

Cameron gripped his steering wheel between his legs as he pulled a pen out of his back pocket and leaned over to the passenger seat and grabbed a piece of paper out of his briefcase. A second later the wheel slipped and his car headed into oncoming traffic. Two horns blared at him.

As he yanked the wheel to bring his car back into his lane, he lost his grip on his cell phone and it smacked against the gear shift before settling to the carpet at Cameron's feet.

He fished it off the floor, breathing in rapid little puffs. *Hello, Mr. Death. How are you today? I was just thinking about coming to visit you.* "Ann, you still there?"

"Are you all right?"

"Other than coming within inches of meeting another Three Peaker head-on, I'm dandy."

"Those horns were for you?"

"Yep. I was driving with my legs and the wheel slipped. Then I dropped my phone."

"Driving with your . . . You're insane. Don't you use a Bluetooth?"

Heat burned his cheeks. "When I remember to bring it with me."

"You're breaking the law."

"Sorry."

"Buy another one for your car. I don't want anything—"

No. He couldn't let her say she didn't want anything happening to him. He didn't need those emotions stirred up. "Can we get back on track?"

"Sure."

"I'll bet the places with the legend are the Middle East, South America, China, Scotland, Turkey, and Egypt."

"How did you know that?"

"Geology." Cameron pulled over to the side of the road and yanked out his notebook. "There's a seventh location, Ann."

"I know."

"And that seventh location is—"

In unison they said, "—Three Peaks, Oregon."

"Where's your interest meter pegging now?" Cameron asked.

"On a scale of one to ten, probably a twelve. This is getting entertaining."

"I'm headed to talk to Susan Hillman about a rock she gave me, then grab a bite and do some serious Google searches on those spots. Wanna meet me at the Ski Inn restaurant—?"

"Absolutely, say around seven?"

"You're perfect."

"I am?"

Cameron heard a smile in her voice.

Wow, where did that foray in the land of Freud come from? "What I meant is, that time is perfect."

"Hello, Cameron, have you prepared yourself to pepper me with all kinds of questions?" Susan looked up for a moment, then continued watering the baskets of rock penstemon flowers hanging in baskets above the four corners of her massive cedar porch.

"Maybe." He strolled up her steps and stopped at the top. "You weren't surprised to hear from me."

"No, I wasn't." She turned from her watering and tapped her head. "You're a smart young man. But I will admit I was surprised to hear from you as quickly as I did."

"You thought it would take me longer to discover the significance of the rock I chose?"

Susan nodded and set down her watering can. "I could suggest you keep delving deeper into the mystery of the stone, but you've already found out what you needed to discover in that arena. And I suppose I should confirm that Taylor Stone is one of the more significant keys to your quest. But again, you've figured that out by now."

Susan clapped her hands together. "So since you're already doing all the right things, I'm not sure what help I can be, but I'm certainly willing to try."

Two white wicker chairs sat at forty-five-degree angles to each other and Susan motioned for Cameron to sit. After asking him to hold his first question, she went into the house and returned a few minutes later with two Arnold Palmers.

"Here's how you can help immensely," he said after taking a sip of the iced tea-lemonade mixture. "While I'm enjoying my scavenger hunt, picking up one clue here, another there, I would not mind in the least if you simply told me the exact location of where the book sits." He cocked his head.

"Would you mind if we played a little game together?"

Cameron shrugged.

"The rules are simple. You ask me a question, I answer as honestly as I can. I ask you a question and you extend the same courtesy toward me."

"All right."

"You start." Susan brushed a strand of brown hair off her face.

"You just implied that the stone you gave me is connected to the Book of Days. Is it?"

"Of course."

"How?"

Susan shook her head and smiled. "My turn. What do you hope to gain by finding this book?"

Life. He wanted life instead of the agony of losing Jessie. He wanted answers, meaning, purpose. He wanted there to be a reason his dad left this world too soon. He wanted peace to replace his frustration . . . He wanted to relive the days and years Jessie and he had shared together . . . He wanted his mind to be restored—all the emotions converged into one.

"I want hope."

Susan's eyes misted over as she nodded. "What do you hope for?"

"Unh-uh." He wagged his finger. "My turn again."

Susan bowed her head slightly and opened her palms.

"Is the book real, or just some New Age dream, or some pseudo-scientific concoction like the Oregon Vortex?"

"I suppose many things are possible that we're tempted to say aren't." Susan held his gaze for a few seconds before looking down. "But I do believe there is a book in heaven—God's book—in which He has recorded each man and woman's life."

"What do you mean—?" Cameron cut himself off. "It's your turn."

"Go on. Ask. The question game is a silly one, only fun for the first few minutes, don't you think?"

"Jason said the Book of Days exists on a spiritual plane that he claims he's tapped into. Is that what you mean?"

"No."

A quiet confidence played in Susan's eyes.

"You think there is a God, and you think that He records every moment of every life? Even future events?"

She didn't hesitate. "Without question."

"You're saying you know it absolutely to be true?"

"People who claim to know there is a God and those who claim to know there isn't a God are more similar than either side would like to admit. I believe, yes, but do I know? For certain?" Susan shook her head, a gentle smile on her face. "No one can with

100-percent certainty, Cameron. Not till our days on earth end. So while I will be surprised if that book isn't in heaven, I won't know definitively till I get there."

A hummingbird hovered near Susan's feeder full of sugar water, flitting back and forth as if wondering if Cameron could be trusted. Finally it began to drink, but only for a few moments before streaking away again.

"That bird is the only species that can stay in one spot as it flies. The speed with which it moves its wings is mind boggling, up to ninety times per second. Some would say that ability came after millions of years of adaptation; others would unequivocally state the hummingbird is proof of intelligent design."

Cameron shifted and crossed his legs. "Which is it?"

"Man has longed to touch the infinite—or explain Him away—ever since Adam and Eve left the garden. In the end, as I suggested earlier, it comes down to what you choose to believe."

"Susan . . ." Cameron paused. The look on her face was not one of pity, but of longing. For what he couldn't tell. But it wasn't for herself. It was for him. "Thank you, once again, for your time and your wisdom."

She leaned forward and took both his hands in hers. "Let me say, for me, the critical question is not whether God's Book of Days is here on earth or in heaven, but if it does exist, what kind of lives are we recording in it?"

As he stood and contemplated Susan's musings, the hummingbird returned, not hesitating to drink more of the nectar, even though Cameron had leaned closer to the feeder.

"I have always celebrated men and women with passion, and I see you have passion." Susan smiled and her head fell back. "The path life takes us down isn't always where we would choose to go, but in the end, it is possible to wind up where we wanted to be anyway."

He wanted his brain back. Was that possible?

CHAPTER 23

He set the seven bullets on the mantel above his fireplace three inches apart and watched the light from his candles dance on their copper tips. Seven was the number of perfection. But he wouldn't need that many.

One for Cameron.

One for Stone.

Banister? Maybe. He grinned and set her picture next to ones of Taylor and Cameron already on the mantel. Probably.

He slid his knife out of its sheath and licked the blade. Nothing like the taste of steel. Unless it had a bit of flavoring. He smiled again. Maybe he'd do it that way. Time would enlighten as to the best method.

After placing the knife to the right of the bullets, he settled onto his leather couch, closed his eyes, and opened himself to the universe.

Soon, it told him, and he believed.

Cameron sat waiting for Ann in the Ski Inn, soaking in the smell of fried onions and sautéed mushrooms, thinking about Susan's words. What kind of life *was* he recording?

His dad's trips to Africa, the free medical treatment he gave to thousands—definitely worth recording. And the joy his father brought to people with his universal acceptance and uninhibited laughter? *Write it down.*

Jessie's volunteering downtown at the Union Gospel Mission, taking those kids from the cancer center up flying? Leading that Bible study for those girls? *Pen and paper time.*

Following God gave them purpose.

But Cameron's life? Sure he coached the kids in Little League and gave extra attention to the boys who didn't have a dad at home, but there wasn't much else.

He plopped his briefcase in front of his silverware and let his head slump forward behind it. It reminded him of hiding behind snow forts as a kid. Why couldn't the days be that simple again, his quest nothing more complex than smacking another kid in the head with a snowball?

Cameron took a drink of his ice water and smacked the glass back down loud enough to get the couple three tables down to look his direction. What hard evidence did he have after talking to Susan? He yanked his notepad out of his briefcase. Nothing.

Describing his emotional state as frustrated was an understatement. He wanted to rip the town apart and force them to give him an answer. Was he the Fool on the Hill? Was he crashing through the underbrush, chasing smoke, trying to find a fire that didn't exist?

Internally he swore at Susan, Taylor, Jason, and everyone else he could think of. Why wouldn't anyone give him a straight answer?

He was finding clues but too few and not fast enough. One led him to another leading to another like a stack of Russian babushka dolls, except this stack never seemed to end.

Cameron sat up and rubbed his ears with the palms of his hands, then his eyes. As his vision cleared, he focused on the yellow pad in front of him. Five pages of notes, plus a reconstruction of the ones that were stolen. Sometimes he could remember every line; sometimes he couldn't remember a quarter of what he'd written down. He circled a few lines in red ink, then closed his eyes and let his head fall back against his chair.

Was the memory loss accelerating? He refused to let himself think about it.

He glanced at his watch—6:50—then closed his eyes. Ann should be here in ten.

"You look tired."

Cameron jumped and opened his eyes. Taylor Stone stood in front of him, arms folded, smile on his face. He had his signature Oregon Ducks hat on, this one crisper than the one he'd worn at the creek. Probably even had one with a little bow tie on it for formal events.

He had to snap out of his descent into desolation. He wouldn't get much pity from Stone, and people didn't reveal their secrets to Eeyore. Be charming outside, even though his insides felt like grapes in a winemaker's vat during crushing season.

"Don't you know as a self-respecting Husky I should rip that thing off your head?"

Taylor opened his eyes wide. "Huskies respect themselves? I learn something new every—"

"Do all Ducks have a proclivity for talking in cliché's? Or is it just you?"

"'Proclivity.' Is that really the way video producers talk in Seattle, or are you trying to impress me?"

He offered his hand and Taylor grasped it in a warm handshake.

"Good to see you. Is this a regular hangout for you?" Cameron said.

"No. It's just where I knew I'd find you."

"And how would you know that?" Cameron leaned back, twirled his pen, and gazed up at Taylor's knowing smile.

"I didn't." Taylor chuckled. "I actually had no clue. This is the fourth place I looked."

"Would you like to sit down and tell me where I can find the Book of Days? Or can I simply abduct you at gunpoint and force you to tell me what you know about it?"

Taylor stared at Cameron.

"At some point you're going to trust me." Cameron took a long look at Taylor and smiled. "I know it won't be this moment, but think about it."

Taylor sucked in a quick breath. "You and I need to go for a drive, my Husky friend."

"Sorry, I can't. I'm meeting someone here in a few minutes."

"Your choice."

Cameron clicked his teeth together. Ann would understand. "Let me make a quick phone call."

"I'll be outside. If you're not standing beside me in two minutes, I'll assume you don't want to talk."

"I'll be there."

Finally. Taylor Stone was going to grab a can opener and let the beans spill.

As Cameron walked out, he spied Kirk Gillum and a woman sitting at the bar.

"How's your search going, Mr. Vaux?"

"Not a lot of progress, but I'm still looking."

"Good for you." Kirk took a drink of what looked like scotch and soda. "Listen. I'm sorry about the day we met if I was a little rude. I've been burned, you understand."

"No problem."

"I hope the book fairy tale comes true for you, and you find what you're looking for."

Cameron frowned. "I thought you were one of Jason's followers."

"I am, and the idea of the book is real. But the book isn't real. Do you understand?"

"Yeah." But he didn't understand. If Jason was pushing the book as genuine to his disciples, why wouldn't Kirk support that belief? And why did he care what Cameron believed?

Kirk turned back to the bar. "Take care, Mr. Vaux."

~

The inside of Taylor's Toyota Tundra matched the outside. Spotless. It didn't have that new car smell but looked like it should.

Neither man spoke as they pulled into traffic and headed for the east side of town. As the Three Peaks High School football field came into view, Taylor broke the silence. "I bled and danced on that field. Three golden years. Even had a few scouts send me letters, small college only, nothing impressive, but I did love the game."

"I understand you were pretty decent at basketball too."

"I see you've been conversing with Arnold Peasley."

Cameron smiled and nodded.

"That there?" Taylor pointed to an old mechanics shop with a 1912 Model T Ford sitting out front. "That's where Mr. Gowner taught me to tweak on cars till they purred like well-fed tabby cats.

"Look at those freestone peach trees over to your left. Tending to them was my first summer job. Thirteen years old and they told me to plant them in perfect rows. From smooth tender shoots to hardened, twisted peach trees in forty-five short years." Taylor sighed.

"Kind of like you, huh?"

Taylor jammed his forefinger at Cameron. "Watch it, punk."

"I've heard it said confessing to a stranger is often easier than those closest to you."

"For some. Am I about to be glad or regretful that I don't know you?"

Cameron propped his elbow on the open window and laughed.

"What? You think if you confess something to me, I'll be obligated to reveal one of the dark secrets you imagine I carry?" Taylor said.

"Something like that."

"First, I don't have any secrets, dark or otherwise. Second, I'm not in the habit of confessing to anyone. Nice try."

Cameron watched the river bordering the highway churn and pummel its rocky bank. "After my wife Jessie died, I did my job every day, never missed work, but I was drunk every minute for six months."

Taylor glanced at him. "Did you wind up taking a ride on the alcohol-addiction wagon?"

"No, I suppose I just wasn't made that way. I never had to have it, but I sure wanted it. If I'd gone by the AA definition, I was a full-blown member of the drinking consignetti. But when I stopped, I quit cold turkey, no temptation to overindulge again."

"What made you hit the brakes?"

"Almost making my car into a toaster oven with me inside. And I knew it would break Jessie's heart to see me that way. My dad's too. I vowed to them I'd never drink again."

"Oh, really? You think they see you from the great beyond?"

"I'm an agnostic, not an atheist." Cameron put on his sunglasses. "So I don't know what's out there. Sometimes I think I feel her, feel my dad. Spirit world, heaven, maybe they're there right here now. I wish I knew for sure."

"Me too."

Cameron cocked his head. "I thought you were a God person."

"I am. That doesn't mean doubts don't sometimes worm their way into my mind." Taylor pulled into a deserted park on the outskirts of town. The sun was starting to set behind thin clouds as they got out of Taylor's truck and walked across the parking lot.

"So what's your current drug of choice, Cameron?"

"Rock climbing."

They trudged along a path that wound up the side of a hill, putting them two-hundred feet higher within fifteen minutes. After they both caught their breath, Taylor pointed out the three peaks the town was named for. The mountains—snow covered even in the heart of summer—were framed by two ponderosa pines that stood thirty feet in front of them. Postcard perfect.

"Do me a favor and stand right . . . here." Taylor stood behind Cameron holding his shoulders and moved him back a few feet to the right. "Take a close look now."

Cameron stared at the peaks. Taylor had brought him here for a reason, but Cameron doubted if the man would tell him why. Like a rabbit that bolts at the slightest movement, he sensed the man would clam up the moment he pushed him.

He'd seen the peaks hundreds of times since coming to town: on postcards, placemats, and around every corner of Three Peaks. But something here was different. The angle? The time of day? He couldn't tell. It reminded him of something and made him wish for his notebook.

There. That was the difference. The angle of the sun on the mountains formed a shadow that mimicked an arrowhead perfectly. And the arrowhead shadow pointed to a spot that looked like a tunnel burrowing into the mountain.

A moment later the sun sank lower in the sky and the illusion vanished.

"Let's go." Taylor turned back the way they'd come.

"What did you just show me?"

"Nothing." Taylor rubbed the back of his neck. "What's the toughest part about your wife's death?"

"You're not going to tell me why you stood me in front of the mountains?"

"No." Taylor scuffed along the dirt path, kicking at pinecones. "Sorry, Cameron."

Cameron stuffed his hands in his coat pocket. Was Stone part of the plan to drive him out of his mind? "The toughest part? The regrets. Stuff you wish you could take back, wish you'd done or said. The things you wish you could forgive yourself for."

"There are some things you should never forgive yourself for. With some things"—Taylor bent down and picked up a rock—"it simply is not possible."

"Really?"

Taylor hurled his rock at a tree twenty yards below them. It smacked into the pine dead center, the sound reverberating through the park. "Really."

The sun had given itself over to twilight by the time they reached Taylor's truck. Neither spoke till they were halfway back to the Ski Inn.

"I like you, Cameron. You're strong. You've lived through pain and sorrow. Now stay strong. And for your own sanity, get out of Three Peaks now. And until you leave, stay away from Jason."

"What's the history between you two?"

"None of your business."

Taylor didn't speak again till Cameron stepped out of the older man's truck and ambled toward his MINI Cooper.

"Cameron!"

He turned to look at Taylor who leaned out his window.

"I'm serious. I'm only looking out for you." Taylor pointed his forefinger at him. "Stay away from Jason, for your own good. Got it?"

Cameron didn't answer, but on the other hand, Taylor didn't wait for a response. He peeled out of the parking lot and didn't look back.

CHAPTER 24

On Wednesday morning Cameron stood at the bottom of the library stairs and peered at Ann over the top of his triple-shot latte, trying to stop the butterflies from playing rugby in his stomach.

"You coming up?" she called down to him.

"Eventually. I need another sip of wake-up juice first." He took another drink of his coffee and climbed the stairs.

Her auburn hair was pulled back, and it didn't look like she was wearing makeup. It should have made her less attractive, not more. Why couldn't she be ugly?

When he reached the top of the stairs, he toasted her with his coffee and made a choice. Today he wouldn't beat himself up for his growing attraction toward Ann. He'd stay in the moment. No projecting what might happen in the future. They were feelings, nothing more.

He walked over and opened the library door for her. They

settled at the back of the library at a large polished table that looked like it was constructed from old barn siding.

"This kind of table would be cool to have in my house," Cameron said.

"I have something just like it in mine."

"Really?"

Ann nodded.

Interesting. The same taste in furniture too.

She scooted her chair closer to the table. "Did you get anywhere looking into those rock spots?"

Cameron grimaced and clacked his teeth together. "Nothing. Yes, those six places around the world have this type of rock, but I couldn't find any mention of a legend similar to the Book of Days. I don't know where Jason snagged his information, but it doesn't show up anywhere on the Internet or in any history book in this library."

"So let's—"

"Let's not. I need to take a break from thinking about the book, and I promised I'd help you look into your family's past."

"Really?" Ann's face brightened.

As she spread out her notes on the table, Cameron said, "Why don't you give me a quick recap of what you know for sure and what you suspect."

"I don't know much for certain. I don't even know my mom's maiden name."

"You never asked her?"

"I was a kid; it wasn't the most pressing question on my mind, and I don't ever remember her talking about her history except one time when I overheard her say, 'When I lived in Oregon.'"

"So how can you know Three Peaks is the part of Oregon where she lived?"

"Because of this."

Ann pulled out a photo that showed a girl—eleven, maybe twelve years old—who had just let go of a tire swing out over a river. Her long arms and legs were splayed in spread-eagle fashion, lit like gold by a late afternoon sun. Her features were obscured by her thick reddish blonde hair, but you could tell she was smiling.

A boy and another girl stood on the bank watching her, one pointing at her as she flew through air. But they were bathed in shadows, the light too dim to make out their features.

"Your mom?"

"Yes." Ann turned the picture over. "Look."

In blue ink was scrawled, *Jennifer flies! July 22, 1963.*

"Where'd you get the picture?"

"It's the only photo I have of her. I barely remember what she looked like as an adult." Ann tossed the photo onto the table. "Not that I'll ever care."

"What you do you mean you won't ever—?"

"Are you kidding?" Ann stared at him as she squinted and gave little shakes of her head. "She was drunk almost every night, and on the nights she wasn't, she was 'riding the horse.'"

"The horse?"

"Heroin."

Cameron nodded. "Is that what she ODd on?"

Ann rocked back in her chair, arms folded. "Yep. All of a sudden I was hearing about lots of things I'd never heard of before. It was quite an education for an eleven-year-old kid."

"I'm sorry."

"Yeah, me too."

Cameron took her hand. "Really, I'm sorry."

Ann flushed and pulled her hand away. "Thanks, but it's eons in the past."

"So you've forgiven her?"

Ann shifted in her chair.

"You need to forgive her."

She gazed out the window, then eventually looked at him. "I know."

"Remember what Jessie always used to say about bitterness?"

"It's like cutting yourself and thinking the other person will bleed to death."

"Something like that." Jessie didn't just say it. She lived it, always forgiving people who didn't deserve it. And she'd taught Cameron you couldn't be free without forgiving people, including yourself.

Ann steepled her hands and rubbed her forehead with her forefingers. "Do you mind if we focus on my history?"

"No problem." Cameron picked up the photo of Ann's mom. "So how does this prove—?"

"I've memorized every part of this picture, every shadow, every ripple on that river, the contours of the bank, the mountains in the background . . . I'd recognize this spot no matter if it was winter, summer, spring, or fall. And I've used Google Earth to look at every image of every river in all of Oregon."

A second later it struck Cameron like thunder. It was close to the spot on the river where he'd first met Taylor Stone. "Oh, wow, that's Whychus Creek."

Ann nodded. "I've shown this picture to a good chunk of the people in town. No one recognizes my mom, or if they do, they're not admitting it."

"How would someone recognize your mom when you can't see her face?"

"I know it's a long shot, but three other people were there the day the picture was taken. Don't you think one of them would remember it?"

"I only see two others on the bank."

"Someone else had to take the picture."

He stared at the photo. Would anyone remember a tire-swing adventure from over forty years ago? Maybe. Maybe not. "So what's my mission, should I choose to accept it?"

"Help me find old school photos, someone who recognizes my mom in this picture, someone who will admit it, find the other kids in the shot . . . There has to be something or someone who can tell us about this picture."

"I'm on it."

Ann stood. "I'm going to grab a stack of old newspapers from the early sixties. The local swimming hole might be profiled in a small-town paper and that's the kind of shot they'd put next to the story."

She sauntered off and Cameron watched her go. Her mom's overdose wasn't eons ago. For Ann it was seconds ago. She needed to let it go.

"Finding everything you need?"

Cameron's head whipped around to the source of the voice. Susan Hillman stood to his left. She worked here? She must have told him. Why couldn't he remember? Rhetorical question. *Think!*

"I forgot you worked . . ."

"You forgot I work here? I never told you, so you're forgiven."

"You didn't tell . . . ? I mean . . . right, I remember that you didn't."

"Are you okay, Cameron?"

"Great. And you?"

Susan just smiled. "How goes the quest?"

"Actually I'm not here for me; I'm here for a . . . friend, who is doing some research."

"Is your friend five-seven, auburn hair, leaning toward red, nice figure, and piercing green eyes?"

He laughed. "Possibly."

"She's a pretty gal. Seems sharp enough too. And from what I've seen, kind as well."

"Wait till you get to know her."

Susan swatted Cameron on the shoulder and chuckled. "Can I point you in a helpful direction?"

"If you're offering, yeah, you can. Take a look at this."

Susan sat in a chair next to him and he slid the photo of Ann's mom in front of her. "Do you know who this girl is?"

Susan's face flushed and she pressed her lips together. After a few more seconds, she stood. "I'm so sorry, Cameron, but I can't talk to you about this photo."

"What?" He squinted at her. "Are you joking?"

Susan licked her lips and glanced around the library. "I don't think it would be right for me—"

"Why can't you tell me about this picture?"

"I can't."

Cameron rapped the edge of the table with his palm. "It's important!"

"Out of respect for . . . an old friend, please don't ask me about it again." She walked off, her soft-heeled shoes making muted clicks on the floor.

He ground his fingers into the top of his skull and smacked the table again.

A few minutes later Ann returned without any papers in hand. "Guess what?" She slid into her chair next to Cameron and sat sideways in it, her legs crossed. "The microfiche of the *Three Peaks Post* from May of 1963 to September of 1963 seems to have vanished."

Cameron didn't answer.

"What's wrong?"

"I want to strangle somebody."

"What happened?"

"Susan Hillman knows the people in your picture, but she won't talk about it."

Ann's face went slack. "She won't? What? I mean, she does?"

"Without question."

"Why won't she talk?"

He rubbed his temples. "No clue. Once again we bump into the Three Peaks' Wall of Secrets." Cameron leaned back. "Susan won't talk. Taylor won't talk. Jason is a psycho. And I'm losing my mind. Literally."

"So what are you going to do?"

"Slip some truth serum into the town water supply."

"Seriously."

He had to hold it together. Going crazy wouldn't get him to the book or help them figure out Ann's history, and something told him the two were connected somehow. "Someone removed the microfiche from the summer of '63 because of that picture. So all we have to do is get a hold of hard copies of the paper from that time period."

"Taylor Stone ran that paper for eighteen years. He might have copies," Ann said.

"He would've been only eleven or twelve when that picture was taken."

Ann slapped her hands on the table and leaned in. "Let's go to the paper."

"Somehow I think they'd be missing those issues." Cameron drummed his fingers on the library table. He blew out a laugh. Of course! He knew exactly who to talk to. Unbelievable. Maybe his memory was returning.

It was time to pay another visit to Arnold Peasley and his newspaper museum.

CHAPTER 25

After saying good-bye to Ann, Cameron sat in his car determined to find something to take his mind off Jessie, his memory loss, the book, Ann—everything. Even if it wasn't good for him. Yes, he and Ann were making progress on her history—Peasley had agreed to see him Friday afternoon—but he was still buried in six feet of Three Peaks dust in his search for the Book of Days.

The Peak Me Up Bar & Grill flashed into his mind. The sting of Jack Daniels and Wild Turkey had led him down a path of emptiness for six months till he'd broken its hold, but when there was little to live for, the city of Empty wasn't a bad destination. A few drinks couldn't hurt.

He pushed open the maple-colored bar door and ignored the voice inside screaming to walk away. Maybe it was Jessie's voice. Maybe his dad's. Maybe his own. It didn't matter. He was going to get plastered, kiss the world good-bye for two or six hours, and love every second of it. Or at least give it an Olympic effort.

The bar was empty except for two fortysomethings who racked balls on a faded green pool table and the bartender who stared at a television that wasn't turned on.

Cameron sat at the bar on a maroon stool with silver legs that looked like it had been minted yesterday. No balls dropped on the break, so the second man stepped up and tried to sink the six ball in the right corner pocket. He sank the eight ball instead.

The perfect commentary on Cameron's life.

"You're Cameron Vaux." The bartender said it as if he were required, no emotion behind the greeting.

"Yeah, and you're the bartender."

The bartender nodded, as if slightly perturbed.

"Sorry, I'm probably not happy enough for happy hour right now."

"What can I get you?"

"Mr. Jack. Double shot."

Thirty seconds later the drink sat next to him, its mellow whisky smell tempting him. But really, there was no temptation. The battle was over. Daniels had won.

He slid his fingers around the shot glass and watched the liquid bounce against the sides like a miniature pond in the wind.

Just a little liquid to set him free.

Cameron carried the drink over to a booth in the darkest part of the bar and stared at it. It was a good choice. As long as he was forgetting things, he might as well forget the futility of his life for a while. He ignored the voice still yakking away in his head and lifted the drink to his mouth.

"Nothing compliments a double shot of Jackie D better than a double-decker mushroom and Swiss burger over at The Sail & Compass."

Cameron whirled to find the source of the familiar voice.

Taylor Stone stood to the left of the front door, next to the electronic dart board, arms folded, one ankle crossed over the other as he leaned back against the wall, a little knowing smile on his face.

"Mr. Stone. Good to see you."

Taylor sauntered over to the bar and sat next to him. "I suppose I could go through all the 'you don't want to do this, and are you sure this is the best choice right now speech,' but you're too smart for that to work. So let me just bluntly say you know where this road leads, so before you toss that double shot down your throat, why don't we get some food in your stomach?"

He stared at Taylor, then at the glass. Taylor Stone, his rescuer. Irony rears up to take a bow. Taylor Stone, the thorn in his flesh. Taylor Stone, the man with hidden answers about the Book of Days. Taylor Stone, the man with his own demons.

"Will you talk about the book?"

Taylor pushed himself up from the barstool and folded his arms again. "You coming?"

Why not? Cameron took another look at the shot glass. He threw down a twenty-dollar bill, set the drink onto the middle of Abe's face, and strode with Taylor out the front door.

When Cameron stepped outside, he stopped to let his eyes adjust to the sun pounding down and turned to Taylor. "The burgers are decent?"

"The best. Let's go."

The Sail & Compass carried its theme throughout the restaurant. Pictures of sailboats adorned every wall, a drawing of an ancient-looking compass covered the front of the menus and the napkins. Even the ceiling was covered with the night sky, little white dots representing the constellations—nature's map for sailors.

They ordered and watched a Seattle Mariners' game on the big screen inside the bar while waiting for their food to arrive.

When the game went to commercial break, Cameron turned to Taylor. "It seems odd to have a sailing themed restaurant this far inland."

"Maybe this is the closest people around here will ever get to the water."

"They could take a drive. It can't be over one hundred and fifty miles to the ocean from Three Peaks."

Taylor tilted his head to the side. "Want to bet?"

"Sure, loser pays for the burgers."

"One hundred and fifty-seven miles to Newport. I win. You lose."

Cameron tossed his cardboard coaster at Taylor and hit him in the stomach. "You want to know why most of our conversations start off okay but drift into the realm of animosity?"

"Sure, enlighten me." Taylor grinned.

"Probably because I get too close to the truth, pick away too much of your scab that covers it up, and you can't handle the pain."

"Probably true."

Cameron expected Taylor to respond with anger, but he didn't.

A moment later their plump waitress with her megawatt smile shimmied up to their table with their meals. As soon as Cameron's plate skidded to a halt on the table, he grabbed a handful of French fries and shoved them in his mouth.

"What are you doing there, sailor?"

"Trying to counteract the effects of Mr. Jack."

"Uh, hello? You and Mr. Jack didn't end up meeting this afternoon." Taylor laughed.

"What?"

"You didn't throw down that shot, Cameron. Are you okay?"

No. Not in front of Stone. Think. Did he swallow the drink? That's right, Taylor came and he . . . paid for it but didn't . . . Oh, wow. Cameron's stomach knotted like he'd swallowed a sixteen-pound bowling ball. He had to get a grip, keep Stone from seeing him panic.

"I guess I was so determined to have the drink when I went in, I thought I . . ."

"Relax; it's an easy thing to forget." Taylor's mouth said the words, but his eyes and tone of voice disagreed. He stared at Cameron as if waiting for a confession.

"I haven't been sleeping well since I got here."

Taylor grabbed the ketchup and squirted what looked like half the bottle in between his double-decker mushroom and Swiss burger and his fries. "I know you want to talk about the book, but let me throw out a wild idea instead. You can decide to shoot me down in flames or go along for the ride."

Cameron squinted at him. "Okay."

"Let's pretend you don't care about the Book of Days' legend, and I don't care that you have an obsession with it. We'll pretend we're old friends telling stories of the insane things we did in our late teens and early twenties. Hmm?"

He shook his head and gave a weak smile. How could Taylor know Cameron and his dad shared those kinds of stories with each other a few years after the disease took hold? Like how his dad set the unofficial record for getting from West Seattle to downtown by running every stoplight and stop sign along the route. How he swam across the bone-numbing waters of Hood Canal on a whim in the summer of '78.

Cameron rubbed his face. He missed those talks. He missed his dad.

"What's wrong?" Taylor said.

"My dad and I used to tell each other those kinds of stories."

"Hey, we don't have to—"

"Nah, let's do it." It might be the closest he could ever get to talking with his dad again.

By the time he was done with his hamburger—which was as good as Taylor said it would be—Cameron had told him about everything from the time as a teenager where he and two friends had filled up fire extinguishers with water and spent the night soaking everyone on the street they could find, to how in their early twenties Brandon and he had parachuted into the middle of a Dave Mathews Band concert at the Gorge Amphitheatre in eastern Washington.

Taylor arched an eyebrow. "I'll bet the aftermath of that stunt was interesting."

"It was a stupid thing to do. But we only spent one night in jail."

After Taylor told of his rock concert days, experiments with drugs, and the time he outran a cop in his 1963 Chevy Impala SS, Cameron smiled. "You were a certifiable wild child, Mr. Stone."

"It was the sixties, there was no choice." Taylor downed the last of his third Coke. "And I have to say, based on your stories from the early nineties, you would have, uh, fit right in with my group of friends."

"I'll take that as a compliment."

"It was meant as such." Taylor raised his glass of now only ice and Cameron clinked his against it.

"To life."

"To life," Cameron agreed.

After their waitress took their plates, Taylor pulled out his wallet. "Just so there's no argument, when the check comes I'll be paying."

"Really. Why's that? I'm the one who needed rescuing from the bottle. You rescued; I should pay. Plus I lost the bet."

Taylor wiggled his ears. "First, because I asked you, second, penance for lying to you the other day at the jazz festival."

Cameron frowned. "How?"

"When I said I didn't know anything about a note threatening you if you didn't leave Three Peaks."

"You didn't lie; you didn't say anything."

"I knew the truth and didn't speak it. It's the same thing as lying."

"So you did send the note."

Taylor stared at him with a thin smile.

Cameron pushed himself back from the table, teetered back in his chair, and smiled. "It's okay. I knew you sent it. Knew you were lying."

"Oh, you did?" Taylor threw his Visa card onto the table and the waitress snagged it a few seconds later. "I believe it. Most people are human lie detectors. Did you know the people who have the most trouble spotting a liar are other liars?"

"No." Cameron shook his head and leaned forward in his chair. "So you feel bad about the lie?"

"For the most part, yes."

"Does this mean you're going to tell me what you know about the book?"

"On that count, I'm afraid I'll have to bring you a bit of disappointment." Taylor looked at the ceiling and pursed his lips. "But I do promise not to lie to you anymore, as long as we close the book on the subject. Pun intended."

"Lousy pun."

"So do you agree? The subject is closed?"

"I can't. I have to do this."

Taylor stared at him, hands folded on top of his head. "You're a good kid, Cameron. Really. But a secret is kept by one. However I will tell you this. No matter what you hear from anyone else, there is no Book of Days that you can leaf through like an old Sears catalog. Never was. Never will be. You can hang out here in town the rest of your life for all I care. In fact, I think I'd like it."

Taylor lowered his hands from his head and leaned forward. "I know I'd like it. But you'll never find a book where God has written down in heavenly black ink every moment of every man and woman's past, present, and future, no matter how long you search."

"But you know more than you've told me."

Taylor sighed and leaned back.

"You can trust me."

Cameron saw the battle going on inside Taylor. Part of him wanted to talk. But it was like sneaking up on a three-point buck. The more noise he made, the quicker the deer would spook and bolt away.

This was a hunt Cameron had to let play out without crashing through the woods like a rookie. The more he backed off, the better chance the war going on inside Taylor's eyes would turn in his favor. But Cameron was running out of time. The waitress brought their bill and Taylor's Visa card back.

"It's been a pleasure to serve you today, Mr. Stone."

"Thanks, Sandy."

Taylor signed, slid the bill to the edge of the table, spread his palms, and leaned in. "All right, I'll tell you a few things I know. Then will you leave it alone and head back to Seattle?"

Cameron lifted his head and stared at Taylor. Was it possible he would finally open the door, even a crack?

"I'll tell you three things about the book if you promise that will be the end of it. Any further search is something you do on your own. No more questions. Agreed?"

"Yes."

At the sound of heavy shuffling feet next to their table, Cameron looked up. No. This couldn't be happening.

"Filling his head with more of your lies, Stone?" Jason stood too close to the table, his thighs pressing into its edge.

Cameron rubbed his eyes. Perfect timing.

"Care to join us, Jason? We'd enjoy gleaning some of the wisdom you have stored up inside that massive cranium of yours."

"Someday, Stone, the falsehoods you've weaved since childhood will fall on you like a net on a bird. Someday the curtain will be thrown back in a flourish and the mighty and powerful Oz will be revealed for the charlatan he is. I will dance in the streets that day, as I will one day dance on your grave."

"Wonderful to see you too, Jason."

Jason squatted and turned to Cameron. "You might not like me. You might not like my methods or personal beliefs. But I don't lie. I speak truth, seek the truth, and press on toward truth." He glanced at Taylor, then focused back on Cameron. "I suggest we talk again, sooner than later."

Cameron watched the big man stride away before turning back to Taylor. "I'd heard you two didn't like each other. I didn't realize how potent the animosity was."

"Powder-keg potent."

"You've known each other for a long time?"

"We grew up together."

"Why the hostility between you two?"

Taylor propped his elbow on the table and rested his head on the palm of his hand. "I never cared about being liked."

"But Jason did."

"Since our junior year of high school, Jason has been trying to one-up me."

"Has he ever done it?"

"I don't know, maybe. I never paid much attention. But if you ask him, he'd probably say never."

It explained so much. "So finding this book would put him on the map, and you'd finally be in his shadow."

"What people do doesn't put them on the map except for a short time; it's who you are that people remember."

"So who are you, Taylor?"

"Someone a lot like you. Someone trying to find answers to the questions rolling around inside his brain."

Cameron glanced around the restaurant. "Thanks for being willing to help me with some of mine. You were about to tell me a few things you know—"

"Like I've said a number of times before, I like you, Cameron. And that emotion got the better of me and turned into a moment of weakness." Taylor wiped up the water on the table with his napkin and set it next to the salt and pepper shakers. "I'm sorry, but as I said before, a secret is held by one."

"Taylor, please I—"

"Be strong." He stood and shuffled toward the door of The Sail & Compass.

Cameron sat for a long time staring at the restaurant's logo—a sail with a compass in the middle, the needle pointing north, unlike the needle on his compass, which was spinning out of control in the middle of the ocean, with no sailboat on the horizon.

That night he dreamed again. Of a sailboat.

Two Years, Three Months Earlier

Jessie and Cameron had spotted four Dall's porpoises as they navigated their rented sailboat through the salty waters of the San Juan Islands, two hours north of Seattle.

In a rare declaration the weatherman said the sky would be brilliant, and it was. The fresh air mixed with the pungent smell of seaweed swirled around them, and Cameron drew it into his lungs in deep gulps.

The seagulls seemed to caw in an intentional rhythm with the wind digging into their sails as they sliced through the gentle swells.

"Another—"

"—crystal day." Cameron finished.

It was their word for a pure day, unencumbered with thoughts of shooting videos or editing or fixing the water pump on his MINI Cooper. And for Jessie, no emergency calls to come in and cover a shift at the hospital or having to think about teaching her aerobics class at the gym.

They sailed on with no need to talk. Only a need to soak in the chaotic pattern of the waves that seemed to drain away the stress of the week.

They stopped at a little cove just south of Limekiln State Park. The Olympic Mountains shimmered in the distance to the west, and looking north they could make out Vancouver Island.

After anchoring their sailboat and taking a small skiff onto the rocky beach littered with periwinkle shells, they found a sun-bleached log to sit on as they ate their tuna salad sandwiches—sandwiches splashed with the tiniest bit of Tabasco sauce. Cameron had teased Jessie about that for six months before he tried it and had to admit she was right. It made the sandwich.

After they finished, Jessie stood and shuffled toward the edge of the water. "When dreams come that feel so real you don't know if they're dreams, are they real?"

"Too many hours watching the philosophy channel?" Cameron laughed.

"Probably." She laughed with him and looked north toward Vancouver Island. "And what should you do when something so fantastic happens in real life you're not sure if your subconscious mind turned it into a dream because that kind of thing never happens in real life? Has it turned into a dream, or is it still real?"

"I'm not sure I followed every speck of that, but I'm going to vote for it's still real." He smiled on the outside, but inside he worried. When Jessie talked like this, he didn't know how to respond. Playing along with her meanderings felt like the wrong decision and the right one at the same time.

"So you'd believe the fantastic?"

"How old were you when the fantastic happened?"

"Ten."

"What happened?"

"I saw something." She turned and walked back to the log Cameron sat on.

"Are you going to tell me about it?"

Jessie squatted down in front of him. "I saw something about us. And something about me."

Cameron touched her cheek. "So that's how you knew to accept my invitation for that first date."

"Yes. I saw you, and your father, and I saw you and me. So years later when I met you and met him, I didn't hesitate to get involved with you."

"Did you see Spider-Man and the Fantastic Four too?"

"This is serious, Cam."

"I am being serious, I'm just . . . Okay, I'm not, but you have to admit it sounds a little woo-woo that you saw me, my dad, and us when you were ten. Even if it was in a dream, it would be weird."

Jessie sank down and sat in the sand with her back to Cameron. "It wasn't a dream. It was real."

"Okay, Jess." Score a point for Mr. Insensitive. "I'm sorry."

"I also saw someone die." She drew in a quick breath. "Someone we both know."

"Who?" Cameron leaned toward her. "Who, Jessie?"

She didn't need to answer. He knew. Where did her visions come from? She would say God; he would say from her fertile imagination. Whichever it was, it didn't diminish the emotional impact.

She turned toward him and wrapped her arms around his waist. "Tell me it was just a dream."

"It was a dream from a ten-year-old. Let it go." That was all it could have been.

"It's gone." She leaned her head on his shoulder and started to cry.

Cameron woke up gasping for air. "Jessie!" She was there. Right there!

He slid his legs over the bed and grabbed his notepad off the nightstand. But by the time he clicked his pen, the memory of the dream had vanished.

Cameron slammed his fist into the mattress. "I'm sick of this!"

The clock read six fifteen. Time to get up and go meet Ann. Why did he agree to go climbing with her? He wasn't sure. Something about it didn't feel right.

CHAPTER 26

Climbing with Cameron was probably a poor use of time.

He drove them east on Highway 126 early on Thursday morning. They should be trying to find the book or working on her family history. But when she'd suggested they try a climb together, he'd agreed immediately. What was she thinking? She refused to allow her heart to answer.

As Cameron took the exit that would take them to Smith Rock, Ann looked at the temperature gauge on the MINI Cooper. Even though it had been in the mideighties the night before, it was now only fifty-nine degrees. Being in the high desert and sitting at thirty-one-hundred feet meant cool mornings even in the heart of the summer. But morning climbing meant less possibility of wind, and wind was not a climber's friend.

When they arrived, Cameron parked the car in front of a sign that pointed them toward the route they'd decided to climb.

Within five minutes she had her pack and gear slung over her shoulder ready to rock 'n' roll.

The narrow trail would take them to the base of a climb rated 5.9, which was perfect. Challenging enough to be fun but with little chance of trouble since there were two of them and they'd be double belayed.

She watched Cameron's black hair silhouetted against the seven o'clock sun that streaked into her eyes. She half jogged a few steps to put the shadow of his head between her and the rays and pulled in a lungful of the thick air full of morning and pine.

What was she doing here with him?

Yes, she'd resolved the matter of their relationship. She wouldn't get involved, but why tempt her feelings by being around him when she didn't have to?

On the other hand, what was wrong with enjoying herself for the moment?

She loved him, yes, but so what? It didn't mean she had to act on it. She *wouldn't* act on it. Ever.

Even if he did start following God, what about Jessie? Would he ever be able to push past that? How could she know how long it took to get over the death of a spouse?

Ann turned her focus to the wild white orchids lining the trail. A meadowlark flew overhead and she tried to send her thoughts of a future with Cameron away with the bird. Stay in the moment.

"There's our spot." Cameron pointed to a sheer rock face looming in front of them.

Gray nimbus clouds moved in as they took out their climbing gear and carried it the final hundred yards to the base of the climb.

"Ready?"

"More than." She smiled. "Let's have some fun."

Their first move was twenty feet up to a wide ledge, which they did without ropes. Their guide book said the first step was moderate. It turned out to be simple and Ann raised her eyebrows when they'd both caught their breath. "Pretty easy so far."

"It was practically stairs. But it's time to get on rope."

"I would agree."

"Do you want to take the lead?"

For the next fifty feet Ann didn't speak except to communicate her holds and check to make sure Cameron was ready before moving higher. They moved into a smooth rhythm.

"How are you doing, Cam? Can you talk and climb?"

"Yes, but don't try to throw me a piece of gum."

Ann smiled. "Do you have any updates on the book we should talk about?"

"I'm headed to Arnold Peasley's tomorrow to see if he has any newspapers from the early sixties."

"Who is Arnold Peasley?"

"Didn't I tell you about him?"

"No."

"Are you sure?"

"Positive." Ann looked down in time to catch a pained look pass over Cameron's face. "Are you okay?"

"It's the memory thing." Cameron shook his head, as if shaking water out of his hair. "I met him when I first got to town. He considers himself Three Peak's unofficial historian. And his home is stacked beyond the rafters with old newspapers. I bet they go back to the early sixties."

"He'd have to have been collecting them since he was a kid."

"Let's hope he did the paperboy thing." Cameron wiped his forehead with his forearm. "It's worth a shot. I was going to save it as a surprise, but I couldn't wait."

"Can I come?"

"No, Arnold is a little quirky. Plus if there's nothing there, you won't have searched for hours only to be disappointed."

Ann grabbed a pencil-thin ridge with the tips of her fingers, and hoisted herself up another three feet. "Careful, we've got a crimper here; I hope the tips of your fingers are in good shape."

"Got it." He grunted as he closed the gap between them.

"What about Taylor?"

"Stone knows volumes more than he's saying. I almost got him to talk, but Jason showed up and destroyed the moment."

"Mr. Creepfest himself, huh?"

"In all his glory."

"You're not going to back down from this quest, are you?"

"I don't have a choice."

"Not to be cold, but aren't you wasting your time?" She reached into her climbing pouch and pulled out a handful of chalk, the powder spilling out from between the cracks in her fingers and floating away on the slight breeze. "You really think whatever Taylor Stone is hiding can make this book poof into existence?"

"Probably not, but I know people, and too many things about Stone don't add up."

"Like what?"

"His reaction to you at Jason's gathering at the community center. His—"

"Hold it. What do you mean his reaction to me?"

"Didn't I tell you about that?"

"No."

"It was weird. As soon as you got up onstage, he went white and doubled over like he'd been gut-punched. He and his wife left a few minutes later."

"You're kidding."

"I was standing close to him. After one look at you, he did the white-as-a-sheet thing."

"You have no idea why?"

"No clue."

Ann tried to remember if she saw someone leave right after getting onstage. Maybe. She shook her head. "All right. You have my attention. Anything else?"

"When we met the first time, he exploded after I left and he didn't think I saw him. It was right after we talked about the book. Then he tells me to stay away from Jason. And he writes that note trying to scare me into leaving town. His coming close to telling me things he knows about the book, then shutting down like he has secrets that would make the CIA gasp."

"That doesn't make the book real, Cam."

"There's nothing that could make you even start to believe, huh?"

"It's like something out of a comic book. I think we landed on the moon. I don't think Kennedy was killed by the Mafia. I don't believe little green men buzz the planet and borrow some of us for experiments. I think there's a rational explanation for why ships and planes disappear over the Bermuda Triangle. And sorry, I don't believe in a nine-hundred-pound book that has recorded the past, present, and future of every soul on earth." *Sorry, Jessie.*

"Nice speech."

"Thanks, I've been practicing."

Ann turned and climbed higher. She had been practicing. If she could rip the idea of searching for the book out of Cameron's head, she would do it. The whole search for the book brought up her own regrets. Jason was right. Jessie had told her about the book in more detail than she'd ever told Cameron.

How Jessie knew the year and season she would die but nothing specific enough to prevent it.

How Jessie had seen Cameron after she died, standing in silhouette holding another woman and laughing.

How she knew for certain Ann would find her Wesley someday and her *Princess Bride* poster would come to life.

All through their teens and early twenties, Ann teased Jessie about believing in a magical book that revealed all these things when she was ten. Ann had done it so frequently Jessie stopped talking about it, even when Ann asked for forgiveness and to hear more of what Jessie had seen.

"The last part is too precious to tell you when I know you don't believe me," Jessie had said.

"I do believe!" Ann protested.

Jessie smiled. "No you don't, but I'll still love you when the sun buries itself in the sea forever."

Jessie was right. Ann didn't believe.

She still didn't.

The Book of Days couldn't be real.

She stretched her leg to its limit to reach a knob that jutted out from the wall a quarter inch and pushed herself another two feet up the sheer cliff.

"So, what if it turns out this book exists on Earth? Will you believe in God then?"

Cameron burst out laughing. "Welcome to the climb, Ms. Conundrum! You crack me up. Twenty seconds ago you're telling me to pull my head out of my proverbial sandbox, and now you're saying the book could be real."

"I'm not saying it's real or even *could* be real; I'm just asking if it would change what you believe." Ann reached into her climbing bag for more chalk. "And I'm finding this intellectual banter helps me climb better." She swung her right leg up to a ninety-degree angle and shoved her foot into a crack just wide enough for her big toe to slide into.

"Nice move," Cameron said.

"I'm serious. If the book is real, is God real? Or is life still arbitrary?"

"No, if the book is real, then God has to be real."

"So you're like Thomas, wanting to see the nail marks in Jesus' hand before he believed."

"You're right. I do."

"His love is an ocean, Cameron. It's so vast you can't take it all in."

He didn't respond. From the frown on his face it was apparent her question needled him.

Cameron scowled, more at himself than Ann; although he didn't care if she saw it. Talk about going for the soft underbelly. Deep down he'd always envied Jessie's and his dad's faith. It gave them meaning. It gave them purpose. It was probably why Jessie had that inexplicable look of peace on her face when she died.

Part of him had always wanted to believe. Ever since he could remember, his dad had loved him fiercely. The idea that the supreme being of the universe felt the same way about him was almost overpowering. The being that made all the stars in the universe loved him?

But there was no proof. *Take it on faith, take it on faith, God is real.* Sorry, faith wasn't enough.

If the book was real, he'd get back his memories of Jessie. He might be healed of the rampage taking place in his brain. And it would mean God and heaven exist, and Cameron would see her and his dad again.

But what if his path ended with a much more realistic outcome? The book being just an idea, a spiritual state of consciousness like all the other religions of the world? What would he do then? Comfort himself with the fact that neither Jessie nor his dad was anything more than dust, just a few years ahead of him?

Deep in his gut he knew the book couldn't be genuine. When would he admit it enough to go home and slowly watch his mind fade into nothingness?

Out of the corner of his eye he saw Ann's weight shift, and he focused on the small outcropping her left foot now rested on.

Oh no.

"Cameron!"

The crack that started the moment Ann put her full weight on the tiny nub, snapped a second later and she fell. As she careened past him, her weight wrenched him backward and his anchor slipped from its crack in the rock.

He reacted without thought and lunged up to where he could grab a handhold. If he didn't make the jump, Ann's weight would yank him off the tiny ledge his toes were on and they would fall at least thirty feet—if his other anchors held. Thirty feet was enough to badly injure them.

If the anchors failed, the fall could be enough to kill them.

Come on! If he couldn't get a hold before the rope snapped taut . . .

Got it! Yes.

The rope went stiff an instant later and the pressure ripped Cameron's right hand off the ledge. "Arrrgh!" Pain sliced through the fingers of his left hand like a knife but he held on, then lunged with his hand and caught hold again. "Ann!"

No answer. Not good. She could have slammed into the wall and been knocked unconscious. He couldn't keep this hold much longer.

"Ann!"

Time slowed to a crawl, the strain on his fingers faded into the background as an epiphany washed over him in a moment brilliant of clarity. In seconds the weight of Ann's body would force his fingers from their cling to life, and slipping off the clothes of mortality would become a distinct possibility.

He would join Jessie at last. It would finally be over, and his question of whether she was waiting for him would be answered.

But in that moment a revelation coursed through him—he didn't want to die. It wasn't time. It wasn't right. Not yet. No matter what was happening inside his brain, he would fight for life.

Time stopped as a feeling appeared as if a massive red theater curtain had been drawn back. An emotion he buried at the moment of Jessie's death. Hope.

Hope for life, hope he could feel joy again.

That he could love someone and be loved by someone.

That he could live a life that would make Jessie and his dad proud.

"Ann!"

"Uhhh." A moan floated up to him.

"Stay with me! Can you hear me?"

"Cameron?" It was just above a whisper, but yes! she was conscious.

He risked a look down, but the ridge jutting out blocked his view. "Can you move?"

No answer.

He had to hold on!

A gust of wind whipped against his face.

"Perfect. All we need now is some rain. Is this in Your book, God? Then stop writing!"

"Cameron." It was more a moan than his name, but it was a streak of hope.

"Ann, you have to secure. Now!"

Silence.

God, if You exist . . .

He focused on his knuckles, shifting his gaze rapidly back and forth between his two hands. His left hand started shaking first. A moment later his right hand joined in. It wouldn't be long.

His left fingers slipped down a quarter-inch.

No!

Drilling in on the second hand on his watch, Cameron promised himself he would hold on another forty-five seconds.

Fifteen seconds later he heard the faint scrape of metal on rock, and he knew Ann was securing a nut into the wall below him. Silence. Then the sound of another nut being wedged into place.

He didn't blame her for securing two; he would have done the same thing. He heard the click of the carabineer as she clipped in, then suddenly the weight on the rope eased and Cameron sucked in a quick breath of air. "Ann!"

"I'm secure. Are you all right?"

He nodded and then realized she couldn't see him. "Stay there. I'm coming down."

After securing an anchor into the rock and clipping his rope into it, he belayed down the thirty feet to where Ann hung, her face white except for where a large bruise had started to form on her right temple.

He reached out and touched Ann's temple with the tips of two fingers. "Are you okay?"

"I'm fine, really," she said in between breaths. "I'm sure it looks worse than it feels." She stared at him. "You saved my life."

"And you returned the favor by waking up. I figured I had about five seconds left when you secured that first nut."

Cameron stared into her eyes, both of them still breathing heavily.

He'd heard you could know a person more intimately after looking into their eyes for thirty seconds without speaking than you could in an hour of conversation. After the half minute was up, he agreed.

"Let's get off this rock."

They sat at the base of the cliff in silence, the only sound was Ann's deep breaths in concert with his own.

The adrenaline had stopped pumping fifteen minutes ago, but perspiration still seeped through his shirt. His legs twitched and his arms felt like they'd been shot up with a triple dose of Novocain.

"Do you want to talk?"

Ann shook her head, her eyes moist.

Without thinking Cameron scooted next to her, put his arms around her shoulders, and drew her in. Ann pressed in hard against his chest without hesitation and sobbed.

"It's okay . . . it's okay." Cameron stroked her hair and repeated the phrase over and over. He didn't know what else to say. After a few minutes her tears stopped but she didn't move. He pulled her in closer and kissed the top of her head.

The chattering of a squirrel filled the late morning air.

Something about the sound brought peace, and Cameron took his first breath that didn't feel like a gasp for air. After a few more minutes he glanced at his watch. They'd been off the mountain for over an hour. Why did it feel like minutes?

"Ann, talk to me."

She stirred and mumbled something.

"What?"

"Don't leave me."

"I'm right here." He squeezed her tight as her tears came again. "Right here."

Twenty minutes went by without any movement from Ann. She could have been asleep. Cameron wouldn't have cared if twenty years went by. Something about sitting here, holding Ann was very right. Very good. Very true.

Did she think the same?

After another five minutes she stirred, stood, and walked a short distance away. Her auburn hair rose and fell on the breeze slaloming through the trees, and her climbing clothes accentuated her figure. If her hair were darker and she were a little shorter, it could be Jessie standing there.

When Ann finally turned back, her tears were dry and she gave a slight smile. "Thank you."

Her simple thanks filled him. *Anytime. I'm here.*

Cameron fired up his MINI Cooper and turned to Ann. "Was that written in God's book? Before it happened, was it written down?"

"Yes."

"So God gives us no choice. What is, is."

"Choice is God's greatest gift to us, Cameron."

"If it's already carved in stone, how is that possible?"

"It's not in stone, and I'm guessing God's book operates a little differently than ours." Ann gathered up her hair and put a scrunchie around it. "We chose to climb that cliff today. Our choice. No one else's. It wasn't some preordained plan that we had no part in."

"Do you mind if we have a soundtrack for our conversation?" Cameron pulled onto the road and slid a Jack Johnson CD into his player.

"Good call, H."

Cameron glanced at her. "H?"

"Did you ever see that movie *K2*? It was about these two climbing buddies. One of the guys was named Harold. So his partner called him 'H,' and was always saying, 'Good call, H!'"

"Good movie?"

"It was all right."

Ann leaned back against the seat and closed her eyes. It seemed so natural for her to sit next to him. Maybe God should keep writing this chapter.

"Listen," he said, "if we say for a moment this Book of Days is real—was that whole thing we just went through together on the cliff written down ahead of time? Before it ever happened?"

Ann didn't answer and he glanced at her again. She opened her eyes and frowned at him. "What are you doing?"

"What do you mean?"

"You just asked me that."

"What?"

"You just asked me virtually the same question two minutes ago."

He bit both sides of his tongue with his back teeth. He couldn't lose it now. His mind had been doing better the past few days. "Sorry, I'm a little stressed still. A lot stressed."

"Is your memory loss getting worse?"

Cameron clenched the steering wheel and ignored the vise grip around his stomach. "It's getting better."

When they reached Three Peaks, Cameron said, "I hope the emergency room isn't crowded."

"What?"

"You're getting that head looked at. You were out cold."

"I told you I'm fine. I meant it."

Cameron shook his head.

"Really, I've been knocked out before. If I had a concussion, it would have shown up by now."

"Even if I let you talk me out of going to the hospital, there's no way I'm letting you stay by yourself tonight."

Ann touched the bruise on her head and sighed. "So what do you suggest? Have me sleep next to the night manager in the lobby of my hotel?"

"You can do that?"

"Funny."

It was a good question. Neither of them knew anyone in town well enough—Cameron grabbed his iPhone.

"Hello?"

"Hi, it's Cameron. Would you be willing to have a mildly injured houseguest overnight tonight? She's very well mannered."

"What happened? Is it Ann?"

"We had a bit of an adventure during our climb today, and Ann got a head injury—"

"It's a bump, not an 'injury.'" Ann whacked Cameron on the arm.

"Is she okay?"

"I think she's fine. But I don't want her by herself tonight."

"I'd love to have her; I've wanted to meet her for a long, long time."

"Thanks, Susan." Cameron hung up. "Done."

"What'd she say?"

"She's wanted to meet you for a long time."

Ann frowned. "What does she mean by that? I just got here a few days ago."

"You should ask her."

"Will she tell me?"

"I doubt it." Cameron smiled. "She's good with secrets. But if she opens up, ask her about your mom's photo."

"That would go over well." Ann laughed. "I'll find out what I can. And we'll meet up tomorrow?"

"I'll call you as soon as I'm done seeing Arnold."

"Find me something good, okay?" She winked at him and Cameron winked back.

He dropped her off at Susan's, then gazed at the front door long after it shut behind Ann. Find her something good? If Cameron's suspicions were right, he would find her something *very* good in Peasley's mountainous piles of newspaper.

CHAPTER 27

Tricia Stone strained to draw back her bowstring till the pulleys kicked in and made the final few inches easy. Just like life. Always a tipping point where the perseverance paid off.

She concentrated on her target, a root beer can hanging by a string from a pine tree forty yards away. The air was still as it often was in the middle of the day, and the only noise was the occasional call of a Wilson's Warbler that had settled behind her. No one to bother her. No one to interrupt her scattered thoughts. It was strange that she'd developed this passion for shooting arrows into pop cans or pinecones or plastic milk cartons in the middle of the woods.

Not the expected hobby of a middle-aged empty nester, and friends teased her about it. Some called her Robin Hood, at least none of them called her Friar Tuck. Taylor never teased her. He even encouraged her practice, but then he had his own target practice: fly-fishing.

Here she knew the answers, or if she didn't, it's where she could find them and fix the flaws.

As the pop can rotated slowly to the left, the sun hit it and flashed into her eyes. She blinked, then closed her eyes and saw the can in her mind.

Breathe in. Now hold it. Focus. See the can. Trust your instinct. Right there. Focus deeper. Release.

The arrow sang through the air, and Tricia didn't open her eyes till she heard the tip of the arrow rupture the can with a screech.

"Impressive shot."

Tricia whirled around to see who had spoken. There was no one. Wait. Over to the left, halfway behind a large pine. Jason Judah. "Thanks for sneaking up on me."

"No, I didn't do that." He rose from the boulder he'd been sitting on and ambled toward her. "I found you right as you started your routine. I didn't want to disturb."

Tricia glared at him trying to convey that's exactly what he'd done.

He didn't pick up on the hint. Or more likely he did and ignored it. "Mind if I join you for a few minutes?"

"Yes."

"We haven't talked just the two of us for years have we now? Hmm?"

Tricia half walked, half jogged to the can she'd just lanced to get her arrow. She didn't trust Jason. She'd never trusted him. And given his erratic history with Taylor, her heart pounded with the thought that they were miles from anyone.

Before she was halfway back, Jason called out, "What does Taylor know about the book?"

"What do you want?"

"To know what Taylor knows. Do you think he'd be willing to lead me to it?"

"That's a ridiculous question, Judah." She shuffled back up to her shooting spot and started packing her bow and arrows into a forest green bag.

"You know you're the only one who still calls me by my last name?" Jason laughed. "Did you know that?" He paused and leaned back against one of the pines surrounding them.

Tricia didn't answer. She wanted to leave, much sooner than later.

"Why is my question ridiculous?"

"Even if I knew what Taylor knows, I wouldn't tell you."

"Ah, so he does know more than he's letting on."

"Judah, I have no idea what my husband knows, if anything. But if you're so convinced he knows something, then ask him yourself." Tricia threw the last of her pop cans into her bag, yanked it onto her shoulder, and started striding the sixty yards back to her Jeep Cherokee.

"I did."

"And what did he say?"

"The truth about him will come out at some point."

"What truth is that?" She didn't look back.

"About his covering up the accident."

Tricia spun and glared at Jason. "For thirty years you've been hinting and hemming and hawing about Taylor. If you have something on him, why not just tell me. If you don't, simply keep that obnoxious maw of yours shut."

"Whoooweee!" Jason slapped his leg. "A little bit of fire coming out of the belly there. I'm impressed."

"I'm serious."

"Oh, I know you are." He narrowed his eyes. "But then again, so am I. Taylor knows more about the accident than he's ever let on. How do I know this?" Jason leaned forward. "He told me. In a moment of weakness, when for a moment he thought we were still friends, he told me. He said, 'I did it to her. I did it.' And I'm convinced whatever it is he did, is tied to the book. I'd bet my life on it." Jason rubbed his chin. "Did you know he told me that?"

Tricia's face flushed. The possibility that Jason knew more about Taylor's past than she did melted her heart. "The past is the past. What happened then is over."

"You're a believing woman, in God Almighty above. Aren't you? And you believe eternity is real? That there is a realm outside of time? A place where the past, the present, and the future can exist together?" Jason smirked. "So don't try to tell me the past is over. The past is right now."

"Are you finished?" Tricia pulled her keys out of her pocket.

"What does Taylor know about the book?"

She opened the back door of the Jeep, tossed her gear inside, and slammed it shut. "You might fool your followers, Judah, but not me. I see who you are. And it isn't about truth."

She got in, fired up the Jeep, and mashed the gas pedal to the floor, kicking up a curtain of dust that blocked Jason from sight in her rearview mirror.

If only making him disappear for good was that easy.

Ann had just finished forty-five minutes on a treadmill at the Three Peaks Women's Gym—which did wonders in erasing the fear of yesterday's climb—when a voice behind her said, "Excuse me, you're Ann Banister, aren't you?"

Ann turned to see a woman probably in her late fifties, with wavy shoulder-length brown hair and a face that looked familiar.

"I am, and you are?"

"Tricia Stone, Taylor's wife."

The wife of the mysterious Taylor Stone. Interesting. "Good to meet you."

"I feel the same way. I've been hoping to bump into you ever since you arrived."

"Really?"

"Yes, and—I don't mean to pry—but speaking of bumps, that's a doozy you have on your forehead there."

"It looks much worse than it feels. I battled a cliff yesterday. The cliff won." Ann touched her forehead. "It's a little tender but that's all."

"That's good to hear." Tricia handed her a small card with an address on it. "I'm sure a home-cooked meal would do wonders for your recovery."

"You're inviting me over for dinner?"

Tricia nodded.

Ann smiled as she wiped the sweat off her forehead with a hand towel. This could be providential. It might be a chance to discover a few of the mysteries Taylor knew about the Book of Days and find out about his reaction to her at Jason's gathering. "This might sound rude, Tricia, and I hope it doesn't come across that way, but why do you want to invite me into your home?"

She smiled. "Good for you. Don't worry; I appreciate people who are straightforward, so I'll be the same." She took Ann's arm and led her away from the row of treadmills out of range of the three other women doing an early morning workout on the machines.

"When you got up on stage during Jason's little shindig the other day, Taylor's face turned the color of freshly fallen snow. He wouldn't talk about it, but I know something about you crumbled his Oreos."

"I heard about that."

Tricia's eyes widened.

"Cameron Vaux told me."

"Ah." Tricia nodded. "When I asked Taylor why seeing you made him go all goofy, he clammed up like a Mafia boss on the witness stand." She grabbed a heartbeat monitor off a stand next to a row of elliptical trainers and strapped it to her wrist.

Ann smiled. "I see. So your plan is to ambush him when I step through that door where he's trapped and has to give some kind of explanation about me?"

"Oh no, I would never do that. Of course not." Tricia patted her on the shoulder. "I plan on giving him a full ten minutes of warning before you arrive."

Ann shook her head and smiled again.

"Can you make it tonight, say around six thirty?"

"I'll be there."

"Wonderful. I'm so looking forward to it."

Ann would be there, along with a certain picture from her mom's childhood. Something told her the Stones needed to be asked about that photo.

As Ann left the gym, her eyes locked on to a man with a baseball hat sitting directly across the street on a dark brown bench. She glanced away, then back to the man. He was watching her.

She reached into her purse to grab her keys, and when she looked up again, his gaze was still fixed on her. She glanced up and down the street for cars, then jogged across Main Street directly toward him.

"Hello. My name is Ann. What's yours?"

The man looked Native American. He smiled, and his dark brown eyes danced. "I hope I didn't frighten you just now."

"You didn't, but why were you staring at me?"

"It is important I see you. Meet you."

"Why?"

"To see."

"See what?"

"I'm sorry. I'm not able to explain that to you right now." The man stood, put on gold-rimmed sunglasses, and gave a slight nod. "It was a pleasure to meet you. And again, I regret the possibility of having disturbed you."

"Who are you? What's your name?"

"Good day, Ms. Banister. I wish much life on you."

Great. Another creeper to add to her collection.

CHAPTER 28

It's a Wonderful Life played though Cameron's head as he drove toward Taylor Stone's house late Friday morning. "I want to live! Clarence, I want to live!" Cameron smiled at his abysmal imitation of Jimmy Stewart.

What was that overused line from *Dead Poets Society*? *Carpe diem*. "Seize the day." He wanted to *carpe liber*. "Seize the book."

The climb yesterday had made him want to live and, at the same time, freed him from worrying about the future. Death could come in any moment, why not live it to the full in the moment he was in? His brain could short out tomorrow, so why not rip the envelope into pieces while he still had the chance? That meant planting his feet in front of Taylor Stone and finding a way to get him to reveal his secrets about the Book of Days.

Cameron pulled up to the curb in front of Taylor's house and tried to formulate a plan. After five minutes he still didn't have one. It didn't matter. He'd know what to say when he got there.

After ringing the doorbell three times and getting no response, he eased around the side of the house into the backyard.

In the southeast corner, Tricia set paving stones in an undulating pattern as she worked toward a wishing well that looked brand new.

"Hi, Tricia."

She turned and stood. "Hello, Cameron." She shook off her gardening gloves and grasped his hand tightly. "You're looking for him?"

He looked back at the house and nodded.

"He's fishing."

"I should have known."

"But I'll answer any question I can." Tricia did a faux curtsy.

Not a bad idea. He might learn something new.

She led Cameron over to a well-worn maple bench framed by a trellis covered with lavender wisteria. She brushed the bench with the tips of her fingers. "My thinking, talking, and kibitzing bench. All ready for you."

"Thanks." Cameron sat. "Is Taylor acting differently these days?"

She smiled. "Video directors are observers, aren't they? He's been acting strange ever since you showed up. But it was nothing compared to the reaction when Ann Banister stepped onstage."

"No kidding. That, I'll remember. Any idea what that was all about?"

"I don't know. Yet."

"You're on a mission to find out?"

Resolve shone in her eyes. "Most definitely. Ann's coming over for dinner tonight."

"My Ann? I mean, Ann Banister?"

"No, Anne Frank." She flicked his leg. "Of course Ann Banister."

Cameron smiled.

"Her visit should be interesting. I'll give you a full report."

"I'd appreciate that."

"I like her." Tricia took off her shoes and knocked them together to get rid of the dirt that clung to them. "I can see you like her too."

"Hmm."

She turned on the bench toward Cameron. "Are you going to do anything about it?"

He'd come to ask the questions but ended up with the Three Peaks version of Barbara Walters sitting next to him. "No."

"Why?"

"I wouldn't do that to Jessie."

"If you knew you were dying and Jessie would live many years beyond you, would you want her to live her life alone, hanging on to the cloud of your death and your memory? Or would you want her to be happy?"

"Point taken."

Tricia tossed her shoes onto the lawn. "I need to stop shoving myself into areas that are none of my concern. I'm sorry."

"Don't be."

She patted Cameron's leg. "Good man."

Time to bring the subject back to Taylor. "So Ann's appearance at Jason's—"

"I doubt Taylor would've been any more shocked if Elvis had stepped up to that microphone. He tried to tell me it was a sudden bout of stomach cramps, but of course I didn't believe him. He hasn't had a stomach cramp since, well, I don't know if he's ever had one since we were married."

"Five years ago."

Tricia nodded. "Yes."

"You haven't been married that long."

"Well, I didn't want to be a widow the rest of my life, and Taylor and I have been friends for eons, at least since second grade. So after I'd grieved for far longer than I should have, we started having coffee together, and dinners at Kokanee Café, and hikes up to Whychus Creek Falls . . . and before long he slipped a ring on my finger, and here we are."

"Do you still think about your first husband?"

"All the time." Tricia patted Cameron's hand. "But the pain is muted."

Mute his pain? Sounded wonderful. But how long would it take to get there? So far the pain of losing Jessie still screamed in his ear every day.

"What about Taylor? Ever married before you?"

"Yes."

She paused so long Cameron thought that was all she would say.

"He was married at twenty-three. They were perfect for each other. It only lasted two years."

"Why?"

"He was widowed as well." Tricia looked up toward the ivy crawling over the redwood trellis and covered her mouth. "Whew, I don't think about the accident too much anymore." She blinked rapidly.

"Accident?"

She stood, pulled the lavender scarf off her head, and moved over to the rosebushes next to the trellis. "Taylor blames himself for her death. He's never come right out and said that, but I can tell that he does. I can tell." She plucked at the roses that were encroaching on her side of the bench. "He's never told me why he feels that way. I stopped asking a few years ago."

"What was her name?"

"Annie."

Window-crank Annie. One mystery solved, three thousand to go.

"He changed after Annie died. There was a big group of us that hung out together. Kirk and Arnold, and Annie and me, and at least ten others. Taylor was our leader and had a spontaneous streak that kept us all in trouble most of the time. After two or three months, the playful part came back but the thoughtful Taylor was gone. At least on the outside. We all tried to talk to him about Annie's death, but he wouldn't speak about it. Ever.

"We'd see him sometimes, sitting in the field where he proposed to Annie, weeping. But around us it was only jokes. He worked so hard at covering up his pain, at some point he couldn't even get past the veneer himself." She smiled. "And now God has brought you and Ann into his life to stir it all up again."

"That's a good thing?"

"It's wonderful. You have to clean out a wound before it can heal properly."

Cameron waited for her to finish deadheading the roses and sit back down before he spoke. "Can I ask you a personal question?"

"Yes, of course."

"Does it bother you that Taylor keeps so many secrets from you?"

Tricia's smile was sad as she shook her head. "No. Because I believe it is a divine plan that I am in Taylor's life the way I am. And I also know beyond a shadow of doubt that he loves me. Deeply." She patted Cameron's hand again. "And I love him back the same way. Some day all secrets will be revealed."

"Does Taylor know something about the Book of Days he's not saying?"

"If I were in Las Vegas with millions to burn—which I don't have—and I were a betting woman—which I'm not—I would have to put my money on the answer being yes."

"What does he know?"

"I haven't a clue." She shook her head.

Cameron hadn't planned on interviewing Tricia about the Book of Days. He assumed Taylor would block any attempt, so he'd put little hope in the idea. But now that he was here, and she answered every question so openly, he'd begun to think he would get an insight or a clue or at least an indication about the true depth of Taylor's knowledge of the book. Now that it was apparent Cameron would get nothing, frustration swirled around him.

But Tricia could help with another mystery tied to the book.

"Can you tell me about Jason and Taylor? Taylor says Jason's been trying to one-up him since high school."

"Since their junior year." Tricia sighed. "But before that they were best friends. All through grade school and junior high, and through the first two years of high school. The best of pals."

"You've got to be kidding." Cameron snorted out a laugh.

Tricia arched an eyebrow. "That amuses you?"

"These days they'd be the last pair cast in a buddy movie." Cameron took out his notepad and scribbled in it. "There must have been a radical turn somewhere along the road."

"Yes." Tricia sighed again. "Over a woman. They both loved the same one." She reached down and pulled two straggling weeds poking up out of a crack in the circle of stones on which the bench sat.

"Annie."

Tricia nodded. "Taylor won her heart over Jason. Up till then, it had been okay that Taylor was the better athlete and more popular, better at school . . . But after Jason's heart was broken, Taylor became the villain, and no matter how hard he tried, Jason wouldn't let go of his bitterness. He was drafted after high school and went to Vietnam. Taylor hoped he'd be different when he came back but he was worse.

"Taylor married Annie right after college, hoping Jason would be his best man, a way to mend the wound, a way to put the pain behind them and move on, but Jason refused.

"Two years later she died, and Jason blamed Taylor for her death. He tried to prove it in all sorts of ways, but of course it was simply a horrible accident. A month or so later, Jason vanished. Nobody heard a whisper about him till twelve years ago when he moved back fully immersed in the New Age movement and determined to see the future and create a new world. He's been looking for ways to humiliate Taylor from the moment he returned. He hasn't succeeded, but it's made Taylor bitter toward Jason."

"I can't say I blame him for that."

"Unforgiveness is like taking a daily poison tablet, expecting it to hurt the other person."

"Jessie used to say something like that." Cameron thought of Ann. Hadn't he just talked to her about forgiveness? "You're saying he needs to forgive him."

"He must. He has to."

"Do you think Jason can ever forgive Taylor?"

Tricia looked up at Cameron with storm clouds in her eyes. "I'm not talking about Jason. I'm talking about Taylor."

Cameron bent down and pulled up a few strands of grass. "Tell me about Taylor's wife, Annie. Who was she? How did she die?"

"I should let Taylor tell you that part of the story." Tricia stood and brushed the dirt off her knees. "Not that he'll tell the tale easily."

"Did her death have anything to do with—?"

"Don't you think we've talked enough for one day? I do."

No, he didn't. He wouldn't feel that way till he stood in front of the Book of Days reading its pages. But he followed her lead, thanked her for the time, and walked to his car.

Onions, Cameron thought as he drove toward Arnold Peasley's

house. Ogres might be like onions, but people were too—always another layer underneath the last one.

Taylor was turning out to have more layers than most.

He had to find a way to peel back every one of them.

CHAPTER 29

He listened to a late-night talk show—almost too soft to hear—as he clipped his nails close and stared at them. No. Not close enough. He always liked to see a little blood when he finished. Not a lot, just a thin red line outlining each nail.

He clipped another nail and watched the blood seep from his pinky finger.

Perfect.

Nine to go.

If only it were that simple to find the book. How many more days did he have to wait? Nine? Eight? Twenty? He couldn't control the answer and it frustrated him.

Why was Cameron rock climbing and talking to Stone's wife? Why was he helping Ann Banister find her history? All of that was time wasted. And there was no time to waste.

Cameron could dig where he couldn't so he could be patient.

He'd waited years; he could wait a few more days, or even weeks, for Cameron to lead him to the book. But not months.

He flicked off the television and the lights, sat in the dark, and breathed in the warm summer air.

As soon as he stood in front of the book, he would kill Cameron, kill Taylor, and there would be a worthy guardian of the Book of Days once more.

CHAPTER 30

Tricia glanced at the clock on the dining room wall wondering how much longer should she wait before upsetting Taylor? It was 5:50. She would wait a few more minutes before telling him who was about to show up for dinner.

She set down a crystal vase full of scarlet gilia from her yard, then adjusted a cluster of five lilac-scented candles in the middle of the table. That one needed to go just a pinch farther to the left. Ah yes. Perfect.

She scuttled back into the kitchen and checked the oven and the stove top. Everything looked right.

"Dinner for three? And in the dining room?" Taylor stood leaning against the doorjamb leading into the kitchen and raised his eyebrows.

"Yes."

"Would you care to elaborate?"

"We'll be having chicken dijon, asparagus, and Asiago cheese bread, but we'll start with a salad and—"

"Hah."

She picked the stem stumps from the flowers off the kitchen counter, tossed them into the trash, and rinsed off her hands in the sink, her back to Taylor. "It wouldn't be a surprise if I told you, now would it?" She sidled up to him and wrapped her arms around his waist and squeezed.

"Who is coming to dinner, my dear?"

"Ann Banister." She looked up and smiled.

"The TV woman? What for?" Taylor's mouth sagged, his eyebrows furrowed. "Are you kidding? I don't want her here."

"So it wasn't just stomach cramps that made you react to her like she'd snapped your favorite fishing pole in two."

Taylor jammed his hands into his 501s, wagged his head, and started to say something three times before giving up.

"She admires you. Your column might not have ever hit national syndication, but she tells me she used to read it—"

"—in *The Oregonian*."

Tricia nodded.

"And she's coming to dinner." Taylor paced. "I need a drink."

"You don't drink."

"I could start." Taylor held his breath. "She can't come here."

"Why, because she reminds you of someone?"

Taylor stopped pacing and stared at Tricia.

"Tell me who." She returned the glare.

Five books on the fireplace mantel leaning to the left suddenly grabbed Taylor's attention, and he strode over and straightened them up.

"You might as well get it over with. I already know who anyway. As if I couldn't figure it out with my own eyes."

"Fine! She reminds me of Annie, okay? She looks enough like her to be Annie's twin. I'm sure you noticed. Do you feel better now that you dragged it out of me?" His back was to Tricia.

"Yes, I do."

Turning toward her, he puffed out a disgusted breath and shook his head. "I really don't need her here, reminding me of Annie with that little hair flipping thing she does, talking like Annie, looking like Annie. We'll end up talking about Annie with this Banister woman—"

"What's wrong with talking about Annie?"

Taylor flopped down in his leather recliner. "I'm tired of talking about Annie. It seems like the only thing we talk about these days."

Tricia swiveled to face Taylor, hands on hips and—she hoped—lightning coming out of her eyes. "Knock it off. Annie's name has come up once, maybe twice in the past three weeks. Before that, never. Not since it happened."

Taylor folded his arms, snorted, and stared at the beige carpet. "Her dying was the most painful experience of my life. I would think you could—"

"She brightened a lot of people's lives in this town, not just yours. Why can't you share memories of this person with her friends who are still alive?"

The question hung in the room like a spotlight. She folded her arms and waited. Taylor blew out a long breath and locked eyes with her but said nothing. Finally he grabbed the remote and flicked on the television.

She'd never pressed him. Annie was the love of his life, and her death was tragic, but it was thirty-three years ago. After they'd first married, Tricia had tried to talk about Annie, but he always shut her down immediately. Once he'd hinted at why he wouldn't talk about it, something about "the power and horror of choice," but he'd refused to say more than that ever since.

When Taylor and she had started dating five years ago, Tricia only saw the charismatic charmer she'd known since they were children. The darker side didn't emerge till they'd been married half a year. Dark? No, that was the wrong word. Better described as a shadow that often hung over him; a cloud that appeared without warning, then left again just as suddenly. A gray streaked fog that had appeared with surprising frequency ever since Cameron showed up.

And had turned into a storm cloud when Ann Banister arrived in town.

Ann stepped onto the porch of the Stone's home at six o'clock sharp and rang the bell. The scent of roses from a bush on either side of the door filled the air. Next to that was a hand-painted sign—from the artists-under-seven set by the look of it—which said Welcome to My Grampa and Gramma's House.

"Good to see you, Ann." Tricia welcomed Ann and motioned her inside with swift hand gestures.

After Tricia took her coat and they had a bit of prerequisite small talk, Tricia called out for Taylor to join them. "Our guest is here, the rest of your article for *Fish Fly* can wait."

"In a minute," came a muffled reply somewhere toward the back of the house.

"He still writes?"

"Not much for publication. Just for a few fly-fishing magazines, a couple of Web sites, and a couple of blogs."

Taylor stepped into the living room and held out his hand. "It's a pleasure, Ms. Banister."

"No, the pleasure is mine, Mr. Stone." Ann glanced around the room. "You have a lovely home."

Taylor gave a razor-thin smile. "I see you have your manners. I can certainly appreciate it, even if the house isn't that impressive. I'm sure it's nowhere close to a big-shot TV host's home."

"I never say anything unless I mean it." Ann's eyes locked on to Taylor's.

His face stayed sullen, but his eyes twinkled for a moment as he moved his head a millimeter to the side.

Tricia cleared her throat. "If you'd like to take a seat, dinner is ready."

Ann settled into her chair, but Taylor stood and watched Tricia waltz into the kitchen. He glanced at her and his face reddened. Embarrassment? That didn't make sense. Fear? No, it looked closer to shame. Before Ann could decide, he excused himself, walked out of the room, and didn't come back till after Tricia returned with a plate piled with chicken dijon.

"So, do you like being a celebrity?" Tricia sat and spread her napkin on her lap.

"I am so not a celebrity." Ann laughed and as she did, Taylor blinked as if he'd been shocked.

"Are you all right?"

"Yeah. Muscle spasm. Fine." Taylor patted his chest.

Taylor sat on her right, Tricia on her left. The hidden looks Tricia kept giving Taylor weren't well concealed. She was obviously concerned about something going on in her husband's head. And it was evident the something had to do with Ann. His strange behavior was definitely an interesting little subplot to add to Cameron's quest.

"I read your columns in *The Oregonian* growing up, and now you're writing for fly-fishing magazines?" Ann said. "Is fishing a hobby of yours?"

Taylor answered by springing from his chair and trotting over to the built-in oak bookshelves next to the fireplace. He returned with a large blue photo album and flipped it open on the table next to Ann. The pages were filled with pictures of Taylor fly-fishing, captions underneath with dates scrawled in a blue pen, and the names of at least forty different rivers throughout the western part of the United States.

As Ann flipped through the pictures, Taylor asked, "Why didn't you take the NBC job when they offered to buy out your contract? I know your show is national, but NBC had to be offering you more money than you're making now."

Ann looked up in surprise. "Wow, you really did do some research on me."

"I've been a newspaper man for thirty years. It's hard to get it out of the system, you know?" Taylor filled up Ann's water glass.

"I think success should be measured in wealth of friendships, not things. And I wanted to keep my portfolio intact as much as possible."

Tricia answered with a smile and a nod. Taylor didn't respond.

For a few minutes the only sound was the clink of forks and knives.

"So you're in Three Peaks to help Cameron look into the Book of God legend?" Taylor finally asked.

"Book of *Days*." Ann took a bite of salad and turned to Tricia. "That is excellent. The walnuts make it, don't you think?" She turned back to Taylor. "You didn't come to Jason's reception, obviously."

"We had to leave early," Taylor said.

"I'm mainly here on a personal matter, and I'm giving Cameron a little bit of help when I can."

"So do you think it exists? The book?" Tricia asked.

"Well—"

"Let's jump off before we go too far down this track. Talking about that book is a complete waste of conversation." Taylor folded his arms across his chest.

"I thought you just asked what she thinks about the book—"

"No, I asked her why she was in Three Peaks, not what—"

"Let the girl speak." Tricia gave Taylor a light smack on his wrist.

Ann pushed a piece of asparagus across her plate. "No, I don't think there's any chance that something like that could be real."

"Finally. Maybe you can talk some sense into the kid."

"I'm trying, Taylor." She smiled.

Tricia excused herself to get dessert and Ann got up to help clear off the table. Both Taylor and Tricia protested, but Ann carried the dishes into the kitchen anyway.

As she made her way back and forth between the kitchen and the dining room, Ann considered Taylor's neonlike reactions to her. Tricia was right; Ann certainly made him feel uncomfortable, but why? She couldn't come right out and ask him, and he wasn't giving away any clues. And his odd responses to the subject of the Book of Days? As Cam suspected, Taylor was undoubtedly involved. How deep wasn't easy to guess. At least not yet.

Dessert was chocolate torte, served along with decaf coffee and French vanilla creamer. Ann struggled to eat it slowly. It slid down her throat like edible silk. Chocolate was her bane but at the same time a tremendous motivator for rock climbing to torch the unwanted calories. As long as you lived long enough to climb again.

After they finished, Tricia asked about Ann's personal reason for being in Three Peaks.

"I lived in foster homes from the time I was a kid till I went off to college. My mom abandoned me when I was eleven, and I didn't want to know anything about her." Ann sipped her coffee. "And I didn't care about where I'd come from."

"But something changed your mind?"

"Three months ago I moved from my apartment into a house. The last box I unpacked was covered with silver duct tape so old it was brittle. As I yanked open the box, I realized I hadn't seen what was inside since I was eleven. Books. All my books from childhood, full of the worlds I escaped into when I was a kid. Pippi Longstocking, Anne of Green Gables—who I've always imagined I was named after—Judy Blume's stories . . . I sat for three hours taking lap after lap around memory lane. The last book I opened—*Treasure Island*—was one I never read. I was a bit too young for it, I suppose. As I leafed through its pages, a picture fluttered to the hardwood floor and landed facedown.

"The back had my mom's name written on it and the date the photo was taken. I turned it over and looked at the only picture I have of my mom from when she was a kid." Ann swallowed and stared at her plate. "It's the only shot I have of her period."

"You decided it was time to find out where you came from."

Ann nodded at Tricia and took another sip of coffee.

"And that picture led you here?" Tricia said.

"Yes, and I think this picture is worth one-hundred-thousand words. If only I could get it to talk."

"What do you mean?"

"I think I know where the picture was taken, but I have no idea who the other kids in the photo are. I would love to find out. Because they might still be alive and they could tell me who my mom was and where she came from."

"Did you bring it with you?"

Ann excused herself to get the photo from her purse. This was it. Time to see if her intuition had been sending her right signals when it told her to get the photo in front of Tricia and Taylor.

She eased back into her chair. It felt like she was stepping onto a six-inch ledge five-hundred feet above the ground.

Ann slid the facedown picture into the center of the table and flipped it over.

An instant later Taylor's fork slipped from his hand and clanged onto his dessert plate.

"Thank you for a wonderful evening, Tricia." Ann stood on the porch and zipped up her Windbreaker more out of habit than need. The temperature felt like it was still in the upper sixties at least.

"Would you like to take a little stroll together? We could take in some of the night air." Tricia leaned in like a seventh grader about to describe which boy at school she had a crush on.

"Sure, I'd love to." Ann breathed in the pine-scented evening air and held it. Portland beat every other place on earth when the sun shone, but she was beginning to think Three Peaks was a close second.

"I'm sorry once again for Taylor traipsing off into his writing room right in the middle of dessert. I don't know what got into him."

"I upset him; I'm sorry."

Tricia stifled a tiny laugh. "Yes, I think you did, most of the evening." She leaned toward Ann. "I loved it."

"Do you mind me asking, does Taylor always drop his fork when thirtysomething women show old photos from when their moms were kids?"

Tricia shook her head and smiled. "That reaction convinced me of something I've suspected since the moment I first saw you."

"And that is?"

"I wonder if people get tired of me saying, 'I think Taylor better tell you more about that'?"

"Without question."

She laughed and Tricia joined in.

They walked in silence, in a warm kind of comfort. Was this what it felt like to take a late evening walk with a mother who cared about you?

"So tell me about Taylor and the Book of Days," Ann said after they'd strolled another block down the street.

"He's always felt the same way about it as you do. That it's nothing worth spending a breath on. At least that's what he's always said."

"What do you think?"

"I'll tell you what I told Cameron. My husband's been acting strange ever since the two of you came into town."

"Cameron thinks whatever the Book of Days' story is, Taylor holds the key."

"I sure hope the two of you feel that way." Tricia's smile almost turned to laughter. "If you hadn't figured that out, I'd have worried you weren't as bright as I thought."

CHAPTER 31

Two Years, Six Months Earlier

Cameron's Christmas present to Jessie that year had been a trip to Disneyland with another couple. All four had gone nonstop from the time the gates opened each morning till the fireworks of brilliant greens, blues, and reds exploded over Cinderella's castle each night. The lines were long but they worked their Fast Passes with precision, and by the end of third day, they were all wiped out but basked in the fun of being kids again.

"Great memories," one of the men said as they strolled toward Disneyland's Main Street on their way back to the hotel.

"I'll never forget this trip," his wife added.

"But we won't remember every moment of our lives, will we?" Jessie asked.

"Not all. We'll cut out the boring parts, but we'll definitely remember the highlights," Cameron said.

"So where do our memories go when we forget them or . . . when we die?"

"Oh boy," chimed in the other man. "Look out, Jessie's going deep again."

Cameron's smile faded. He'd said almost the same words to his dad the last time he saw him six years earlier.

"Where do the memories go?" the wife of the other couple said. "I thought everyone knew they went to Tasmania."

The other couple laughed. Cameron didn't and stopped walking.

Jessie stopped as well, but the other couple kept moseying along, plunking blue cotton candy into their mouths.

"Are you all right?"

"Great." She forced a smile and bonked Cameron on the head with her Mickey Mouse balloon.

"Wow, I like that, keep doing it please."

Jessie slumped onto a bench, a statue of Walt a few yards behind her, and Cameron slid down beside her and wrapped her in his arms.

"What's going on? Are you bummed because Pirates was shut down this trip?"

"I'm fine, Cam, really."

"And I'm Goofy, really."

She pulled her Mickey balloon into her chest. "Maybe God writes our memories down, hmm?"

As Cameron crossed his leg, the loss of his father welled up in his heart. Yeah it would be wonderful if God did.

He missed his dad so much. His laugh, his kindness, his quirky sense of humor. Where were his dad's memories? When he was losing his mind, did the memories float into nothingness, or were they stored somewhere for eternity?

Cameron hadn't thought about his last conversation with his dad in months, maybe a year. A book with all days in it. He sighed. If only it were true.

A hundred years from now, even fifty, would anyone remember his dad answering his phone at home with "Joe's Bar and Grill, Joe speaking"?

Would they remember the swimming contest he had with his best friend's son in the community park? Would they recall the banner hanging over the pool that said, Old Age and Wisdom Beats Youth and Hair Every Time?

"Sitting in this park where make-believe comes true, you could almost convince me your God does exactly that. I wish He did."

Jessie turned and looked over his shoulder toward the lights of Space Mountain. "What if it's true? What if it could be more than a wish? What if He does write down what happens in our lives, in everyone's life?"

"Like some cosmic high-school yearbook put together by the supreme being of the universe?"

"Something like that." She turned away.

Cameron shook his head and gave what he imagined was a melancholy smile. Jessie sure could stretch her imagination beyond the confines of normal human cogitation. "I love your insanity. One of the countless reasons I'll love you for eternity."

He watched the back of her head, the breeze making her hair wave like ribbons, waiting for her to look up at him.

"Baby?" Cameron reached out and touched her elbow.

Still no turn back.

"What is it?" He shifted till he saw her face. A pair of tears wound their way down her tanned cheeks. "Talk to me."

"Life is so short."

"Not for us. Twenty-eight now means you're stuck with me for a least another fifty years. Maybe sixty."

"So short."

Her hands were cold as he took them.

"Why are you saying that?"

"I'm okay, really." Smiling, she took his hands and placed them on her cheeks. "I'll tell you later, okay?"

"How about telling me now?"

She stood and offered her hand. Cameron took it, raised her long fingers to his lips, and kissed them.

"Just promise me you'll remember this conversation, okay?"

"I will. Always and forever."

CHAPTER 32

Cameron sat in Java Jump Start on Saturday morning tapping his foot in double-time waiting for Ann to arrive, wishing for a better camera than the one on his cell phone. One iPhone with a two-year contract? $99. A Three Peaks white chocolate mocha? $3.75. The look on Ann's face when he told her what he'd found? Priceless.

He sipped his drink and skimmed a brochure on white-water river rafting and another one on joining Broken Top, apparently one of the premier private golf courses in the area.

Where was she?

He glanced at his watch again.

Five minutes later Ann walked in with a knowing smile. She winked at him and ordered what sounded like an extra hot caramel macchiato.

After getting her drink, she slid into the dark brown chair next to Cameron. "I had a riveting dinner last night with Taylor and Tricia Stone."

"And I had a fascinating search party with Arnold Peasley." He toasted her with his cup. "Do you want to go first?"

"Sure, even though I can tell you're about ready to explode."

"Guilty as charged. But I promise to contain myself."

"I'll give you the headlines. First, Tricia confirmed that Taylor definitely knows more than he's telling about the Book of Days, and second, when I showed them my mom's photo, Taylor just about had a heart attack. He actually got up and left the room right after I pulled out the picture. I asked Tricia about it, and she said me describing that photo convinced her of something she suspected from the moment she first saw me."

"That's it?"

Ann flicked him on the forehead with her ring finger.

"Hey, that hurts!"

"Good." Ann took a drink of her caramel macchiato. "What do you mean 'that's it?'"

"I was trying to be funny."

Ann gave him a plastic smile.

"You want to hear about my visit with Arnold?" He folded his hands and leaned forward on the table.

She nodded.

"We didn't do any digging."

"You mean he wouldn't let you look, or he didn't have any papers from the sixties?"

"I mean, we didn't *have* to do any digging. Not only did he have the papers, old Pease went right to the three papers in question so quick I think he should rename himself Dewey."

"What?"

"Dewey Decimal, don't you remember that from library when you were a kid?"

"You're getting off track, Cameron. Tell me what you found."

"Right, we were talking about . . ." His mind went blank. Was it libraries? Why would he and Ann be talking about libraries? He took a long drink of his white chocolate mocha as the bowling ball returned to his gut. It was a nice slice of pop psychology to tell himself not to worry about the future because life could end at any time. But it didn't work so well when the loss of his mind made living in the present a nightmare.

He grabbed the edge of the table. Tight. Maybe it was time to see a doctor. Find out if his memories were disappearing because of stress or because his mind was truly—

"Do you want me to insert a drum roll here?" Ann said. "Are you thinking drawing out the suspense will make it more exciting when you tell me?"

Think! He was telling her about . . . basketball? No, was it? Someone who used to play . . . Peasley! Arnold's newspapers. Yes. The article from the sixties.

"Are you sweating?"

He wiped his forehead with a napkin and tried to smile. "Coffee that's too hot always does that to me."

"So are you going to tell me about what you found?"

Yes, he would tell her. And she would know about her history. And then they would find the book. His memories would return and his mind would be healed. *Now snap out of it. Focus on Ann. Upbeat. This will rock her world.*

"Are all four legs of your chair securely on the floor?"

"You think this is going to knock me over?"

"It might." He leaned in on his elbows. "Thanks to Arnold, I know who your mother was, who your grandmother was, along with a few of your other relatives."

"Are you kidding?"

"You ready for this?"

"Tell me!" Ann punched Cameron in the arm.

"Your mom's maiden name was Coffee, spelled just like the drink, right?"

"Right."

He waited for her to react but Ann sat with eyebrows raised, as if asking why this was a revelation.

"I don't hear any bells going off yet."

"And your grandmother was named Josephine. Last name Coffee."

"Okay." Ann still didn't react. The anticipation on her face remained.

Was she in shock or not surprised? How could she not be surprised?

"You're acting like this should mean something to me."

"Don't you get it? Coffee."

Ann held her hands wide with a bewildered look on her face. "I'm sorry; I'm still missing a piece of the puzzle."

"Annie's maiden name was Coffee."

"Taylor's Annie?" Ann's face went white and she covered her eyes. "Oh my gosh. Are you saying . . . Annie is my aunt?" She said it half as a statement, half as a question. "She was my mom's sister."

"Yes."

"That means . . . Taylor Stone is . . . my—" Cameron nodded as Ann fell back in her chair and clunked her drink to the faux marble table. "He's my uncle."

"Yes, he is. Uncle. Or uncle-in-law. Does he stay your uncle even though Annie isn't living?"

"Unbelievable." She put her face in her hands. "Taylor Stone is my uncle."

"Looks that way."

Ann slumped further down in her chair as her arms fell to her side. "Wow. That's about as weird as you can get." She let out a long, low whistle. "How did you figure it out?"

Cameron pulled a copy of the *Post* from 1963 out of his briefcase and slid it in front of Ann. On the front page was the same picture of her mom she'd showed Cameron three days earlier. The caption read, *Summer in Three Peaks Always Means Kids and Swimming.*

Ann snatched up the paper and skimmed the story. "Swimming spot . . . rope swing . . . where the kids . . . Jennifer and Annie Coffee, Jason Judah, and Taylor Stone enjoyed an adventure together on . . . Oh my." The paper fluttered out of Ann's hand.

She looked up at him, eyes wide. "I should have seen it. Maybe Taylor did. Maybe he's known about me my whole life."

"I don't think so. I watched him when you came onstage at Jason's reception. He looked like he'd seen a ghost, not a long-lost relative. And I think I know why."

"Tell me."

"This is the part I'm glad you're sitting down for. And the reason Taylor reacted like he did. Ready?"

Ann nodded once, her eyes riveted on his.

"Take a look at this." He held out another yellowed newspaper.

She reached out her hand but Cameron didn't hand it to her. "It would be easier to look at it if you gave it to me."

"Just making sure you're ready."

"I told you, I'm ready."

"This is a picture printed in the *Post* a few years later."

Ann squirmed in her chair and stared at Cameron, anticipation spread over his face. "Will this freak me out?"

"Maybe. It might be a bit of a shock, but you need to see this."

Ann looked down at the picture and her pulse spiked. It was a wedding announcement and a photo of the couple about to be married. Her head instantly felt like she'd taken a huge bite of Thai food with five-star seasoning.

She was looking at a picture of herself standing next to Taylor Stone.

"How in the world did they . . . ? It's me. Why would someone—?"

"No, it's a picture of Annie."

Ann pulled the newspaper closer and rubbed the grainy photo with her finger. "I can't believe . . . this is too strange . . ." She trailed off not knowing what to say.

"Explains a lot, doesn't it?"

Ann nodded, not sure she could trust her voice.

"When Taylor first saw you it was like seeing Annie, as if she'd come back from the dead."

"But why wouldn't he come talk to me about it? Meet me, tell me who I looked like?"

"I don't know."

"It makes no sense, Cameron. When I showed him the photo at dinner, why didn't he tell me who I was and who my mom was?"

"Excellent questions." He shook his head and shrugged.

Ann set the paper down and scooted back from the table, the legs of her chair sending out a screech like a wild falcon. "I've got to talk to Taylor."

She stood and stared at Cameron. "I've gotta talk to him right now."

CHAPTER 33

Ann wasn't sure if she should have come. Yes she was. Without question she needed to have this conversation.

She trudged over Creek Bank Park's lush green lawn, only sporadic russet strips showing where the sprinklers apparently hadn't reached with enough water. Tricia had said he'd be here; it was one of his thinking spots.

How should she open a conversation like the one she was about to have? *Hi, Taylor, just thought I'd let you know I'm your long-lost niece. Would you like to catch up on the past thirty-two years?*

Given Taylor's reactions to her so far, he might refuse to talk at all. She stopped and once more considered returning to her car and driving away. Finally she plodded on, scanning the park for her . . . for Taylor.

As she came around from behind a large spruce tree, she spotted him. He stood on a deck that hung over the Metolius River like the lady on the prow of a ship. A continual bath of spray misted the beams supporting the deck every few minutes from the small waterfall just beyond it, making it look like he and the deck rested on wispy clouds.

Ann watched him for a few minutes before wandering close enough for her cleared throat to be heard over the rush of the river. He turned.

As she approached, he lifted his Oregon Duck's hat off his head, placed it on his chest, and gave a slight bow. "Have you come for a time of potentially awkward conversation? If so, I think I can help."

"Is that your way of saying 'I wish you weren't here, but since you are, I'll at least be civil toward you'?"

"Blunt today, aren't we, Ms. Banister?"

"As with most days. I apologize."

"No, it's refreshing."

Ann waited till Taylor gave the invitation she suspected would come. "Why don't we stroll the perimeter of the park, and we can chat without having to look at each other every moment."

"That sounds good."

Taylor turned slightly as they strolled down the gray gravel path. "It's actually a welcome surprise to see you."

"Really?" Ann said as she crunched along next to him. "I wasn't sure how you felt about me."

"Why is that?"

"Are you kidding? Let's just say I felt more welcomed by your other half last night. And the dancing fork bit, and the subsequent vanishing act made me think—"

"That's one of the reasons I'm glad to see you. I've been thinking we could use some time to make the air between us a mite clearer."

"Good, there are a number of things I want to talk to you about."

"Do I get to see the list?"

They sauntered down the path that ran along the riverbank to their left.

Taylor Stone had charm and wit, but she guessed there was a sadness that came out when the doors were shut and the lights dimmed to black. She saw it in his eyes when he laughed.

She'd always been good at seeing the story behind the story, the mark of a good investigative reporter and television host. If she was right in this case, Taylor had a story going on so deep, she wouldn't be surprised to find Jules Verne at the bottom of it.

"Since you inspired the creation of the list, of course you get to see it. And don't worry, it's short. Only three items."

Taylor looked at her with one eyebrow raised and one eye closed.

"That's a good look."

"Thanks. I've done it since high school. Some people seem to think it's wearing thin." Taylor put his baseball hat back on and pulled it back so most of his forehead showed. "The three items?"

"First is the reaction you had when you saw me at Jason's reception."

"You didn't buy the stomach-cramps scenario?"

"Second is the Frosty the Snowman reception I received at dinner—"

"I was a little cold, you're right. But during the time I showed you my fly-fishing journal, I warmed up to a nice temperature."

"I agree."

"And the third?"

"Your dinner fork."

"Yes, that." Taylor turned and looked at her without expression. But something in his eyes moved, maybe it was behind his eyes. She'd read somewhere that the eyes were the window to the soul, and in Taylor's case at least, it was true. He was a man who wanted to talk and wanted to stay quiet in equal measure.

"Can we talk about it?"

The firm shake of his head said no, but after thirty seconds with no sound but the crunch of their shoes on the path, he apparently changed his mind.

"Yes, let's talk. But instead of me telling you why I did those things, why don't you tell me. I have a feeling you already know the answer."

"In other words, you've figured out who I am," Ann said.

"I suspected immediately." He coughed. "The moment I saw you on that stage."

"I didn't figure it out till this morning."

Taylor nodded, stared at the path in front of them, and kept walking.

Ann had expected some kind of reaction. Certainly more than nothing. It was her turn to punch the mute button on the conversation. Did Taylor want to ignore it? She looked back expecting to see a pink elephant stomping along behind them. What was the best way to bring the animal to front and center? She was glad walking down the path gave her an excuse to keep looking straight ahead.

After another minute she said, "If you know who I am, why have you been pushing me away? What is it about me you dislike so much?"

Taylor sucked in quick breath. "Ann," he started to say, and then stopped to snatch a gnarled pine branch off the ground and turn it into an impromptu walking stick. "Don't think that even for a second. I do like you, very much. It has nothing to do with you.

"But . . . seeing you stirs up a number of memories I'd rather not deal . . . I'd rather not think about. It's God's way of rubbing my nose in the past, not letting me forget my sin, poking me in the spot where it hurts most."

They continued strolling through the park in silence, Ann wanting to know so much but not wanting to press into Taylor's pain without invitation.

They continued, the scuffing of their shoes on the path the only thing breaking the silence.

"Ask me what you want to know, and I'll tell you," Taylor said a few minutes later.

"Why did my mom leave Three Peaks?"

Taylor sighed again, stopped walking, and turned to Ann. His face was white and he swallowed like someone who was choking. "Years ago I made a horrible choice, and because of it someone died."

"Annie."

Taylor nodded and rubbed the bridge of his nose. "Yes. Your mom left town—angry at me, angry at herself, angry at the world. I decided to stay. I wrote to Jennifer five times during the next three years begging for her forgiveness, but she never wrote back."

Taylor took three long breaths.

"I never heard from her again. I'm not sure what I would have said if she had responded. I didn't know if she got married, had children . . . There were times when I almost got in the car and drove up to her last known address. Finally I gave up. It would only bring the memory back on both of us."

Ann drew a finger across her mouth. "Why did she become a drug addict?"

"The pain. A way to deal with it."

Pain? It was the only legacy her mom had left. Ann shook her head. But she was still her mom. Ann couldn't stop from asking the question. "Will you tell me about my mom?"

"What do you want to know?"

Was it possible to loathe someone and love them at the same time? "Everything."

"She was quiet. With one or two friends she talked with such intensity, but in public she was shy." A sad smile appeared on his face. "She was a natural athlete but preferred reading and learning to playing sports. As you might imagine she was smart, straight A's all through school."

Like mother like daughter. "What else?"

"Jennifer had a dry sense of humor. And she was very loyal."

"Loyal? To whom? She must have lost it on the drive up to Washington, because I never saw it."

"I'm sorry." Taylor shoved his hands into his coat pockets.

"She worked two jobs. Not to feed me. To feed her heroin habit."

Taylor's shoulders slumped and he let out a long sigh. "I didn't know."

"One day she shot up too much and never came home. That was her loyalty to me."

"I'm sorry, Ann. So sorry."

They tramped on, their shoes scrunching into the gravel in the same cadence.

"Have you forgiven her?"

Ann shook her head. She didn't trust her voice.

"Whether she was able to tell you or not, the Jennifer I knew would have loved you. Deeply. She always talked about wanting kids."

Ann rubbed her forearms with both hands. "Then why didn't she ever show it?"

"When Annie died it changed her. It changed me too."

Ann rubbed her hands across her cheeks. "I'm named after Annie, you know."

"Yes, of course."

"So seeing Annie in me is both wonderful and painful at the same time?" A tinge of warmth crept into Ann's face.

Taylor nodded. "Precisely."

"Do you want me to leave?"

"No." Taylor dug a hole in the gravel with the toe of his leather boot. "Of course not. God is in this. At least I know that in my head, if not my heart."

Taylor started walking again and kicked a pinecone off the path, then turned to Ann. "I need to talk about something different now. It will take a while to stuff my insides back into my chest cavity, and I don't want Tricia to see me this way."

"I understand." Ann smiled.

"Tell me about Cameron. Do you like him?"

"Are you playing Yente?"

"Who?"

"Yente from *Fiddler on the Roof*. Supposedly it's an old classic. I had a boyfriend in high school who made me watch it three times."

Taylor smiled. "I agree on your definition of it being a classic, but old? I was nineteen when that movie came out. So are you saying I'm old?"

"Yes. Ancient."

Taylor burst into laughter, and the mood around the man changed in an instant. "While I appreciate the humor, that doesn't excuse you from telling me about Mr. Vaux."

"He's complicated."

"All compelling men are. Are you interested in him?"

"I've loved him for seven years." Ann's face grew hot in an instant. What was she thinking? Why did she confess that? Were her emotions that close to the surface? Ugh. She needed to keep a tighter rein on them. Bury them. Treat her interactions with Cameron more businesslike. Cool, calm, collected. Please.

"Ah, I see. Don't worry; I'll keep that information to myself."

"Thanks."

"What do you see as his complications?"

"Two things. First, he doesn't follow Jesus—"

"Which is why you can't do anything about your feelings."

Ann nodded.

"And second?"

"Even if he were a Christian, he wouldn't be ready for a relationship. He wears a band of pain around his neck." She glanced at Taylor. "The same band you wear."

"Really? Which one is that?"

"One of hanging on to a past love, not able to let go of her, and letting the burden of carrying that weight affect everyone around him."

"You're doing the blunt thing to me again."

"I'm sorry, would you like me to stop?"

Taylor shook his head. "No, it reminds me of someone I knew a long time ago."

By the time they finished their third lap around the park, Ann had fallen for Taylor Stone. Would her sentiment ever be returned? Even if he wasn't a blood relative, he was her uncle; he was family.

The only family she had.

Over time he could tell her more and more about her mom, and in time she might be able to listen. But forgive? She pushed the question out of her mind.

Ann leaned into Taylor and he gave her a quick sideways squeeze. It was enough. Ann didn't care what he knew or didn't know about the Book of Days. She just hoped she'd found a friend.

CHAPTER 34

Two Years, One Month Earlier

Cameron was in the middle of voicing a corporate video for Wiley's Water Ski Shop when his cell phone rang.

Great. And the take had been perfect so far. He needed to remember to put his cell on mute when he was cutting tracks. "Hello?"

"Hey, it's me."

"Hi, babe. Love you. What's up?"

"Can you talk?" Jessie said.

Cameron glanced at Brandon sitting in the booth drumming his fingers on the mixing board. He pointed at his watch and then made a motion like he was handing out dollar bills.

"Not really, I forgot to shut my phone off. We're in the middle of recording a voice-over and this studio isn't cheap. Someday we'll get our own—"

"No problem. I'll talk to—"

"Wait, Jess." Something in her voice said it was important. "Talk to me." He held up his forefinger to Brandon as if to say "one minute."

"I want us to go to Oregon."

"Uh, we've been to Oregon, honey. Remember the coast last summer?"

"Soon, we need to go again soon."

"Sorry to repeat myself, but we've been there. You okay?"

"Central Oregon. We've never been there together."

"Can we talk about this when I get home?"

"I'm sorry, Cam. I know you're in the middle of work. It's bad timing on my part, but it's time to go."

"Why?"

"We need to look for something, find something there."

"What?"

"Something I saw when I was a kid."

"What? The thing you saw when you were ten? That thing?"

"Yes."

"Why?"

"To see if it's real."

"If what is real?"

"I can't tell you over the phone."

"You took trips there when you were a kid, right? Girl Scouts?"

"Yes."

"Why the sudden interest in going back?"

"I'll explain when we get there."

"Yeah, but what is the something?"

"I told you, I can't tell you."

"Listen Jess, I'm not tracking. I'm in the middle of this VO. Can we yak about this when I get home tonight? I mean, we can go there if you want, but I gotta get this thing done, all right?"

"Sure."

"Okay, love. See you then."

When he'd gotten home that evening, Jessie was asleep and she didn't bring it up in the morning. He didn't either and the conversation faded from memory.

~m~

Cameron stood with Ann on Sunday morning at the base of a 5.10 climb, fear pinging around his stomach like a gyroscope. "Are you sure you're up for this?"

Ann nodded but didn't look at him. She'd been cool the entire drive to the climb site, responding to him with one-word answers, her head turned toward the passenger side window.

So much for the thawed-out Ann he'd enjoyed the past few days. The Ice Queen returneth.

He stared at their climbing gear laid out in front of them. They'd checked and double-checked to make sure they had a full climbing rack of carabineers, nuts, cams, and quick-draws as if that could make the fright of the last climb fade away.

The accident three days earlier had shaken both of them. But the longer they waited to get back on a cliff the more doubt would grow in the fertile soil of fear.

Ann took a deep breath. "Do what you fear most and you conquer fear."

"You believe that?"

"No, but it's one of my favorite clichés anyway." Ann frowned and jiggled her hands up and down as if she held a set of reins. "And I do know we need to get back on this beast."

Cameron nodded. "Okay, let's ride. It's the perfect way to kick off the first day of August."

Two hours later he sat next to Ann on a ridge 350 feet above the ground, the rush of the climb seeping out of him, replaced by a deep sense of satisfaction.

He stole glances at Ann as the sunlight danced on her skin. She was gorgeous. And intelligent. Intriguing in ways so different from Jessie. Tricia's words floated back to him:

"If you knew you were dying and Jessie would live many years beyond you, would you want her to live her life alone, hanging on to the cloud of your death and your memory? Or would you want her to be happy?"

The problem was Ann didn't care for him. Yes, she'd warmed up for a few days from "I despise you" to "I think I could almost be friends with you," now today back to "I'll tolerate you." Not a great romantic foundation. Plus why would she want to be with a man losing his mind? And finally, while Tricia might be right, he couldn't—he wouldn't—let his heart turn from Jessie to anyone else. He needed to get back to reality.

"We make a decent team," Ann said.

"What?"

"We climb well together."

"I agree."

Ann cleared her throat and ran her fingers through her hair. Then swallowed. Twice. "Will you ever be ready to give love another chance?"

"You mean date again?"

"I mean fall in love again."

He stared at a prairie falcon circling above them and wished the pain of losing Jessie could soar away that easily.

"I always told Jessie I could never love anyone after her."

"What did she say?"

Cameron's mind buzzed. He remembered talking to Jessie about this. Didn't he? When was it? Years ago. She'd said something strange, as if she knew she would die before him. *Think*. Did they talk about it, or did he only dream it? He needed the book. *Please be real. Please.*

"Cam?"

"Right here."

"I thought I lost you. I called your name twice." Ann tapped the top of his climbing shoe with the sole of hers.

"Sorry, I think Jessie and I talked about this. I was just trying to remember what she said." He looked down at the slight tear in his climbing shorts. Like the tear in his mind. "I'm guessing she said I'd love again."

"And?"

"And what?"

"Will you?"

He tried to drag the memory out of the corner of his mind. Where did Jessie and he have that talk? "Will I what?"

"Are you with me here? Do you think you'll ever love anyone else again?"

"I can't get her out of my heart."

Ann sighed and pulled a climbing rope slowly through her palm. "I don't think you ever have to get her out of your heart, but what about getting her out of your head?"

"She's leaving my mind. Faster every day."

Ann put on her sunglasses. "Jessie will always have a place in your heart, but as long as you keep holding on to her in your mind, you'll never be fully open to anyone else who comes along. You have to let her go."

"I know, but I don't know how. It's not like a button I can push."

"All I'm saying is if the possibility of love is in front of you, you need to open yourself to see it. And holding on to Jessie too tightly is like walking around with blinders on."

Cameron didn't respond and a few minutes later Ann suggested they head back down. After the seconds hand on his watch whirled around ten times, they stood on red-brown earth. It had been an excellent climb, without anything of note happening except how seamlessly they worked together.

"Good climb. Good call on getting us back up there, H," he said. "Are you glad we did it?"

Ann didn't answer.

The falcon swept by overhead and screeched. Cameron cocked his thumb. "At least he agrees."

Again Ann didn't comment. She picked up one of their ropes and coiled it in swift, tight motions, tied it off, and tossed it toward the car almost violently. He walked over to her and bent down to grab another rope.

"You want some help?" Cameron slid his hand around the rope on top, but Ann yanked it away and walked toward the car, coiling it herself.

It was obvious the thaw on top of the mountain was temporary. And it was getting tiring having her travel back and forth from sun to snow.

"Did I do something? Taking a wild guess here, but I think you're ticked off at me."

"You're a genius. You should write a book on picking up on women's subtle emotional clues. Book sellers would catch on fire it'd sell so fast." She dumped the rope in the trunk and strode back toward him.

"And *why* are you upset with me?"

Ann shook her head as she marched past him.

"Come on. Are you going to let me know what I did, or are we going to have as quiet a ride back to town as we did on the way up here?"

"Do I really have to tell you?"

Yes, she did.

"I'm sorry. You're right. It's not your issue, it's mine. You haven't done anything wrong." She picked up her day pack, strode back to the car, slammed it into the trunk of his MINI Cooper, and ambled back toward him.

"Then what's the problem?"

Ann placed both hands on her hips, and her eyes drilled into him like a laser. "You really and truly don't understand what I was trying to say up there three-hundred feet over your head, do you? You didn't pick up on any clues as we sat looking out over the valley?"

Cameron squatted down and drew circles in the dirt with his forefinger. He had every excuse to say no. Her hints would have sailed over the head of a lot of guys. But deep down he knew. During the past week and a half, her eyes had been saying the same thing they'd said years ago when he first met Jessie and her. She liked him. Wanted to be with him. And then he'd chosen Jessie, and the light in Ann's eyes had gone out. Until now. "Yes, I knew what you were saying."

"But you just let me sail it out there, gave me no response . . . let me feel like a complete fool."

"I'm sorry, I'm just not ready to let go of Jessie."

"You need to consider something, Cameron Vaux."

He looked up.

"Do you think you're the only one who misses her? You're not the only one who lost someone two years ago. She was my best friend. The sister I never had." Ann kicked the ground. "At a certain point you have to get on with life."

"Before I get on with life, I have to know if there's going to be a life to get on with!"

"What's that supposed to mean?"

Cameron rolled his eyes.

"You know what I think? I think you're losing more than a few memories here and there, which all of us do. You've lost a lot. You're terrified this thing will accelerate into losing your mind completely.

It's why you cling to the idea of this book, even though you know there's ninety-nine percent chance it's a farce. It's a way to avoid ever really looking reality in the eye."

Ann marched over to a pine tree, folded her arms, and leaned her shoulder against it, her back to Cameron.

"I'm not losing my mind!" Cameron flung his arms wide. "You have no way of understanding what I'm going through. Just because I'm not willing to tell you about all the demons I'm wrestling with, doesn't mean I'm not facing reality. And yes, the book gives me hope in the midst of the nightmare I've lived in since Jessie died—one that I'm living more vividly now than I ever have."

Ann whirled back to face him, her eyes full of fire.

"I know. You gave your heart away to Jessie and life stole her from you. So focusing on the book keeps you from the risk of giving your heart away again. Tell me, if you could do it all over again, would you have still loved her? Still swam in the beauty of that relationship?"

She strode over to him and popped his shoulders with her palms, making him stumble back two paces. "Climbing is life, Cameron. Figure it out. At a certain point you'll have to go beyond climbing 5.10s and risk climbing 5.11s, 12s, 13s. Whether it's with me or someone else."

"What are you saying?"

"Brilliant video producer dies because he can't see the picture right in front of him. Film at eleven." She turned and strode toward the car. "You know exactly what I'm saying."

Two emotions slammed into his heart at the same time. Betrayal, of Jessie; and his growing feelings for Ann. "I'm just not ready to go there with you, with anyone." He rubbed his head with both hands. "I can't—"

"Won't." Ann turned, strode to the car, yanked the door open, and got in.

He ground his teeth together. Nightmare. Wondrous. He couldn't tell which emotion was stronger.

Cameron glanced at Ann as they bumped along the road, his car throwing up clouds of fine brown dust behind him. Was she crying? He couldn't tell with her face turned toward the window. There was no manual in the glove compartment for this kind of problem.

What could he say? *"Uh, I think maybe I could feel the same way about you. In fact I'm sure I do, but you're right about my mind. It feels like microscopic drops of acid are being dropped into my mind burning away my memories. And why would you ever want to be with a guy with that problem? And I'm not over Jessie, but I think maybe kinda sorta want to pursue a relationship with you."* No, would not happen.

After riding in twenty minutes of silence, Cameron said, "I'm sorry, Ann, I—"

"Forget it. My fault." She turned and gave a big smile that didn't reach her eyes. "We're wrong for each other on so many levels. We couldn't ever be together. But I needed to get what I told you out in the open, but now that it is, I'm truly good. Trust me. You and I as friends is the way it's supposed to be, and it's the way we'll go forward from now on forever and ever, amen."

"What do you mean we couldn't ever be together?"

"You know why."

"Enlighten me."

"My whole life centers around Jesus."

"So."

"Yours doesn't at all. It's not exactly a match made in . . . you know."

Cameron rapped his fingers against his steering wheel. "It never was a problem for Jessie and me."

Ann arched an eyebrow and looked at him. "Oh, really?"

"Yes really. We worked through it."

"No you didn't. You worked through nothing." Ann pulled her knees up to her chest and wrapped her arms around them. "You never saw how much it ate at her, knowing she wouldn't see you in heaven."

"How do you know there is a heaven?"

"Don't change the subject, Cameron."

"How can you be so sure heaven is real?"

Ann's gaze bore into him. "How can you be sure it isn't?"

They rode the rest of the way in silence. Ann was right. Friends only would work. He'd make that work. For both of their sakes.

"So are we still on for tomorrow?" Cameron pulled into the parking lot of Ann's hotel and helped her carry her gear to the trunk of her Prius.

She shut the trunk and smiled. "Sure. I have a little more research to do today, and if I find what I'm looking for, tomorrow I'm going to blow your mind."

CHAPTER 35

Cameron sat in the corner of Java Jump Start just before ten on Monday morning, debating whether to order a third latte or go for straight black drip when the bells on the front door jangled. He looked up. Ann. She swept inside, stopped, and glanced to the left then the right.

When her eyes found him, the corners of her mouth turned up a millimeter. She waltzed toward him, as if she knew without a doubt he'd be sitting there ready to hear what she'd discovered.

She twirled in a tight circle and, while still two paces away, tossed a bundle of papers toward him, spinning them like a Frisbee.

"Hey!" Cameron lifted his coffee and leaned back as the package smacked onto the dark walnut table and slid to a stop with a third of the papers hanging off the edge.

"Time to connect the dots." Ann grinned at him, hands on hips, sunglasses dangling from a cord around her neck.

"Apparently you're providing the pencil?"

"I am, and the pencil is a number ten out of ten. I found what I was looking for. And you will like it. A lot." She bounced on the balls of her feet and rubbed her hands together like she was starting a fire.

He looked back and forth between her and the bundle. "You've found something."

"More than something." She plunked down into the seat next to him. "Open it."

He untied the twine holding the papers together and spread three pamphlets and ten or so pages of notes out on the table along with two maps—one of the world and one of the night sky. The world map was marked in seven spots with dots of red ink.

Leaning back in his chair he took a sip of his coffee and gave Ann a little smile. "We know the seven spots on this map are the only seven spots in the world where I'd find a certain kind of stone."

"Right."

He looked from the map of the world, to the map of the night sky, back to the map of the world. "Unbelievable." He rapped his knuckles on his forehead and grinned at Ann.

"What is?"

His hands shook as he drew lines between the dots.

"What's unbelievable?" she repeated.

He looked up and her eyes told him she already knew the answer. "That I didn't think about doing this earlier."

After he finished connecting all the dots, Cameron held up the map and studied the pattern.

"You've already done this exercise, haven't you?"

"Yes. But I thought you'd like the rush of doing it yourself." She smiled.

"Now we look for the constellation that matches the pattern of the stones."

"Go on."

"And once we figure out which constellation it matches, it gives a major clue as to where we're going to find the Book of Days."

"Congratulations, Cameron, you've just won the daily double."

He smiled and compared the pattern to the picture of the night sky. Five minutes later he looked at Ann. "I'm not seeing it."

She had a smug look on her face.

"You're already ahead of me on this, aren't you?"

"Miles."

"And you've enjoyed the last five minutes of me flaying about, yes?"

"Immensely."

"So now that the fun is over, you're going to tell me what you've known for the past twenty-four hours."

"Past fourteen." Ann slid an acetate drawing of the pattern of the stones and laid it over the map of the night sky. "Do you see the pattern of the stones matching any of the constellations?"

"No, that's what I'm saying. There's no match."

"So what's your next guess?"

"Maybe it's not a constellation. Maybe it's latitude and longitude, maybe—"

Ann shook her head. "No, I took three astronomy classes in college, I actually did okay in them and if you—"

"Great idea. I'm clueless when it comes to astronomy, but I have a friend at UW in the astronomy department. I can e-mail him this pattern. He'll probably get back to me within half a day with the possible constellations this pattern could represent. If he can't give us anything, we'll move on to the latitude-longitude theory." He kept his eyes riveted on the map.

"Cameron."

"Because it might even be a combination of constellations we're not seeing."

"Cameron."

"Have you tried—?"

He was interrupted by a rolled-up newspaper hitting him in the head.

"Ow!"

"You're making me feel like I'm in a Three Stooges movie. Didn't you hear me? Now be quiet and listen."

He rolled his eyes.

"Buddy, you roll your pupils at me again and I'll whack-smack you so hard, you won't remember tomorrow." Ann looked like she was trying to keep the grin off her face but failed.

Cameron gasped. The exact words Jessie used to use when they were bantering back and forth and she wanted to make a point stick. His stomach roiled. "I have to get out of here for a moment."

"What's wrong?"

"Nothing."

"Where are you going, Cameron?"

"Be right back."

He walked down Main Street to the end of the block and stood staring at the summit of Broken Top, feeling like its jagged ridge was a picture of his mind. Maybe his heart as well. A heart in no condition to be opened up to anyone. But Ann was blowing up his steel-enforced walls with everything she said and did. He'd hardly slept last night as he wrestled his emotions for Ann into submission. Until a moment ago they'd laid dormant, but now they swam through his head like a school of maniac dolphins.

No. It wouldn't happen. He would reconstruct the walls. For Ann's sake. For Jessie's. He drilled his fingers into the back of his neck, trying to massage the ropes of tension into surrender.

He took two strides back toward Java Jump Start, then did a 360 and clipped back the way he had just come. A few seconds later he turned again. He clenched his jaw and marched toward the coffee shop. There was no debate. The argument was over.

By the time he got back to Java Jump Start, his walls were back in place and thicker than ever.

"Are you going to tell me what you know?" he said to Ann as soon as he plopped down beside her.

He couldn't decipher the look on her face. "Are you going to tell me why you left?"

"Can we get this thing done?"

She stared at him for a full ten seconds. "Sure." She scooted her chair closer to the table and leaned in. "No problem."

"Sorry."

"For what?"

"For being . . . for not . . ."

"Don't worry about it." She tapped the table with her pen. "Let me show you what I think. I was stumped for a while too because I assumed it would be one constellation. But it's more than one; it's a combination just like you guessed. Whoever put this mystery together apparently wants us to work a little harder, but not much. Do you want me to show you, or do you want to take another run at it?"

"Run." Cameron went back to work and within two minutes had the answer. "It's a combination of Vela and Pyxis."

"Yes."

"So now we figure out what these constellations have to do with the areas of the world where the stones are or what it has to do with the legend of the book, and we're on our way to discovering its resting place."

"Or it leads us to another part of an elaborate goose chase someone has cleverly devised that will never get us to the end of the rainbow."

"True believer, aren't you?" He smoothed out the map of the

night sky. "Since you've had some time to think about this, what are your theories?"

Ann bobbed her head and smiled slightly. "Three ideas so far. One, of course is what you just said; that the pattern points us to Vela and Pyxis and something about those constellations is a clue. Two, it's a map or pattern you lay over each area where the rocks are found and it guides you somehow. Or three, and the most likely, it's the model of a four-dimensional portal we can build with cereal boxes and a roll of duct tape that will instantly transport us to the nearest Book of Days."

"Can we stay serious for a moment?"

Ann crossed a leg underneath her and leaned in. "If you're ready to get serious, I'm more than ready."

"What's that supposed to mean?"

She waved her hand at the map, the papers, and the table. "Do I really have to convince you this whole thing is a hoax? Don't you know, right here?" Ann tapped his chest.

Cameron didn't answer.

"If you're excited about this connect-the-dots exercise because it means we're drilling down to the answers to an elaborate puzzle, great. If you think we're close to exposing a game that's been perpetuated on Three Peaks, fine. But that look in your eyes tells me you really and truly believe the book could exist."

"It could."

"How, Cameron?"

"Are the stones real?"

"Yes."

He raised his eyebrows, leaned back in his chair, and flipped open his palms. "Well?"

"Come on. I can show you evidence Kennedy was shot by seven men or the CIA or the Mafia, depending on what stack of facts I want to haul out. I can prove to you, not in theory but using photos and conversations and hardcore evidence, that we never landed on the moon."

"And your point is?"

Ann glared at him.

"Maybe you're right. But does it really matter? Say it's all faked. You're curious. I'm curious. It means we both want the same thing: to find out where this thing leads. It's a great story either way. And I have to hope this book is genuine."

"Why?"

He closed his eyes. "You know why."

"Why?"

"Can't you imagine for a moment it's real?"

"No." She took a sip of Cameron's coffee. "Did you see that movie *The Game* with Michael Douglas? It involved an *elaborate* setup that took him all over the globe hunting down clues and putting his brain through a psychological blender. Coincidences and patterns were in place that looked impossible for someone to have set up. Things were real and then they weren't, upside down, right side up."

"I saw the movie."

"Did you know it's based on real life? That there really is a 'game' where Mensa-level intellectuals race against each other? It's like a PhD-caliber scavenger hunt sponsored by guys like Bill Gates. Teams of four to six people get clues they have to solve leading them to the next clue. A lot of time the clues are so intricate and choreographed they're like small theatrical productions, with hired actors to pull it off."

"What are you driving at?"

"Someone has created an elaborate game out of this Book of Days legend. He's probably waited years for someone to discover it. And we're about to win. But we won't win the chance to see our past or our future. I think the only prize we'll get is the chance to say we figured out the clues and have some mysterious game architect pat us on the back."

"Taylor Stone's clues."

Ann nodded. "That's where I'd place my bet."

"So Taylor is the architect?"

Ann shrugged and raised her eyebrows.

"You're saying Taylor traipsed all over the globe planting rare rocks to concoct—?"

"No, I'm saying he searched until he found something unusual—those rocks—and tied it all together."

"Why take all the time and energy and money to concoct something like that?"

"I don't know, Cameron! Maybe he got bored. Let's just follow the bread crumbs. I don't believe—you do—but like you say, it doesn't matter." She grabbed her purse and stood. "Listen, I have to go."

"Go? Now? You can't go; we need to figure out what the constellations mean. Where do you have to go?"

"I have a massage appointment. I'll be back in an hour and a half max."

"Massage? How can you get a massage when we're in the middle of all this?"

"If I don't work out the kinks after rock climbing, I'm sore for days." Ann flipped her hair and laughed. "Plus massages make me more beautiful."

"You're already beau— I mean you look fine."

"Thank you." She smiled.

"When will you be back?"

She sniffed out a laugh. "I just told you, in an hour and a half or less."

He lied and said, "I remember." He mashed his forefinger into his lips. Concentrate. He needed to concentrate better.

Ann sat back down, a concerned look on her face. "You're right; I do know why it's so important for you to find this book. I nailed it yesterday after the climb, didn't I? I saw it in your face then and I'm seeing it again right now. You truly are losing your mind, aren't you?"

Cameron held his breath till he had to let it out. "Yes."

"And the book will heal you?"

"That's my hope."

She squeezed his arm. "I'm sorry, Cameron."

"It's okay."

Why couldn't he tell her the truth? Okay? No. It wasn't. He didn't want to wind up in an assisted-living facility in two years, ten years, forty years—ever. He wanted a life!

~~~

Ann wove her way up the street around tourists in bad hats worried about nothing more than finding another summer adventure.

How should she navigate the one she was on with Cameron?

She'd suspected his mind was slipping more than he'd let on, but she hadn't been around him for an extended amount of time for years and didn't know how the stress of Jessie's passing might have affected his brain.

No wonder he was so desperate.

The bells on the spa door jangled as she stepped inside and stopped. "All right, God, I get it. He needs me to help him find this thing—whatever it is—so I'll do it, with everything in me. It doesn't mean I have to believe the book is real."

~~~

As soon as the front door of the coffee shop closed behind Ann, Cameron squeezed his temples, as if the pressure could jump-start the memories deep inside his brain. A soft groan escaped. He was losing it. *Come on! Remember!*

Cameron wiped his forehead, leaned back in his chair, and forced his breathing to slow. If only he could get more sleep. Maybe he should . . . No. He wouldn't see a doctor. Had he ever considered that? Forget it.

He was fine. He would be fine.

After pouring over their notes for ten minutes and getting nowhere, Cameron stepped outside Java Jump Start to take a break and a short walk. As he strolled north on Main Street, the sensation of being watched crept up his spine.

He did a slow spin studying the people on the street and even the windows of the stores across the street. Nothing.

Wait.

A man in a baseball hat and gold-rimmed sunglasses sat on a bench forty yards away at the end of the block. The man stared straight ahead, but he could have been looking at him a second before.

A moment later the man turned and, yes, his gaze was drilling Cameron from behind his sunglasses. He was sure of it.

As Cameron started to trot toward him, the man stood. It was him. The figure from the park. No question. Same height. Same build. Same gait.

Cameron broke into a sprint as the man ambled down a side street, then ducked behind the Grand Palace Hotel.

Cameron rounded the corner of the building. "Hey!"

The alley was empty except for an old Pepsi can rocking back and forth in the slight breeze.

The man had vanished.

CHAPTER 36

"You can't hide from me, so why hide it from yourself? Whether you admit it to me or not, you and the Book of Days have a deep connection." Tricia thrust her shovel into the soil and heaved another pile of dirt out of the trench she was digging. Why did she love the man so much? He drove her nuts at times. Most of the time.

"Are you positive you don't want a hand with that?" Taylor said from the cast-iron bench he sat on in their backyard.

"One hundred percent."

"Building a pond is a great idea."

"Don't try to change the subject." She pointed her forefinger at him. "You know something."

"So what if I do? I don't see how that obligates me to tell you."

"What makes you come to the conclusion I'm talking about me?"

Taylor blinked and turned away.

"You have a newly found niece. And a young man she likes. And he likes her. And they're looking for this book which is probably a fake. But it really doesn't matter because you're not going to lift even your pinky to help them." Tricia scooped out another shovelful of dirt and tossed it at Taylor's feet. "And it's wrapped up in something you've carried around in the dark ever since Annie died, and it's time you lay the burden down and forgive yourself for whatever it is you think you did."

"Are you finished?"

"I'm just getting started, Taylor."

"Great."

"You lose Annie when you're young, Cameron loses his wife when he's young—don't you think that's an interesting coincidence? Have you considered for more than a passing moment that God might have something to do with putting you two together? That maybe He's asking you to give Cameron a little help?"

"I wouldn't be much help."

Tricia shoved her shovel into the sod and trudged over and sat next to her husband.

"We both see it, so I might as well come out and say it—Cameron is headed down the same path you've been on for too many years. Holding on to the past with a grip even death would have trouble releasing, unable to get past the tragedy of losing someone he loved.

"Helping him find this book of his would go a long way toward getting him to open up to you, and then maybe you can talk some sense into him that you haven't been able to talk into yourself."

Taylor sighed. "There are some things you can't forgive yourself for. Things you shouldn't forgive yourself for." He rose from the bench, grabbed Tricia's shovel, and started digging.

"It's amazing to meet someone greater than God."

Taylor frowned. "What's that supposed to mean?"

"He's willing to forgive everything you've ever done, or ever will do, but since your wisdom is much greater than His, you know you shouldn't accept that kind of love."

"And if I forgive myself?"

"It would give you the ability to forgive others."

"Who haven't I forgiven, Tricia?"

She shifted on the bench, took off her work gloves, and tossed them onto the grass. "Your best friend."

"I don't have a—"

"Jason. You need to forgive Jason too."

"You're not going to start talking about that again, are you?"

"It would set you free."

"That's what you've told me."

Tricia took off her sunglasses. "It's true."

"The past is the past is the past. I'm not going back there."

"If you've forgotten the past, why do you have a vacation home there?"

Taylor dropped the shovel onto the dark soil and strode over to the edge of their property, hands on the cedar fence, face turned to the sky.

Tricia let him have a few minutes of solitude before strolling over to him. "Hello, my name is Tricia. What's yours?"

"I'm guessing there's a point to this."

"You're not you."

"Uh, I think I am." Taylor whapped his stomach with his palm. "Yep, still me."

"Do you remember when you and Annie and Susan and I were all around thirteen years old and you blindfolded us and took us down to Munson's Bridge and had us get out on the edge? You were so excited. It was only twenty-five feet up, but it felt like two hundred. You jumped first and watched as each of us jumped, but only if we wanted to. And of course we all wanted to, and when we'd all leaped, you gathered us on the shore?"

Tricia waited till Taylor looked right at her. "Do you remember what you said?"

He didn't answer.

"You said, 'I was so scared to jump, but I was even more scared to tell you I was scared. But if we can't tell each other our greatest fears, then what would our friendship be?' That was profound wisdom coming from a thirteen-year-old. Do you remember?"

"Yes." He looked back to the sky.

"I don't see that Taylor so much anymore. Do you?"

Silence.

Tricia took his hands in hers. "What happened when Annie died? And why is this book business turning you inside out?"

Taylor leaned back against the fence and sighed again. "Maybe I'll never open up. Maybe this is who I am now. Maybe it's all I'll ever be. Am I so bad?"

"You are wonderful in so many ways. But there is still so much more inside you."

"Maybe there isn't, Tricia. Maybe that part died along with Annie and is impossible to resurrect."

"I don't believe that."

"Maybe you should."

Tricia trudged up to the house and tossed her work gloves on the deck. She glanced back. Taylor walked to the shovel and picked it up again. For a few moments she watched him work up a sweat, trying to pay penance for the rooms of his heart he'd shut her out of.

"Break him open, Lord. There's gold inside, but no one can get to it but You."

Cameron glanced at his watch. An hour and a half had come and gone. At an hour-forty-five the bells on the coffee shop door chimed and Ann walked in.

"You're late," he said when she reached their table.

"Are you going to dock my pay?"

"Sorry, I'm a little hyped up here. You won't believe what I'm going to tell you."

"You could use a massage too." Ann slid into the seat next to him and squeezed the back of his neck. "You're tight."

He didn't need that. Cameron shifted in his chair and pulled away from her touch.

"Sorry."

"While you were gone, I did a little research on Vela and Pyxis."

"And?"

Cameron leaned further over the table and tapped his pencil against the constellation map like a woodpecker. "Guess what the translation of Vela is?" He slid a piece of paper in front of her.

"The Sail," she read off the paper.

"And here's the translation of Pyxis." He slid another small piece of paper in front of Ann.

"The Compass."

"Now take a look at this business card from a well-known Three Peaks restaurant."

Ann eyes went wide. "The Sail & Compass Bar & Grill. Oh, wow."

"Great burgers. But we're in the middle of the high desert. Why would someone name their restaurant Sail & Compass when it's 160 miles from the ocean? Bronco Billy's, sure. Pine & Post Bar and Grill, absolutely. But Sail & Compass? It doesn't fit. Unless they were sending out a New York-sized neon sign."

"We need to find out who started the restaurant."

Cameron nodded. "My thinking precisely."

"You already know."

"Yes, I do." Cameron bent the Sail & Compass business card in the middle and spun it on the table like a top.

"Tell me."

"Take a wild guess."

"Taylor Stone."

"He sold the restaurant three years ago, but Taylor still owns—"

"The building."

"Correct. Owned one-hundred percent by him and him alone. No partners. It's the perfect place for him to store all his large secrets." Cameron gathered up his papers.

"Are you saying the Book of Days is inside that building?"

"I'm saying we should head for the courthouse and look at the blueprints of the structure. It wouldn't surprise me to find a basement."

"Are you hoping to find blueprints that say 'Book of Days' room?"

Cameron grinned. "That would be nice."

Ann and Cameron stepped into the county courthouse at two o'clock. A large sign on the door told them the building would close at three. Plenty of time to find what they needed.

As they approached a tall counter with a black and white Information sign, the floorboards creaked, as if they were about to snap, but the bespectacled middle-aged man behind didn't look up.

After clearing his throat three times, each time raising in volume but eliciting no reaction from the clerk, Cameron looked around for another way to get the man's attention. A bell sat at the far end of the counter and Cameron stepped over to it.

A tiny sign matted down with yellowed Scotch tape said, "Ring bell for service." He looked at Ann, shrugged, and gave the bell a sharp rap.

The clerk instantly looked up from his Dean Koontz novel and smiled. "Hello! Nice to have you here today. How can I assist you?"

"We're selling hearing aids, are you interested?" Cameron said under his breath.

Ann elbowed him. "We'd like access to some public records."

"Sure, what of?" He set down his book and stood.

"The building where The Sail & Compass restaurant is."

The clerk frowned but trudged off and came back six minutes later with blueprints of the building.

"Be careful with those, please. That's Taylor—" The clerk stopped himself as if he'd been caught taking a cookie out of a kid's lunch box.

"We know Taylor Stone owns the building." Cameron spread the blueprints out on the counter and studied them.

"Do you know him?"

"What?" Cameron looked up.

"Do you know Taylor Stone?"

"Yes." He turned back to the plans. "We both do." He glanced at Ann who had a look of intense concentration on her face. "Are you seeing what I'm seeing? It looks like the basement has—"

"Does he know you're looking at the plans?" The clerk leaned in almost close enough for his head to touch Cameron's.

"I don't think so. I didn't think we had to ask permission to see items of public record."

The clerk leaned back and tapped his foot. "No, I suppose you're right. But don't you think it would nice if you asked? I do."

"We will next time. I promise. Now do you mind if we take a quick look at these without interruption? And then we won't bother you anymore."

"You're not bothering me." The clerk cleared his throat. "Much."

"We just need a few more minutes, thanks." Cameron smoothed out the plans and scanned them again. He looked at Ann and found her staring at him with a little smile on her face. She had to be thinking the same thing. The plans showed a basement with two levels with a number of large rooms.

The perfect place to hide a Book of Days.

"Could we make a copy of these plans?" Cameron said.

The clerk's face paled. "No."

"Why not? They're public record."

The clerk smacked his lips with a series of rapid pops, as if it would help him make up a story as to why not. "The copier's busted."

"Really? I used to work on them," Cameron said. "I bet I could—"

"It's, uh, time for you two to leave."

Ann puffed out a breath. "The sign says you close at 3:00 and it's only 2:20."

"I have a lot to do to close up."

"But this is a government building. You can't lock the doors until the hour stated on your sign."

"Oh yes, yes, yes I can. If I have a government errand to run, which I do, I can lock up early."

"I could get the copier fixed in a few minutes."

The clerk waved his hand at Cameron, as if shooing away a hornet. "You have to leave. Right now."

"We'd really like to get a copy."

As the clerk kept shooing them away with his hand, Ann whispered, "We don't need a copy, trust me."

"Why?"

"I'll tell you later. Let's get out of here before the clerk has a coronary."

Cameron smiled. The bees didn't buzz unless you whacked the hive. And he wouldn't stop till he and Ann found the honey.

The clerk picked up his phone on the first ring.

"What did they want?"

"The layout of Taylor's restaurant." The clerk squeezed the tip of his pencil as beads of sweat broke out on his forehead.

"Interesting. I was right." The phone hummed. "And did you make it seem like Taylor wouldn't want them to see those plans?"

"Yes. I think I convinced them."

"Good." The line went silent. "You've been an extremely loyal disciple, and that means a great deal to me. Thank you."

"You're welcome."

"But just so we're clear, if you tell anyone anything about the, uh, observing you've been doing for me—and I mean anyone—I will slit your throat. Will that work for you?"

"Yes. We're clear."

"Excellent. I appreciate you."

The line went dead.

"Taylor has influence in this town, I'll give him that," Cameron said as they walked out the courthouse doors.

"Considerable influence." Ann batted him on the arm. "Did you really work on copiers at one time?"

"No."

Ann smiled. "So what's our next step?"

"I think we need to do a little late-night exploring."

"You mean a little late-night breaking and entering." She glared at him. "Are you serious?"

Cameron smiled. "But it's only a little exploration in a good friend's building. You think he'll mind?"

"Hello?" Ann knocked on her head. "Yes, I think he'll mind."

"I agree, but I can't worry about that. Tonight we're going to find an amazing book. I can feel it."

CHAPTER 37

A strong wind whipped down Main Street, powerful enough to give a slight bend to the lampposts spaced at twenty yard intervals. Cameron's parked MINI Cooper lurched back and forth as the wind buffeted the car. His window was open a crack and the wind whistled through the opening, as if it was trying to speak a warning.

Ann scrunched down in the passenger seat—matching Cameron's own posture—giving little shakes of her head. She looked at him. Her eyes asked if they were really going to do something as ludicrous as break into Taylor's building. He imagined his own eyes said, "I'm not sure" in return.

It was one in the morning; most of the town had been shut down for three hours. The only building still open was Take a Peak Tavern a quarter-mile down the road at the end of town, and there had been only three cars in the lot when they drove by ten minutes earlier.

"I can't believe we're doing this," Ann said.

"Why?"

"Why?" She coughed out a laugh. "Other than the fact I could get fired for doing this and we could both wind up in jail, no reason at all. I'm sure the police would be sympathetic and Taylor would certainly understand why we ended up inside his building at this hour."

"Early breakfast?"

"We're going to be careful, right?"

"Like little elves on Christmas Eve."

"Elves make the presents, they don't deliver them." Ann shifted in her seat and pulled her knees up to her chest. "Sorry to repeat myself, but I don't want to end up in jail."

"Then why are you doing this with me?"

"I'm doing it for Jessie."

"What?"

"I can't believe I'm going to confess this." Ann rubbed her face with both hands. "I don't want the book to be real."

"What are you talking about?"

Ann turned and looked out the passenger-side window. "A few months after Jessie and I met in that foster home, she said she knew when she would die. Said she'd seen it when she was a kid. She didn't know the day, or method, but she knew the month and the year. I told her she was crazy."

Ann hugged herself. "Over the years she'd bring the subject up, trying to tell me it was part of God's plan, and I mocked her for it till she gave up."

"Wow." Everyone had their secrets.

"If the book turns out to be real, how do I tell Jessie I'm sorry? Even if it's not real, how do I tell her?"

"She forgave you a long time ago." Cameron flicked his fingers. "It's gone."

"I know it. I need to believe it." Ann patted her knees once. "Shall we go?"

"I'll go in alone. You should stay on lookout—"

"We already decided to do this together; don't go back on me now."

"Ann, there's something I need to tell you first. We might be into something more dangerous than I thought. There's a guy who's been watching me."

"Sunglasses, baseball hat, looks Native American?"

"He's stalked you too?"

"Well, I wouldn't say stalked exactly, but yes."

"We need to be more careful than the elves."

"Agreed."

Cameron slowly squeezed his door handle, opened his door, and slid out. He pulled out his pack from the backseat, looked at Ann, and raised his eyebrows, as if to say one more time, "Are you sure?"

Ann nodded, got out—her pack in hand—and darted across the rough asphalt street, Cameron close behind. They sliced through the alley between The Sail & Compass and the Three Peaks Hotel around to the back of the building.

"I'm an idiot," Cameron said as they knelt next to the back door.

"Why?"

"I didn't remember to bring a glass cutter. We're going to have to break a window."

Ann scrunched up her face. "Are you teasing me?"

"What do you mean?"

"We talked about not having to worry about bringing tools to break in."

"We did?" Great. Another missing song from his brain's CD.

"We did. Watch." Ann pulled out an eight-piece lock-pick set from her pack and grinned at Cameron. After a quick study of the lock in the doorknob, she chose two picks and leaned in, her ear millimeters away from the lock.

She closed her eyes and seemed to be talking to herself. In less than thirty seconds the door was open. Ann bowed her head and extended her palm in invitation for Cameron to enter the building first.

"Another unknown skill of the resourceful Ann Banister."

"From when I was a teenager. Before I met Jessie and Jesus. Don't ask."

Neither spoke till they'd stepped inside and shut the back door behind them.

"Not to be paranoid, but let's lock that."

"Done," Ann said as she locked the door. "I need you to explain a mystery to me if you don't mind. If the book is genuine, why would Taylor hide the book in the heart of town where someone is more likely to go down to the basement and find it? Why not hide it in the basement of his home? Or in a cave out in the middle of nowhere? Or bury the thing in the ground?"

"Two reasons. The first is Poe."

"What?"

"Edgar Allan. 'The Purloined Letter.' The best place to hide something is—"

"Right out in the open," Ann finished. "I wouldn't call the basement out in the open."

"All I'm saying is you wouldn't expect him to hide it on his own property right in the center of Three Peaks."

"And the second reason?"

"The same reason we're here in the middle of the night. With this place filled all day long, seven days a week, it would be a little tough for someone to explain why they were headed to the basement, especially if it's locked, which I'm guessing it is."

Cameron moved through the restaurant's kitchen and looked for a door leading to the basement. "Taylor owns the building and The Sail & Compass?"

Ann stared at him, concern etched into her face. "No."

"But he started it, didn't he? The restaurant?"

Ann nodded. "Yes."

"I'm supposed to know this, aren't I?"

"Yes." She hugged him and whispered, "It's going to be okay. We're going to find the book and you're going to be healed."

A few moments later they found the stairs to the basement and Cameron started down them. The restaurant's dim night lights illuminated enough of the pine stairwell for Cameron to see his way down, but not much more. Two thirds of the way down he stepped on a stair that screeched like a catfight.

He glanced back at Ann. "I think you might want to avoid that step."

"Good call, H."

The quote from the *K2* movie. Cameron smiled. He remembered.

At the bottom of the stairs was another door, this one with a double lock. "I'll take this as confirmation we're on the right track."

After Ann did her lock magic, they stepped through the door and snapped on their flashlights.

They stood in a large room filled with dusty cobwebs hanging from rough-hewn dark wooden beams. A light brown carpet, which might have been white once, covered the floor.

"It's a museum; no one's been down here in years," Cameron said.

"Museum is right."

Along the far wall was a series of shelves piled with an extensive assortment of Native American artifacts: arrowheads, clothing, tools, bows, cooking pots, animal skins, and numerous photos.

While Cameron studied the collection, Ann made a clean sweep of the room. "We need to go down to the next level. But I don't know how."

"You didn't find a door?"

"Not an obvious one."

"Let's start a little light stomping." Cameron started in a corner of the room, stomped the wood floor with the heel of his boot, scooted a few feet forward, and stomped the floor again. Ann did the same at the opposite corner of the room. They both coughed from the small tornado of dust they kicked up.

A little over half the room had been covered when Ann said, "I found it." She took a silver-handled Swiss Army knife out of her pack, knelt on the carpet, and sliced a perfect square in four quick strokes and peeled it back.

"Let's go a little deeper, aye?"

"Aye, captain."

Cameron bent down and pulled on the trap door. It didn't budge. Not even a quarter-inch. He yanked it again. Nothing. After grabbing a screwdriver from his pack and wedging it into the microscopic slit between the door and the floorboards, he put his full weight on the handle of the screwdriver.

A second later the door popped open and a whoosh of stale air filled the room.

"Why do I feel like we're about to lower ourselves into our own crypt?" Ann said.

Cameron flopped the trapdoor over onto the carpet, shone his flashlight down into the opening, and peered in. The concrete floor below was at least twenty feet down. "No stair, no ladder. Get ready to climb."

"This is a pretty remote location for a wine cellar," Ann said.

"It would be nicely aged by now. I think it's been a while since someone took a stroll in the bowels of The Sail & Compass."

Ann tied her ropes to one of the thick wooden beams so they could repel into the darkness. Two minutes later Cameron dropped through the opening, flashlight clamped securely in his mouth.

"The water's fine, come on down," he called out twenty seconds later.

After Ann reached him, Cameron did a slow scan of the room with his light. It was small and square, maybe six-feet across and eight-feet wide. He expected it to be damp, but other than smelling a bit musty, the room was dry. Long tapestries of mountain scenes hung high on three of the four walls, running all the way to the floor. The rest was empty.

"There." Ann pointed to a narrow black opening in the uncovered wall to the left, not more than twelve-inches wide and five-feet high.

Cameron bent down and shone his flashlight into it. "I hope your claustrophobia insurance is paid up."

Ann massaged her temple and he realized she didn't find it funny. "Sorry."

"Let's do this." Ann slapped her hips with her palms.

Cameron turned sideways and slid into the opening, with Ann close behind. He shone his light on the wall inches from his face, illuminating jagged cracks in the concrete that ran from floor to the ceiling.

"How much farther?" Ann asked after a few seconds.

"It can't be much more."

"You don't see the end yet?"

"Sorry, it curves slightly up ahead. You doing okay?"

Ann didn't answer, and for the next ten seconds the only sound was their feet scuffling along the narrow passageway.

What were they doing? Breaking the law like this was insane. All for a book that logic said wouldn't be down here or anywhere else.

But Cameron had left logic land fifteen days ago.

Moments later they stepped into a room the same size as the one on the other side of the tunnel.

"Feel better?" Cameron asked.

"Much." Ann shuddered and licked her lips. "If the book is here, how would he have gotten it through that passageway?"

"Maybe Stone built the tunnel after he got the book down here." Cameron did a slow spin on his heel as he shone his light on the walls from left to right. There was one door, directly in front of them. He stepped up to it, stretched out his hand, and slid his palm down its wooden surface till it came to rest on the brass knob.

"Here we go. Ready?" His heart pounded like a jackhammer. Could this be it?

"Are you sure you want to open that door?"

"I just realized . . ."

"I know. When you open it, you'll either be overwhelmed or devastated."

Cameron nodded. "Exactly."

There was no point in waiting. He curled his fingers around the doorknob, let its coolness seep into his damp palm, and pushed. It didn't budge. A little harder and it creaked open.

He stepped through and shone his flashlight around the room. It was large, maybe twenty by twenty feet. The room was thick with the smell of old musty papers. In one corner stood a small lamp that looked like it was made in the 1930s. A broken stool lay in the middle of the room. Two old oak desks rested next to the stool.

Nothing else was in the room.

Cameron leaned up against the wall and slid down to the floor like sap oozing down a pine tree. Why did Stone do it? Why the clues? Why would he put this whole charade together only to have the end of the puzzle result in nothing?

Cameron slammed his fist into the wall behind him.

He'd believed in the book because he had to believe; in his dad's and Jessie's God, in sometime beyond this life. If he didn't, what kind of future was left for him?

He'd had to believe he could answer his dad's final request, find his memories of Jessie, and be cured of this insidious disease.

Cameron glanced around the room. So what would he do now? He banished the question from his mind. "Are you going to say I told you so?"

"I'm sorry." Ann sat beside him.

"At least I know, and it won't haunt me the rest of my life, wondering what I might have found."

They sat in silence for three or four minutes. Then Ann patted his leg. "Are you ready to go, or do you want to sit here a little longer? I doubt we're in any danger of being caught if we haven't been already, but still, I wouldn't want to be found down here."

"You're right; we should go."

But Cameron didn't want to go. He wanted to stay and watch God's Book of Days magically appear before his eyes. He wanted to remember every moment he'd spent with Jessie and relive days with his dad—to bathe in the glory moments they'd had together.

He wanted to remember the important things Jessie had told him before she died that pounded at the back of his mind but refused to take shape any longer.

He needed to remember them. They were tied into the things going on in Three Peaks right now. Things somehow he knew he needed to know but couldn't dredge up no matter how hard he willed himself to do so.

Suddenly Ann stood. "I can't believe I almost missed it."

"Missed what?"

"I don't know what I was thinking." She paced and pressed her fingers against her temples. "Yes, yes, of course." She closed her eyes. "I can see it."

"Talk to me."

She whirled to face him. "This is the outer room, not the inner."

"I'm not following."

"There's another room in this basement. A big room."

"There's a slight problem with that." Cameron swung his flashlight around the room in a slow arc. "There's no door. No opening. No curtain for the wizard to emerge from behind."

"There has to be."

"There isn't."

Ann pulled a folder from her backpack. "Take a look at this." She knelt down and spread a two-by-one-foot piece of paper on the floor. "Did I tell you I have a photographic memory?"

Cameron hesitated. Did she? "I don't think so."

"It doesn't always work for remembering conversations or places I've been or people I've met, but with photos and papers I've seen and things I've read, I retain 90 to 95 percent of what I see."

"So?"

"Look." She pointed to the paper she'd smoothed out on the dust-choked floor.

"After we got kicked out of the courthouse, I sketched out the blueprints of this building." Ann tapped the paper. "This is where we are now. If I'm right, there has to be another room on the other side of that wall."

"You didn't think to mention your photographic memory till now?"

"Did we need it till now?"

He leaned forward and shined his flashlight inches from Ann's paper. Her simple line drawing definitely showed a room on the opposite side of where they knelt.

Moving slowly along the north wall, Ann rapped her knuckles against the wall every few feet. After Cameron figured out what she was doing, he started at the opposite wall and did the same.

Boom!

The hollow reverberation sounded like a cannon in the stillness of the chamber. He shined his flashlight on the spot. No door. He rapped the surface in front of him again.

Boom!

"I think you found it," Ann said.

Cameron ran his fingers over the surface of the wall feeling for an edge. Nothing. Ann did the same on the other side, where the edge of the doorjamb would be if there was one. "He put Sheetrock right over where the door would be."

A low whine filtered down from above them, almost too soft to register.

Ann looked up. "Did you hear that?"

"Sounds like a blender from two miles away." Cameron spun his flashlight around the ceiling. "Or three stories above us."

"And?"

"No idea, but it's pretty late for anyone to be whipping up a smoothie."

They held their breath and listened. Nothing.

"Let's get this done."

He dug into his pack for his climbing ax as Ann did the same.

The blender started again.

"You want to keep digging and I'll go check out whatever is making that noise?" Cameron said.

"Good plan."

The noise stopped the moment he turned. They listened. Again nothing.

"I'm going anyway."

Ann nodded.

He eased through the narrow hallway, stopping every few feet to listen. On his fifth stop the whine started again. Then stopped. He didn't hear it as he scrambled up the rope through the trapdoor into the first level of the basement, up the stairwell into the restaurant.

The sound didn't start again till he stepped around the back corner of the building into the shadows in the alley in between. A streetlight strobed and the element inside whined. It sounded like their blender.

How could that—?

As he followed the pole down into the ground it made sense. The pole was probably directly above where they were, and the vibrations carried down into the basement.

A car drove by and Cameron tried to push himself into the wall of Taylor's building as it passed. It didn't slow and didn't speed up. He stood in the shadows for a minute, watching the other shadows, watching for . . . nobody.

There was nothing out here. Paranoid for no reason.

Finally he shook his head, as if he could shake off the unsettled feeling flitting around his mind, and crept back into the restaurant, down the stairs, down into the second level of Taylor Stone's basement.

The light from Ann's flashlight lit up the narrow passage as he shimmed through it and the luminescence drew him like a moth.

"I see you're still among the living," Ann said as he pushed through the small opening at the end of the passageway and stepped into the room.

"Just a streetlamp burning out, sending the whine down into the ground." Cameron coughed as the cloud of dust swirled around him. "Wow, nice progress."

A pitch-black hole in the wall roughly six feet by two gaped next to Ann. "Not bad, huh?"

"Not only that, but I couldn't hear you doing it from above, which means this vault is deep enough that we can relax a bit. Any noise we make down here won't be heard above."

Adrenaline pumped through Cameron. This had to be it.

He grinned at Ann and she returned it with one of her own. "You want to go first?" he said.

"Not a chance."

As Cameron stepped through the opening, he flicked off his flashlight and turned back toward Ann. "If it's real, we should see this at the same time."

She followed his lead and shut off her flashlight before stepping through the opening.

Silence surrounded them. If he didn't know Ann stood three feet from him, he could have felt like he was the only person alive on earth. Was this what death was like?

"Are you ready?"

"Yes."

Their feet scuffed the floor as they shuffled forward a few feet.

"Let's do this." Cameron snapped on his flashlight.

A moment later Ann's flicked on and their lights filled the room. They stood in a large domed space with faded cedar paneling. The back wall was covered from floor to ceiling with shelves that held piles of parchments, each stack weighted down by familiar-looking rocks.

Cameron pulled Susan Hillman's stone out of his pocket. It was smaller, but it was the same as the stones on top of the parchments. Blood pounded through his head and adrenaline pushed through his body.

In the middle of the room a thick gray canvas covered a rectangular shape at least ten-feet long and five-feet wide.

Cameron looked at Ann and grinned. She raised both eyebrows and returned the smile.

The Book of Days. It had to be.

"Taylor Stone is worthy of an Oscar. He almost had me

convinced it was only a legend." Cameron interlocked his fingers. "Shall we?"

As they stood at either end of the canvas, ready to throw it back, Cameron said, "Whatever is under here, thanks for going on this journey with me."

"My pleasure."

"Ready? One, two, three!"

They yanked off the cover, a snow storm of dust dancing in the glow of their flashlights.

Yes!

Cameron's knees went weak as his lips curled up.

They'd found it.

Cameron stared at the book almost afraid to approach it for fear it would vanish off the rough-hewn table it sat on. The dark brown leather cover looked ancient. Cracks ran throughout the surface and the leather strap that bound the book shut was graying. At the far left end of the book, cords the color of damp straw wound through the cover and the pages.

Cameron blew out a long, slow breath. Unbelievable. A tingling sensation ran up and down his arms. His dad's and Jessie's words were true. Answers. Finally.

"We did it, Ann."

She shifted from one leg to the other. "I want to know, even at this size, how every event, past, present and future, of every life is supposed to be contained in this book."

"Maybe the words are really small." He smiled and circled the massive tome slowly. "Maybe the words appear and disappear depending on who looks at the book. I'm serious. This is God we're talking about. Have some faith." He winked at her.

A title six inches high ran across the top of the page in a language Cameron didn't know. He stared at the book wondering what to do next. Open it of course. But to where? How would he search for his memories of Jessie in a book this size? How would he read the words if they weren't in English? It didn't matter how. He would figure it out even if it took years.

"Come on," Ann said. "Let's open it."

"My thought exactly." Cameron moved to the end of the book. He reached out and touched the corner of the cover. Like his father and Jessie had done?

He closed his eyes as they lifted the cover and set it on the table. "For you, Dad; for you, Jessie."

After a moment of silence he opened his eyes and looked at the first page. What? It couldn't be. A sensation of fire started in his feet and moved up his body in surges. By the time it reached his head, he felt ready to throw up.

He swallowed, looked up at the ceiling, then back down at the paper in front of him.

It hadn't changed.

The parchment was still blank.

He turned to the next page.

Nothing.

And the next.

More pages.

More nothing.

There was no writing on any of them.

CHAPTER 38

A dry heave pushed up from Cameron's stomach and he doubled over, then lurched forward and caught himself on the table.

"No." His knees buckled and he slumped to the floor and bit his lip. "This can't be happening."

"I'm sorry." Ann put her hand on his back.

"Where are the words? Where are they!"

"I don't know."

"I believed, I did. I believed the book was real."

"Shh, I hear something."

"I needed that book to be real. There has to be something we did wrong. There has to be some way to unlock it, some prayer we need to say, some code, maybe it's like invisible ink . . ."

But he knew none of those things would make words appear on the faded pages.

"Let's close it and get out of here."

She was right. It was over, time to go. He was too numb to argue.

They closed the book and packed up their gear.

As Cameron slung his pack over his shoulder he said, "It makes no sense. Why would—?"

Ann snapped her hand up to cover his mouth. "Our blender has grown feet," she mouthed. "Listen."

The faint scuffle of shoes or boots echoed off the concrete walls of the outer room.

"Cameron!"

The voice rang out like a gong and he knew instantly who it belonged to: Jason Judah.

A moment later Jason stood in the opening, bowing, grinning, and bouncing lightly on the toes of his dark green military boots. "Wowee!" Jason took a slow look around the room and then settled back on Cameron, a mocking smile on his face. "I must express my great gratitude for leading me here. It is highly appreciated."

Jason stepped through the opening and continued grinning as he stared at the book. "The Book of Days, in all her glory, resting peacefully in Taylor Stone's basement. Why doesn't that surprise me even minutely?"

Jason kept his flashlight shining on the book as he strolled around it. "As you know, Cameron, I had little belief there was an actual physical book till you came along. But your dad saw it when he was a child. And children often tell more truth than most adults. Taylor Stone for example." Jason leaned back and laughed. "I love to be proven wrong and to be proven right."

"How did you know we were here?"

"I've been following you, of course." Jason studied his fingers before looking up at Cameron and Ann. "Now please, how did you figure it out? I'm curious is all."

Cameron glanced at Ann. She was pale but stood as solid as the concrete at their feet. It looked like she was holding her breath.

"You are not going to tell me. I understand. Keeping all your secrets secret, right?" Jason motioned toward the book. "Do you mind if I . . . ?"

Cameron stepped away from the book. "Not at all, I'll be interested to see what you think."

Jason looked at the cover of the book. "Did you translate it?"

Neither of them answered.

"It's Hebrew. 'The Stories of All Times.'" He ran his fingers across the cover like he was touching silk. "God's book. Thousands and thousands of years old at the least. And thousands of years still to come. Will you help me open it, Cameron?"

"Sure."

As they lifted the cover he kept his gaze locked on Jason's face to see the moment when he realized the truth.

After they set the cover down Jason started turning pages. One. Ten. Twenty. "Is this a joke?" Jason pulled back from the book and blinked. "What is this?" His eyes switched back and forth from Cameron to Ann. "Where is the writing?"

"There isn't any," Cameron said.

"Explain to me where the words are. What do you do to make them appear?"

"There are no words."

Jason stared at them for twenty seconds before pulling a knife out of his belt and flashing his light over the blade. "This is an Mtech tactical bowie knife. It's extremely sharp." He lasered his eyes on Cameron. "Tell me how it works."

"What do you want me to say? It's a fraud. There are no words on any of the pages."

With one stride Jason grabbed Ann, yanked her back, and pressed the blade into her throat. "I've always liked you, Cameron, but I will gut her right now unless you tell me how to read the book."

"I told you! There's—"

A voice pierced the darkness behind them. "From the beginning, Jason, you've understood correctly what the Book of Days is. An idea. Only an idea."

Taylor Stone stood in the doorway.

"Put the knife down. They can't tell you anything."

Jason laughed.

"Now, Jason."

He released Ann and shoved her to the side. "So you're finally going to be the answer man, Stone?"

"Try me."

Taylor walked to the book, his eyes focused on Jason. "Get farther away from her."

Jason eased a half step to the right and pointed the knife at Taylor. "There, now talk."

Taylor looked at Ann. "Are you okay?"

She nodded, her face pale.

The instant Jason let Ann go, Cameron wrapped Ann in his arms. "Are you sure you're all right?"

"That's more adrenaline than I've ever gotten during a climb."

"Cameron," Taylor said, "I tried to keep you from finding this because I knew it would dash your dreams. I'm sorry."

"Stone, I want answers," Jason said. "What game are you playing?"

"No more games."

"Then talk." Jason motioned toward the book. "What is this thing?"

"There is an old Native American legend in Central Oregon that tells of a book of stories of every man's life. So I've always guessed that settlers from the early- to mid-1800s learned of the myth, tied it to Psalm 139:16, and created this book to symbolize their beliefs. You were closer to the truth than you knew."

"Why the charade all these years? Why not tell me instead of hiding it, denying you knew anything about the Book of Days?"

"Because until Cameron came along you were content in your belief that the book was an idea, and as you can now see, you were right. But if you discovered this symbol that was created to represent a spiritual crock-pot idea, you would try to get the book declared a historic artifact and fight me to get it moved out of here into your possession. Then you and your followers could worship it and draw more followers into your cancerous religion."

"Which I will do."

"Fine. Try it."

"When did you find it?" Jason asked Taylor.

"I think you should be more worried about Ann pressing charges than when I found an old pretend book."

"I'm not going to press charges; I just want him to leave."

"Answer me," Jason said.

"Ann?" Taylor asked.

"I'm fine."

Taylor glanced around the room, then ran his palm over the surface of the book. "I haven't been in this room for more than twenty years. It is a marvelous piece of history." He cracked his knuckles. "I found it in my midthirties and brought it here shortly after."

"Where did you find it?" Cameron asked.

"That is a story for another time."

"Is this what my dad saw when he was a kid?"

"I would imagine. It's the most plausible explanation for what he told you."

"You are a platinum piece of work, Stone." Jason ran the bowie knife up and down the side of his pants.

"Thank you." Taylor stared at Jason.

Jason started to say something to Taylor, then stopped and turned to Cameron. "I still say the man is a liar and can't be trusted." He pointed at Taylor. "We're not finished."

"You're right." Taylor took a deep breath. "I need to say something to you."

Jason glared at him.

"Forgive me."

"What?" Jason shook his head.

"Forgive me." Taylor opened his palms. "For many things. For my ego, for letting myself look good and allowing you to look bad after we fell apart. For not acknowledging the pain you felt when Annie chose me over you. For not letting myself care what happened to you when you went off to war. For keeping you in your place through my silence. For carrying a bitterness toward you all these years. It's poison. Lead weights." He looked up, then back to Jason. "Forgive me."

Jason stared at Taylor for over half a minute, his eyes betraying the struggle raging in his heart. Finally he spoke. "You've got to be kidding. What do you want me to say? Let's kiss and make up? You stole Annie from me, you destroyed my life, and now you've stolen my hope of finding a real Book of Days."

"I'm sorry; I've been wrong." Taylor stretched out his hand. "Bitterness destroys the vessel it's kept in. Let's bury it, release it. Let it all go, old friend. Please. For both of us."

"I . . ." Jason's gaze darted from the book to the floor to Taylor. "You're asking me to . . ." For a moment his eyes softened and his body shuddered. He shut his eyes, then they snapped back open. "Never. I'll never forgive you. This isn't over."

"Yes, it is."

Jason pointed his knife at Taylor. "What is between you and me won't be finished till one of us is dead."

The big man turned and strode out of the room.

As soon as the echo of Jason's footsteps faded, Cameron yanked on his pack, glanced at Ann, then glared at Taylor. "Now that that's over, it's answer time. Why the elaborate game? The clues, the rocks, the whole setup?"

"Like I said, I tried to keep you away from the heartbreak of all this."

"You did a lousy job." Cameron kicked at a clump of dust on the floor. "Why didn't you just tell me from the beginning that the book existed but only as a symbol? Why let me waste all that time and stir up all my hopes?"

"Because you wanted to believe your dad and Jessie so desperately. Unless you followed the clues and went down the path of discovery for yourself, you wouldn't have accepted the truth. And also, your search these past few weeks—whether consciously or unconsciously—has been about far more things than the Book of Days."

"Oh, it has? Are you going to enlighten me as to what those things are?"

"You're searching for eternity. For meaning. For hope. You're entertaining the possibility that you can let Jessie go and move on with your life." Taylor glanced at Ann. "None of these quests would have started if you hadn't come to Three Peaks and completed your search for the book."

"But I have no answers to any of those questions."

"I don't think your journey is over yet." Taylor touched the blank pages of the book.

Nice try. How would he know? "When the path ends at a stone wall, the journey is over."

"I'm sorry. I know how much you wanted it to be real. And I believe there is a real book with pages we will open, full of words where everyone's story is written down and recorded by God's own hand for all of eternity, but it's not on this earth and it's not for the eyes of mortal man to see. Someday I believe I will see it, but not in this age, not in this life. And I believe your memories of Jessie and your dad are hidden and safe in that book."

Cameron glanced at Ann. "Let's get out of here."

He walked past Taylor without looking at him.

Cameron and Ann sat in his car, neither of them speaking. What was there to say? It was time to go back to Seattle, but he didn't want to. Go back to what? If his condition continued to worsen, he wouldn't have much of a mind to work with back home anyway. He wanted to stay in Three Peaks. But do what? Search out the Native American legend that would only lead him back to Taylor Stone's basement?

What should I do, Dad . . . Jessie? What should I do, God?

"I'm sorry." Ann touched his hand. "Truly sorry."

He rubbed his upper lip and stared at The Sail & Compass logo on the outside of the restaurant, at the needle on the compass pointing to the North Star. If only he could find a north star for his life.

Jessie would say the only North Star was Jesus. As would his dad. And Ann.

"What are you going to do now?" Cameron asked.

"I'll spend a few more days down here, then head back. I want to hang out with Tricia and Taylor for a bit. I'm still trying to wrap my brain around the fact that he's my uncle." Ann turned toward him in her seat. "And you?"

"I don't know. I should probably head back in the morning and try to get on with my life. Start working on that bid with Brandon."

"May I make a suggestion?"

"Sure."

"Tell Brandon everything that's happened. If he's any kind of friend, he'll understand why you need two more days. Then do something for yourself tomorrow. And keep your fly-fishing lesson with Taylor the day after tomorrow. You're blind if you can't see he cares about you."

Cameron fired up his MINI Cooper and pulled into the street.

She was right. His life was ending anyway. It wouldn't end any faster or slower if he returned to Seattle two days from now.

A moment later he knew exactly what he needed to do the next day.

CHAPTER 39

Two Years, Two Weeks Earlier

Cameron made himself a raspberry-and-banana smoothie and plopped down in front of the television Sunday afternoon.

Jessie clumped down from upstairs. "I'm headed out to spend a little time in the sky, but I want to show you something first. Do you have a minute?"

"Sure, always," Cameron said, but kept watching General Maximus Decimus Meridius lead the Roman legion against the German barbarians. "We haven't watched *Gladiator* together in a long time."

"I'm not big on the violent parts."

"Neither am I, but it's such an epic flick."

"I need to show you this."

"Uh-huh."

"This is important, Cam-Ram."

He paused the DVD and turned toward her, the light from the big screen casting a warm glow on her face.

"Sorry."

"I need you to take a good look at this." She reached into her coat pocket and held out what looked like a highly polished stone about the size of a large grape. It was slightly oval and russet colored with a small hole bored through the top, a thin leather cord threaded through it. As she handed it to him, Jessie settled down next to him in their blue two-person chair.

"It's beautiful."

Jessie nodded.

Cameron turned it over in his hand and ran his forefinger over the surface of the smooth stone. There were scratches on it, but they weren't random. It looked like some kind of pattern or writing. "Where'd you get this?"

"I found it when I was a kid. It's Native American."

Something was off. There'd never had secrets between them. "How long have we known each other?"

"A long time."

"And you're just now getting around to showing me this? I thought I knew everything about you." He winked and patted her leg.

"It wasn't the right time till now."

"And what makes now the right timing?"

"It just is."

"Okay." Cameron put his arm around Jessie and pulled her close. "And these markings?"

"I think it's some kind of language."

"What's it say?"

Jessie shrugged. "I have no idea."

"It's cool, I like it." He started the movie playing again and tried to hand the stone back to her.

"No." Jessie pushed his hand away. "I want you to have it. You need to have it."

He paused the film again. "This stone means something to you." He brushed a strand of hair away from her face and studied her eyes. They were puffy. "What's going on? Why have you been crying?"

She shook her head. "I needed to give it to you just in case."

"Tell me what the stone means."

"I'll tell you when I get home, I promise."

Pressing her wouldn't make her tell him, but he had to ask. "Just in case what, Jess?"

She placed her finger on Cameron's hairline and slowly ran it down his forehead . . . nose . . . chin . . . neck . . . chest till she stopped on his heart. "I will always be here, you know. No matter what happens in the next few weeks."

He pulled her in close and kissed the top of her head. This wasn't like her. Quiet, hidden, melancholy. And holding on to a secret that had her living in a world she rarely visited. She wouldn't tell him what the stone meant? Okay, he'd give her time. But he didn't want her to be alone today. He didn't want to be without her today.

"Are you sure you don't want to stay here today? Hang out, you and me?"

Her gaze dropped to her lap. "I can't stop living and I need to get some hours in the air."

"Tell me, Jess."

She stood and buttoned her Gore-Tex jacket. "Good-bye, Cameron." She flipped her tan scarf over her shoulder, the one he'd given her so she'd look like Amelia Earhart, and shuffled toward the door.

He squinted at the back of her head. "You sure you don't want to stay?"

"I'll be fine. I'm sure I got all worked up for nothing." She opened the door halfway and stopped, her hand resting on the knob. A few seconds later she turned and looked at him, a sad smile creasing her face. "I love you, Cam. Always and forever. Remember."

"What is it?"

She dropped her head and shook it. "Fine, I'm fine." She opened the door the rest of the way. "So are you. Always."

The front door clicked shut and the blast of cool air that had swirled around him for the last few minutes died.

CHAPTER 40

Early on Tuesday morning Cameron looked at his directions again, wondering if he'd missed the cutoff. The guide at the climbing store said the trail was tough to see, but was right past the huge boulder shaped like a peach. He wanted to find a climb no one had been to in years. A place he could be alone on the mountain.

Wait. There.

He slammed on the brakes and made a quick U-turn.

At the base of the rock was a faint trail. It looked like it had been eons since anyone had used it. Perfect. He didn't care if he remembered the climb, didn't care if he forgot it.

He just wanted a place to figure out his next move. Maybe even attempt another conversation with God.

After hiking for a little over an hour, he reached a cliff that looked at least 250 feet high. Other than a single crack that meandered up the rock face, there were no holds he could see for at least the first fifty feet. It would be a challenge. Good. He was ready.

By the time he was halfway up, sweat dripped in a steady pattern off his forehead, down his nose, then either onto his burgundy climbing shirt or slid past him to splat onto the ground 120 feet below.

He was almost bored by the time he reached the top. The climb was strenuous, but the crack had widened after the first twenty feet providing an easy hand and foothold all the way to the crest of the ridge.

Cameron sat at the top, his legs dangling over the edge. Little zings of fear bounced through his stomach as he teased himself by looking down.

"Are you alone?"

Cameron spun at the sound of the voice and his heart rate spiked.

Behind him, twenty or thirty yards away, sat an elderly man in a plaid shirt, jeans, and hiking boots. His long, jet-black hair hung to his shoulders. He looked Native American. And familiar. Had he seen this guy before?

"Wow. Didn't expect to meet someone else up here. Yes. I'm alone."

"I ask your forgiveness for startling you."

The man stood and eased toward Cameron with a slow gait. Without question he'd seen that walk before.

"You looked strong during the climb."

"You were watching me?"

"I've watched you for a while now." The man smiled and sat on a small boulder. "I pulled back from the edge a few minutes before you crested. I didn't want to scare you as you came over the top. To lose your grip just before the point of success could be extremely unsettling."

"Agreed." Cameron smiled, knowing the man was talking about more than climbing.

"My name is Grange."

"Cameron Vaux."

Grange looked out over the valley, then down the cliff Cameron had just ascended and yawned. "It makes me tired thinking about the climb you just finished. I did it often years ago, but no more."

"How did you get up here?"

"This is my land. I live here on my twenty-three acres of paradise." Grange pointed behind him with a gnarled finger. "Go far enough that way and you'll find what you might call a road. I certainly never drop by the store for an impromptu gallon of milk."

"I'm sorry; I didn't mean to tres—"

"You need offer no apology. I see very few people up here anymore." Grange closed his eyes and bowed his head. "You are welcome here, Cameron Vaux."

He offered Grange a Powerade from his pack, and they sat on a rock near the edge of the cliff.

"Why did you choose to attempt this particular climb?"

"I don't really know. I was looking for something different. Something off the beaten path to explore, somewhere to get away, to get some time to think."

"Maybe you were brought here by the guidance of a higher power."

"Why do you say that?"

"Might I trouble you to look at the stone you wear around your neck?"

The guy wanted to see Jessie's stone? Grange's eyes were intense as he gazed at Cameron's chest, and they didn't leave the stone as he untied it and handed it to the man.

Grange turned the stone over in his palm. "Where did you get this?"

"My wife got it years ago. She gave it to me before she died."

"I'm sorry for your loss."

"It's an unusual rock I'm told." Cameron took a long drink of his Powerade.

Grange nodded.

"Apparently it's rare."

Grange nodded again.

"But I don't know where she got it."

"I do."

"Really? Where?"

Grange's only answer was to give tiny shakes of his head.

"She thought the scratches on the back were some kind of writing, but she didn't know what language it was or what the symbols said."

"I didn't think it would be found during my lifetime." Grange studied the stone for over a minute, the midday sun sending off little flashes of light as he turned it slowly in all directions.

"Do you mind?" Grange stuck out his tongue and licked the stone, then studied it again. "I mean no disrespect; the darker shade helps me see certain nuances more clearly."

"No problem, but maybe next time you could use some of the Powerade?"

"That I would find to be too sticky."

Cameron nodded. "Good point."

After twenty seconds, Grange said, "Your wife was correct. It is a language." He turned and squinted at Cameron.

"Whose?"

"Mine."

"What?" Cameron blinked.

"It is the old markings. My grandfather was fluent in it. I can speak a little. I'm better at deciphering it."

"So you can translate the markings?"

"I already have."

"And?"

"Before I answer, I need to apologize for possibly disturbing you. It was not my intent to be seen."

Two memories splashed into Cameron's mind. The figure in the park and the one in the truck. "You've been stalking me."

"Not stalking. Watching. You and Ann. I needed to see you two. I needed to watch you for the coming time."

"What coming time? What are you trying to say?"

"As I said before, I think a power beyond yourself guided you here today. Maybe you are the new guardian?"

"Guardian of what?"

Grange tilted his head back and held the stone up to the sky. "This was marked over four hundred years ago. It tells of the place where the stories of time are told."

"Stories of time? What are the stories of time?"

"Memories. Of the past. Of the future."

Cameron stared at the stone, and his heart pounded faster than it had during the climb. He grabbed his climbing pack and rustled through it, even though he knew his notebook wasn't inside.

Hadn't Jessie said something about the stone and the book? Weren't her last words about the stone having to do something with the book? The memory flitted in and out of his mind like a dragonfly.

He needed God to come through.

If You're real, help me remember.

A moment later her death flashed into his mind.

"You have the stone?"

"What stone?"

"You must not lose it. It's the key . . . use it to find the book, okay?"

She'd known. A chill sprinted down his spine. Cameron closed his eyes and rubbed his face with both hands. She'd known where the stone would lead him.

"It's a place that records the past, present, and future?"

"One might use that word to describe it, yes."

Unbelievable. This had to be the Book of Days' legend Taylor had spoken about. Cameron wiped his hands on his pants and swallowed.

Stone had lied.

"It's real? This place?"

"Yes."

His heart rate kicked into another gear.

"Can you tell me how to get there?"

"It is a special place. It is not for everyone." Grange held Jessie's stone by the leather cord and let it settle onto Cameron's palm. "It is only for a very few."

"I need to go there."

"Why?"

How could he explain the reasons to a man he'd just met? For Jessie, for his dad, for himself. To know there was meaning to life, that there was something beyond what he could see, beyond the chemical reactions residing in his mind he called memories. To be healed.

Cameron closed his eyes and let his chin fall to his chest. "For the love of my father and the love of my wife."

"Is there anything else?"

"Just before my wife died, she told me to use the stone to find the book. And that someday I would know it's okay."

"I see." Grange stared out over the valley, sitting on the palms of his hands. "If you choose to go, please note that it is a long hike. The hike is not hard, but it is four miles from an obscure trailhead not frequented much any more. Consider giving yourself enough time to make the journey. And give yourself enough time to be there as long as is necessary."

Grange picked up a small stick from the ground and sketched the Three Peaks Mountains in the dirt at their feet. "Start here." He pointed to the base of one of the peaks. "This is where you will find the trailhead."

Wait. Grange's sketch reminded him of something. A view? Taylor . . . Didn't Taylor show him? Yes. That day at the park. Stone guided him to a specific spot at a specific time of day to look at the Three Peaks. And he'd seen a shadow that looked like an arrowhead pointing to what looked like a tunnel in the same spot Grange had just drawn.

Cameron shook his head and smiled. Taylor had been telling him where to find the book.

"Do you know Taylor Stone?"

Grange nodded. "We are friends."

"Has he been there? To the place where the Stories of Time are told?"

Grange patted Cameron's shoulder. "Let me show you what to look for along the way." And he continued drawing in the thin layer of dirt at their feet.

When he finished he asked Cameron, "Do you understand?"

"Yes."

"I pray you are able to discover your path and find the Stories of Time."

Cameron's adrenaline didn't stop pounding till he reached the bottom of the cliff and started the two-mile hike back to his MINI Cooper. He'd found it. The Book of Days and the Stories of Time were one and the same. He clutched the stone around his neck. Tomorrow he would take Ann and find his memories of Jessie and see his father again. Maybe even be cured.

After that he and Taylor Stone would have a very long talk.

CHAPTER 41

The next morning Ann called Cameron at 7:40.

"Are we still on for coffee?"

Cameron rolled over in bed, grabbed his iPhone, and punched up his calendar. SEVEN THIRTY. ANN: COFFEE AT JAVA JUMP START. Whoops. They'd set the date the night they explored Taylor's building, but he'd forgotten to set his alarm. "I spaced. Yes, we're on. I'll be there in ten."

"Good, we have to talk. There's something bothering me about Taylor's basement, and I want to work through it with you."

Ann had a white chocolate mocha waiting for Cameron when he walked into the coffee shop.

"How was your climb yesterday?"

Climb? Right, yesterday he'd gone for a solo. *Wake up, Cam.*

"Excellent. Great workout and great view from the top." At least there probably had been.

"Were there any other climbers?"

"Nope, my solo climb stayed solo."

Was that right? He didn't see anyone, did he? Another climber? No, but he'd seen someone . . . Cameron squeezed his head.

"What's wrong?"

"Nothing."

"You look like you just forgot what day it is."

"I . . . think I did meet someone." The flash of a conversation flitted through his mind. There was someone at the top. Was that right? A wave of panic flashed through him. Something deep inside said it was critical he remember who he talked to. And what they talked about. Was it a man? Yes, he was certain it was a man. A moment later he wasn't sure he'd talked to anyone.

"Who'd you meet?"

"I can't . . ." Heat filled his body. "You have to help me." He looked up. "It's important for me to remember this." He kneaded the back of his neck. *Remember!*

"Was it a man? A woman? A kid?"

"I talked to this person about the Book of Days, I know it." Cameron stood and immediately sat back down. "Help me."

For the next few minutes Cameron tried to recreate the event of the previous day, but nothing more than a vague recollection of talking to someone at some point during or after or before the climb was all he could grasp.

"It'll come back. Give it time."

He didn't have time. And it wouldn't come back. "We need me to remember it now. I have to."

"Let it go."

"I can't." Cameron turned and stared out the window of the coffee shop.

"It seems like whatever it was, it's let go of you." Ann took his hands and rubbed the top of them. "It'll be okay, Cam-Ram."

He fell back in his chair as another wave of heat washed over him. "What did you call me?"

"Cam-Ram. Has nobody ever called you that before?"

He gripped his chair. "Jessie called me that."

"Hey, I'm sorry. I didn't mean to call you something she—"

"No problem." Ann calling him that? As strange as it was, it felt right.

She squeezed his hands. "Can we talk about Taylor's basement? I think I've found something that might help us in this crazy quest."

"What quest? It's over."

"Probably, but maybe not."

"Give me a minute to clear my head."

Ann stood. "No problem. Those éclairs have been tempting me for three days. So I'm going to get rid of the temptation by eating one."

Ann seemed to move in slow motion as she weaved through the knot of people waiting to order their java jolt. When she reached the pastry shelves at the back of the coffee shop, she reached in and pulled out two chocolate éclairs and pretended they were dancing with each other.

When she got back, she said, "This éclair will do wondrous things for your mind and to your taste buds."

"Wouldn't that be nice?"

Ann took her first bite and wiped her mouth with a napkin. "I think Taylor wanted us to find the book."

"What do you mean?" Cameron took his first bite of the éclair. Wow. Tasty.

"Didn't you think it strange he wasn't upset that we broke into his building?" Ann took another bite. "He didn't even mention it. And did you see the look of satisfaction on his face as we left?"

"No."

"Trust me. It's a girl thing. Any other woman would have seen it too."

"And?"

"It was as if he'd accomplished something he wanted to see finished."

"Which was?" Cameron clicked his pen and pulled out his notepad.

"I think he wanted to keep us from finding anything else in that basement."

"Like what?"

"Something we missed."

"And that is?"

"Another room we should have seen, that should have been there but wasn't, but had to be but we didn't see it."

Cameron rubbed his forehead. "English please."

"According to the blueprints, there is one more room in that basement we didn't see. My photographic memory, remember?"

No, he didn't. "And you remember what?"

"When we dropped down to the second level of the basement, we could only go left. But there should have been a room just to the right. There wasn't."

"How big?"

"At least ten by ten, maybe bigger."

Cameron ran his fingers through his hair. Was it possible? He couldn't stop hope from stirring in his heart. "Hidden from sight just like the book room."

"That's what I'm thinking."

"You think he's stashed something in the extra room? A real Book of Days?"

"You won't be able to push me that far, Cam, but I think we're going to discover some fascinating things about Taylor Stone."

"I'm going back. Soon."

Ann dug her hands into her hips. "You mean *we're* going back."

"Really, even after that run-in with Jason?"

"Yes."

"I think I like you." Cameron smiled.

"It's mutual."

Finding the additional hidden room proved easier than finding the first. Behind the tapestry to their right was a small door with three ancient-looking padlocks. Time for Ann to apply her special skill again. She winked at him and two minutes later tossed the locks to the concrete floor.

"Ready?" Ann asked.

"More than."

The door scraped open and they stepped into a room the size of a small den. Cobwebs hung like layered curtains from the ceiling covered by a fine coating of dust.

"Ugh." Ann brushed them aside with her flashlight. "Someone forgot to call the cleaning crew."

"Amazing." Cameron took a slow spin, shining his light on the room's contents. "I have a whole new set of questions for Mr. Stone."

A large stack of newspapers were piled on a large oak desk directly in front of them. Hundreds of photos were tacked to the wall above the desk. On the left-hand wall was a map of Deschutes County. On the right wall hung a world map with a familiar set of dots and next to it a map of the night sky with the Vela and Pyxis constellations lined out with a white pencil.

Cameron rapped the map with his fingers. "We have just found—"

"Game headquarters."

"Take a look at this." Cameron pointed to a framed picture on the desk. It was a copy of the photo of Ann's mom flying through the air on the tire swing.

"All the secrets of Taylor Stone on display."

He continued to search the right side of the room as Ann explored the left. A few minutes later she walked back carrying something. "I think you're going to want to sit down for this, Cam. Maybe lie down. Stone created more than a game." She shone her light on an old notebook in her hand.

As Ann flipped the pages of the notebook, Cameron felt like a dentist had shot his body full of Novocain. Page after page was filled with scrawled notes on how to make leather look and feel hundreds of years old, how to hand-make parchment paper to look hundreds of years old, and notes of the fonts used in the early eighteenth century.

The realization flooded over him. "He made the book."

"Yes."

"The whole thing."

"The question is why," Ann said.

Cameron rummaged through the rest of the notes on the desk. "Native American legends of the Northwest, Native American languages, burning letters into leather . . . unbelievable. He could publish *Creating a Book of Days for Dummies*."

Ann didn't speak till they'd left the building, clomped the quarter-mile to Cameron's car, and slumped into their seats.

"Any ideas why Taylor would go to all the effort to manufacture that book and set up the clues? This is more than a game to him," Ann said.

Cameron stared out the window. A sick game.

"I'm guessing you'll be keeping your date with Taylor tomorrow morning."

That's right! Taylor was going to teach him to fly-fish.

"Absolutely. He'd better be ready to catch much more than fish."

CHAPTER 42

Cameron got up Thursday morning with fishing on his mind. He was the hook. Taylor Stone was the trout.

They reached the trailhead to Whychus Creek at five o'clock, meaning Cameron had lurched out of bed at a horrendous time, but Taylor said they had to get to the river early if they wanted to catch any rainbows. This didn't jell with Taylor's penchant for dropping his flies on the river at all hours of the day, but Cameron didn't argue the point. It was the perfect place to confront him about his creation of a Book of Days, and if getting up before God was awake was the price, so be it.

Here there would be no distractions. Nowhere for Taylor to walk away to. And Cameron had written down the details of what they'd found under The Sail & Compass the night before, so if he needed to be reminded of anything, he could access it in an instant.

By six o'clock they'd tied their first flies and Taylor had coached him on the fluid back and forth motion needed to cast correctly. The hole Taylor had chosen was no bigger than a large inner tube. Cameron only hit the spot two times in ten casts, and bites from the brown trout under the translucent water eluded him, but he loved it.

The only sound was the rush of the river as it meandered its way through the stones, and the smooth swish of their rods through the air.

"Slow down," Taylor said, "you're not going to whip the fish into submission by casting like that. Let the fly settle on the water and then take it back up after a two count."

Cameron slowed down.

"Much better."

After he caught and released his first trout, Taylor said, "How many years were you and Jessie married before her accident?"

"Too few." Cameron drew back his rod and made a perfect cast into the hole. "Five."

"You were with her when she died?"

"Yeah." Cameron slogged through the water back to the rocky beach and set his rod down. "All the clichés you hear on the radio and see in the movies were bottled up in her like love-lightning. Being with Jessie was like opening that bottle in every moment."

"I know that love."

"You and Tricia?"

Taylor shook his head. "I love Tricia and don't deserve all the things she's done or tried to do for me." He cast five more times before he continued. "I'm talking about Annie."

Finally he would get the story on Annie.

"Ann was named for her as you know." He stopped casting and drilled Cameron with his eyes. "I'm not sure how I feel about you falling for my niece."

"I'm not falling for her."

Taylor adjusted his U of O hat. "Uh-huh."

Cameron rammed his hands into his back pockets and didn't answer.

"Annie was all grace and toughness. Pretty as all get-out but could run faster than half the boys growing up. Vanishing from my life almost thirty-three years ago, you'd think my memories would have faded, but Annie was the type you never forget."

Taylor finished releasing the fish he'd just caught and set it back in the river. It spurted away, disappearing downstream. "Of course not being able to let go of her makes for a pretty heavy burden to carry, you know?"

Cameron knew. "How did Annie die?"

"In a car accident." This time Taylor cast eight times. "Like you, I loved the old muscle cars. And I found a favorite. When I looked at the horses under the hood of that beat-up Mustang, I knew I was the one to tame her." Taylor turned and stared at him. "You understand, don't you?"

He nodded.

Taylor yanked back on his rod, a rainbow trout dangling on his line, and pulled it in. "I bought that beauty two summers before the accident happened. That car was my passion." Taylor trudged back to shore and set his rod down. "It took me the full two years to restore it. Ran as smooth as a maple seedling twirling to the ground when I was finished."

Taylor stopped talking for so long Cameron thought he'd fallen asleep standing upright. When he spoke again, his voice was like smoke in sunlight, and he could barely make out the words.

"The morning after I'd finished it, I had to go somewhere and Annie asked if she could take the car for a drive. Of course I agreed; I'd restored the car for her."

He sat next to Cameron and rubbed his face. "A 1970 Ford station wagon with three high school juniors inside ran a stop sign going like a whirly-wind and T-boned Annie. They say she probably died instantly."

Cameron shook his head.

"Are you all right?"

"Remember me telling you I restored a '65 Mustang and gave it to Jessie for Christmas one year?"

"I do."

"She only drove it once." He breathed deep and imagined he smelled the water, a pure crystal smell with no imperfections. "On the way to the airstrip. On the day she died."

Taylor put his arm around Cameron's shoulder. "Life is funny the way it puts certain people together, isn't it?"

Taylor stood and waded into the river, the water swirling around his waders. He cast in perfect rhythm, nothing moving except for his right arm.

He was a good man, a friend even, but he'd hidden the truth. It was time to confront the lie. It was time to find out exactly what Taylor knew.

"I want to talk to you about why you created a Book of Days."

"I suppose it's time, isn't it?"

"We found the hidden door."

"I thought you might." Taylor continued casting.

"Why go to all the trouble to create that elaborate set of clues and a false book? Why did you do it?"

"I had to. It was the only way to convince anyone searching for a real book that the Book of Days was only an idea." Taylor glanced back at Cameron. "I expected they would follow the clues I'd laid out, find the symbolic book, and prove to themselves the book didn't really exist. It wouldn't be a good thing for most people to find the real book."

He gathered up his rod and smiled at Cameron. "And then you came along out of nowhere, knocking over apple carts every which way, and tracked the thing down. Well done."

Cameron stared at him. "What did you just say?"

"Yes, I did say 'real book.'"

"Are you telling me—?"

"But as smart as you were, you must extend a great deal of credit to Ann, don't you think? I don't believe you would have gotten where you did without her."

"The book is real?"

"She was an interesting twist to the puzzle." Taylor shook his head. "Having a niece show up after all these years is a definite mind bender."

Taylor turned and sloshed out of the river till he reached a boulder the size of a small ottoman and sat on it. "That stone around your neck, can I see it?"

Strange. Someone else asked to see it recently, hadn't they? "Sure." He lifted it from around his neck and handed the stone to Taylor.

Taylor studied it. "I'd lay odds these markings are Native American."

Suddenly the memory of his climb two days before surged into his mind. "Grange!"

The image of Grange studying the stone just as Taylor had filled his head. The questions about why Cameron wanted to go to the place of stories. The directions . . . He'd told Cameron exactly how to find the place. What was it called? Time Stories? The Stories of Time?

"He told me how to find it." His heart beat picked up.

"He must have liked you. And trusted you. He's probably been watching you since you got here." Taylor nodded. "Grange is a good man."

"You know, don't you? You know what they are. The Stories of Time and the Book of Days are the same thing, aren't they?"

"Yes." Taylor handed the stone back to Cameron.

"Why did you lie to me?"

"I'm sorry, Cameron, forgive me. I had no choice."

"We always have a choice."

"What did Grange tell you?"

"He said few are chosen to see the stories."

"True."

"And you were one of the chosen." Cameron tossed a rock into the swirling water.

"Yes, to my eternal regret."

"Do you care to explain that?"

"After I found the book, I used it." Taylor slid his reel down to the river rock at his feet. "I used what I saw."

"You're telling me the Stories of Time truly do tell the future?"

Taylor nodded.

"Why didn't you tell me the truth?"

"I wanted to tell you. I did." Taylor rubbed his face and sighed. "I did try to tell you in my own way."

"When?"

"In the park, when I showed you the arrowhead shadow pointing the way to the book. I've wanted you to find it for a while now."

Oh, wow. The memory swished through his mind. That's right. Taylor had tried to show him.

"But I couldn't go any further than that. I swore I wouldn't ever put someone in the position to go through the regret I've lived with for thirty-three years."

"It all comes back to Annie, doesn't it?"

"I found the book when we'd been married for two years. We had the same type of relationship you and Jessie had." Taylor shook his head. "Perfect. Even after we were married, I loved backpacking through the mountains around here by myself for days at a time. A part of me has always been built for solitude.

"One early morning in July over thirty years ago, I explored an area of the mountains I'd never been to. I came to an opening in the rocks and somehow I stumbled through them to the prettiest slice of earth you'll ever find.

"There it was lying out in front of me like a mirror. As I gazed at it I saw the past, saw the present, then I saw the future. A future where my dad would lose his legs in a logging accident the next afternoon.

"Annie was out of town and I couldn't reach her so I came home and told my sister-in-law about what I'd seen and she never doubted me."

"Ann's mom?"

"Yes."

"She told me I had to save my dad. I agreed." Taylor rubbed his face with both hands. "I was supposed to wait for Annie to get home the next afternoon, but I left her a note saying I'd gone to see my dad.

"So I tried to stop the accident. And I did; my dad never lost his legs. People wondered for years how I knew that tree would fall the wrong way. But what I set in motion . . ."

Taylor stopped and swallowed as tears seeped onto his cheeks. "What I did caused Annie's death in the moments after my father lived."

"Because she didn't go to Bend with you."

Taylor nodded.

"So you made a book and created a series of clues—"

"I realized if I could create something that people would have to work to find, I could end it right there. In the case of Jason, it worked. I don't think he'll ever figure out . . . But you, it seems you're one of the chosen."

Cameron didn't know what to believe. Was it real? Was it another part of Taylor's game?

Taylor turned to him. "You didn't tell me your wife asked you to use the stone to find the book."

Cameron frowned at him.

"You're wondering how I knew?" Taylor said. "Grange told me."

Taylor tossed a rock into the river. "Don't you think it's time to come clean?"

"About what?"

"About why you're forgetting pieces of conversations. About why you didn't start your search for the book right after Jessie died. About why you didn't think her story was more than the jumbled thoughts of a dying woman until three weeks ago."

"Because . . ." There was no spin he could put on an answer that would satisfy Taylor.

"Why didn't you remember what Grange told you?"

Cameron watched the river rush around and over the rocks, as if it knew exactly where it wanted to go. Where it needed to go.

"I'm losing my mind. My memories flit in and out of my brain like sparrows. Eight years ago my dad died of the disease, and the last thing he asked me to do was to find the book for him. His dying wish. I thought he was talking nonsense.

"Then two years ago I started noticing my memory wasn't as sharp as it had been. Little things like reading notes I'd just written and reading them as if for the first time. Not remembering if I'd brushed my teeth or not. Telling my partner the same thing three times in one morning.

"Then I started losing memories of Jessie. What we'd done, where we'd gone, important conversations we'd had."

"I'm sorry." Taylor looked at the sky. "Okay, God, I get it."

He turned and stared at Cameron for a long time before

nodding twice. "I am going to do something I swore I would never do for the rest of my life."

"Return to the Book of Days?"

"Yes." Taylor massaged the back of his neck. "And take you with me. But I should warn you. You might not like what you see."

CHAPTER 43

I'm taking him to see it." Taylor sat in front of his workbench and stared at a map of the Three Peak wilderness as he spoke into his cell phone.

"When?"

"Tomorrow morning."

"Do you feel at peace with that choice?"

"Yes." Taylor paused. "Your counsel helped."

"I'm glad. Is there anything else I can do?"

"I need you to be ready for Jason if he tries to follow us." Taylor ran his finger along the route Cameron and he would take.

"You believe he'll try?"

"I'd be surprised if he didn't. His skills with knives and guns are far greater than mine. And I have little doubt he would kill to possess the book."

"I agree. Do not worry. I will look out for you and Cameron."

"Thanks, Grange."

"Yes, my friend. Yes."

Cameron didn't speak as Taylor drove up the rutted logging road, only a hint of gray dawn painted across the sky toward what he said was the genuine Book of Days.

Cameron hadn't set his alarm the night before. He'd never gone to sleep. He'd considered telling Ann about his conversation with Taylor and his claim that the book was genuine, but what if it wasn't? What if it was another one of Taylor's games? Or nothing more than a beautiful spot in the mountains where Taylor felt God gave him impressions that seemed real?

Sure, Taylor's story of saving his dad seemed like proof, but what if it was nothing more than a hunch he'd acted on?

But then again, Cameron had his dad's story to go on as well as Jessie's to bolster his belief. It didn't seem as if both of them could have hallucinated about the same thing. And then there was Grange and the stone.

He sighed. His brain was exhausted from trying to analyze everything he'd gone through over the past two and a half weeks.

Something Taylor believed to be God's book was up there, but what would a book be doing in the middle of the mountains? Sure God's book would be rainproof—it could be anything proof—but it didn't make sense. Was it in a cave? Was it two thousand feet thick? Logic wasn't helping and Taylor stayed mute about the book's description.

At least he hadn't let his emotions leapfrog on him. He'd shut down any hope of seeing anything more than a stunning setting hidden in the mountains.

"How could my dad have seen this thing when he was a kid?"

Taylor shrugged. "It's a long hike, not a hard one. He probably was up in the mountains with his dad or a friend, who knows?"

"And how did Jessie find it?"

"Think about her childhood if you can. Did she ever mention Girl Scouts or—"

"She was a Girl Scout. She talked about them doing a lot of things outdoors, taking trips—maybe she even told me she came down here . . ."

"There you go."

Cameron stared at the ponderosa pine trees rushing past and thought about the last time he saw his dad. "*You must find the book. Everything will make sense to you then.*"

I'm ready, Dad.

"Is the book real?"

"I've told you it's real. You don't need to hear me say it again. You need to choose to believe or not."

"How much longer?"

"Probably an hour before we reach the trailhead and a good three hours of hiking before we get there."

"Will you tell me anything about the book?"

"You'd like a preview?" Taylor grinned.

"Yeah."

"It's possible that some people have seen the book and not known it."

"How can you see the book and not know it's a book?"

"You'll see." Taylor paused and grinned again. "I hope you'll see."

"What does that mean?"

"You'll see."

Cameron frowned. "Stop saying that."

"You will."

Ten minutes later they turned onto a dirt road that wasn't even one car wide. Branches scraped the sides of Taylor's truck as they inched along the narrow road, but he didn't seem to notice.

When the trail ended, Taylor threw the gearshift into Park. "Let's go."

He led Cameron up what looked like a game trail. After an hour and a half of steady climbing, Taylor heaved himself up onto a large slab of granite.

Cameron joined him and looked out over the forest below them. The only sound was the pounding of blood rushing back and forth through his veins, the air as still as it had ever been since coming to Three Peaks and the scent of dry pine needles filled his nose.

A hawk screeched high above and behind them.

"How did you find the book?"

"I was praying." Taylor shifted on the rock and stretched out his legs.

"Praying?"

"Like I told you on the river, I wanted to go someplace I hadn't been before and chose this trail. I came up for some reflection, some alone time with God. I wanted to figure out where my life should go. Where Annie's and my life should go."

Taylor stood and took a long draw from his water bottle. "As I hiked along pouring my heart out to God, I reached a spot where I got an impression to stop. So I stood in the silence for a few minutes. I looked around and suddenly got this feeling I should walk toward what looked like solid rock. It wasn't a voice in my head, just the thought that I should walk right up to it. So I did, my nose inches away from the wall. That close I saw it wasn't rock. It was an optical illusion. Nature's way of hiding an entrance that was there the whole time.

"I'll let you discover the rest of the experience for yourself when we get there. Let's get moving. We're burning daylight."

CHAPTER 44

His eyes darted back and forth, back and forth, searching for the little clues telling him exactly where Taylor and young Cameron had gone. As he slogged along he massaged the handle of his knife with one hand, the handle of his gun with the other.

It was always good to check to see that his two friends were still with him, even though he knew they were. They were loyal, they could be trusted to follow directions, and they never talked back or tried to force him to listen to a dissenting opinion. And when they were called on to persuade people to his way of thinking they always performed well.

He nicked his pinky finger on the tip of the knife and watched the small bead of blood pop to the surface of his skin. After licking it, he wiped the finger on the back of his neck and slowed his pace.

Stone wasn't trying to be discreet; tracking him and Cameron was almost as easy as following a dirt bike up the mountain. And there was little point in getting close enough to be seen should one of them look back and have the right line of sight to see him.

He fell back to what he estimated was a fifteen-minute gap and tried to quell the adrenaline pumping through his body.

But this was the day he would fulfill his destiny. Finally. How much longer? An hour? Two at most?

He wouldn't enjoy killing them. There would be no joy in it. But once he knew where the book lay, it would be the right decision.

CHAPTER 45

After hiking another ninety minutes, Taylor stopped at the base of two intersecting hills "We're almost there."

A thick grove of pine trees framed Stone, who stood with his hands on his hips. A slight smile bounced over his face.

Cameron glanced at their surroundings. "I don't see any pages."

"Not yet." Taylor laughed.

"For a guy about to revisit a place that rocked his world to its foundation, you seem to be in an okay mood."

"You're perceptive, Mr. Vaux. And you're right. I am feeling good. I made a decision about something last night."

"What's that?"

"You'll see when we get to the book."

They trudged on through the trees, Taylor's stride growing wider and lighter. Whatever he'd decided must have taken a huge weight off.

Two minutes later Taylor stopped and grinned. "This is it."

"The book's location?"

"Yes."

Heat coursed through Cameron's body and he sucked in a quick breath. Stone was serious. Cameron glanced from tree to forest floor in a slow 360. Nothing. "Where?"

"I need to explain something before we take the final steps to get there." Taylor closed his eyes for a moment before continuing. "When Adam and Eve chose to disobey God in the garden, it wasn't just man's immortality that was destroyed. The earth itself fell from its original design."

"What does that mean?"

"As stunning as the earth can be, its current beauty is a shadow of its original splendor. God says the earth itself groans, longing to be restored to its original design. And one day it will be. There will be a new earth restored to its former glory. Far more beautiful than what man sees now."

"What does that have to do with the book?"

"Maybe it's my imagination, but I believe this place we're about to step into has retained much of that original design. At the very least, the presence of God is here in a way I've never sensed anywhere else."

Cameron gave a wry grin. "Should I expect a bush to start burning?"

Stone's eyes narrowed. "The ice has grown thin under your feet, Cameron. Be careful. God will not be mocked."

Cameron's face flushed. "I shouldn't have said that."

"Let it go."

"I'm sorry—"

"It's all right. Truly. He is a God of vast mercy. Vast forgiveness." Taylor smiled. "Let it go. He has."

Taylor pointed over Cameron's shoulder. "Do you see anything through the pines?"

He turned. "I see a rock wall on the other side of them."

"That's where we're going. Right through the rock."

He followed Taylor through the ten yards of trees and stopped just beyond them. Taylor motioned toward the wall. "What do you see now?"

"The same thing I saw a moment ago. A rock wall."

"That's what I see too, even if that's not what's there." He winked at Cameron. "Watch this." He took half steps up to the rock and then seemed to vanish. A moment later he was back. "Now that's an illusion worthy of David Copperfield. Are you ready to try? I'll be right behind you."

Cameron stepped forward till he was inches away from the wall.

"Step forward; trust me you'll be fine."

He took another step forward and laughed. His eyes said he was stepping through solid rock, when in reality he was stepping in between two narrow rocks so perfectly aligned and with colors that matched so precisely he couldn't tell where one ended and the other started.

He was in a thin path, between the rocks. The walls narrowed at the top creating the sensation of walking through a tunnel. Sunlight shone through the other end like a beacon.

When he exited the path he stumbled to a stop. A gasp escaped. The scene before him was staggering. They were in a small valley the size of two football fields. The jagged, snow-capped peaks surrounding them shot up at least a thousand feet on each side. Pine trees lined a crystal clear lake so still it was impossible to distinguish any difference between the real mountains and sky from their reflection in the water.

The silence during the moments of rest they'd taken on the climb up seemed like the roar of the ocean compared to this place.

A sense of peace immersed him like an ocean wave, and Cameron took in long breaths, pushing his lungs to take in more of the mountain air than possible.

"This is . . . astonishing." Cameron turned to look at Taylor.

Stone shook his head and smiled wide. "I'd forgotten how beautiful it is."

Cameron glanced at the sky. "Is it me, or is the sun getting brighter? This whole valley is—"

"It's not the sun. Look." Taylor pointed across the lake to the far shore.

A circle of light the size of a pinecone hovered in the air over the water.

"What in the world . . . ?"

Taylor shrugged. "I'm not sure."

Even from fifty yards away it was so bright Cameron had to shield his eyes.

Through his fingers he watched the circle split and streak around the lake toward them, then split again and sprint toward the sky. And again and again till there were thousands of trails of light into and through and around each other till they filled the valley, arching over them and surrounding them like an ocean of light.

A roar like thunder exploded against his ears, and he covered them while at the same time holding his elbows up to his eyes in a vain attempt to block the increasing brilliance.

An instant later he lay facedown on the lake's shore, the light pressing him down and into his back, as if the weight of a thousand planets were on top of him.

And unfathomable love. He felt it. He was immersed in it . . . He opened his mouth and drank in this Presence . . . now inside him, filling him, overflowing . . . A Being so magnificent he would follow Him anywhere.

A moment later everything vanished.

The weight.

The light.

The Presence.

Cameron sat in the aftermath for what might have been minutes, or might have been hours. All he wanted was for the light to return.

Taylor sat cross-legged, looking like he'd been caught up in an F5 tornado and loved every moment of it.

"What was that?" Cameron said.

"This is a holy place."

"I felt Him." He frowned at Taylor, then smiled. "I felt God. He was . . . in me."

"Yes."

Cameron shuddered. "I . . . I don't know how to explain it."

"You don't have to."

"He's real." Cameron covered his face with his hands and blew out a long breath. "He's found me."

Taylor yanked Cameron into his chest. "Welcome to life."

After their embrace Cameron glanced around the lake, still swimming in the intensity of the moment. "Did this happen last time you were here?"

"It was different, but also the same. I'm not sure I can explain it. And it lasted much longer last time. And didn't vanish so suddenly." Taylor frowned, then smiled. "But that's okay. I'm not sure I could have taken much more anyway."

A moment later his smile vanished and his face hardened into flint as he stared over Cameron's shoulder. "We have a problem."

A voice rang out from behind Cameron along with the cocking of a gun. "Yes, you do." Laughter. "I would say you most certainly do."

Cameron spun as the figure above them twirled a knife around the fingers of his left hand and held a gun in his right as he tramped down the slope toward Cameron and Taylor.

"You're going to teach me all about the Book of Days, Stone. Then you and Mr. Vaux will unfortunately need to die."

It was Kirk Gillum.

CHAPTER 46

Kirk Gillum gazed around the valley and grinned before focusing on Cameron and Taylor. "I appreciate you two. Truly." He winked at them.

Cameron glanced at Taylor. If he was surprised at Kirk's appearance, it didn't show. Where was Jason?

"First, thank you for validating the belief I've had in a real book all these years. Not even Jason believed me till you came along, young Cameron. And second, thank you for leading me right to it; although I admit it took me a while to follow your tracks through that last part." He bowed and laughed.

"The book is the lake, right?" Kirk scratched the underside of his chin with the barrel of his Glock. "It makes sense. While I always thought a genuine book existed, I never thought it would be literal paper and ink. That's much too prosaic for God, don't you think?" He raised both eyebrows and jutted his head back and forth, as if to taunt them with the question.

"Give the idea even the slightest consideration and you realize it would have to be an immensely large book to contain the story of all the lives that have lived and are still to live, hmm? And when Jason gave me the full report on the adventure in your basement, well, that seemed awfully convenient to me."

Kirk had been speaking in a singsong voice, as if talking to children, but suddenly he leveled the gun at Taylor's head and spoke in a monotone. "Okay, playtime is over. I'm ready to dance. Back away, Stone. I'd like to take a good long look at the future."

Kirk stepped up to the edge of the lake's shimmering surface and glared at Cameron. "We could have shared this, you know. Jason never lied to you like Stone did. He even offered you friendship. Truly, I did originally consider sharing it with you, but you've clearly sided with Stone, so now the book will be mine alone."

"Yours alone?" Cameron said.

"You thought I would share this with Jason? Really?" Kirk laughed and wagged his finger. "No, no, no. He wanted the book for the wrong reasons. Besides, toward the end of this little jaunt, he got downright pushy with his opinions and that was unacceptable. In any case, it would be impossible to share the book with him at this point since he's no longer with us. So sad. But I do appreciate the work he did for me. I don't think I've ever seen someone play the front man with more passion."

Cameron's stomach lurched. Gillum was insane.

Kirk kept the gun pointed in Taylor's direction as he gazed into the pool, expectant rapture on his face. The silence of the valley pressed in, the only noise was his steel-toed boots shuffling over the shale surrounding the pool as he sidestepped along its edge.

"How do I read it? What should I be seeing?"

"It was never real in a literal sense, Kirk."

"Nice try, Stone. Tell me how I get it to work." He pointed the gun at Taylor's head again.

Taylor walked toward Kirk.

"Stop!"

Taylor opened his hands. "The few who find this place do hear from God, but only when they slow down long enough to listen. He is alive and this"—Taylor motioned to the mountains surrounding him—"testifies to His glory and the magnificence of His creation. But there is no magic in the pool, no special chant that will tell you your past or present or specific details about the future unless you are willing to—"

"As you've probably figured out by now, I'm willing to do anything."

"No, Kirk, you're not. You must choose—"

"Shut up!" A shot whizzed by Taylor's head a foot to the right and splintered a tree behind him. "Tell me how it works!"

"You're not here to kill me."

"Really?"

"All right, if you are, then shoot me." Taylor took another step toward Kirk.

"What?"

"If it's truly what you want, shoot me." Taylor put his arms out to the side. "Go on."

Rage, sorrow, and fear passed over Kirk's sweaty face, all three emotions blazing out of his eyes in seconds. Then only rage remained. "You're ready to eat a bullet?"

"Yes."

Kirk's trigger finger shook.

"He's lost it, Taylor," Cameron said. "Don't make him snap."

Kirk snorted. "You're next, Cameron." He waved the gun back and forth between Cameron and Taylor, his finger still twitching. "Tell me what I need to do and we can all live happily ever after."

"You can put the gun away. And both Cameron and I will forget you ever came here."

"I'm finished with your games, Stone." Kirk's gun exploded

with another shot, this time the bullet streaked by Taylor's head by no more than six inches. "Will you start talking, or do you want to see how close I can get to your head with each progressive shot?"

"There's nothing here for you to see."

Kirk turned and walked back toward the pool, glancing over his shoulder at Cameron and Taylor every few feet. He stared at the water as his eyes grew cold. When he finally turned back to them, the blood had drained from his face.

"Not acceptable. This doesn't make sense. This can't be all there is. The book has to be real." He bent down and touched the lake, then stood and flicked his fingers, drops of water arcing against the sun.

"I'm going to count to one. After that I will shoot you in the leg. If that doesn't convince you to talk, I'll shoot you in the arm, then the stomach. If that doesn't scare the cat into letting go of your tongue, I will start shooting Cameron." He grinned and spun toward Cameron. "In fact, maybe I should start with your new young friend."

Kirk turned the Glock on Cameron and moved his finger over the trigger.

The sensation of floating surged through Cameron and his mouth opened. He gave a tiny shake of his head and whispered, "Not yet."

As he glanced from Kirk's trigger finger to his face to the barrel of the Glock, time slowed.

It's not time. I'm not ready to die, Jessie.

An instant later something large smashed into Kirk from the side knocking him to the ground. A blur of clothes. A man, now on top, blocking a punch, driving his knee hard into Gillum's throat, and in the same fluid motion grabbing the gun out of his hand. The man bounced to his feet and took three rapid steps backward, the weapon trained on the mayor's head.

Dark hair, wiry build—it was Grange.

The Native American turned to Taylor, breathing hard. "Gillum has talent. He lost me for a time and his tracks were difficult to follow."

"My friend." Taylor grasped Grange's forearms as Grange clasped Taylor's. "Thank you."

"Of course."

Kirk lay moaning, holding his neck with one hand, his ribs with the other. Cameron guessed at least a few of them were broken.

Grange held the Glock with both hands and said to Kirk, "Get up. We have a long hike ahead of us." He looked over his shoulder at Taylor. "I will explain to him in detail the way things must be."

Taylor nodded and they watched Kirk stumble up and out of the valley, Grange following, the gun steady in his hand.

Cameron stared at Taylor. "What is that little smirk on your face for?"

"It's not a smirk. It's a smile."

"Why?"

"Forgiveness." Taylor eased over to a boulder and sat. "For Kirk."

"Are you kidding? You're okay with what he just did to you?"

"I'm letting it go."

"What if he tries to come after—?"

"He won't. Grange will keep an eye on him. And once they trace Jason's murder to Kirk, the mayor's schedule will be full for a very long time."

Forgiveness.

Cameron stared at the craggy top of the highest peak surrounding the lake, locked his hands behind his neck, and paced back and forth.

Could he do it? Right here, right now? Could he forgive Taylor for telling him the book was real and bringing him here only to shatter his hopes? He'd believed. Taylor had convinced him the Book of Days existed.

But he'd felt God. He was real. Maybe it was enough.

"So the book is a place of beauty and solitude." Cameron spoke it more to himself than Taylor. "And a place of holiness. A place of God's presence. But not a place of memories and not a place where the future can be seen."

Taylor gazed at Cameron the way his dad used to. With joy, pride, and love shooting out of his eyes like lightning. "You are a good man, Cameron. We will talk about the book in a bit. But first the lake and I need to do some business."

CHAPTER 47

Taylor walked to within a few paces of the water and squatted. A moment later tears fell from his cheek and dropped onto the dirt at his feet.

"Do you want to be alone for this?"

"No. I'd like you to be here." He motioned Cameron to join him and waited till they crouched together on the edge of the pond.

Taylor reached into his pocket and pulled out an oblong object wrapped in a powder blue handkerchief. He motioned to it. "One of Annie's handkerchiefs from when she was a little girl." He unwrapped the object slowly, as if to lend some anticipation to what was inside. But Cameron already knew.

Taylor twirled the window crank around his fingers to catch the reflection of the sun, but he closed his eyes as the sunlight flashed off it, flared against his face. He let it settle into his palm. He sighed, and without opening his eyes brought the handle to his lips and kissed it.

Then in one quick motion he flung the crank out over the water like a discus thrower, tiny swooshes of air echoing back at them as it floated through the sky. Time seemed to slow as the handle spun clockwise, perfectly horizontal with the water's surface.

Then it was gone, the ripples fading fast, as if time had sped up, and silence filled the air. A silence of peace. Of forgiveness, of hope.

"Good-bye, Annie."

Taylor stood and nodded. "Take a moment, my friend, more than one, and let this place talk to you. Soak it in."

"Who is doing the talking?"

"Often I find that depends on who is listening."

"It was never real, was it?"

"The book? We will see. I want to give you the time you need. The time to possibly do some business with the pool of your own."

Cameron sat back on the turf that ringed the edge of the lake, listening to Taylor's fading footsteps as his friend thumped along the shoreline to his left, leaving him with his thoughts.

When Taylor reached a spot directly across the lake from him, Cameron decided his friend was right. He'd known it since the night before, maybe longer. It was time.

He took Jessie's stone out of his pocket, held it in his palm. It felt lighter than it usually did. Then heavier. A few seconds later he couldn't tell how it felt.

He held it out over the lake, his palm up and open, stretching his hand out till his arm ached and still he pressed harder.

Letting go wasn't letting go of her. It was releasing himself to live whatever life he had left, with whatever memories he could hold on to. Even if there wasn't a Book of Days, it didn't matter. Even if there was no direct portal into the mind and heart of God, telling of the past and what the future would bring, it was still the perfect place to choose freedom.

The lake was glass. No ripple, not a hint of wind. The mirror image of the surrounding peaks and wispy clouds was so brilliant, the images seemed more real than what it reflected.

Cameron glanced across at Taylor, then back into the lake. He saw why Taylor had convinced himself that the pool gave visions of what was recorded in the heavens. The presence he'd felt in this valley was real, and it was a place he could imagine God speaking.

Cameron drew back his arm—held it still for a moment—then flung the stone toward the center of the lake as hard as he could. It arced across the sky, a black dot against the sun, then fell in slow motion toward the water, almost seeming to stop before it melted into the deep and disappeared.

Once again the ripples faded almost instantly, and the lake returned to its reflection of a perfect mirror image of the craggy peaks and cobalt sky above him.

"Always love, Jessie. Always and forever."

Suddenly an image appeared on the surface of the water. Cameron's heart surged.

What?

The clouds and mountains vanished, replaced by a 1965 Mustang driving along a wet street, its lights ramming into a pounding rain. It was daylight, but the rain buried the scene in a blanket of gray.

Cameron staggered forward and braced himself against a tiny pine tree.

It seemed so real. The clarity was better than HDTV could ever hope for.

Jessie?

But it wasn't her Mustang, was it? No, Jessie's was different.

"Taylor, get over here!"

The view zoomed in from a wide shot where Cameron saw the street and the car to a close-up of the driver who seemed to be singing.

It wasn't Jessie.

It was . . .

Ann?

It couldn't be. The driver wore a tie-dyed T-shirt with every color of the rainbow and a scarf straight out of the seventies. Not Ann, the hair was too dark. But the eyes, the nose, the shape of her mouth, so similar . . .

He glanced at Taylor jogging toward him, now only ten yards away. Cameron kept his eyes on the image as he heard Taylor's footsteps thud up to him. "Look."

Taylor struggled for air, would have sprawled onto his backside if Cameron hadn't steadied him.

"Annie," he whispered. "It's my Annie."

Annie's diamond ring flashed as she took a corner, her hands smoothly turning the wheel, then reaching to adjust the radio. She flipped her hair back and joined in with whatever song she'd switched to. The light ahead of her was green and the car sped up.

As she reached the intersection, the scene slowed and the view pulled back. A station wagon plowed into the intersection to Annie's left.

She looked to her left—her face full of fear—and slammed on the brakes, but it was too late.

The scene slowed further as the look on Annie's face turned to one of wonder.

Her smile seemed to fill the lake, then her head fell back and laughter poured out of her.

She nodded once to whatever she was seeing and turned to look up, seemingly out of the lake as if searching for someone, light radiating from her face.

"It's time. Don't hold on. Let me go."

Cameron could read her lips. He didn't hear the words, maybe Taylor did. It didn't matter. They were as clear as if they'd been shouted.

Annie smiled, closed her eyes, then slowly opened them. *"I love you, Taylor Stone."* She closed her eyes for a second time and didn't open them again.

Just before the station wagon smashed into the Mustang, the image faded back into the surface of the water.

"Taylor?"

Taylor looked through him, as if he was still seeing Annie talking to him, and staggered backward, his eyes watering, his hands groping out behind him as though he might fall at any second.

He turned and found a pine tree to lean against as he gasped for air, and words sputtered out of him, too soft for Cameron to make out. But the peace in his eyes as he looked back said enough.

Movement out of the corner of his eye made Cameron whirl back to the lake.

He gasped as a new image formed on the surface.

Jessie and he sat on top of Mount Erie in northern Washington, gazing at the lush green farmland five hundred feet below them.

"What if I told you something you'd never believe?"

"I'd believe it."

She tickled him. "God is real."

"You have proof?"

"I've seen something He made. Something amazing."

The scene faded into the time they sat on the shores of Lake Chelan, the remains of barbecued salmon on plates to their right.

"You know how you always said you couldn't live without me?"

"True."

"You can."

"Uh-oh. This is where you tell me you've fallen in love with your old high school tennis coach and you're about to leave."

"You'd make it without me." Jessie gazed up at him, eyes sad.

"I'm not going anywhere and neither are you."

"Okay." Jessie buried her head in his chest. "I want to believe that."

"Why wouldn't you?"

"It's still years away. I'm not going to think about it."

She nuzzled in tight to his chest and he stroked her hair. "I love you, Jess."

"Always, Cam-Ram. Always and forever."

He glanced at Taylor who sat at the base of the tree, legs crossed, smiling. Cameron turned back to the lake.

The scene shifted and Jessie and he were sailing in the San Juan Islands.

"How old were you when the fantastic happened?"

"Ten. I saw something about us. About me."

"So that's how you knew to accept my invitation for that first date."

"This is serious, Cam."

"I'm being serious. I'm just . . . You have to admit it sounds a little woo-woo that you saw us when you were ten."

"I saw someone die." She drew a quick breath. "Someone we both know."

"It was a dream from a ten-year-old. Let it go."

The surface of the water shifted again.

"What's going on? Are you bummed because Pirates is shut down for the night?"

"Maybe God writes our memories down, hmm?"

"Sitting in a park where make-believe comes true, you could almost convince me God does exactly that. I wish He did."

"What if it's true? Not a wish? That our lives are written down, recorded, everyone's life?"

"Like some cosmic yearbook put together by the supreme being of the Universe?"

"Something like that."

"I love your insanity. One of the countless reasons I'll love you for eternity."

The scene ended and melted into Cameron taking a call on his cell phone as he recorded a voice-over with Brandon.

"I want us to go to Oregon. We need to go soon. We need to look for something, find something there."

"What?"

"Something I saw when I was a kid."

"What? The thing you saw when you were ten? That thing?"

"Yes. To see if it's real."

The scene shifted once again and Cameron watched the scene from the day Jessie gave him the stone. The day she died.

"I want to show you something."

"It's beautiful. Where'd you get this?"

"When I was a young kid. It's Native American."

"And these markings?"

"They told me it's a kind of language."

"What's it say?"

"I have no idea."

"It's cool; I like it."

"You need to have it."

"This stone means something to you."

"I need to give it to you just in case."

"Just in case what?"

"I'll tell you when I get home, I promise."

"Just in case what, Jess?"

"I will always be here, you know."

"Are you sure you don't want to stay here today? Hang out, you and me?"

"Good-bye, Cameron."

"You sure you're all right, babe?"

"I love you. Remember."

"What is it?"

"Fine, I'm fine. So are you. Always."

The scene on the surface of the pond shifted once more and the final moments of Jessie's accident played out in front of him.

"Promise you'll find it." Her eyes closed. "No tears, Aragorn."

"No. You can't leave me, Jessie."

"I have to. It's going to be all right, I promise. I love you, Cameron. Always and forever."

A moment later he vanished from the scene but Jessie remained. There was no blood and her face was more radiant than he ever remembered it. He couldn't tell if she was still in the airplane or somewhere else, but a moment later the scene changed again.

A man in a white T-shirt, his back to Cameron, sat on the stern of a sailboat, sun streaming down on him, wind whipping through his thick dark hair.

A shiver shot down Cameron's back as the man spun to face him. It was his father. Young. The way he looked when Cameron was a little boy. A massive grin broke out on his dad's face, and he threw his arms wide and spoke to the sky.

"All my memories, You've stored them for me, Lord." His dad was so full of joy it seemed to shake the rigging. *"Draw Cameron to Yourself. I long to see him in eternity. And let him know I'm so proud of him, okay?"*

Cameron shuddered as tears threatened to spill onto his cheeks.

The scene shifted and when the images came back into focus, he again looked at the top of Mount Erie in midsummer. But the colors were brilliant, too full to be from earth.

A woman sat with her back to him, looking out over the farmland and lakes and Puget Sound to the south. The wind tousled her hair, as if fingers were lifting it off her shoulders and setting it back down.

Jessie.

She turned and her gaze seemed to be searching for him, her eyes like diamonds, throwing off light. Was she older or younger than when he'd last seen her? Both maybe. Cameron couldn't tell. She laughed and somehow he heard it in his head.

"When I come to You and he remains, tell him it's okay. In a way he won't doubt. Let him know I'm where I'm supposed to be. And that I want him to join me. Not now. Not for a long time. But in time. Help him to seek, to choose life in the years that have been recorded for him on earth, and might he always love. Always and forever."

Jessie's face melted into the water and only the mirror image of the mountains surrounding the lake remained.

Cameron slumped back off his knees to the ground.

"I'd forgotten. Every one of them. She'd been trying to tell me all along."

"Are you okay?" Taylor stood next to him.

"I don't know. Maybe. Yes, somehow . . . How can I not be?" He looked up at Taylor.

"What happens if the memories of Jessie fade again?"

"It doesn't matter. She's right. It's okay." Cameron smiled as he cradled the back of his head with his hands.

"I think there's more for you to see." Taylor motioned toward the water.

The reflection of the mountains melted into another mountain, a different one, bathed in early morning sun. A climber clung to the side of it, too far away to tell if it was a man or a woman.

The view moved in.

Could it be?

Yes, it was Ann, laughing as she scaled the sheer face of a cliff, which ended in a domelike rock.

He knew the spot. It was Liberty Bell, right off the North Cascades Highway in northern Washington. Just a few days earlier

Ann and he had talked about how she'd never been there and that they should climb it together. The view widened. Twenty feet below her was another climber. Male. The scene moved and he was now looking at a profile of Ann and the other climber. Himself.

Adrenaline filled his body; it felt like he was floating as he watched himself pull up toward Ann, a smile plastered on his face.

The image of Ann and he climbing Liberty Bell—was it the future, already recorded in God's book? Her future with him in it? Two weeks from now? Two months? A year?

But why would he do that to her? It wouldn't be right to burden her with his disease. No, maybe God had written it down, but Cameron would rewrite future history just as Taylor had.

The water swirled and he stared at a New York skyline as if from a plane. The view zoomed in to Ann sitting at a dark wood table at a restaurant with a man who toasted her and laughed. As she raised her glass, Ann's mouth smiled but her eyes didn't.

The scene shifted again and Ann sat in her car staring at a picture of Cameron taped to the dashboard. She sighed and yanked the picture free and stuffed it in her glove compartment. She dabbed her eyes with the backs of her hands and shook her head.

Another shift and Ann lifted an Emmy above her head.

The water changed again and Cameron watched himself editing a video in what looked like a home office, the clock on the wall reading 1:07 a.m. Three awards lay stacked on their sides on the desk next to him.

Another shift. Ann sitting at a dinner table with two beautiful girls who looked like her and the fourth spot at the table empty. Then the phone rang and Ann answered saying she understood, pain in her eyes as she hung up the phone, her back to the girls, then turning and forcing out a smile.

Cameron again, hair gray and thinning, sitting in a dim room alone watching television, a slight shaft of daylight piercing into the shuttered living room. Piles of books. A dusty coffee table. Bloodshot eyes.

So the future would be as bleak as the past. He wouldn't end up with Ann. With anyone. Sad. Her future looked better than his, but he couldn't shake the image of the empty chair at dinner. Was it him missing? Or the man he'd seen with Ann in the New York restaurant?

It was okay. It was his destiny to be alone.

Cameron squatted down, his head slumped forward, and a soft moan seeped from his lips. He sank deeper into himself to the quiet place where he couldn't lie to himself.

He loved Ann. And he couldn't stop loving her.

If she would have him, diseased mind and all, he would go to her and pour his heart out to her for the rest of his life.

He looked up. Taylor's eyes were riveted on the water. "Look."

Cameron turned.

The lake boiled for a moment, then cleared. Scenes of Ann and Cameron flashed across the surface.

She and Cameron stood on a ledge overlooking a tropical valley, an azure sea beyond that. "I think I like Costa Rica," she whispered. Her head was wrapped in small golden and crimson flowers, her turquoise dress was whipped by a strong wind, and Cameron held a diamond ring between his fingers.

A Christmas scene with Ann and him skiing the Swiss Alps with two other couples. The following summer they would rent a houseboat on Ross Lake, and Cameron would get so sore water-skiing he would slather BenGay over his entire body.

A child was born: a boy. Then another boy and a year later a daughter.

Now Cameron was speaking to a packed house at UCLA film school. Ann sat in the front row, her hair up, face radiant.

"What did you do?" Taylor grabbed Cameron's arm.

His lips slowly separated as he turned and stared at Taylor. What had he done? He'd changed his mind, surrendered to the longing inside and dreamed of building a life with her.

"I didn't do . . . I decided if she'll have me, I'm going to love Ann the rest of my life."

Speaking it out loud made him shiver. He shouldn't have said it. That made it real and real was too frightening.

Cameron closed his eyes and shut down the feeling, then shut down the choice to move forward. No. He couldn't do that to her. Even if she chose to be with him . . . So much better for her to find someone whole.

"It's changing back again," Taylor said.

Cameron opened his eyes and stared at the lake.

The scene had changed back to the one with Ann in New York with a smile and sad eyes. The man at the table opened a Tiffany's box and she nodded.

Cameron standing on the top of El Capitán alone.

Ann dropping off the girls for a weekend with their father.

Cameron old and flipping through channels on a television screen that covered his entire wall.

The water shifted and there was nothing to see except the placid still waters. Cameron watched and waited for five minutes but no other scenes came.

Cameron stared at Taylor as both men let what they'd just witnessed sink in.

"I saw myself years into the future, still alive. I was doing things you have to have a memory to do. Does that mean I'm going to be okay?"

"I don't know, my friend."

"Have I been cured?"

Taylor shook his head. "I don't know."

"I need to know."

"I don't think you can."

Cameron rubbed his face and stared at the surface of the water. "Tell me," he said to it, even though he knew there would be no answer.

Jessie. She was right. It was his choice to live or not to live.

Cameron gazed at the mountains, the trees, and finally the lake before looking at Taylor.

"So what future will you choose?" Taylor finally said.

"I don't know."

"Yes, you do."

"Life."

"Does that life include Ann?"

"I don't know. She has her choices to make. I have mine."

"Well said."

Cameron closed his eyes, lifted his head, and drew in a long breath of the pure air surrounding them.

"We need to head back," Taylor said.

As they made their way out of the valley, Taylor threw his arm across Cameron's shoulders. "You're free, my friend."

"As are you."

Taylor turned for a last look at the lake. "I'll see Annie again soon."

"But not yet."

"No, not yet."

CHAPTER 48

"I didn't hear you leave this morning." Tricia shook out the porch mat and flopped it back down next to the front door as Taylor meandered up their walkway. The setting sun framed his silhouette. And even though his face was obscured, she saw something about him had changed.

"I left rather early."

"Just you, or did you bring along a guest?"

"I brought a guest." Taylor rubbed his chin with his forefinger.

"Where did you and Cameron go?"

"I took him to see the Book of Days."

Tricia smiled and took his hands in hers. "And what did you find?"

"I made an amazing discovery." Taylor grinned and wrapped her up in his arms. "I found the Taylor Stone you used to know. Apparently there is nothing that can't be forgiven."

"I've suspected that for a long time." Tears welled up in her eyes as she squeezed him as hard as she could.

After separating, Taylor stood with his hands in his coat pockets, rocking back and forth on his heels. "How would you like to go for a walk with me?"

"On a gorgeous summer evening, why is that something I'd want to take the time to do?"

"Because you love me."

She reached into his coat pocket and slid her hand into his. "Well, there is always that."

They strolled down the street, Tricia not knowing where they were going and not caring. Her husband had come home. The change in his countenance was stunning. Even the air around him seemed lighter.

Taylor slid his hand into hers and squeezed twice as they continued down the road. She kicked a stick out of their way. "So the Book of Days *is* real."

"Very."

"And it shows you every memory and your entire future."

"No, the book shows you what you need to see. I didn't need to see the future, but I did see some things from the past."

"Like Annie."

Taylor nodded.

"And?"

"It's okay." He squeezed her hand again. "I'm okay."

"Why do I sense a hint of regret in your eyes?"

Taylor massaged his forehead, then left his hand covering his eyes for a long time.

"It looks like Kirk Gillum killed Jason."

Tricia stumbled. "No . . . no."

Taylor nodded and told her what happened at the lake.

"I'm sorry." She leaned into his chest. "Are you all right?"

"I will be. Even though Jason didn't . . . we didn't . . . I found my peace." Taylor sighed. "Let's talk about Cameron, okay?"

"Did he see his future?"

"Yes."

"So he knows what will happen?" Tricia asked.

"He knows he has a choice."

"So will they choose each other?"

"I'd love to eavesdrop when they talk, but I don't think we're invited."

Cameron and Ann's future. It would likely be set during their next conversation. She prayed they would choose wisely.

CHAPTER 49

The two o'clock sun warmed Cameron's back on Saturday as Ann and he sat at the top of the cliff where a little over two weeks ago, her silhouette had stopped him from trying to join Jessie early. He dug into his backpack, pulled out two blackberry PowerBars, and offered one to Ann.

"Thanks." She took it with a smile.

"Did I ever mention you saved my life here?"

"No."

Cameron unwrapped his bar and stared at the forest floor far below. "I gave considerable thought to 'losing my grip.'"

"You're serious."

"Yeah." Cameron started to put on his sunglasses but turned and looked Ann in the eye. "When I looked up and saw your silhouette, it stopped me from . . . Thanks for making the climb just before me."

"My pleasure."

"Apparently I have a few more pages to add to God's book."

Cameron had led them up the face and to the top in a leisurely fashion, taking time to savor the brilliant early August morning, feeling the magnificent strain on his arms and legs as they worked together in a smooth rhythm—clipping in carabineers, roping and unroping, suggesting holds and routes, and tossing smiles back and forth across the cliff face.

Now sitting at the top of their climb, having told her how close he'd come to killing himself, he let the peace of the moment settle over him. Only one more confession to go. But not right away.

"It still amazes me that the Book of Days is real." Ann breathed deep. "It's hard to let go of how insensitive I was to Jessie about it. I refused to believe her."

"So you haven't forgiven yourself for that?"

"Are you my spiritual advisor now?" Ann punched him lightly in the shoulder.

"How about forgiving your mom for what she did or didn't do?"

She leaned back, bracing herself on her hands, and smiled. "As a matter of fact, I have. I let it go. What my mom did to me . . . what I did to Jessie."

"How does it feel?"

"I feel free." Ann smiled and looked at the sky.

Cameron let the scene around him soak into his memory. A memory he might be able to hold. If not, God would hold it for him.

"Taylor says when he and Grange are gone, someone needs to be the guardian of the book. I think he handed the baton to me. I wouldn't mind having a partner in that venture."

"You're asking me?"

"Would you like to go there?"

"To the lake? Without question." Ann grabbed his hand. "Will I see anything?"

"Yes, I think so. I . . . I don't know." Cameron fumbled for the words. "It's not like I had any control over what it showed me or didn't show me." Cameron smiled. "I would love to see what it would show you."

"And you couldn't see everything it contains?"

"I thought I'd be able to. I thought it would tell the story of every soul on earth. That I'd be able to access every memory I'd ever had and look into my entire future. But the book is far smarter than that. I only saw glimpses, quick scenes of what was, what is to come, and what could come. Like I said, it only showed me what it wanted to show me."

Ann arched an eyebrow and quirked her lips. "It?"

"God."

"So He's real, then?"

"Most definitely."

"What are you going to do about that?"

"Learn, explore, follow Him."

Ann laughed, threw her arms around him, and squeezed tight. "As soon as you picked me up this morning, I knew it. It's all over your face." She pulled back and studied him. "It's over all of you."

"That's a good thing?"

Ann nodded and squeezed him again. "Would you mind terribly if I called you Wesley? It sounds so much better than Farm Boy."

He knew those names. Where were they from? He laughed. Of all the things to remember. "*The Princess Bride.*"

"Yes." She leaned her head against his shoulder. "What did His book show you about us?"

"That we have a choice to change what might become."

"You sound like Dickens."

"What does that mean?"

"Scrooge changed things after his visit from the three ghosts, didn't he?"

"Ah yes." Cameron slid his arm around her and pulled her into his chest.

"So the future is fluid."

"If you like those words, yes."

"In this fluid future, if we both choose the way you'd like us to, where would we end up?"

Time for his final confession.

"I had hoped God would cure me at the lake. I have no idea if He did. It feels like something has changed, but that could be only my imagination." He took her hands in his. "I never thought I could let Jessie go." He reached for the familiar sensation of the stone around his neck, but his fingers found nothing. "But I have. And even though my mind might be gone in a month or a year, whatever time I have left, I want to spend it with you."

Ann didn't respond for a long time. When she did, she stood, pulled him up, and held both his hands in hers. "Do you regret the years you spent with Jessie? Even if you'd known the future, would you have pushed her out of your life, or would you have still savored every moment?"

She gazed toward Three Peaks in the distance. "I met a guy once who had a near-death experience. He was a white-water rafting guide on the Rogue River in southern Oregon. Going through Blossom Bar, he made a rookie mistake and ended up underwater for five minutes. They revived him and now he goes around speaking about living life to the full today because tomorrow it could be gone."

Ann slid her hands up Cameron's arms. "At the time I wrote it off. *Carpe diem* and all that has always seemed like a cliché to me. But it changed when you and I were on the side of that cliff dancing with death.

"I have no idea if we'll be dead tomorrow. We could die tonight. But I do know every moment we don't live to the full now, will be a moment we regret for the rest of our lives; however short that might be. So let's live, Cameron. While we have today—let's live."

Cameron smiled. "That's a good speech. Maybe just a hint of melodrama, but overall an excellent speech."

Ann whacked him on the head, and he pulled her in tight.

Wind whipped through his hair as he lifted her chin and kissed her for a long time. A very long time.

"Ann Banister, let's go record an amazing life together."

Dear Reader,

Why do we take hundreds of pictures of our spouses, kids, and friends?

I believe it's because of a universal desire to record our lives, to somehow keep the ravages of time from eroding our most treasured moments.

It was around 2000 that my family realized my dad had started losing his most treasured memories. As parts of his mind slipped away, it only caused the joy inside him to be released in fuller measure—that part was a gift. Even so, the pain of watching him walk down the path of the long good-bye was wrenching.

As the disease progressed, I started to wonder where my dad's memories were going. Were they mist? Or could God somehow, someday restore them? When I found Psalm 139:16, it was a huge comfort. I knew that his memories would be returned to him when he crossed over into eternity. God had recorded them in His book.

Then I thought, what if God's book could be found on Earth? From that question *Book of Days* was born.

If the mind of someone you loved or love is melting away, my desire is you find hope in this story, that you will embrace the idea that not one of the treasured moments you shared together is lost.

In the age to come God will restore memories and relationships, and He will revive the most joyful events of our lives to be celebrated again and again.

With great anticipation of reading His Book of Days in eternity,

James L. Rubart
www.jimrubart.com

DISCUSSION QUESTIONS

1. What character in the book can you relate to most? Why?

2. Which character in *Book of Days* most surprised you?

3. What themes did you see in the novel?

4. Cameron is losing his memories of Jessie and it terrifies him. Do you worry about losing some of your memories? Read Psalm 139:16. What does that say to you about memories in light of eternity?

5. If God has forgiven our sins, do you think those parts of our lives will be edited out of God's Book of Days? (See Psalm 103:12.)

6. Both Cameron and Taylor Stone have to let go of their late wives to be free. Why do we hold on to things from our past that weigh us down? Is there anything or anyone you've been holding on to that you need to let go of?

7. Taylor Stone likes Cameron from the start, but he tries to push him away because of the memories that are stirred up. Have you ever shunned a friendship because of a painful memory it reminds you of? What keeps you from dealing with painful memories?

8. Have you ever had a Jason Judah in your life? How did you deal with them? What did it teach you about other people? About yourself?

9. We tend to be harder on ourselves and offer far less forgiveness than other people give us. Why do you think that is? Are there areas of your life you need to forgive yourself for? (See Col. 1:13–14.)

10. Ann has to choose to be with Cameron or not be with him even though his mind might slip further away and their days together might be few. What would you do in such a situation?

11. Do you think Jessie made the right choice by trying to tell Cameron about the Book of Days and her future slowly? Or should she have told him all at once in clear language?

12. If Jessie had told Cameron bluntly, do you think he would have believed her? Why or why not?

13. Do you think the future is fluid, as *Book of Days* implies? Can we change the future by our choices, or is the future already set?

14. Were you surprised when you found out what the Book of Days really is? Why or why not? Did you like or not like what it turned out to be?

15. Have you thought about the idea of recording a life? What kind of life do you think you're recording? (See Eph. 2:10.) On a scale of 1 to 10, is it the life you had hoped to record?

16. What do you need to change to record a life you'd be more proud of? (See Matt. 25:14–30.) In light of this parable, consider what one thing you would like to do differently from this moment on.